FROSSIA

by the same author

TOMORROW WILL COME
an autobiography

POLONIAE TESTAMENTUM
a poem

FROSSIA

E. M. ALMEDINGEN

HARCOURT, BRACE AND COMPANY
NEW YORK

CONTENTS

FROSSIA

CHAPTER ONE

SNOW ON STONE

The man took a handkerchief out of his pocket, stooped, and covered the face on the floor. Frossia, watching, knew she would always remember it. He was bending, she could not see his face, but the fitful light caught his hands into its pallid web, and she thought, Somehow these hands are the loveliest thing in this train, in the country, in the whole world. They are rough, calloused, badly shapen, nothing in them to admire really—but they are lovely and kindly . . . she thought, observing the big square of grubby grayish cotton. It briefly fluttered in the air, the face was covered, and things were suddenly clothed with decency as though one man's grubby handkerchief had wrought an invocation in the small overcrowded space. The airlessness notwithstanding, Frossia breathed deeply and freely.

I should so much like to see his face, she went on thinking, now, this second—and only for a second. Why, he is raising his head—she waited, all eagerness and excitement, but the man swiftly slipped back into his shadowy corner. Yet his hands are still there. Those lovely, kindly hands— Frossia reminded herself.

There had been more than enough chatter before. Now silence stole across the small overcrowded space, and in the peace broken by nine people's loud breathing Frossia found herself remembering odd things.

"You should always keep calm, particularly in novel surroundings, and take careful stock of them so that they do not overwhelm you"—so prim, thin, slightly dusty Fräulein Eltz had preached to her in the past which need never have been at all, thought Frossia, and wondered what the Eltz would have made of surroundings which to her, Frossia, were novel, baffling and certainly overwhelming. "*Schrecklich! Unglaublich* . . ."—the Eltz would have murmured, her bony hands steady and her mind more than half-occupied with some ameliorative scheme: anything *schrecklich* found but temporary lodgment in her tidy world, Frossia remembered.

But the Eltz could not be imagined alone. Frossia could almost hear her grandmother's imperious request for smelling salts, her brother's terse dictum "Why, this is history in the raw," and her uncle's curses. Yet none of them could have turned a cattle truck into a railway carriage, nor done away with those four dirty, squealing, hungry babies, nor yet—and here Frossia forbade herself another look at the grimy floorboards—nor yet brought that poor stilled body back to life.

It seemed queer. They had all chattered, all busily offered their crude little requiems—except the man in the corner whose face she could not see. His handkerchief fell on the quieted face, and all of them stayed silent.

Frossia must needs look down again. She was being stupid and morbid, she knew that, but looking seemed preferable to thinking and, certainly, to remembering.

Dead, the girl looked more decent than any of them. Grubby cotton lay lightly on the upturned face. Frossia could guess at the sharp contour of shoulder bones under the thin pink muslin of a soiled blouse. The shabby dark green coat covered the worn body up to the breast, and the girl seemed enclosed in a world of her own, separate and no longer embarrassed by demands and limitations of flesh. Strange, said Frossia to herself, why can I not look without thinking? Just consider this pink muslin. . . . What an odd thing to be wearing in winter. . . . Yet her coat looks warm enough, and it is dreadfully hot here. I wonder where she bought this blouse. . . . It is shabby and faded, but it must have been a bright salmon pink once. . . . It is the last thing she will ever wear.

Frossia had not even noticed the girl at the beginning of the journey. It had all been such a terrible scramble and scuffle, the train leaving Kiev with people hanging on to steps and buffers. It was after they had steamed out of some station, when the few tallow candles, supplied by more provident passengers, had given out, that they were all shaken by the sound, neither scream nor moan, but brief laughter. The laughter had made Frossia wish to get up, move, run away, but nobody could have moved. Then there came that queer gurgling noise, a thud, and the fat woman in a malodorous astrakhan coat produced a jealously hoarded stump of a candle, someone fumbled for a match, and they had enough light to watch the face twitch for a few seconds. Nobody did anything except watch. Soon all was over, two soldiers doffed their greasy caps, the mother of the four babies crossed herself, the astrakhan coat sighed a slow fat sigh, and all were silent.

4

But the unnatural stillness could not last. The astrakhan coat grew voluble, ready to offer a probably imagined story.

"I met her the first time in Kharkov—some time ago. She was all right then. Later I ran into her in Kiev, and I found her broken-hearted. She told me she had heard about her young man being shot in the South, somewhere near Tsaritsin, she said. He was in the Dragoons. She said she had her poison all ready. Poor little thing, but I ask you—what was there to do?"

Nobody replied until Frossia murmured in a small trembling voice: "Why did you not tell us?"

"Well, was it my business? And you cannot always believe what the young tell you. They will say anything that comes into their heads. Besides, she is far better off as she is—"

The soldiers gruffly assented. The mother of the babies whimpered in a thin gray voice: "Yes, much better off."

Frossia wanted to say: "No, you don't really mean it. Nobody could be. No matter what life is like, it is still life—with room in it for effort and hope, always for hope." She wanted to say: "I know it. I mean it"—but she said nothing at all because she knew that her words would fall limp and poor, just mere words, whatever the excitement in them. You cannot convince anyone with words, she thought.

Was it an hour ago? A few minutes ago? She could not be sure. It seemed to have happened in another world. Every moment suggested coming into a different world from the last she had seen. Nobody possessed a watch, and nobody troubled about time. They had stepped into the train, and time must have ceased then. Twilight, darkness, dawn, all came and went. Now once again the timid dawn was painting fields and woods ocher and dun, and the train stopped. It had stopped so many times since leaving Kiev that nobody took much notice of those halts. Frossia sat in her corner, thinking that even the Eltz, always so definite and reassuring, would have seemed fantastic in such a world. Petrograd—where they might or might not arrive before nightfall—seemed equally unreal. So was everything she heard, touched, smelt, and saw. Only a tiny thing within her remained stubbornly real and even beautiful in that whirling dance of the fantastic.

Nonsense, she admonished herself, I am tired and very dirty. My right arm is cramped. If I had known the girl had poison in her pocket, I would have stolen it from her and drunk it myself. No, no . . . I am wrong. . . . We may be all mad, but I mean to live. Only it is all so queer. I should have screamed or fainted when it happened. I just sat and watched. They all did the same. What has happened to us? It is not that I have forgotten. I shall always remember. The drawn curtains, the logs in the open fireplace, Eltz by the door, Grandmamma and her phials, Papa's trembling hands, Paul looking so fierce, and Uncle Nicholas shrugging his shoulders. Then Grandmamma said: "Euphrosynia, all is over. We may be shot in a week. We must not give them the chance. Your father and I have therefore decided . . ." Grandmamma went on talking —but it was not just her words. It was that slow unstoppering of a thin rose-colored phial. Someone whispered, probably poor Eltz, "It will be instantaneous, child. It will not hurt you at all. Your father did think of pistols, but the first shot might attract attention. The house is surrounded," and then Grandmamma's voice again, "Come, Euphrosynia, of course, you understand." And what did I say? "Grandmamma, you are mad. They might shoot us, they might not. But I mean to live," and I ran, ran, ran—

Frossia had run. There was a dead house behind her, and no kindly hands to cover those faces.

Poor Grandmamma! How could she help it? Yet it was all fantastic. . . . It is so still. Perhaps, not having died with them, I am no more alive than this girl—just a husk of me with a head that aches and a stomach like jelly. Perhaps I am dead—without knowing it—differently dead. I must be. I should either be screaming or laughing, and I am quiet. Tired, but quiet. Why should I be quiet?

The soldiers rubbed their eyes and buttoned their dirty frayed tunics. The gray-faced mother woke up and began nursing the smallest baby. One of the children sneezed, stirred, whimpered, and went to sleep again, its unkempt flaxen head in a soldier's lap. Light broke over the fields and invaded the dirty crowded carriage. Frossia glanced at the farthest corner. The man was asleep, his head slightly bent. She saw a young tired face with a firm stubbly chin. It was an oval, ordinarily chiseled face with nothing in it to remember or to admire. The thin brown hair was cut *en brosse,* peasant-fashion. He wore a sheepskin coat and high brown boots. All about him was worn, soiled, and had an odd tired look, as though his very clothes had been in exile for so long they had forgotten the mold of any human body. His hands were folded in his lap. Frossia thought:

What did I imagine about him in the night? That his hands were lovely and kindly? Well, they still look kindly, but there is nothing extraordinary about them.

The astrakhan coat turned to her.

"We are moving again," she said unnecessarily.

"We are." Frossia was polite.

6

"We are certain to stop at Velikiye Luki. Then we must call in the guard and have it taken out."

"Have *her* taken out."

"Well, yes, but she is just a corpse. Have you been to Petrograd before?"

The woman's face was like a fat cushion of shining pink satin. Somewhere in the depths of that glossy satin were buried two tiny eyes, hazel, or brown, or gray—so small they were you could not tell their color. The curiosity in her voice had something soiling in it.

"Petrograd? Oh, yes—"

"Have you any people there?"

"Rather," Frossia replied with not a hint of hesitation, since a lie meant nothing at all.

"Well, I must say you are lucky. Life is a hard business for pretty girls with nobody to look after them. Tell me—what do you do to your hair?"

"Do to it?"

"Yes." The astrakhan coat grew impatient. "Dye it, do you? I have never seen such gold with bronze in it. And the way it lies about your head—just like a casque."

"Well, it has always been the same."

"Some people don't know their luck," muttered the astrakhan, and Frossia stayed silent. The greasy fat woman seemed far worse than the evil-smelling soldiers and the still body under their feet. The soldiers led their own kind of life, hard and muddled, the girl had begun another, but the astrakhan thought of life in all too obvious and sickening terms. Frossia looked away from the large, slovenly painted face. The astrakhan found a sticky fruitdrop in the depths of a black oilskin bag, sucked it loudly, and went on:

"Yes, my girl, you are lucky indeed. But if you ever find yourself in any difficulties, you might do worse than come to me. With a face like yours you need never go hungry. Have you a pencil on you? Now write it down carefully: Sergievskaya Street, No. 39, Madame Touras—I believe my husband was a Lett," she added vaguely. "Just let me know how things are going with you, and I might be able to help you." She pushed the sweet further behind her fat cheek and went on whispering hoarsely: "Relations, you said? My dear, one's flesh and blood are not much use in these days. Everything is upside down. Fend for yourself is my motto, and things generally turn out well. You see what I mean?"

"Oh, yes."

Frossia wished she might giggle or smile. But her mouth kept

7

obstinately grave. Yet the astrakhan coat was ludicrous and pathetic in her determination to add one lump of mud to another, stuff it into a dirty rose satin cushion, and call it life. She was a good liar, Frossia reflected, the kind of a liar who had long since ceased to distinguish between truth and falsehood. She was probably kind after her own odd fashion. And it would be unkind to touch her dirty fat hand and to say:

"You know I am also a liar. There is nobody at all expecting me in Petrograd. In fact, I have nobody left in the world. You understand—not a soul—except for a few cousins who are goodness knows where. Please ask no questions. I might go mad if you did. I might also come back to life. I believe—at least I hope—that I am asleep. Can you make use of a body when mind and soul are asleep? Or perhaps you can only use it when those are asleep? Forgive me for this abruptness. I have written down your address, but how could I forget it? I suppose you have put in a lot of faded crimson plush and hung cheap lace curtains everywhere. The rooms would be reeking of stale scent and tobacco. And Grandmamma never let anyone smoke there. . . . She never used scent. The air was pure, very pure—"

She broke off her reflections. Madame Touras whispered on: "Of course, you will start looking for work. But honest work is so hard to come by, my dear, and life goes on just the same. Here I am trying to carry on as best I can. Men never change. You just tell me of any revolution that could meddle with human nature? Rusbish. No man can do without a woman—be he bolshevik or capitalist. Mind you, things are very difficult in Petrograd. In the old days, a hundred rouble note to the police inspector, something for the sergeant, and you were left in peace until such time as another bribe became due. Now, most of those Tcheka men would shoot you if you suggested such an arrangement. They are not yet what you might call civilized. Also they have cleared the streets, my dear, which adds to all the other difficulties. And there is food. . . . It is more than enough to make your hair turn gray, I assure you—"

"Oh, I suppose so—"

"You will not forget. Sergievskaya, 39. I shall always be pleased to see you." Madame Touras looked at the floor. "I had my eye on *her* at Kiev, but she would not have really suited me. She seemed far too temperamental. And you must not be temperamental on this job. You look quiet enough."

"Do I?"

Frossia bent her eyes. A bit of very dirty paper lay in her lap. 39, Sergievskaya, and Madame Touras with a husband she believed to have been a Lett. . . . Another touch of the fantastic, but she had herself welcomed the fantastic, greedily, eagerly, running away from the unstoppered rose phials in that beautiful doomed room. They, about to die, had decided that life would be unbearable in the chaos, and she had challenged their decision; so she must not try and run away now, even though a soiled woman lorded it in the rooms where she, Frossia, had lived.

The train groaned, jerked, and at last came to a halt. Someone, very gray and dirty, grumbling and bored, opened the door and pulled out the stiffened body on to the platform caked with damp beaten snow. There followed an interminable wrangling about documents. Men's hands ran over the thin body, fumbled in the pockets of the green coat, fluttered bethumbed squares of flimsy grayish paper in the softly gathering twilight. Snow began falling flakily, negligently. Documents were read and pocketed. Another paper was drawn up. The people in the carriage gave their names and addresses. Frossia's turn came last. She must invent a domicile in an instant, and did so quite nonchalantly. No other questions were asked; a guard slammed the door, and the train moved off. The astrakhan coat, bored with Frossia's monosyllables, sought out the man in the corner.

"It was kind of you to cover her up," she began, breathing heavily. "Well, the curtain has fallen on her, and that is a fact."

"Perhaps, it is only just up," he replied quietly, and Frossia started.

The astrakhan coat opened her thick lips, but the man's eyes were once again closed, and she must needs nudge Frossia and touch her dirty forehead with a finger. Frossia saw and shrugged.

"Perhaps, it is only just up."

Inarticulately she prayed for stillness to come to the carriage. Offended by the shrug, Madame Touras turned away, and Frossia was left free to ponder both on the voice and the words spoken. It was a deep voice with no culture in it. A man of Grandmamma's world would not have used such a "perhaps." He would have said *"Mojet byt."* The man in the corner had merely jerked a brief *"moje,"* and the word excited Frossia in that it certainly painted one corner of a huge blank canvas. A tradesman, not a farmer, not even a schoolmaster. . . . But there was certainly beauty in the voice. And what did he mean? Did the curtain go up for all of them when . . . here she checked herself brusquely.

In a wet, woolen twilight, the weary engine breathed its last inside Nicholas Station. Frossia counted her luggage, two heavy suitcases, one bag to go on her back, one small bundle and another . . .

"You will not forget," rasped the voice she could not escape—"Madame Touras . . . Sergievskaya, 39. . . . It is quite easy to find . . ."

Politely Frossia halted on the slippery platform and listened to a detailed description of the whereabouts of the house where she was born and had spent twenty-four years of a life which now held little but a nebulous meaning. Fantastic again? Well, she had accepted it all, the fantastic and the real and the inevitable, herself neither living nor dead, and the tall slim husk, registered in her name, went down the perilous station steps, and was soon engulfed in the wet glitter of Znamensky Square.

2

The square looked wet and hostile. She could think of no possible sanctuary in its neighborhood. She peered, trying to make out the heavy bulk of an equestrian statue facing the station. Instead she saw a hurrying processional of shadows, wet and shimmering against a dark winter sky. A woman brushed past her, close to one of the few street lamps, and Frossia saw a thin hand rubbing a cheek, and instantly she knew that neither the square nor the shadowy reaches beyond were really unfriendly, nothing in the great city could be hostile to her, its child. She did not really know why, and she looked behind her, she peered ahead, trying to catch a glimpse of the worn sheepskin coat and the rough bared head. Of course, she saw nobody, and she would have marveled if she had. Back in the train, it had been a flash of light, briefer than the life of a match, something imagined rather than seen. Now she must learn to see things happen and put them all behind her tidily.

Were she to cross the huge square, go down Liteyny Prospect, take a turning to the right and another to the left, she might still come to No. 39, Sergievskaya Street, and to Fyodor, and to his fat bearded face, the genial voice, all of him a nice soft pillow of happily blended friendliness and respect. To Fyodor Frossia could say anything, and she had her story ready. At the very beginning of her endless journey she had been busily rehearsing words and gestures, easily imagining herself in that small cubbyhole, tucked inside the archway of the great courtyard, a cubbyhole which always smelt of old leather, sunflower seeds, stale air, and cheap tobacco.

"Fyodor," she could say, "you knew Grandmamma, and Papa, and Uncle Nicholas, and Paul, and Nina Petrovna. Also Fräulein

10

Eltz. You remember Fräulein Eltz, Fyodor? You must remember her—she is not, she was. Grandmamma was terrific. She went on believing in things which never moved. She was caught in a whirl. So she put on her finest black velvet and all her diamonds, had us called into her small blue drawing room, and spoke to us. She said we must die, Fyodor, because when the Reds got to us, they would shoot us, and this would be an infamy. They all agreed—except me. Red, white, pink, or green, Fyodor, I don't care which it is—I merely want life and people and everything. So I ran away and I hid somewhere for three days. Then I heard about them. They had done it. I ran on to Kiev, and I found a train. The Reds were there. They looked murderous enough, but they did not interfere with me at all. Now I am all alone, Fyodor, and I had to come here, to my own beloved place. So please, Fyodor—give me a corner with a nice clean bed. The train was so dreadfully dirty, and we had days of it—"

It would have been easy enough to go to Fyodor, and he would have nodded his great unkempt head and said: "Well, *baryshnia,* perhaps her Serenity was right for herself and others, and you were also right, and certainly, I have a corner for you." But Fyodor would not have crossed himself in the old fashion because he was a *dvornik,* a porter, and nursed an ingrained respect for such powers that were, but, time-server or not, Frossia knew Fyodor had an affection for her.

Now Madame Touras was in the Sergievskaya house, Frossia could not go to Fyodor.

She drew level with the wide mouth of Liteyny Prospect, and caught sight of a roughly timbered stall. A tiny oil lamp, set in an earthenware crock, gave her a glimpse of a stained counter, littered with mugs and saucers and a round basket covered with a dirty, fringed napkin. Behind the small island of light a dim shape drew near, and Frossia saw a girl's face framed in an enormous dark shawl, a face somehow remote from the counter, the basket, and the lamp. Frossia asked shyly:

"Is there anything to eat? Or, perhaps, something hot to drink?"

The girl seized a mug, turned back into dimness, and presently gave Frossia the mug filled with hot dark-brown liquid. Then she uncovered the basket. The bun looked hard and yellow, and tasted of burnt chicory and potato peelings.

"That will be forty," said the girl in a deep voice, and Frossia tendered a dirty slip of pink paper, her heart suddenly lighter. Life seemed cheaper in Petrograd. In Kiev she had paid seventy-five roubles for a mug of water and a potato cake half the size of the bun she was nibbling now. She smiled at the girl. But the shawl-framed face stayed remote.

"You will be a visitor here?"

"Well, I was born here—"

"Have you been away?"

"Almost four years—"

"You would hardly know the place." The deep voice fell to a husky plaintive whisper. "You don't know if you are dead or alive. My aunt Catherine was selling little patties by Kazan Cathedral. They say it is allowed. Well, would you believe it?—She was arrested for illegal trading, all her patties confiscated and eaten by those men on the spot, and the next day they found out it had all been a mistake, but the patties were gone, and my aunt is so frightened now she would not leave the house if you bribed her with a pound of caviare to do it—"

"I am sorry," said Frossia wearily, finished her bun, murmured "Good evening," and moved off.

She was truly sorry for the dim, shawled girl and for her aunt. She was also sorry that her own heart had no deeper reserves of sympathy. She ought to have said, "How very dreadful! Yes, life is unbearable," yet she did not have it in her to say such things. Life was indeed a strain, and death, all too often, came in so shocking a garb that one's imagination recoiled from it. Yet none of it could be unbearable. At least she could not believe it to be.

Last time we drove to the Sergievskaya from the station, five years ago, was it?—we passed a blind girl selling violets, and Paul wanted to stop and buy some, but Grandmamma told the coachman to go on. "What a silly idea, Paul, violets can be bought in any shop. . . ." "She is blind, Grandmamma. . . ." "That makes no difference. . . ." Stupid, beautiful, heartless, stubborn Grandmamma. "Let them shoot us? Ah, no . . . I prefer my own way, and I expect you to follow it." "I prefer mine." Frossia could still hear her own voice shouting in the small blue room, and she could see her grandmother all but freezing her with a stare. "Your way? What can you expect of life here—now? Please explain yourself." Frossia could not explain. She merely muttered: "Oh, just life"—and Grandmamma smiled. "Child, there would be no life for you—there would be a Calvary." And Nina Petrovna echoed obediently: *"Rien qu'un Calvaire."* And Frossia said: "Those are such big words, Grandmamma. I suppose it will all be strange and hard, but, perhaps, it may be good—in the end." "And what will you do?" demanded her Uncle Nicholas. "Well, teach . . . Anything. I might teach dancing. . . . I could always teach French." Her brother Paul went white

12

with anger. "Teach French? You will be teaching commissars how to wash their necks—"

Frossia plodded on down the wide Liteyny Prospect, toward quays and bridges, all the time guessing at the loved landmarks, memory rather than vision conjuring up the familiar gracious scene of spire, façade, dome and railing, all out of shadows, shadows, and more shadows. Her own self was at one with those shadows, walking, as she firmly held separate from her kind, preferring her own smoking lamp to the world's bright chandeliers. They had been, they were, and they would always be like that poor stilled body on the carriage floor, having no real part with her, and suddenly Frossia knew why to her the entire upheaval was something to welcome rather than run away from: it made for easier separation, it offered more and more opportunities for remaining within the four walls of her own house, her thoughts uninterfered with, her secrets inviolate, her joy and grief alike unspoiled by the crude invasion of anyone's imperfect and fussy understanding. Now she thought she would be free to choose her own intimates, or else have none, if she so wished. People would not be forced on her simply because they went to the opera and pinned diamond stars in their hair. If I find few or none, she thought, her rough-shod feet beating an uneven measure on the swiftly hardening snow, nobody would call me either odd or unsocial.

She walked on, and the shadows thickened, and the world around her lay still and empty, silent as though everything were drained out of the cold air, the earth, and the water under the ice. "*Rodimy,*" she murmured, raising her head and looking ahead where she knew the river would be. "*Rodimy,*" she whispered again and again. *Rodimy,* a word akin to the stranger's brief *moje* in the train, a word not ordinarily used by educated lips in elegant drawing rooms, a word of the soil, a word born of sweat and pain and toil, a hard, unpolished pebble of a word, nothing in it to show the fiery passion latent in the very sound. *Rodimy,* which means familiar, beloved, one's very own, flesh of one's flesh and bone of one's bone. "*Rodimy,*" Frossia whispered for the third time, unaware that her very passion for the city which bore her, warred against the separatist in her, and the city replied to her with its silence as comforting as anything she had ever known.

Frossia had left Petrograd in the late autumn of 1916. Her people had then insisted on going to the Ukraine. "The place is getting more tiresomely disturbing," decided Grandmamma, and the great jeweler's shop in Morskaya Street was handed over to a capable manager—but not before a huge black leather trunk had been

13

brought into Grandmamma's bedroom, and Frossia must stay and write a neat inventory on sheets of expensive thick white paper. Slowly, precisely, Grandmamma dictated, and her small pale hands went on opening one green velvet box after another. All Bozert jewelry was housed in impeccable green velvet boxes, lined with discreet gold satin. Gradually the vast bedroom was crowded with mounds and mounds of moss, and Frossia thought of churchyards, and shivered in spite of the heat in the room.

Grandmamma went on with the dictation. The inventory was purely factual. No comment was to find any place in it, no history of any single gem added to the sere commercial recital. "And yet," mused Frossia, her fingers busy with the pen, "they must have a story behind them all. Some of them were old before Papa's people reset them." Dutifully she wrote:

"Necklace, pearls, pink, clasp—a square emerald set in brilliants. 64 pearls. A." She slowly wrote out the huge distinctive capital at the end of the entry. All jewelry was graded at Bozert's—"A," "B," "C," and "D"—the latter lacking entirely in the inventory Frossia was making.

"Necklace, pink tourmalines, 3 opals in clasp. 45 stones. B."

"Necklace, 25 diamonds and 10 sapphires. A."

"Necklace, 39 rubies, clasp 3 diamonds. A."

"One cabochon ruby set in pearls. Platinum chain. B."

"One sapphire cross, 12 stones. Pearl chain, 50 pearls. A."

"One anchor of rubies, 15 stones. Chain of smaller rubies, 47 stones. A."

Here she raised her face from the paper. She could see green velvet boxes all round her, Grandmamma's white hands all the paler against the dark velvet, Grandmamma's thin ivoried face intent upon the gems scattered on the tiny tulipwood table. Grandmamma had several faces—one for the food she ate, one for domestics and their broils, one for Frossia's father, one for church, and the one for church was the same she had now—intent, all gathered-in, all absorbed in the shining things under her hands as though the jewels of heavenly Jerusalem and the trinkets from her son-in-law's store were fashioned from the same materials.

"This anchor," said Frossia, "must be very valuable."

"It is," Grandmamma replied briefly from a distance, and picked up yet another green box. "Write, Euphrosynia, a crescent of emeralds, 10 stones, chain of—"

But Frossia had no concern for emerald crescents. She put down the pen.

"What are you going to do with them?"

14

Grandmamma's delicate frown was a swift reminder that questions were never welcomed in her room, but Frossia disregarded the frown, and her pen lay idle.

"A crescent of emeralds," Grandmamma repeated with grim emphasis, glanced at Frossia's motionless hands, and said icily: "You might send for Nina Petrovna if you feel bored. I must have this inventory finished today."

"Grandmamma, are we taking these things to Kiev?"

"Do I then have to ring for Nina Petrovna?"

Frossia went.

Later, in the Ukraine, through the first turmoiled days of March, 1917, she heard the old nurse say on a dim landing:

"In all truth—this must be the day of Anti-Christ—"

Through an opened doorway Frossia heard Nina Petrovna moan in eager agreement. Nina Petrovna was born forty, shrunken, timid, a fully trained companion to rich old women.

Nina Petrovna and the old nurse never agreed. They could not. The nurse was a domestic by right and by birth, so she said. Nina Petrovna, scoffed the nurse, was a domestic by misfortune. Nina Petrovna disliked the nurse who despised her. But now they could chant in happy unison.

"Anti-Christ's day," wailed the nurse.

"The end of the world," crooned Nina Petrovna, gathered up her narrow silk skirts and click-clicked her way into the dining room for the morning tea. There she sat down, unfolded the napkin, and repeated piously:

"The end of the world—"

"No world could end quite like that," ventured Frossia.

"Euphrosynia Pavlovna, what are you saying?" In horror and confusion Nina Petrovna went on piling peach jam on a white china saucer.

"Well, it may be the end of peach jam for all of us. But jam was finished for nearly everybody ages ago. There were bread queues in Petrograd when we left—"

"Euphrosynia Pavlovna, this is—why, it is socialism. You talk as though you had been to that dreadful university."

"I wish I had. But it is not politics. It is merely a question of living. We have lived for generations. Others have not. They must have a chance. It is only fair—"

Nina Petrovna stopped eating her jam.

"Your Grandmamma would have a heart attack if she heard you. To hear you saying such dreadful, impious things! You—Euphrosynia Pavlovna, of all people—"

15

Frossia laughed.

"Nina Petrovna, why do you always flatter me? We are not aristocrats. Papa is a very clever jeweler. But how does his passport describe him? A merchant. A—"

"Of the first Guild—"

"Yes, that is important, of course, and my tailor belongs to the second Guild, and the grocer to the third, and the ironmonger to the fourth—but they are all the same, really, merchants, *kuptzy*—"

Nina Petrovna's thin face went a nervous mottled red.

"You forget that your father married—"

"Yes, a prince's daughter, but his marriage did not ennoble either him or us. And did Grandmamma like it?" asked Frossia. "Do our exalted cousins take any notice of us? Rarely—except when they need money. Why, take our lovely incomparable Marianne. Do we know her? No. She comes into the shop in Morskaya Street, she buys things, she always buys a lot. She is known to have bought seven fitted dressing cases in as many years. And so many other things. She is no relation of Papa's—except by marriage—but she is Grandmamma's great-niece. She is very important. She buys jewels from her contemptible uncle by marriage—but she does not really buy them, Nina Petrovna. She takes them, and then ignores the bills. If Papa were to sue her, Grandmamma would say "What an outrage!" He could never do it. . . . And Marianne—now that this business has started—will probably escape to safety abroad on the jewels stolen from us. . . . Yes, stolen, Nina Petrovna. And I shall say it again—the word pleases me—lovely, patrician Marianne, daughter of one prince, wife of another, knows how to steal. . . ."

"Euphrosynia Pavlovna—"

Nina Petrovna wept. When she wept, she looked like a bird with crippled wings, left too long out in the rain, and Frossia went away with a shrug. But Grandmamma heard fragments of the discussion and sent for her.

"How can you possibly talk about that *canaille* being given a chance?"

"Why should they not?"

"You are so young. You do not seem to realize the necessity of careful social grading. Now a world is lying about us in ruins and—"

"Well, it may be a catastrophe, but so many of us asked for it. Look at Uncle Serge—"

"Your Uncle Serge was badly wounded in the war. . . . How dare you?"

"Yes, but before the war he used to light his cigars with hundred rouble notes, and there were always people who starved—"

16

"Rubbish! Nobody need starve in this country. There is plenty for everybody."

"Is there?" she demanded passionately. "Has there ever been?"

But she received no answer. Nobody could argue with Grandmamma. You had all your own arguments ready, you had them strung as faultlessly as a necklet of pearls, you knew you could clothe them with fierce and beautiful words, but Grandmamma's manner was like layers of thick cottonwool thrown over the fierceness and beauty. She said little. She could merely say "Rubbish," and your words lay shriveled and useless, even though you knew she was wrong. Grandmamma regarded life in terms of birth, behavior. Birth meant blue blood to her, behavior was expressed in a sequence of rigidly determined social gestures. There was nothing else in Grandmamma's vision. Certainly there were no ideas. An idea was like a bomb to her. Ideas came from places like universities where students, their necks unwashed and their hair uncut, wasted time in waving red flags down streets and quays. The red flag was certainly an idea.

"Rubbish," she said again. "Nobody need starve. Your brain is full of most fantastic nonsense, Euphrosynia."

"Well, my brain would not be in such a muddle if you had let me go to college."

"That is stupid, Euphrosynia. You are extremely well educated. You had most expensive governesses. Also you went to a very *comme il faut* private school. No granddaughter of mine could possibly have gone to a university."

Grandmamma was something more than an anachronism. She was a beautiful and incredible muddle. She belonged wholly. She had no links with the mushroom-bred crowd fobbed off with titles in the eighteenth century. Grandmamma was a Rurikovich, a far nobler and more ancient lineage than the Romanovs. She had the right to ermine on her coat of arms. Her people had begun in the mistiest beginnings of Russian history. "More than eight centuries ago, from father to son," and she would pore exultingly over the frayed parchment of a pedigree copied by a monk of a great abbey in the neighborhood of Kiev, and Frossia, impertinently unimpressed, murmured back: "From Adam onwards it must have gone on from father to son. It is nothing but a name, and are names much more than labels?"

"Of course," Grandmamma spoke icily, "I always forget that you do not quite belong—"

That was where she proved herself at once a muddle and a contradiction—in her strangely colored vulgarity. Nearly all her traits

17

ran counter to most traditions of her race. Grandmamma cherished her pedigree. She also loved jewels and money, and she possessed neither. However, she had a daughter, and at seventeen the daughter was married to one of the richest merchants in the country, and Grandmamma clothed her greed in several flimsy explanations: "It is a love match. *Elle est folle, mais je ne m'y opposerai guère. Je l'aime à la folie. Du reste—*" she shrugged, laboriously explaining that Paul Bozert was of very good French descent. Grandmamma never narrated the more obscure details: an ancestor of Frossia's father did come to Tula from a slum in Marseilles some time in the reign of the Empress Anne, about 1736. He was no artist, a mere undistinguished worker in copper and brass, and he got himself apprenticed to a second-rate firm of samovar makers.

Paul Bozert lived for his trade which was pure art to him. Grandmamma possessed herself of the children even during their mother's lifetime. Anna Bozert had so often been told about her fragility that she ended by believing in it. Frossia had known and adored her mother but from a distance; someone beautiful, always thin, always speaking in a murmur, a person etched in faint pastel colors both in mind and body. Her father was different. He was tall, dark, substantial both in voice and manner and, in spite of his prodigious success as a court jeweler, always happy to get back to his bench. But Grandmamma succeeded in domineering even him. She would never openly recognize the Bozert wealth, though, herself impoverished, she later lived in grandeur made possible by her son-in-law's bounty. She had her own grievances. Herself the last of her line, she had asked the Emperor that her grandson, Frossia's brother, might be allowed to bear the old title, and the refusal had certainly soured her. It had all been rather piteous because, in reality, she did possess the splendor of many generations living in her. She was well versed both in history and in legend of her race, and she cheapened both by her attempt to compromise with her innate greed.

Between the great house in Sergievskaya Street in Petrograd and the huge place near Kiev, Frossia had lived, full of love and hatred also, admiring, criticizing, rebelling, accepting. Grandmamma always occupied the very center of that glittering scene. Then there were uncles, a superior, though lovable cockerel of a brother, himself annoyed at being denied his grandmother's dignity, a succession of fussy and snobbish governesses, French and English, engaged solely on titled references, and she, Frossia, always a shuttlecock, with her vagueness, her impossible ideas, her frequent and absurd rebellions, her stubborn refusal to develop into a pleasant and creditable social specimen, and her disastrous talent for making friends who could never be invited under the family roof. "You may, if you wish, call the postmaster's daughter by her Christian name but, of course, I could never ask her to the ball," and, secretly irritated, Frossia would parry: "Of course not, Grandmamma. Poor Mania would be bewildered and utterly bored. She does like real fun, you know."

There they had been, sometimes irritating and often absurd, but the end had splendor as well as tragedy in it. Of that end she dared not think too much, though, inevitably, it stayed near her. She could not escape such thoughts because, in her own way, she had loved them all.

3

In the still darkness she went down Palace Quay. The morning would come in time for her to see the beloved place, undoubtedly broken and charred, its beauty wronged by flame and bullet. Petrograd, as they had tried to convince her in Kiev, was a hotbed of sniping, looting, massacres, wholesale raids, and worse. Instead of a bedlam Frossia had found a churchyard.

She had already passed the dead curtained face of Marble Palace. Now she reached the corner of a tiny lane running away from the Quay to Millionnaya Street, and turned into it. She had earlier remembered that there was a private house with a garden fronting the lane, and a small gate in the wall. In the garden stood a summerhouse. It had a bench. She had some matches in her luggage. Now that she was in Moshkov Lane, she knew herself spent; she had plodded all the long way from the station, a heavy suitcase in each hand, a sack on her back, and there had been but slender chance of a rest during the endless journey from Kiev.

Tired, Frossia could not find the gate. The shadows had by now thickened to an impenetrable dark, and the relatively hardened snow of the granite quay pavements was here turned to slippery mush. Frossia made an uncertain step forward, lurched against the wall, and stood still, cold stone close to her cheek. If this is the wall, the gate must be quite near, and she ordered her shaking fingers to go on with their fumbling and searching even though her feet kept on stumbling and slipping. Snow, swept away from the quays by the wind and, probably, occasional labor, lay here and there in high uneven mounds, wet, slippery, treacherous. Once she fell, and for an instant she could not get up. When she did, her outstretched hand groped and found nothing but air. The wall had vanished, and her body seemed hers no longer but something alien, an encumbrance which must be got rid of without delay.

19

"Find the wall. You have got to find the wall again," Frossia commanded her left hand, and groped blindly until the benumbed fingers once again brushed against the cold wet stone. Another moment slipped by, she felt wood under her touch, and her heart beat faster. There was the latch. She lifted it. Now she was inside. Cautiously she made her way to the summerhouse, found the door, and sank on the floor, pulling the sack off her shoulders and fumbling for a match. The pale yellow bud of the flame gave her the tiny refuge, rich in cobwebs and dust. A sodden, half-rotten rug still lay across a low marble bench. Overhead the roof caved in rather drunkenly. "But it is a roof," Frossia said, pushed the bolt in the small door, supped off a sour milk tart and a hard-boiled egg, got a rug and some shawls out of the sack, snuffed out the candle, and slept; a vagabond come back within her own gates.

4

She was still asleep when the gray fingers of a winter dawn crept through the dusty latticed window and stroked her grimy cheek. And, across the ice-shackled river, life began to stir in a small room on the sixth floor of a derelict house on the 15th Line of the Vasilyev Island. The 15th Line may have had some pretensions to gentility at its beginning, between Nicholas Quay and Bolshoy Prospect, but the derelict house stood cheek-by-jowl with the unsavory avenue known as Maly Prospect, and its dirty ocher walls, tiny windows and murky staircases were so many admissions of its humble status. "I am just a tenement block, and don't let us argue about it," it seemed to say to every passer-by.

The room was small, warm, dark, tenanted by odds and ends of decrepit furniture. All of it, bed, chair, table, and cupboard, expressed the same theme. We were not here yesterday, we might not be here tomorrow. If logs run short again, we might walk into the stove.

The old woman was the first to rise from under a mass of indeterminate blankets and rugs in a corner. She was small, like the room, and her hair shone white in the candlelight, but she moved about briskly and lightly as though neither years nor cares lay on her thin shoulders. She moved softly, set a match to a smelly kerosene stove, filled a saucepan from an aluminum pail on the floor, and set the saucepan on to boil. Her fingers were red and stiff. She breathed on them, murmuring, "I must not rub them. It hurts so." She stood watching the saucepan, a small woman, with a small

20

winter apple of a face and sunken brown eyes. Then she turned back to the dim corner and spoke in a clear loud voice:

"It is time to get up, Vanichka. It is almost seven. It is market day," she added, her eyes on the saucepan. "The water is nearly boiling."

From under an avalanche of rugs and rags, a swollen bluish face turned to her. The eyes were barely open, but the mouth was smiling.

"Nearly boiling? Mashenka, my angel, you do look after me. Now just fancy—I had a dream about our wedding day. No, not a dream, a real memory, just as it happened, you dropping the gloves, and the colonel picking them up, and my batman forgetting to pack the razors. Do you remember?"

"As though I could ever forget!"

"Let me see—my best man did something dreadful."

"Yes, he trod on my train and tore off a flounce. What a to-do! But his mother was so nice. She sent me six yards of the best Valencienne. Do you remember? I had my brown silk dress trimmed with it."

"Yes, Mashenka. And do you remember the lemonade at Ymatra? It had not enough sugar, you said, and you wanted to sweeten it, and you put in some salt by mistake—"

He gabbled on, half in bed, half out of it, a little shriveled man with mouse-gray hair, a stubby chin, and a very old cotton nightshirt. He gabbled on, time was slipping, but she had not the heart to check him. She listened and smiled as she poured boiling water over a carefully measured spoonful of dried black currant leaves, and cut a piece of rough rye bread into two purposely unequal portions.

"Mashenka, this dream must be a good omen. I, Ivan Petrovich Parnikov, retired infantry captain, may be seventy-two, my pension has gone and our savings are spent, but we never whine much, Mashenka, do we . . . unless—"

A different note crept into his wife's voice:

"We never whine, Vania. But come on. This tea will not keep hot much longer—"

He shuffled up to the table.

"There is always room for a miracle, Mashenka, if you hope hard enough for it. The worst about all of us is that we do not hope hard enough. Hope is good fresh milk, and we must always water it down. Why, a commissar's wife or else some foreigner might notice the beryl pendant and buy it, and then we shall have no worries for months."

21

"Yes, Vania."

The tea drunk, he dressed himself slowly. His coat needed careful handling and, struggling into a patched sleeve, he stood still, the timid sunlight of the dream already stealing away from him.

"A retired infantry captain, Mashenka . . . And I used to think I would have a brigade—at least, the day I married you. You should have been a general's wife. I never had any luck. Mashenka, are you not tired of me? Look, I have even lost my pension."

"How could you help it, my darling? It is the revolution—"

"Yes, but Lilian . . . Mashenka, you know I think it is all my fault about Lilian. . . . Had we not been always so poor—"

This time Maria Nikolaevna spoke sternly: "Vania, really, it is time we went—"

"Yes, yes." He fumbled with a scarf round his thin throat. "And we must be careful on those stairs. They are so slippery and there is nobody to clean them now. You know I am a coward, Mashenka. I simply dare not go near the House Committee."

"They are such dreadful people, Vanichka, the Domkom men. They always bully you, and you are a gentleman."

"I am a fool," said Captain Parnikov, watching her spread a darned handkerchief on the table. Candlelight caught and held the beryl earrings so that he must smile again. "Mashenka, that ball at Krasnoe Selo . . . You wore them—"

"Let us go," she said briefly.

The wide unswept street welcomed them with a gust of wind and powdery snow. He shook his head, sniffing. "North again . . . In late March . . . Even the weather has changed. . . ." Then he remembered her dislike of conversational effort in the streets, and was silent. They passed people hurrying to queues and people hurrying to jobs, and people hurrying just anywhere as if swift movement offered them solace they might not seek elsewhere. They passed thin flocks of obviously homeless, bedraggled children, drab brown bundles of them, slinking along, making for queues and market places, hoping for crumbs to be picked, begged, or merely stolen. They passed girls, competent in look and certain of gait, clothed in shabby khaki, and Captain Parnikov shifted his eyes when he saw them. They passed men and mere boys, clothed in queer clumsy uniforms, rifles over their shoulders, home-rolled cigarettes hanging wispily from their lips. Everybody hurried, everybody went about with the air of saying that their business was exclusively theirs, and nobody must interfere with them: and yet, nonetheless, everybody, including the Parnikovs, walked that gray scene profoundly and achingly conscious that someone could and did interfere with the least thing they had a mind to do. The day of carefully patterned privacies was over. The dawn of genuinely communal sharing had not yet broken.

At the corner of the 15th Line and Bolshoy Prospect, a young girl stood, a tray with tiny brown rolls swung from her shoulders. She stood erect, still, silent, expecting passers-by to purchase her admittedly appetizing wares, but not daring to solicit such purchasing either by word or glance. They hurried past her, Maria Nikolaevna shaking her head. They disapproved of such ventures. It was foolhardy to offer things all alone, at a street corner. There lay some measure of safety in numbers. A market place would be raided often enough, but not everybody was doomed to suffer in a crowd. "Silly," muttered Captain Parnikov. "Mashenka, if anything should happen to me, you must promise never to run such risks."

They reached the traditional market place just off the 6th Line. They were not the first. Here and there, a few straggling lines of roughly timbered stalls displayed what food could still be smuggled in from the country—butter at so many millions a pound, potatoes at so many millions a sack, eggs sold apiece at a dizzy price, various buns and cookies made of rye and barley flour, and even bottles of vehemently colored fruit syrup. Maria Nikolaevna halted to observe some pancakes, and the captain nudged her gently. "Later, my darling, later. . . . We must get our business done first." He did not want to remind her that between them they had not got the price of a single bun.

They had had their perch for months, and now made for it. He fixed a small camp stool for her and stood beside her. She spread a handkerchief over her lap and arranged three or four oddments of tortoiseshell and ivory, a fan, a cardcase, an oval snuffbox. The beryls must stay hidden until a possible and comparatively trustworthy customer came their way.

It was a cold morning. Most people ignored both ivory and tortoiseshell and shuffled past them towards the food stalls. Still Maria Nikolaevna sat, quiet and very straight, her small shriveled face resolutely void of the least expression of anxiety. Her Vania had had a gorgeous dream, and now she let her mind take refuge in its lovingly remembered details.

Suddenly she heard him cry in a voice shaking with pleasure:

"Mashenka, Mashenka, look, look . . . There is Frossia—I mean Euphrosynia Pavlovna. . . . And however you did get here? Why, we thought you were far away, in Kiev?"

23

Frossia dumped both suitcases on the ground and ran, both hands outstretched.

"You—dears, dears." Pleasure outstripped her speech, her eyes burned, her mouth laughed. "Why, I have been to the house in Nicholas Quay, and they said you had left, and now meeting you here—"

Maria Nikolaevna dropped both fan and cardcase. She clung to Frossia.

"When did you come? Let me look at you, please. You are thinner, you are paler, but you are the same Frossia. And you look so grown up, so deepened. . . . Why, I should be calling you Euphrosynia Pavlovna—"

"Never, never. I shall be always Frossia. I came last night. Yes, I came from Kiev. But look, it is so cold. We must not stand here—"

"Have you eaten?"

"Oh, yes. . . . But is that so important? Where is Sasha? and Lilian? And where do you live?"

Maria Nikolaevna stooped to pick up the ivory cardcase. Captain Parnikov coughed.

"Sasha? May the kingdom of heaven be his! Last November a sniper in Nevsky Prospect got him, Euphrosynia Pavlovna. Now we have no children left—"

"But Lilian?"

"We have no children left," he repeated, his voice like a key turning in the lock, and Frossia asked no more. Maria Nikolaevna sat still, her shawled head bent, and Captain Parnikov stood staring at some food stall in the distance, and in the muted hubbub of that market place the three found themselves on an island of silence, and Frossia knew she was shaken by the brief encounter.

For months she had believed—however vaguely—that the whole upheaval was but a beginning to greater and more satisfying orderliness. It had ended some things, she said, but some things were better finished. Now something seemed wrong. Here were the tired, shabby, timid Parnikovs whom, years ago, she had met at an unimportant house in Petrograd, whom she could never invite under her grandmother's roof, whose children, particularly the boy Sasha, a brilliant medical student, had been her friends. These people had not oppressed anyone, could never boast of either riches or rank, they were just ordinary unimportant people. Yet the upheaval had not spared them. They looked hungry, shabby, they seemed dwarfed. They had, obviously, griefs they could not explain, and Frossia wished she might cry—both in bewilderment and in anger, but she had lost all power to cry since a day in Kiev.

"So you came last night," Maria Nikolaevna was saying. "Did you go to Sergievskaya Street?"

"No." Somehow Frossia felt reluctant to mention the summer-house.

"And you must not go there. They looted your flat. Fyodor left ages ago. A nasty woman lives there, Frossinka, you would not understand what I mean—a nasty painted woman. All scented and very loud of voice. . . . They said she was a Lett or something like that. Vania and I went over some months ago, we wanted to hear some news of you, but there was nobody to tell us."

"I shall not go to Sergievskaya Street," Frossia said mechanically, her mind still absorbed in the suddenly born bewilderment.

"Come to us," said the Captain. "Yes, Mashenka?"

"Of course, come to us. There is a small room and a sofa." Maria Nikolaevna looked almost happy. "Now, Vania, you stay here, and I will take Frossia home. See, she is so tired. You leave it all to me," and she dropped her voice to an anxious whisper: "For pity's sake, do sell something, Vanichka, no matter how cheaply. The child must have a meal. It does not matter about you and me—"

They left the Captain in charge of tortoiseshell and ivory and threaded their way out of the market place, Maria Nikolaevna busily explaining:

"Take no notice of what he said, golubushka. Lilian is not dead. It is a man—I cannot even remember his name. She says she is married to him. Vania does not believe it. He is dreadful. He wears a shamelessly new leather coat, lives in scandalous plenty—she told me they even had meat and wine and sugar, and he shoots people by the dozen. They have no home life. Lilian goes all over the place—and always by herself. There are still some cafés left open in Nevsky Prospect where you pay about a million for a cup of coffee. It is a shame and a grief, Frossia. Lilian is not alive. She looks a painted doll and she lives like one. And she is seldom enough sober these days. . . . But I have told you enough. This is not interesting." She glanced sideways. "Now how did you get here?"

"By train. They still run sometimes. Ours was no proper carriage, just a cattle truck. But it had wooden seats of a kind."

"Why did you come, Frossinka?"

"I do belong here, Maria Nikolaevna."

"It is your people I had in mind. Nowadays families get so dreadfully divided, and I heard that you were all together there near Kiev."

"We were—"

25

"Well?"

"Please, Maria Nikolaevna, they are all gone. It is a bit like Ivan Petrovich and Lilian—and yet different. Something happened, and they are not there any more, and I am all alone in the world, but, please, I may tell you some day—"

Maria Nikolaevna said nothing. She stopped, put down the suitcase, made the sign of the cross over Frossia, and kissed her. The kiss was shy and brief, but it said much. It said: "I am here. Use me when you need me." It said: "Our home is yours, and we are your people." It said: "We could not make you forget, nobody could, but we can make you feel you are wanted by us." Finally, the kiss said: "God need never be away from all forsaken people."

The kiss had said so much and Frossia had heard it all. Now she must do something for Maria Nikolaevna and, as soon as they had climbed to the sixth floor and her belongings were taken to the small room with a sofa, Frossia said quietly:

"Maria Nikolaevna, I mean to see Lilian. Today. This morning. Before Ivan Petrovich is back. You know her address, do you not?"

"See Lilian? My angel, why should you see Lilian?"

"I know I could never bring her back, but I can tell her about you two. She might feel ashamed, and shame is good."

"Frossinka, it would not be decent. Why, an old friend of ours went to see her once and found her drunk."

"She could hardly be in the morning. I mean to see her."

She remembered Lilian; ugly so as to appear attractive, with a badly shapen long nose, curiously hooded green eyes, and a large greedy mouth. Lilian expected nothing to come to her in life, she went out of her way to grab at things. Yet there had been something of a friendship between her and Frossia, hers rooted in unashamed greed, and Frossia's in sheer curiosity. Even Lilian's greed was not of the usual kind.

"I mean to see her," repeated Frossia, got the address from the bewildered and speechless Maria Nikolaevna, and went.

She found the house tucked away in a stuffy narrow street off Liteyny Prospect. It was a block of single rooms with loud pretensions to expensive flatdom. There was a liftshaft and no lift, a conciergerie and no concierge, a profusion of appalling stained glass and vulgar veneer on the cheap wood of staircases and doors, smell of cabbage, cats, and an unpleasant dimness everywhere. In a corner Frossia saw a huge sheet of fly-blown paper pinned to the wall and covered with heavily inked names and numbers. She read that Serge Grammère de Garonne inhabited room No. 126 on the fifth floor. This was the only unusual name on the board, and she remembered Maria Nikolaevna saying that the son-in-law's surname was so uncommon nobody could believe it was his. Frossia mounted the incredibly dirty stairs, wondering what she would find at the end of her pilgrimage.

She found a big room mainly furnished with two beds and an enormous table. The table carried a pair of lady's pale suède boots, soiled teacups, a broken accordion, some untidy paper parcels, and a startling green vase. One of the beds, its counterpane pulled off, was strewn with greasy playing cards. From the other a disheveled fair head raised itself, green eyes stared, thin bare arms flashed in the air, and a voice minced:

"It is never—never—my own Frossia—" and Lilian was up in a none too fresh nightgown, sticking bare feet into slovenly slippers. So swiftly did she run across the room that Frossia could not escape a kiss.

"You are here in Petrograd—looking lovelier than ever! How did you get here? And find me . . . Goodness, this is a miracle. Now sit, sit, my angel." She pulled Frossia down on the tumbled bed. "Have a drink? I have two whole bottles of *hanja*. No? Darling, why this grimace? *Hanja* is not all petrol. Have you any cigarettes on you? I have run out of them. Serge said he would bring some. No? Ah, well? One must learn self-control in these difficult days. Darling, I have so much to tell you. Can you imagine me as a married woman?"

She laughed. The room was warm and airless. She crouched on the bed, the pink nightgown almost slipping off one shoulder. Frossia stared at the green vase on the table and asked:

"How did you come to meet him? Yes, I have heard that you were married."

"On the market. Yes, just so. I went to sell an old shawl of Mother's. You have no conception what those two are like. They will not accept the facts. They just sit and whine. Father would not let Mother go to any market place, so I went. Can you imagine the risks? Well, I stood there, and Serge came along, so wonderful in a real leather coat with a fur collar and lovely brown leggings. He said: 'Is that all you have to sell?' I was so sick and tired that day, Frossia, what with those two grumbling at home, and no hot water and no gas, and I had used up my last piece of soap, and I knew my face looked awful, and I did not know what I was saying. Do you know what I said to him? 'All? Well, no, there is myself with a marriage license.' He said: 'You are impertinent,' and went away. The next day I was there again—I could not help it—could I?—I tell you there was not a crumb in the house. He came along

27

again and asked: 'Where do you live?' Of course, I told him I lived at home. He laughed. In a week we were married. He is sometimes a savage, Frossia, but so marvelous. He will go very far. Even commissars are afraid of him."

"Why should they be?"

Lilian tittered.

"Well, I cannot tell you. It is a very great secret. Of course, it is partly his name. It is a wonderful name. Why, he is the last lineal descendant of French kings—"

"I should have thought that would go against him—"

"No, he is not a Romanov. Besides, angel, he is the most blood-thirsty communist, and that is what pleases them all so much—to have an aristocrat turned red."

"How long have you been married?"

"Ten months, I think. Sometimes he goes his way, and I choose mine. But he married me, my angel, because I am a lady and he is particular."

Frossia tried to convince herself that she felt sick owing to the airlessness in the room.

"I suppose he is hard at work," she said, wondering about the nature of occupations left for a descendant of French kings stranded in Petrograd. "And what are you doing?"

Lilian made a strange face. Suddenly Frossia thought of a monkey left out in the cold, its oddly ugly and attractive face pressed against the windowpane of a room it might not enter.

"Oh, we are very happy, but he does not like taking me to all the places he goes to. That is natural. Well, I dress in the afternoon. . . . There are a few cafés in Nevsky Prospect, Chat Noir and Bi-Ba-Bo, and a marvelous place in Moyka, and a hotel down in Gorokhovaya Street—not far from where Rasputin lived, you remember. Someone always buys my meals. Why, I had caviare the other evening. Of course, we never go short here, Serge sees to that. Well, angel, there is still some fun to be had in Petrograd. My old parents refuse to see it. And commissars are most interesting people, forthright, sudden, unusual. They all admire me. . . ."

Then Frossia knew she need not have come at all. Lilian would ask no questions, she never did, and she need never know with whom Frossia was staying, whose stone-graven grief she was even now remembering. And is she worth any grieving? marveled Frossia. I suppose so—in a way. She is flesh of their flesh, but I do wish they might learn that her flesh has wandered worlds away from the ways of their own clean and simple flesh. There is nothing I can say to her. Just nothing. She might perhaps invite a quarrel, shake

28

Lilian by the shoulders, scream sharp abuse at her, drench her soiled shallow mind in the hot wine of fury, and what good would it do? She shrugged in reply to her own thoughts, and rose to go when the door opened, and Lilian's husband was in the room.

For quite five minutes Frossia examined him at her leisure. For quite five minutes neither husband nor wife took any notice of her. Lilian rushed to him, slovenly slippers flopping on her feet, and he buried his face in her bare neck.

He was small and wizened, Grammère de Garonne, as he liked people to call him. He looked cruel. Everything about him was thin—face, body, voice. His small brown eyes peered rather than looked at people. His manner was that of a second-rate shop assistant, though his accent revealed no such social attainment. Frossia knew nothing of his antecedents and had little desire to know them. Details would have told her that he was an illegitimate son of a Petrograd dvornik by an Esthonian milkwoman, an illiterate piece of indeterminate flotsam, also a deserter from the old imperial army, life in the ranks having proved too much for his love of indolence. Ignorant of such details, Frossia guessed at the broad outline, thought of the Parnikovs, and was angry because they had not deserved him.

He stopped kissing his wife and peered at Frossia who immediately thought of some incredible cross between a vulture and a hyena. Then Lilian remembered her.

"Serge, this is Frossia Bozert. Her mother was Princess Martov. You remember her—"

"Of course, they were my father's greatest friends." He spoke in a thin brittle voice, and did not offer to shake hands, and Frossia smothered a tiny sigh of relief.

"Indeed? I am so sorry I do not remember you, M. de Garonne, and I have lived with my grandmother all my life." She spoke with her usual directness and knew that she might just as well have showered open abuse on Lilian. But diplomacy had forsaken Frossia, she was challenging, she spoke in French. A brief pause fell. In the silence she read Lilian's declaration of war and, aware of it, Frossia did not care. "Where did you meet my people? At Kiev? Or here? Or was it your father—did you say? Perhaps it is my own memory that is at fault." Frossia went on hammering out her challenge in fast and flawless French, and Lilian must interfere, awkwardly, clumsily, as though she were trying to retrieve a garter in some public place and the garter kept on slipping through her fingers.

"Angel, I know this sounds ludicrous, there are so many mysteries, but, you see, Serge does not know any French yet."

"Really? That is a mystery." Frossia wanted to laugh, controlled herself, and another gap was bridged by Lilian's sullen voice:

"I am sorry. It must seem a muddle to you. It is not, really. Now what about coming to the Chat Noir this evening? You and I and a few friends. We might find beer or something."

Frossia excused herself. She had not been in Petrograd long enough. There was much to do. Neither asked her questions. She murmured "good-by." Lilian did not offer to kiss her again, and Serge grinned, peering at her. She went. Neither Serge nor Lilian found much to say about her. He emptied his pockets of sweets, cigarettes, liquor. She kissed him greedily. They ate, drank, smoked. Then Lilian poured a cupful of water into the chipped basin, sponged her face, dabbed it with the fringe of a towel, and scrambled into her clothes. Serge swept the cards off the bed and tumbled into it. In a few moments she heard him snore. She was used to his sleeping by daytime.

5

Frossia could not tell much to the Parnikovs, but she knew they would guess all left unsaid by her. The Captain would blame the revolution and Maria Nikolaevna the devil, and Frossia could not say: "Yes, it is awful. You were right. There was nothing I could do, but it is neither the devil nor the revolution. Lilian would have been just the same if Nicholas II were still in his palace at Tsarskoe Selo. Perhaps not quite so crude, but does mere crudity matter in her case? Lilian never had much shame. She was always a glutton. Now she is afraid of missing anything: a cigarette, a free meal, a man, a bottle of spirits. She has always been the same. I once liked her, we were friendly, but she always sponged on me for gloves, sweets, ices, theater tickets, anything."

She could say none of those things to the Parnikovs, and she would have to choose widely different topics, invite Maria Nikolaevna to her room, discuss some plans for the future, show her the things salvaged from Kiev. . . .

Frossia reached Nicholas Bridge, and here she must pause, her hands quiet on the snow-powdered gryphon railings. Below lay the river, calm and incredibly beautiful under her sheath of green-white ice. It had been a severe winter, and now, at the end of March, the ice had not yet begun to show the least sign of cracking. But the deep shackling mood of the winter had already gone from the air and the wind, and the primrose clouds above Vasilyev Island spoke of enchantments soon to be born of April evenings and May nights.

Yet she was not considering the island. Behind her, separated by two or three silent closed-in streets, lay a square. Almost Frossia had meant to go there straight from the station, turning the walk into a pilgrimage, but she had not dared. Even on her second day in the beloved city she felt she must still exercise her self-control, deny herself, even for a while, the sharp incredible joy which would be hers once she stood and looked at the great colonnaded building where her first and truest love had flowered. A date slipped into Frossia's memory, a January date in remote 1914, when Kschessinskaya was Esmeralda and Stukolkin—Quasimodo, when the entire cream-crimson of the Mariinsky Theater burned with lights and jewels because the imperial box was occupied, and she, Frossia, slight and awkward in pale pink tulle, must get up with the rest of the audience because a small spare figure, dressed in green, ran on to the stage. That day was the great Legat's silver jubilee, they drenched the stage with exotic flowers, and someone's thundering voice recited a telegraphed distich:

> "Oh, Terpsichore, thou art rich
> In having given us a Legat."

It was late when they came home, and Frossia pleaded fatigue, refused lemonade and lobster patties, and sought her own room there to seize a pen and write: "Why, I believe all real ballet is true life. There soul and flesh find a point where they can meet and stay together. I think that movement, poised and controlled, should be the world's language. I knew myself as I watched Kschessinskaya tonight, and I felt free and fruitful and all in order inside, and I would have no words to express it. There is something far clearer than speech in such perfect movement—"

She tried it herself, very hard at Mademoiselle Loiret's in Gogol Street, and how direly she failed.

"Your limbs are just bone and iron, Mademoiselle. They should be fluent like water."

Yet ballet had flowed in her, and even now, shabby, dispossessed and alone, running down the deserted Nicholas Square, Frossia felt herself all caught up into the delicate drifts of Tchaikovsky's *Lac des Cygnes,* music as clear and white as the snow over the Neva's ice and as coldly impersonal, and therefore, thought Frossia, utterly satisfying. A poet, she remembered, later than Tchaikovsky, wrote a plangent lyric about an old swan singing in his evening hour:

31

Because on the threshold of all-reconciling death
He had seen Truth for the first time—

Lac des Cygnes was all alive with it. *"Cher Dieu,"* murmured Frossia, stood still, and closed her eyes.

Behind her lay the vast square, and in front stood a shuttered confectioner's shop, a neat row of ordinary houses, with the lime-fringed arrow of the 6th Line running away from the square, things of dark timber and darker stone, comfortably poised in a turmoiled three-dimensioned world, and Frossia's small feet pressed the snow-caked cobbles. But she had her eyes closed to look at other things.

So she had her moonlit wood, a young prince in shimmering green, and his men hunting the swans, the easy, the definite, chasing the hard, the indefinite. . . . But the hunters vanished, the slender prince found himself alone and baffled. Across the clearing broke the shimmer of a lake, and its shining waters bore the swan towards him. The swan was not a Sedova, not even Frossia out of her body, but a disembodied symbol, given a cloud of white-rose plumage to satisfy one's longings for the definite. The swan left the lake, the cygnets joined her, the world became a whirl of fragile rose-feathers, and Frossia opened her eyes.

She had forgotten a dim untidy room back of Liteyny Prospect, as well as its soiled tenants. But she must not forget the Parnikovs. Dreams of remembered loveliness could still be welcome guests of her leisure, but not inmates of all her moments. She must think of the Parnikovs, and settle down in the new environment, and start questing for a job since without work nobody might live in the city. . . .

In the doorway of the great block she saw Captain Parnikov. She smiled at him, saw his underlip shake, and wished she might escape his eyes.

"You should not have done it, Euphrosynia Pavlovna. Mashenka told me, and I thought I would go and bring you back. It was not a suitable place for you to go to. Lilian"—his voice was sobbing now—"why, she has just crossed a river, and she is on one bank, and we stand on the other." Now he looked away as though aware that his candor must needs be blended with a father's shame. "It may be that she has always had something tainted about her. We had not looked after her properly. Cheap boarding houses, poor schools, never much money, and Lilian was always hungry for frippery. Why, I can remember those tiny bottles of dreadful cheap scent she used to buy at Brocard's." He sighed, and Frossia dared not look at him. His pathetic honesty seemed far more terrifying

32

than his anger, and she said nothing. Maria Nikolaevna spared her the ache of any explanations. She stood in the doorway, looked, shook her head, and then flung her grief behind her in manifold anxieties over Frossia's comfort.

"You are still in love with all of it?" asked Maria Nikolaevna, and Frossia nodded.

"Why, I remember. Even when you were small, toys and parties meant so little to you, but a matinée at the Mariinsky, and your Grandmamma would say, 'Now Euphrosynia is in paradise,' and they would take you there, and give you a lovely bonbonnière from Des Gourmets, and back home you would come, the bonbonnière in your hands, and not a single sweet eaten."

"Yes, but I used to gorge—all alone in my bedroom," parried Frossia.

The room was slightly more important than a mere cubicle. It had a table, a chair, a rheumatic sofa, and no curtain to the solitary oblong of a window. Maria Nikolaevna proved herself generous. A pile of rugs, counterpanes, yellowed sheets, and even a shabby green-blue quilt lay all tumbled on the unpainted floor boards. The table was already covered with a square of thin faded rose silk, and somehow dignity was housed in the mean room, and beauty breathed from a pastel portrait in a tarnished silver frame.

"Your great-grandmamma had it done. She probably saw her dance," remarked Maria Nikolaevna.

White-rose skirts billowed from the frame, a tight-fitting bodice of gleaming silver tissue rose above them, the feet were poised on their satin-shod toes, the thin arms were upraised in a clean curve, and neat dark curls ran a whimsical measure all round a pale bemused face. In her home of old chased silver, Taglioni came to reign in a bleak back room of a mean house in the 15th Line of Vasilyev Island. Two things kept her intimate company on the table: a small violet-bound book on old French dances and a slender volume in crimson leather with gold lettering in twisted Old Slavonic scrolls and loops—*The Legend of Euphrosynia*.

Frossia had not yet unpacked. The two suitcases lay open, the bag was thrown on the floor. An erratic impulse to assert some imperishable identity in a crumbling world made her pull out her three main treasures happily salvaged from the catastrophe at Kiev. And now Maria Nikolaevna was looking at them in a slightly amused way. Frossia remembered the spring skies opened to her by the older woman's kiss, and smiled back.

"Yes," she replied, "Great-grandmamma must have seen her dance. In the thirties, was it not?"

"I think so." Maria Nikolaevna began rummaging in the chaotic pile on the floor. "Oh, dear, they say the Mariinsky is still open, and also the Ballet school in Mikhaylovskaya Street. Is it not strange?"

"Why should it be?"

"Because the world has ended," explained Maria Nikolaevna in her gently didactic voice. "Now what about having this rug for a curtain?"

They arranged a bright orange rug for a curtain, and the old sofa was soon converted into a bed. The Parnikovs feasted that evening. From a small bag of flour and a lump of lard Maria Nikolaevna produced a great mound of *bliny,* hot, crisp, golden-brown pancakes, and the Captain rubbed his hands.

"It was the fan, Euphrosynia Pavlovna. . . . Imagine having an ivory fan for supper! We must be very careful not to break our teeth on it. Mashenka, mind, eat slowly. Good old Semyon Parfenovich is dead, and we never had another dentist . . . No, no . . . Mashenka, you were the cook. I shall be waiter." He piled the pancakes on Frossia's plate, handed her knife and fork, and apologized for the salt appearing in a chipped crock. Of pepper there was none, nor of butter.

The food was eaten, the small iron stove, stoked earlier in the day, had warmed the room, and they all sat in frail and shabby armchairs, and Frossia knew that they were waiting for her to speak. They wanted to be told a great many things, in a sense they had a right to know, and she felt she could not even begin. She said slowly and clumsily:

"Ivan Petrovich, you were not there, or were you? I believe I told Maria Nikolaevna that I was all alone in the world—"

"We understood you." Maria Nikolaevna spoke in the voice of someone singing a lullaby to a beloved child. "We understood you, and no more need be said—"

"No more need be said," echoed the Captain, and Frossia was startled. How much had they understood? Or had they heard? Rumor, gossip, news, anything may have drifted towards them. She glanced at the Captain now smiling a little sadly and remotely. She looked at Maria Nikolaevna, and wondered no more.

"And now"—Frossia breathed more easily—"there is a double job to do."

"A double job?"

"Yes. There is the job of earning my living and the job of just living."

"The job of living? Is it a job? And what about the other?"

"I believe so. . . . And the other. Well, I know French and German well. I know dancing, but I could not teach it. I used to keep accounts for Grandmamma, but I always made mistakes—"

Maria Nikolaevna shook her head. The Captain looked thoughtful.

"There are hardly any jobs," he began, but Frossia broke in:

"Surely, there must be. One can find them. Why, there are crowds of buildings—I mean—they are all crowded, telephone girls and typists," she ended lamely.

"Oh, Commissariats," Maria Nikolaevna said dryly.

"Difficult," mused the Captain.

"You could not really go there," his wife said. "They are all hostile. They would blame you for your birth and manners and the rest. Frossinka dear, there need be no hurry. You have saved some things. We have a tiny bit left. We will share and go on together. God is merciful."

Frossia thought, Yes, we will go on—selling a fan today, a snuff-box tomorrow, and she almost saw the three of them tip-toeing to a day when there were no more trinkets left, no more jade or ivory. . . . They would die then, she reflected, but they will never beg from, never work for those who have ended their world. But I must not condemn them. It is just in their blood. It is not cowardice— She looked at them and knew she loved them for their pathetic and beautiful gallantry, and she also knew she could not stay with them. If—no—when I do find a job, and come back to tell them, they would be hurt. Their eyes would look wounded, she thought later, alone in her room, and, looking round, observed its humble furnishings and Taglioni's portrait against the dim rose silk cover. Taglioni belonged to her, but all else did not. She loved the room in all its humbleness, and the thought smote her that her being there at all meant nothing more than a brief sojourn at a wayside inn.

"I want to live," Frossia repeated to herself, rearranging the rugs and quilt on the improvised bed. "Goodness, is it not dreadful, but I care so little about red, or pink, or white?" and, nearly asleep, Frossia remembered Maria Nikolaevna's plans for the following morning. A visit to the market place would begin the day. "You see, Frossinka, we never know how long this may be allowed. Some day, perhaps, they will say, 'You shall have no market places at all,' and it is difficult to sell things through private speculators. They

35

are such dark people, Frossinka, they come, they bully you, they always cheat you, and then they vanish. . . . The market is there on Mondays, Thursdays and Fridays, and we dare not miss a single day. . . ."

6

The city said to Frossia: "Yes, I can give you much, a marble bench in a derelict summerhouse, an hour's reverie on one of my bridges, a roof, a broken sofa, a dome, an avenue, ice splintered all along my rivers, and trees in breaking leaf. Take anything, move in it, dance through it if you can and if you dare. You said there was a double job for everybody—living and working. Prove your words. Use me. . . ."

The city gave much, and within a few days it gave her Nikolashka. Maria Nikolaevna was laundering in the tiny kitchen, Captain Parnikov sat mending a fresh tear in his coat, and Frossia glanced at a stack of soiled crockery, saw the empty pails, and seized them.

"Oh, *golubushka,* you will have to go to the back yard. There has been no water in the house all these years—"

"The taps should go to a museum some day."

Frossia ran down the stairs soberly enough, but she wanted to sing. Spring was coming, she could read that lovely fugitive mood spread all over the city, along broken walls and pitted pavements. Spring had nothing to do with dereliction wrought by man. It danced its soft measure over all the charred ugliness and bleakness and ordinariness. It pushed a blade of young grass here, a tuft of bright moss there, and it commanded them: "Go, grow, spread and multiply until this gaping fissure is decently covered and that skeleton of a wall is clothed in green," and moss and grass grew and spread.

Across the wide 15th Line lay a waste heap where a house had once stood, the local police station burnt down some years ago. The broken jagged walls were covered with thick snow when first Frossia saw them, but now the white pall was no more, and here and there she could observe thin roots of a creeper struggle out towards light and warmth, and she knew that before many weeks were out, the place would stand all greening and hopeful.

She was going to the back yard, but the unmistakable movement under the ground and in the air made her stand still and wonder.

"Nothing could halt spring."

Grandmamma used to say, "You have said it before, and I cannot understand you. Seasons come and seasons go. Why this wonder?

36

You might just as well marvel at sugar being sweet. Of course, once winter is over, spring must come—"

She could not explain properly.

"Yes, always, independent of what happens to you, to me, to the whole world. . . ."

Grandmamma then whispered, "I am sometimes afraid for Euphrosynia, Nina Petrovna. She is such a prey to moods."

The back yard, however, could not be quite forgotten. Frossia slipped under one archway, under another, and found herself in a dank enclosed space, paved in rough cobbles, surrounded by unfriendly blind walls of dull red brick. It smelt of stale and rotten vegetables. The cobbles were slippery. Tenants, pumping their water from the farthest end of the yard, spilt and splashed running back, their pails filled. Frossia slipped and saw an enormous gauntleted hand flash out and steady her.

"These cobbles are a peril. . . . I watched you across the yard. I said to myself, 'Now, Nikolashka, keep an eye on this young lady. She has never filled the pails before, she is certain to slip,' and you have."

He stood before her, one enormous arm swinging her pail, a huge man in a quilted brown coat and breeches, a black cap over his flaming hair. The great red beard burned copper in the sun. Under the cap was a face. Butter, butter, thought Frossia, a nicely buttered bun and two sultanas for eyes, and she smiled because he was smiling, as though the two of them were not standing in an evil-smelling, shut-in yard. Frossia went on smiling, and forgot that presently she must wrestle with the enormous rusty handle of the pump, fill her pails, and carry them back up five steep flights.

"Why, how very friendly of you," she began, and his laughter interrupted her.

The Parnikovs had their sad, remote smile. Madame Touras had smirked and Lilian tittered. Most people either smirked or smiled in that sad forlorn way, but this was mere laughter, loud and unrestrained, all the lovelier because there was no reason for it, and Frossia remembered Turgenev's words "Unreasoned laughter is the best in the world."

"And why should we not be friendly? I know of you. I met Captain Parnikov on the stairs, I lodge just below him, and he said, 'There is a great joy in my place today: a young friend has come back to Petrograd.' So, of course, I know you." He tugged at his incredible beard and the sultanas winked. "My name is Nikolashka, Euphrosynia Pavlovna." He doffed his cap and bowed solemnly,

37

from the hips, and Frossia thought of Ivan Susanin in Glinka's *Life for the Tsar.*

"You know my patronymic. What is yours?"

"Nikolashka it used to be to grand duke, bishop, general, and policeman. And Nikolashka it is today to commissar, red guard, militiaman, and to all my friends." He put down the pail and within ten minutes Frossia knew his story. A surname slipped into the preface, and she remembered him. Nikolashka had owned flour mills and about twenty-five huge bakeries in Petrograd and Moscow. In 1917 he had lost his flour mills. By the middle of 1918 most of his bakeries had to put up their shutters. But Nikolashka, having in his heyday lent money to extravagant grand dukes and drunk tea with bishops, knew other things over and above servility and formal piety. He knew the ways of corn and bread. He knew what could and what could not be done with rye, wheat, barley. "You can live without sheets, shirts, sugar—you cannot live without bread."

"People do."

"They try to, and they make a bad business of it. It will get worse. Corn cannot grow on ravaged land. Corn cannot fly across hundreds of versts. My heart ached last autumn, Euphrosynia Pavlovna, sacks of good rye and millet and *grecha* all rotting away in the South, and no rolling stock available to put them on the tables of hungry folk up here in the North—"

"But what are you doing now?"

"I am a baker. Good bakers are few." He was not boasting, he spoke so simply. "Most bakers in Petrograd were Germans. So many have fled. Well, I am here—"

"Did you not—I mean—did they not—"

"I know what you are thinking, Euphrosynia Pavlovna. 'Nikolashka was a millionaire. Nikolashka lived in luxury. And why did they not shoot him?' Dear *baryshnia,* they shoot people for two things—opinions and wealth. I have never had any opinions, my business lay with corn, flour, bread. My wealth? I did not wait for them to come and take it. I just left it, my house on Kamenny Island, my wife's diamonds, silk sheets, silver, biscuit porcelain, everything—I left it all."

"Are you a communist?"

He laughed.

"I have no opinions. I am a baker. And though I am Nikolashka to the whole world, my daughter is always called Irina Nikolaevna, and do you know why?"

"You must tell me—"

"She agrees with everybody. She has done so all her life. If you were to tell her that raspberries grew on elms, she would merely say, 'Fancy! And I never knew it!'—just like that. It is a great gift. You must meet her. Nobody could quarrel with Irina Nikolaevna. She is too pleasant. In December, 1917, they came to our house in Kamenny Island. You will understand that my dear wife was dead then. Well, Irina Nikolaevna was out in the garden, clearing the snow off the paths. The red guards came and shouted, 'Hey, citizeness, what is your name? Never mind . . . This place is not yours any more,' and she put down the spade and said, 'Fancy you bringing such news. And I never knew it.' You could have knocked those men down with a chicken's feather. Within half an hour she had them all in the dining room, treating them to saucerfuls of cherry jam. No trouble, no rudeness, no unpleasantness. Yes, she is a marvelous creature—"

"I must meet her."

"She is at Velikiye Luki now, trying to pick up a few potatoes for her father here. But she is coming back. I tell you I am lost without Irina Nikolaevna. Yes, you must meet her. I shall then give a party, bread and some fruit syrup—and what more can anyone want?—but in my flat, Euphrosynia Pavlovna, in my flat, not elsewhere." Frossia could not escape his sudden grim emphasis.

"I thought you said you were friends with the Parnikovs?"

"Friendly indeed we are, but they would not think of me as a friend. They are gentlefolk, I am a baker, and they will die remembering the difference that used to be—"

Frossia did not reply. There were her empty pails to turn to in an awkward moment. Nikolashka had them both full in an instant, and insisted on carrying them up. On the landing, in the open doorway, Maria Nikolaevna met them and spoke pleasantly enough.

"This is very kind of you. I felt so worried about Euphrosynia Pavlovna. I wondered if she had found her way to the back yard."

Nikolashka bowed, carried in the pails, and vanished. Maria Nikolaevna slipped back to her laundering, and Frossia followed her.

"I am going to wash up." She rolled back her sleeves. "I thought you were going to ask him in—"

"He was not in any trouble," Maria Nikolaevna said in her exceptionally level voice. "Vania and I would not like to have him come here unless he were in some trouble—"

"Yes," said Captain Parnikov, "I am civil to him when I meet him on the stairs. I am quite natural with him. I told him about your coming. Yes, he is harmless—but, all the same, he is a most despicable turncoat."

"How could he be?"

"He is baker in one of those communal depôts."

"Yes, he told me—"

"Well?" asked Maria Nikolaevna, and the Captain echoed—"Well?" The brief word said, "Is that not enough? If you accept anything like a regular wage from the enemy, you must be on the enemy's side."

Frossia said, drying a cracked plate very carefully, "There is no question of being anything. Why, he said he had no opinions. He may look absurd, but I think he is rather lovable and wise—"

This was an unfortunate word. There stood an invisible gunpowder barrel in the tiny kitchen, and the match of the word fell into it.

"Very wise," the Captain acquiesced heavily. "If he had not been wise, they would have shot him a long time ago."

"But why? Why should anyone want to be shot?" Frossia flung the frayed kitchen cloth away from her, she was conscious of their wounded silence, she knew she would have to leave them today, that very hour, but she hurried on, one word tumbling after another. "It is all a muddle, but can we not get away from politics and all the rest of it? I allow that at the moment it all does look like a bedlam of cruelty and beastliness, and worse. I know—I have seen—I do loathe so much of it, but you cannot fight anything either by ignoring it or else by mere contempt. Can you—dare anyone ignore our country? Or despise it?"

"But the country is dead," murmured Maria Nikolaevna. "You should realize it. You come from a world which is no more. Frossinka, you must be very tired to say such things."

"Can a whole nation die because of a revolution? Or because its government has changed? Please do listen to me. . . . Grandmamma used to grieve over my socialism. But I was no socialist. I hate labels. . . . Labeling anything is just like trying to make a great picture fit a small frame. . . . And I am no communist. I don't know them. I can't say I understand much about it all, but I do know, please listen—I have it in my bones, in my prayers, in everything—I do know that Russia is there, and always shall be whatever people have to sing before a theater curtain goes down—"

Maria Nikolaevna's cheeks went pale. The Captain stood up, his stubby chin trembled, his sunken cheeks flushed mottled purple.

"As an officer of his Majesty's army I protest, and," he began in a loud unnatural voice, then it broke on a thin whimper, and Maria

Nikolaevna's arms were round his shaking shoulders. "Euphrosynia Pavlovna, you must go. . . . I could not bear it. You are a renegade."

"Vanichka, you are not to say hard things to her. You don't know what may have happened to her. People get all twisted in these dark days. Vanichka, you shall not say another word—"

So she went on, but her tired dark eyes were hard as they looked at Frossia who turned and left the kitchen.

She went straight downstairs. Nikolashka was out, but an indeterminate kindly old body, who crept from out the dimness of a passage, mumbled that Frossia could easily leave her boxes in Nikolashka's rooms. She went upstairs and started packing. An hour later Maria Nikolaevna crept into the room. Captain Parnikov had gone out, she stammered. Then she saw the strapped suitcases, and her mouth was folded into a piteous line, but Frossia forestalled all questions.

"Maria Nikolaevna, you will understand. I am going. Now, at once, it would be so unfair—to him, to you, and to myself. You see, I mean to live, I must find a job, there are no private jobs to be had, and you will think of me as a turncoat—"

"But it is so strange of you, Frossinka. You used to be so gentle and patient. Now you are fierce and sudden. . . . And then the things you said! Russia is dead to us, she should be dead to you. You are young, you have been away, you don't know what has been happening. . . . It is a dead country, just a corpse. . . . How could there be a Russia without a Tsar, bishops, policemen?" asked Maria Nikolaevna.

Frossia could not answer her, she shrugged once again, and stole out of the room.

CHAPTER TWO

SHADOWS AND FOOTSTEPS

Frossia stood in the doorway of the huge house. Once again she knew herself a vagabond—yet not in a desert. The city was truly hers, and the desire for an aimless wander urged her to set her face towards the Neva. There were so many familiar landmarks to see and to welcome.

Some of the houses on the once busy Nicholas Quay were blind and scarred, and the granite-fringed pier had no lively scenes to offer her. There was hardly any shipping, and such few begrimed hulks as were there, looked as though they would never weigh anchor again. The very stones of Nicholas Bridge gaped with holes, and shreds of dirty red bunting flew from the splintered window frames of Clark House on the English Quay. Frossia crossed the bridge and turned sharp to the left, towards the Senate, the Admiralty, the forlorn dark red massif of the Winter Palace and, as she walked on, her eyes hungry for the least detail, she knew once again that her very passion for the place was not rooted in shallow sentiment dependent on perfect form alone. She loved it all no less now that its proud beauty lay dusty and ruined.

The huge Palace Square lay behind her. She broke away from the quays, and now threaded her way down Millionnaya Street. Here, if anywhere, dreams would have found an anchorage and ghosts choose their lodgment, but the pale proud houses, with their exquisitely colonnaded porches, had nothing to say about ghosts. They were all tenanted, all seemed busy and alive, and Frossia stared at the men and women who hurried in and out of those same houses where great ladies used to dance and courtiers once thought of love-making and intrigues.

Those men and women were busy. They looked rough. They *were* rough. Their slouching gait annoyed her. Their obvious lack of manners disturbed her. Nonetheless, they attracted her. All down the length of the street they hurried, with papers in their hands. The windows were closed, but she guessed at the sound of telephones and typewriters. The old bureaucracy had gone. The new kind was there—installed in silk-paneled walls. Over many a doorway was an enormous poster, black letters painted on red, and the hammer and sickle in pallid yellow. The busy people, working in those houses, were concerned with food, transport, education, and culture. The modern spelling, the clumsily abbreviated words, irritated her, but she envied the hustle and bustle of those shabby, slovenly men and women who, so obviously, knew how to crowd every moment of their day.

The wet snow was slippery, and in her preoccupation with the scene in the street, Frossia stumbled once or twice. She saw some of the passers-by measure her with a swift, dismissing glance. At the end of Millionnaya a dark-bearded militiaman made as if to stop her, and for a second Frossia stood still. He might ask her where she lived. What could she tell him? She was unacquainted with many laws; these were changed from day to day, she had no idea whether she belonged to the category of such homeless folk, *bezprizornye,* who, when approached by authorities, were immediately sent to some prison or other. She had no domicile. She felt she could not mention Sergievskaya Street, No. 39, for this might ally her with Madame Touras and her business. She went on, deeply uncertain and flushing angrily. But the militiaman, having looked at her, did nothing at all, and, secretly ashamed of her fears, Frossia turned into Moshkov Lane.

She had not really meant to seek again the doubtful comfort of that summerhouse, yet she remembered that an acquaintance, once a friend of her people, had lived in a small flat in Moshkov Lane, a woman much older than Frossia, who had once taken her to the *Lac des Cygnes.* Herself an impassioned lover of ballet, Anna von Packen, daughter of a small Jewish pawnbroker, beautiful and unusual with her fair hair and black eyes, who had married an unimportant, scholarly Baltic baron. Frossia remembered odd things about her; the Baltic clan would not know her, the pawnbroker had disowned her, but Anna triumphantly survived both scorn and neglect, gave her husband ten years of happiness, buried him, and settled down in Moshkov Lane, to enjoy sunsets over the Neva, her Persian cats, and the ballet.

The house was there. Frossia climbed the narrow marble staircase and knocked. There came a great deal of fumbling with bolts, someone's labored breathing, then silence. Frossia dared greatly and knocked again. The door opened slowly, and she saw a face in the dim green light of the hall.

"Frossia? No, it cannot be you—"

"May I come in?"

She stood in the once familiar drawing room, now ruined by an iron stove, its funnel thrust through a hole in the window. The pale gray walls still bore innumerable autographed portraits of Fokin, Diaghilev, and several ballerines. Over a dusty escritoire hung a pair of worn white satin slippers in a glass case, and a pale rose feather drooped behind a picture of Sedova. Anna herself looked dusty, shriveled, thin.

But not as fierce as she used to be. Merely harder, thought Frossia.

"Goodness—where have you come from?" Anna's voice rang almost petulant.

"Oh, I left Priapitzi, and got to Kiev, and here I am."

"But your people—"

"All dead, Anna."

"What?"

"Yes, please, Anna—no more questions—"

"Yes, yes, of course, but, my dear, you should not have come here at all—"

"Well, I do belong here—"

"Does anyone belong anywhere today? We are all adrift. It has started here, it will spread all over the world. You shall see, the red daub of a poster, or a decree will soon cover the whole of Europe—perhaps, the whole world, in ten years, in twenty years. Here life is over. Last year I lived because I had my sables to eat. This year I can live because I can eat a few diamonds. The year after—or, perhaps much sooner, unless I go away or something—well—" Anna shrugged—"I shall go to sleep and be glad of it—"

"Are we not all asleep now?"

"I don't know. When you sleep, you can't think. I wish I could stop thinking. I can't help it. I quite thought you had escaped. . . . I had heard nothing for years. Instead you come here and tell me we are all asleep. Frossia, you are unkind. This terrible life should have taught you that kindness and pity are the only things needed—"

Frossia might have said: "Pity? We must learn to do without it if we mean to live through it all. Pity turns you into jelly, and jellies are feeble things. And mere kindness is not enough—something different, something vaster than kindness has become necessary, only we have no words for it. If you dare show pity to me, I might go mad." She might have said all this and much more, but she restrained herself to a brief shrug. She had forgotten that arguments to Anna were what water is to fish, and Anna looked some-

44

thing like a fish, a plump pale fish, all gray scales, a fish in shabby beige tweeds with faded scarlet facings to the coat, and a dirty green shawl round her sloping shoulders. She does not walk now. She just floats. She seems to have no hold on anything. Sunsets? She would not think much of nature. And cats? Frossia looked around and saw none. Well, then, the ballet, all the photographs look dusty enough, and she might be equally bitter about the ballet. How shabby she is. . . . I remember once, going to an embassy function, she wore something filmy green with a motif of corals. From Paquin. . . . And she argued with Papa about cabochon rubies.

Anna was saying: "It is all pure economics, child. Money is the only criterion of civilized life. Once it goes, civilization is a broken glass bowl. Take sex. Look at all this promiscuity. . . . Marriage is of less importance than a game of cards. They have all gone sex-mad. You will soon hear that they have cleared the streets of prostitutes. Rubbish," said Anna. "Does it matter where one practices harlotry—against a grass hedge or under a roof? All idea of principles is gone. Do you wonder? Because money has gone mad. Today we count in thousands, next week it will be millions, and by next year figures will mean nothing at all. Am I not right?"

"No," said Frossia and wondered whether she might be driven to spend a second night in the summerhouse. "You may hate me, but I must say it. It is not money. Money is a mere token. It is for us to determine its value and importance. We have exaggerated both. It is not money. It is the spirit gone sick—"

"Whose spirit?"

"The nation's."

"You are impossible and provoking," sighed Anna. "All right, we are sick, every one of us. Perhaps, we are. I wash my tin platter, eat my gruel, sell my belongings as furtively as possible, buy more flour and millet whenever I can find any. Also I keep silent. What is there left to talk about?" and she continued at great length.

Shattered by this verbal artillery, Frossia sat still. Presently, she hoped, there would come a pause, and she might ask a question or two about the Mariinsky and the ballet school, or else Anna would remember her duties of a hostess, offer food and, possibly, a bed. Passionately Frossia longed for a nice clean bed, not a marble bench in a derelict summerhouse, or a wooden seat in the train, not even a cobbly sofa, but a nice, static, maternal bed. But Anna went on talking and, aware of being there as a suppliant, Frossia sat in her chair. Anna said there was nothing in the present to talk about, and now she turned to the past.

"I suppose you wondered if I were still here. . . . Me being a

45

baroness. . . . Come to think of it, I never knew why I married Hugo. He had birth and some money, but he was nothing except bones. A palaeontologist should remain a bachelor. He lived with those bones, he almost smelt of them, he always muttered terribly long words in his sleep. . . . But we were not really important. They just left me here. The petty title does not seem to offend them. I never had any political aberrations, and I told them so. Of course, I do loathe them. The banks all closed down. . . . Famine is bound to come. I don't understand anything about distribution and such things, but it is obvious they are making a muddle of everything. But nobody knows much of what is happening—at least, not people like me. I keep quiet. I should hate them to pounce on me—"

"Anna—"

The dusty photographs of ballerines, the stained mauve carpet, the absurdly frilled heliotrope curtains, the very chair Frossia was sitting on, everything lost its moorings and floated about.

I am just stupidly tired, she thought and whipped something like a semblance of energy into her voice to ask, "Would you mind if I stayed here—just for a few days . . . ?"

"You are here. Of course, you must stay. Life has turned topsy-turvy, but you shall stay. And I will ask no questions. Your people are gone. I ask nothing. But this does happen. It is not the banks only. I like to think it is—because I am afraid, Frossia. I bolt my door and I curtain the windows, and I never go out after dark. I am afraid all the time. And you must never, never be out after dark. . . . Mars Square is round the corner, and they say all the thieves and murderers in the city live there, underground some-where. If caught, they get shot, but they are caught so seldom. In winter they wear white from head to foot. They hide in Mars Square and in cemeteries. They say Smolenskoye Cemetery teems with them. . . . There was a baker's wife in Millionnaya Street. They knifed her all over. Yes, things do happen. Have I been chat-tering? Forgive me. . . . But you came just like a ghost out of a buried world."

"This ghost is dying for a bed, Anna. With sheets . . . Have you got any sheets left, Anna?"

"Have I got sheets?"

The stay in Moshkov Lane had its own difficulties. Anna was inquisitive.

"What are you thinking about? Any plans for the future? But this is silly of me. Whoever could make a single plan nowadays?"

"Oh, yes, I mean to work—"

"Have you salvaged anything?"

"A few trinkets. . . . Not much. Just a suitcase or two. I had to leave them at the Parnikovs," Frossia explained carefully, and Anna nodded.

"I can see it all. The Parnikovs are dear, good, noble people, but they refuse to live. So do I—but in a different way. I suppose they cannot help it. And your Nikolashka . . . *Quel drôle de nom.* I have eaten his pies and cakes, and never dreamt the man existed. Is he a clown?"

"Not at all."

"Why ever did they not shoot him? I thought all the merchant princes were dealt with at the very beginning."

"Nikolashka is a philosopher. He has no opinions. He gave his wealth away. Now he is a baker."

"I would not see too much of him, Frossia. You never know with such people. He may be a fool, and fools are dangerous in dangerous times. And never go near that Lilian again. I have heard of her husband. He is a monster. You had better go after your luggage. Come back before dark."

2

Frossia came to the 15th Line and collected her luggage. She met Maria Nikolaevna on the landing. The older woman was courteous but distant. Frossia told her about Anna. "She is a Jewess, they never interfere with Jews," said Maria Nikolaevna bitterly and then turned away. Frossia knew herself ostracized. She wanted to cry out: "But I feel grateful to you. You gave me so much. Please don't turn against me," but she could say nothing to Maria Nikolaevna, and went down the stairs slowly, burdened with her belongings.

Anna's life was circumscribed, yet she knew some people and she wanted Frossia to meet them, and now Frossia realized she would have to tread very carefully. Anna's world was mainly inhabited by people much better circumstanced than the Parnikovs had been, gallant, proud, unbending people, and to such she, Frossia, with her muddled views and rash admissions, must have appeared something of a traitress. They welcomed her warmly, they remembered her own family, they offered pity, and she strove hard to avoid them, until Anna shrugged and remarked that "some people were made to live like hermits."

Frossia now remembered her strange aunt Alina in her summer *dacha* at Terioki in Finland. Aunt Alina's husband was at Russian embassies in Paris, Washington, London. It happened some time in 1908, trouble of a kind nobody would discuss in the open, when Aunt Alina's husband retired at the age of 39. In a room at Terioki Frossia saw an oddly bound book and examined it. The book bore on the fly-leaf: A. Tchertkov, Purleigh, Maldon, Essex, England, 1900—and on the other side: Headley Brothers, Printers, 14 Bishopsgate Without, London, E.C. But the book, printed in England, was in Russian, a novel in three parts. Tolstoy *Resurrection*, Frossia read, Complete version untouched by censorship. Fifth cheap edition, and she cried, "Aunt Alina, how very funny, a Russian book published in England," but Aunt Alina did not think it funny. Her great violet eyes looked sad. She said: "Darling, put it away. You must not rummage among my things," yet Frossia insisted, "But why was it published in England. Is it bad?"

"No, no, it is just—very truthful."

"I want to read it."

"Not yet. You would not understand it. It is sad and lovely—but rather difficult," and the book was locked away, and some sixth sense made Frossia link the English edition of the *Resurrection* with her uncle's withered career. Aunt Alina, Grandmamma insisted, was undoubtedly mad. She had odd evening gatherings in her drawing room, with evil-smelling workmen from the Gutuevsky Factory and wild-eyed unkempt girls from the University. Aunt Alina was no scholar herself, she knew little about factories, and it looked very odd to watch a princess offering tiny sugared biscuits to a rough man in tarred boots and a sweat-stained shirt. Aunt Alina died six years later, and a notebook of hers came into Frossia's hands, and she read: "We must not live in such a walled-in garden. Everything must be shared—our jewels and our thoughts. We must go out, reach the people, break down hostility and misery by love and understanding. We must develop generosity, too, and be ready to surrender our privacy, and our self-imagined superiority." Frossia grimaced, read no more, and prudently burned the book. She disliked it all. Aunt Alina's friends from the Gutuevsky looked such barbarians without grace in their movements or form in their thoughts. They left mud on Aubusson carpets. They broke Aunt Alina's biscuit porcelain cups, they looked suspiciously at food offered them on fragile plates. Once there was a dreadful scene. Aunt Alina took some of them to a matinée at the Mariinsky. It was *Petrushka*, and one of the Gutuevsky men delivered a crisp verdict on their return to wastefully fragrant tea and tiny saffron buns in Aunt Alina's drawing room:

"*Chepukha*—utter rubbish."

Frossia trembled with grief and fury.

"Rubbish? Rubbish? Rubbish? It is you who are rubbish, you blind, thick-skinned fools . . ." And never again was she invited to Aunt Alina's motley gatherings.

All of it happened long ago, and now men from the Gutuevsky and other factories sat on important pinnacles and decreed what she, Frossia, should or should not do. She knew herself belonging neither to them, nor yet to the mournful ranks of déclassés.

"You are sitting astride a trapeze," Anna said, "but I have a few friends left. I would like you to meet some of them. Please, don't be too provoking."

3

In Moyka, not far from the house where Pushkin lived and died, were Pavel Pavlovich and his sister, Paulina, morganatic widow of a minor German princeling. Pavel Pavlovich stood well over six feet in his socks. He had an untidy beard, wore Russian blouses, white and usually dirty, their red and blue collar embroidery tarnished and shredded. He smelt of paint, oils and turpentine, and lived in a vast ghostly room crowded with easels, rags, and mostly unfinished canvases. Behind the bare studio was Paulina's kingdom, two mean little rooms, over-furnished and over-curtained. Paulina was tall, florid, and vague. Her brother lived for art and talk. She inhabited rather foggy heights, searching for what she called ultimate truths. Pavel Pavlovich painted on as happily as though no revolution had ever happened at all. Paulina had a mind above bread queues and unlit streets.

"You may like those two," Anna said cautiously.

Frossia did. The untidy bleak flat in the Moyka was a blissful oasis. Paulina kissed her, measured her with a searching glance, and said:

"You look honest. Perhaps you would like to join me in the quest," and Frossia was rescued from committing herself by Pavel Pavlovich's laughter.

"Leave her alone, Paulina;" and he explained to Frossia, "she has just found another prophet. Some Tibetan monk or other. But he is really a European. He lives in a queer temple somewhere at Ochta. He burns incense and tells his beads most of the day, and sleeps at nights like any other ordinary person. But he is very picturesque, taller than I am, and goes about in striking orange robes. I wish you could get him to come here, Paulina. I should like to make a study of him."

Paulina sniffed loudly into a checked handkerchief.

49

"Paul, you have no respect for my feelings. You forget what it means to me—"

"Go," he said affectionately, "and make us some tea or whatever there is. Now, young woman, let me have a look at you. . . . H'm. . . . Lovely enough, but I could not paint you—just yet."

"Why not?" Frossia challenged.

"I could get the outline—but not you. You don't seem to be anywhere. I am not a Leonardo, my dear. I could not interpret a human question mark," and he turned to Anna, and Frossia looked around. In one corner an enormous easel supported a canvas, all deep violet and gray. She went across to examine it. There were rocks and swirling waters, and, above them, on a boulder, a desolate human figure, chin cupped in huge hands, eyes considering the fury below him. Frossia felt it was good.

"I have christened the picture," said Pavel Pavlovich, *"The Abandoned Titan.* It is not finished yet. I must alter the eyes. They look bewildered. They should not be. He is reconciled to broken rocks and swollen waters." He moved away from the light so that Frossia might not see his face.

Anna was peevish.

"You always annoy me, Pavel Pavlovich. You are intent and busy and full of something. Anybody would imagine life were normal today."

"Life is never normal," he thundered. "Anna Yosifovna, honestly, no life can be normal except for turnip-like minds. Real life is stress and a bit of madness, and agony often enough, and all of it is splendid. Even ugliness can be nice. Look at this." He pulled forward a water color study of a head, and Frossia gasped.

"So you know Lilian—"

"Know her? She sat for me several times. Yes, look at her. A born harlot! And her sweet simple mother wailing about the revolution! Lilian might have queened it in Monte Carlo if revolution had not happened. As it is, things are amusing enough for her here."

"A dreadful woman—"

"You and your labels, Anna Yosifovna. You are always subjective. Lilian has nothing in her but flesh, she does not pretend to a mind. Well, if you like, she is bad, but her badness is genuine."

Anna shrugged. Paulina shuffled back from her cubbyhole, tea came, and some shy sunlight crept through the begrimed skylight. Frossia drank hot dark-brown liquid out of a chipped Dresden cup, and listened to Anna and Pavel Pavlovich arguing about the Rembrandts in the Hermitage. Anna said:

"Of course, these fiends will sell them to America. Let them go. The money would feed a few hungry millions."

"They must not be sold," roared Pavel Pavlovich. "A good picture could not be valued in terms of loaves and fishes. To hell with your bulging cornbins! I am being honest, objective. I do hate going hungry, but I would rather give up my day's ration than see a Rembrandt go across the ocean. Mind you, I would not protest so much if I knew they were going to a museum, a nation's picture gallery, a place open to all, but I will not have them sold privately, to rich and dusty millionaires who buy them for their own pleasure. No," Pavel Pavlovich roared lustily, "I am a true communist in art. Great pictures must not belong to individuals. That is immoral. God did not dole out His sky in small portions, so much square space per each soul. Great pictures are like that—glimpses of skies and—"

"My dear brother," quavered Paulina, "always talks too much. Paul, our guests look weary." She turned to Frossia, "You now live with Anna Yosifovna. That is not too far. You might like to come to Ochta with me some morning. Nothing very strenuous, I assure you. Merely an hour's contemplation of very simple things, like water and clouds. Sometimes a ladybird—"

"No," thundered Pavel Pavlovich, "she shall not go to Ochta. Euphrosynia Pavlovna, you must be careful with your shoe-leather. Fancy sitting in that draughty wooden hut and reflecting on a cloud or a ladybird! You will probably find it is a bug. . . . *Chepukha.* . . . You might just as well go to St. Nicholas' Hospital —the lunatics would give you quite enough to think about."

Paulina withdrew—to wash up, she said with great dignity, and Anna followed her. Pavel Pavlovich sighed.

"I have no tobacco today. Not even a wisp of cheapest mahorka. I would give a fortune for a Lemon cigarette. Do you remember them? Cheap and nasty, the kind *droshki* men used to smoke. No, of course, you could not remember them. Well, young woman, so you have come back here. That is good—" He grinned and Frossia smiled back.

The studio felt warm. Sun went on trickling through the skylight, and the riot of extravagantly splashed color all along the walls added to the warmth. Lilian—from her easel—looked the wanton she was, but she lived. From the opposite corner the abandoned titan offered little enough comfort but, at least, he was a living study of detachment.

"You must not take much notice of my sister," said Pavel Pavlovich; "she is large and kind, even if besotted with her contemplation of ladybirds. And should Anna Yosifovna get too much like a vinegar bottle, you come here, and we may straighten things out together. Some day I should like to read you as though you were a primer. Today you seem like one of those chained books in old libraries—"

"I have a rather tired body . . . a shuttered mind, and not too much of a soul—"

"I am glad of that. Paulina has too much soul. It bulges all over the place, at least, the thing she thinks is her soul. But it is all nonsense about a shuttered mind. A tired body? Well, we are all tired, and sometimes it does one no harm. . . . A shuttered mind," he pulled at his empty pipe, "that is as annoying as Anna Yosifovna's nonsense about the Rembrandts. You walk as though you were in a dream. No, you don't walk. . . . You just move in mid-air. . . . That won't get you anywhere. Either climb up into the clouds or stay a clod upon earth—the thing between is no good. What are you going to do?"

"Find work."

"You mean—find yourself." He laughed, and Frossia, liking him, felt annoyed and embarrassed, but Anna was back, saying in her reedy voice:

"Yes, exactly, Paulina Pavlovna. If you go to No. 14, Grafsky Lane, you ask for Mahmet and mention my name. There you might buy some rye flour. I am not certain, of course—who would be?—but Mahmet is reliable. And his things are not a bit prohibitive. Why, I got ten pounds of barley flour for a very small musquash muff—"

"Leave the address with me," bellowed Pavel Pavlovich, "Paulina's mind is above gruel and muffs. Even if she did remember it, she might carry the flour to her blessed contemplative at Ochta—"

"Pavel, I have never, never starved you at his expense. . . . Of course, he must live, but I would not dream of taking ten pounds of flour to him."

"No, my dear, you never dream of such things. You just do them. Here, Anna Yosifovna, 14, Grafsky Lane, Mahmet. Thank you. . . . Thank you. . . . Come again"—he winked at Frossia—"and some day you shall sit for me."

"He is impossible, but lovable," commented Anna on the way back, and Frossia said nothing.

They talked about ballet one evening. From Anna, Frossia could gather enough and to spare about past glories. The very names flashed like diamonds about the dusty room with its dim furniture and absurdly frilled heliotrope curtains. Fokin, Lifar, Legat, Diaghilev . . . Anna could still drop her voice to gentleness when she mentioned Diaghilev, and the women—Kschessinskaya, Sedova, Preobrajenskaya, Gordova . . .

"They are still carrying on," Anna said negligently. "At least some of them. I believe there is a school in Teatralnaya Street. Vaganova is at the head there, and this dreadful Lunacharsky got the Government to subsidize it. They mostly go in for old material, things like *Esmeralda, Lac des Cygnes* . . . *Petrushka*—though seldom enough. . . . Someone said there were one or two new ones—I have not seen them—*Gardens of Illusion* and *Fountain of Bahchi-Sarai*—"

"What would they be like?"

"I don't know." Anna yawned.

"What is happening at the Mariinsky?"

"Maxim and Zerst are there. They have classes and evening lectures. Once they gave *Coppelia* with Gordova and also *Don Quixote*. They say young Semenova is all the rage, she has done good work in *Lac des Cygnes*. . . . She is a peasant or something. I have not seen her." Anna could be lyrical about the past only.

But Frossia gradually heard a few things about the present. There was a real *corps de ballet* started by some members of *Ratis*, the Peasant Artists' Union, and in Millionnaya, in a building occupied by a branch of the Proletcult, on a tawdry, untidily lit stage, Frossia saw Gordova dance *Coppelia* and heard a thin swarthy stranger give a stilted lecture on the *Lac des Cygnes*.

"The swan," said the lecturer, "is really disembodied. We watch her raising herself on her points, her arms close to the body, both feet together. Now she has folded her wings—only for a moment. Presently we shall see her feet no longer on the ground. She will fly away, separate from us and from the ground. When she comes back, she will have grown doubly intimate because of her having been away—"

Frossia listened, disturbed and bewildered. The little swarthy man read on, frequently consulting an untidy sheaf of notes. He was certain neither of phrasing nor of accent. She liked his eagerness and the taut attention of his hodden gray audience. But she could not follow the exaggerated sentences, and did not go again.

Lilian had told her about the great Soleil Cinema in Nevsky Prospect, Chat Noir, Bi-Ba-Bo, and suchlike doubtful haunts. In Chernishov Lane was a gambling den, in Vladimirsky Prospect another, so Pavel Pavlovich told her. The old Nobility Hall in Michael Street was a concert hall, and the once fashionable Udelnaya Church, cradled among the Admiralty gardens, was another. The great Yussupoff Palace in Moyka was a music hall, and a dancing school was housed in the huge mansion of the Yurievsky princes, that great mass of gray marble and purple granite, its roofs wounded by bullets and bombs, its plateglass windows long since smashed and splintered, its floors, inlaid with nacre and ebony, scratched and muddy. Pavel Pavlovich once went there, and told Frossia about its white satin furniture yellow with mildew and gray with dust, about its ceilings of pleated gold silk and pale pink damask, checkered by ugly gashes. "It is all grotesque, those rose marble fire-places look so incongruous—but the rooms are crowded, young men and girls seem to work quite hard there," he said. Frossia remembered her painful juvenile efforts at Mademoiselle Loiret's in Gogol Street. "Your limbs should be fluent like water. They are bone and iron, Mademoiselle." Frossia did not go near the Yurievsky Palace.

In less than a month she knew that all the stories she had heard about Petrograd were so many fables. And most people told me they had seen things, she thought indignantly. There were dreadful things in plenty, the darkness, the sorry state of city drainage, theft, murders, the several horrors of the Tcheka in Gorokhovaya Street, at König House in Viborg Side, Kresty Prison and Shpalernaya. There were lootings grown so common that people wasted little time on recounting them. There were midnight raids and daylight raids on people and on property. Finally, there was hunger. But life flowed on—apart from queues and cemeteries. Plays were still given at the Mariinsky and the Alexandrinsky. The Hermitage was open at the appointed hours. The Winter Palace was turned into a somewhat mournful museum, and Frossia was astonished to find members of the former household conduct groups of visitors through halls and passages once denied to all but members of court circles. Those cicerones wore no uniform; they spoke little, limiting their explanations to dryly factual remarks, but their very presence seemed to Frossia more or less of a question mark.

She also learned that people still worked at the Academy of Arts and the Academy of Sciences. The University was busy enough. There trembled fear, uncertainty, furtiveness, in all behavior and effort, but, as days spun into weeks, Frossia learned that the Parnikovs and a great many other people lived in small detached houses their own imagination had built. In a sense, Anna, with her constant lamentations about vanished finance, belonged to their company, though Anna refused to admit the death of the whole country. Her own life, as she understood it, was over. As to the people, she frankly said she could not be concerned about them. What difference did it make if a few extra millions lived or died, she asked Frossia.

5

The brief March day had already petered out when Frossia reached the house in Moshkov Lane. It had been a day of no aimless wanderings for her. She had tried for work in a small local Provnarkom—she had imagined herself quite capable of wielding a bread knife—and at the *Gosizdat* in Catherine Street behind Nevsky Prospect, and a few other centers, but she had met with contemptuous rebuffs in all places. It had been the kind of a day when even dreams might not be indulged in for sheer sacrilege; the sleety rain had soaked through her inadequate coat, and she felt small, frightened, and in need of a friendly shoulder to shed her tears on—but somehow she could not think of Anna's shoulder.

In the tiny hall she heard voices coming through the closed door of the living room, and she slipped through to her own little den. It was dark, she must fumble for matches and light a tin lamp.

At first she noticed nothing except that the small place looked somewhat tidier than usual. Her two suitcases, her bag, the few oddments on the table by the window, Taglioni's portrait, the leather bound books, were just as she had left them. Yet the room had an air of saying that it did not altogether belong to her, as though it had been interfered with during her absence, left emptier and poorer. Frossia stopped tinkering with the recalcitrant wick, knelt and pulled out one of the suitcases. The few clothes she possessed lay on the top. She delved deeper, and knew she could not find the green velvet box. She went on rummaging, her cold hands turning icy. She delved deeper and deeper until she came on a crumpled sheet of thick white paper and read the lines written in her own precise round hand:

"One cabochon ruby, set in pearls. Platinum chain. A. One sapphire cross, 12 stones. Pearl chain. 50 pearls. A. An anchor of rubies. 15 stones. Chain of small rubies. 47 stones. A."

There was more. The rest was crossed out. The rest did not matter. She had salvaged just those three things from Kiev, the ruby, the cross and the anchor. She had shown them to Anna, and they

55

had discussed possibilities. Anna had urged her to keep complete secrecy. Such things, according to Anna, were far too valuable for casual speculators. Frossia must not dream of taking them to any Tartar merchant in Chernishev Lane. Anna had appraised them slowly, shrewdly, telling Frossia that, famine or not, she need not go hungry for many a year.

"But you must be very careful. There should be no hurry. I suggest you get them broken up. Nobody could afford a chain of 47 rubies—however small. Now there are still two or three decent jewelers left. I know one of them quite well, he has become almost a friend of mine. We will get him to come here and do the job properly—under our very eyes. Yes, my dear, nowadays you could not trust your own father in such matters."

Frossia's knees shook a little. She felt sick. Now she had nothing at all—neither job nor possessions. She was untrained. She stood alone in a darkened city. Almost she imagined the rose-colored phial in her grandmother's thin hand. . . . And the Parnikovs' plaintive warnings rang in her ears: "Life can be dreadful. You are young. You have had no experience—"

She listened, and heard muted voices, the sound of a door opening and closing. On leaden feet she went to Anna.

"Anna," she began, and stopped.

Anna was sitting in a chair by the iron stove. Her face looked chalk-white, her underlip hung loose, her hands were shaking.

"What is the matter? What have they done to us?"

"They have robbed me." Anna's mouth folded like that of a bitterly hurt child, and she wept vulgarly, noisily. "They have robbed me, I tell you, and I dare not denounce them. It is the man at the Domkom. He has always hated me. They have taken all—the star, the small tiara, the earrings, all the bracelets, the rings. . . . Look, look—" she pulled at a bureau drawer, huge tears cascading down her dirty cheeks—"look, all the cases gone—"

"When did you go out?" asked Frossia.

"This morning. After you had gone. I went to Moyka. I came back soon enough. Of course, I did lock the front door, but those fiends have master keys, I am certain of it. Had I found them at it, it would not have been much use. It is illegal to possess any jewelry. I have no redress—"

"But it is also illegal to steal. They have stolen the things. They should have confiscated them."

"What a child you are! What is the difference between theft and confiscation? What is the sense of bothering about such niceties? No, someone must have denounced me—"

"And me also," amended Frossia, "I, too, have been robbed."

Anna spoke indifferently: "You have, have you? Well, of course, they would have gone all over the place with a fine tooth comb. Now there is nothing left and we might just as well die." She wept, and made Frossia lose patience and grow hard.

"At least you have a roof, and some clothes, and furniture. I have got nothing left."

"Well?"

"And I don't mean to die. For goodness' sake stop crying. We must think. I quite see it would be no good to report it. We should have been wiser, carried the things sewn into our clothes or something. Now we must think—"

"What is there to think about?" screamed Anna. "We dare not tell anybody. Do you not understand? We are really lucky that we are here still. They might come back for us yet. What is there to think about?"

"I was not thinking of the jewels. After all, people can survive anything. But we must do something and live." Suddenly Frossia smiled. "It has become quite stark now, shorn of all complications. I am beginning to see what Nikolashka meant. There are no more props for you and me, Anna."

Anna rose and pursed her lips into a thin line.

"Yes, you might think so," she whispered. "You are in no need of props. Why should you be? You are young. For me it is the end—"

Abruptly Frossia turned and went into her room.

6

Anna had wept over the robbery but, her tears poured out, she seemed to show no further interest in the vanished jewels. She grew calmer, more furtive and secretive. She sat near the stove in the room with its heliotrope curtains, still hugging the green shawl round her shoulders even though it grew warmer and warmer. Anna sat in her room, and Frossia thought she had gone into another country. Anna no longer talked of anything. She behaved as though she and Frossia had had no common interests in the past, and could find nothing to share between them in the present. She has found something for her own, mused Frossia and left Anna alone.

The loss of those three jewels had left her defenseless indeed. She still had her mother's small dressing case with gold and malachite fittings, but the fragile boxes and bottles did not, at least to her inexperienced eye, suggest any important market value. She also had a ring, a slight thing of a diamond loop held together by a tiny square emerald. This again had been her mother's, and Frossia had no wish to part with it. Besides Anna would now have been unwilling to discuss any possibilities of barter. Anna had gone into a separate room, locking the door behind her. When they met, she replied in dry monosyllables to any casual remark of Frossia's.

"Of course, I have not mentioned the loss to anyone."

Anna's black eyes went ironical.

"How could you mention it? Neither of us has a proof that we ever had them."

So Frossia went about searching for work and finding none. Occasionally she found her way to Moyka. There one morning she met Lilian, unexpectedly neat, almost smart in a canary yellow knitted suit.

"You never came again," Lilian reproached her loudly and left a lipstick stain on Frossia's cheek. "Serge was so attracted by you. He told me that he had never met anyone so complete, and you know how particular he is. But you were not very kind to him, Frossia." She stroked her skirt. "Do you like it? Straight from Berlin. You must not ask me how I got it."

"I should hate Euphrosynia Pavlovna to hear the answer," muttered Pavel Pavlovich, staring at an unfinished sketch, and Lilian stamped her foot and went out. Frossia stared after her. Pavel Pavlovich moved about awkwardly, sucking his empty pipe.

"There is Lilian for you. People like me and you are just good enough for her when there is nobody to bring her smart clothes from Berlin. Yet I feel pity for her. Once, months ago, Serge sent her packing from the flat, and she came here, all ugly and shivering, crying, in the middle of the night. Paulina almost turned her out. I could not. I lent her my dressing gown. She arrived in rags, said that husband of hers had sold all her clothes. Well, in the morning she sat for me—and then hated the sketch. 'You have made me look greedy,' she complained. 'I am the most generous woman in the world.' Greedy? Euphrosynia Pavlovna, she is a glutton. Then she went. We missed a couple of teaspoons. Later I met her at the Palace Theater. I said: 'You took those spoons.' She never denied it. She said: 'Yes, you should not have left them lying about. You know what I am like,' and she also borrowed a few odd thousands, to pay a shoemaker, so she said."

He paused, wiping one brush after another on a filthy rag.

"She paid it all back. There is Lilian for you. A wanton and a thief, and yet there is a streak of honesty in her. Euphrosynia Pavlovna, you cannot really condemn any living creature. You see something dreadful, crooked in them, and say to yourself, 'This one is a rogue, that one a thief,' and the rogue comes along with comfort in an hour when you feel like killing yourself, and the thief brings out a reminder of blue skies over your head. It is a queer twisted world all round."

Frossia hesitated.

"Yet I sometimes feel that one should not be concerned too much with any living creature."

He shook his enormous unkempt head.

"Not in these days—at least. High walls belong to a different world," he said, and turned his back on her. "I have no manners at all, my dear. The light is good, and I must work."

When she left, she remembered Nikolashka. Bureaucracy had indeed fallen, but in this strange new world one could not push one's way through without somebody shepherding one to the right door. Pavel Pavlovich was kind, but quite unanchored in any official sense. Sometimes he did posters for the Government, but he worked for them as a free lance, so Paulina had told her. Nikolashka was a baker, in charge of a communal food depôt and, by virtue of his appointment, a fully fledged member of the Narprovkom, the commissariat which dealt with food from corn to caviare.

She found him, laid the brief bare request before him, and he tugged at his huge red beard.

"Ah, everybody is wanting a job these days. Now then, are you rich?"

"I am a pauper," she said candidly.

"And have you any opinions?"

"Plenty of them."

He frowned.

"There you are, Euphrosynia Pavlovna, and how could I find you a job? Now if you could only be like my Irina Nikolaevna, it would be as easy as a plate of cranberry soup. She is a marvelous woman, she has no opinions, she would be safe at the Smolny, she agrees with everybody. You must meet Irina Nikolaevna when she is back from the country. Now this very morning we had a committee at the communal depôt. And one comrade said that if the bread ration is not cut down, there will be none left in a month, and I agreed, and some did not, but if Irina Nikolaevna had been there, she would have agreed with those who agreed and those who did not, and everybody would have been pleased. She has such a way with her, butter is not in it. Well now, Euphrosynia Pavlovna, you are gently bred, you are intelligent, and they will say at once 'Counterrevolution.' That is an ugly word, Euphrosynia Pavlovna. Then they will shout: 'and who brought her along? Why, Nikolashka. . . . To the wall with Nikolashka. . . . His friends are too dangerous. . . .' It will be a plateful of nice thick gruel for all of us. Besides, what can you do? You know nothing of corn, you could not bake bread." He appraised her slender arms. "Why, you could not even cut bread for more than an hour before you got tired—"

"There must be some office work somewhere," she insisted. "Ration cards must be printed and issued, and paper money, and labor books, and what not besides. Why, I have seen buildings absolutely crammed with typists. I have been to some of them. Telephones, typewriters all over the place. Commissariats may be dirty and untidy places, but everyone seems busy. Why, I could work a telephone board if I were taught. And I can spell. I have used a typewriter—"

Nikolashka looked doubtful.

"We have no telephone at the depôt. Nor a typing machine. Wait, though, I must think. I do know of something—it is only your opinions," he added unhappily.

"I promise to lock them up."

"Well, then, come along."

They turned into Maly Prospect and came to a small wooden house. A red painted notice told the few passers-by that the building housed the sub-divisional headquarters of the Vasilyev Island Narprovkom. Nikolashka pushed open an unpainted creaking gate, halted, scratched his head, and muttered: "If only Irina Nikolaevna were here. . . . She is such a marvelous woman—"

But Irina Nikolaevna was still in the country, and Frossia stood there, waiting for him to lead her to an unpromised land. They crossed a small yard, Nikolashka opened a door and went forward into a spacious dim room, warm from a huge porcelain stove. The room seemed littered with papers rather than furniture. Frossia could smell onions, paraffin, and ink. She blinked.

"Comrade Fyodorov," said Nikolashka, "I have brought you a clerk—"

From behind a huge rough table, its shape unrecognizable in the dimness, rose a pygmy of a man with an enormous disheveled head and a neat dark beard. The pygmy wore a soldier's tattered tunic, and Frossia noticed that the left sleeve hung loose. The pygmy yawned and spoke in a deep bass.

"Why, Comrade, this is unexpected." His piercing black eyes swept over Frossia. "Out of work, are you not?"

"Yes," she stammered.

"Registered?"

"Well, I have been to the Labor Exchange—"

"Have you got your unemployment ticket, Citizen?"

"No," replied Frossia, plunged into deep bewilderment. She had never heard of such a document. The pygmy shrugged and spat on the paper-strewn floor. Nikolashka fidgeted uneasily.

"Have you been educated?" boomed the pygmy.

"Oh, yes—"

"Here," he pushed a fragment of thick gray paper towards her, "write something on it, will you?"

Something like generously soaked hemp seemed to live in the ink-bottle, the pen was rusty, but Frossia managed to write her name, address, and what qualifications slipped through her mind. The pygmy picked up the paper, carried it to the window, pondered over the scribbled lines, and turned to Nikolashka.

"Why, she can write. She can spell. Little sister, you are coming here—documents or none—" He seized Frossia's hand and pushed her towards an inner door, bellowing, "Cherny, ah, Cherny, I have found a clerk—"

Frossia turned round, but Nikolashka had gone, and she felt she could not blame him. Now she was in another room with a dirty window, a dirty table, a dusty typewriter, and a man behind the table, a stocky, steely man, badly scarred about the face, with enormous brooding brown eyes. He wore khaki, the tunic was unbuttoned at the throat, its sleeves were too short for him, and the wrists showed, thick, red, also scarred.

"Cherny, here is the clerk—"

Frossia's hands gripped the greasy edge of the table. The man looked at her, she heard his sudden deep laughter, rasping, slashing, and rasping again, and her cheeks turned red.

"Her—for a clerk in this place? Nikita, you are mad! Look at her fingers! She has never done a day's work in her life! *Burzhuyka* . . ."

"She is all right," boomed the pygmy. "Comrade Nikolashka brought her along. He is sound. And what do I care what her people were? There are few girls who can write and spell properly. Have I not inquired at every commissariat? 'Wait,' they keep telling me, 'we have no one suitable.' Yes, I can wait, and look at these papers. They go on growing like mushrooms after the rain. Anyway, Cherny, this is not Gorokhovaya—"

"And Tcheka is not a mere building, Nikita." The other leant back in his chair and stared at Frossia. "Well, and what may your serenity's name be? I wager your father was a prince, was he not?"

"Euphrosynia Bozert. My father was a merchant, a jeweler—"

"Yes, we have heard of him. He married a princess, did he not? Nikita, he was a court jeweler. They lived in Sergiovskaya, in a house with plateglass windows, red carpets and palms all over the stairs. Well, where is he now?"

"All my people are dead," Frossia said levelly, "but you have no right to shout at me like that. I am going—"

"You are not," thundered the pygmy. "Nikolashka brought you. I have engaged you. It is a bargain. I don't mean to waste any more of my time running about the commissariats searching for clerks. You are staying here."

"You are," said the man behind the chair. "I was not shouting at you. It is my ordinary voice. I am a peasant. I have been in the army. Nobody whispers in the army. Well, and how do you find things?"

She drew a breath before answering.

"Terrifying often enough, sometimes revolting, but interesting—"

"Interesting! You say that—"

"And why should I not say it?"

"You are not of us—that is why."

"That is stupid. Your people are always preaching equality."

"Equality!" He broke out laughing again. "Do you mean to tell me that you honestly consider us to be as good as yourself?"

She measured him with a slow glance. She knew she disliked him, his loud voice, his laughter, his roughened scarred wrists, his insistence on awkward topics, and his utter lack of subtlety. Indeed, Frossia disliked him so much that she wished she had it in her to give him a different answer.

"As good as yourself? Why, no, very likely you are much better—at the moment."

"At the moment?"

"Yes—because you are doing things—in your own way. Most of them bewilder me. Some are loathsome but you are doing something, and I suppose I am a mere drone." And she thought: Here I have given them a whole batch of opinions. . . . Poor Nikolashka. . . . Have I really let him down? And she schooled herself to read their faces. The pygmy stood, scratching his unkempt red mop. Cherny bent his head. Neither spoke for a few seconds, and Frossia was preparing herself for something sudden, dramatic, irrevocable, when Cherny said, without raising his face.

"Well, you might do worse than join the Party—in spite of your birth."

"No," Frossia gestured angrily. "I would not commit myself. I hate labels. I love freedom too much."

62

The pygmy yawned. Cherny got up and pushed the chair against the wall.

"The Party is not a label." Now he was on a platform. "The Party aims have been well defined by Comrade Bukharin, who says—"

He continued at great length. Frossia could not even pretend to listen. He went on and on. Imperial or Soviet, she thought, we Russians will never change. We must talk. Sitting or standing, sick or well, tired or fresh, we must always talk. And our words are like so many boughs of an old chestnut tree—they go spreading and spreading. . . . We must talk. If we had no listeners, we would talk to a wall, a tree, a cloud, anything. Most of us would have been ready to number Edison among the saints. Is it because our language is so beautiful? she thought. No matter how roughly pronounced are its accents, it always flows, it is never angular, it never jars. . . . Cherny went on and on, direly mispronouncing terribly long words, stumbling over many a Russianized idiom but lately borrowed from French and German. His audience were no longer Frossia and the pygmy. Cherny was on a platform, addressing thickly serried ranks of intent men and women and young people. Cherny's face lost its uncouthness. Gradually he ceased fumbling with unfamiliar words, and his native eloquence flowed like an undammed river, gathering strength and color with every new phrase. The content wearied Frossia. The manner, the voice, the brooding brown eyes, had a fire in them which could not be altogether ignored, and she could well imagine how such rhetoric would capture crowds and keep them safe in its flaming thrall.

As suddenly as he had started, Cherny finished, picked up his shabby peaked cap, and walked out, slamming the door behind him. He had neither looked at Frossia, nor spoken a word to the pygmy. Probably, reflected Frossia, Cherny still imagined himself on his platform.

"Comrade Cherny likes talking," boomed the pygmy. "He is a very important person at the Gorokhovaya—a member of Tcheka, you understand. And he likes talking—"

"So I have gathered," said Frossia, and asked for a brief initiation into her duties.

7

Now she sat behind the rusty and frequently rebellious typewriter, and typed endless, involved reports at the pygmy's dictation. The work proved interesting, and it pleased and annoyed her at the same time. Nikita Fyodorov dealt with speculation in all its varied branches. Now she learnt that food speculators were by no means the only transgressors of economic decrees; people black-marketed in currency, in timber, in building material and raw chemicals, in leather and in steel. There was a case of a sackful of rough amethysts looted from a mine in the Urals, and a boy of ten was the culprit. He thought that the stones were "just pebbles." He must have known they were not, decided Frossia, reading through the dossier which proved that he had received a consider-able sum for them from an unnamed Armenian dealer. There were other cases, complicated and obscure; some of the documents but served to deepen the central mystery of the case; she could under-stand little, and wisely asked no questions.

She also observed the pygmy who soon proved to be a nursery story, all big print and clear pictures together. He had once had a definite background, keeping a tiny grocer's shop somewhere in a settlement in the Western provinces. Yet that background had grown dim in patches. Now he belonged nowhere, and nobody be-longed to him, though someone must have taken enough notice of him to provide him with such a responsible job. Nikita had come from nowhere, he would, most likely, disappear into nowhere once his usefulness ceased to exist from the official point of view. At the moment he was useful. Frossia helped him write his lengthy dela-tions, his reports of such speculators as happened to cross his path. Yet their many and varied misdemeanors never provoked him to any comment. He would never say: "Well, this devil had best go to the wall. Five hundred pounds of raw glycerin stolen, and there is such a shortage!" He would merely remark: "Have you finished with the glycerin case, Euphrosynia Pavlovna? Was it four or five hundred pounds? Ah, I thought it was five. Now here is the report about those hides from Kazan . . ." And Frossia nursed a feeling that, given different circumstances, Nikita himself might join the ranks of those racketeers he now helped to denounce. To Nikita nothing was black or white, nothing good or bad. Things were things. He troubled himself no further than that. The law provided him with a comfortable livelihood so long as he remained in his post, and he kept the law. She found his stark objectivity rather startling at first. Gradually, she came to like it; there was some-thing comforting in it set against the overbiased attitude of the majority around her.

Her small world received the news of her employment with vary-ing degrees of approval and otherwise. Nikolashka beamed, tugged at his huge flaming beard, and once again implored her to throw all her opinions into the Neva. Paulina Pavlovna said vaguely: "Oh, a job? How very nice. But will it give you enough scope for reflection?" and her brother pressed a whole smoked herring on Frossia.

"Well, there you are! Typing things may be very dull—but never mind, Euphrosynia Pavlovna, a narrow lane often leads to the high road."

Anna was trenchant in her disapproval.

"Working for them? How can you?"

"Why not?"

"Of course, it is a mere point of view, but I could never have accepted their charity—"

"Anna, I am working."

"Precisely. You will not stand aloof from them. Therefore you are helping on their ghastly revolution."

"Anna"—Frossia tried to argue calmly—"this is childish. The revolution has happened. You hate it, and so do I—to a certain extent. But neither of us could have prevented it."

"Exactly—because nobody cared enough to prevent it. Everybody is such a failure. The closing of all banks was the end. You cannot have civilization without finance, and I suppose they pay your wages in kind, do they not?"

Frossia did not reply. She wished she might shout back at Anna: "Failure? Yes, you are a failure. Perhaps, it is just people like you and me who have brought it all about. Nobody did care enough. . . . Most of us have either escaped abroad or else slunk into corners, living on our furs and jewelry. Had it not been for that robbery, I should be doing the same . . . and I can't judge . . . Pavel Pavlovich said that about Lilian. . . . We cannot judge anyone, but judging people is such a blissful relief sometimes." And Frossia wished she might go on shouting at Anna: "Yes, those dreadful, dull, fiendish people have won—or else they are winning because they had enough ardor for their cause. And we are tepid and feeble. I know I am. I am so feeble that I dare not turn to some memories because I am afraid of them. . . . And you, Anna, you have lost your diamonds and have gone to pieces."

Frossia might have said all this and more, but she kept quiet. You could quarrel lustily with an intimate friend, and make it up later with widened warmth and deepened understanding. You could hardly go to war with a peevish, secretive acquaintance. Ballet was now the only link between them, and to Anna ballet was little more than a frail memory from a wan, remote world of ghosts, as fragile and as dusty as the autographed portraits in her small drawing room. When Frossia told her about *Coppelia* at the neighboring Proletcult, Anna exploded with a string of sarcastic remarks, and Frossia was silent. Gradually she found herself invited but seldom into the over-furnished room with its mournful heliotrope curtains, and Anna began closing the door whenever Frossia was in the flat, rushing past her in the diminutive hall, her plump pale face closed in the absurd importance of a secret. Sometimes, on hearing the front door open, Anna would call out that she was busy that evening, and Frossia must seek the shelter of her own tiny den and go to bed for warmth since her room had no stove and the April evenings continued chilly.

She kept away from the Parnikovs, rightly divining that until she had indeed found herself on some sure ground, she could neither face their inevitable reproaches, nor endure their plaintiveness. Sometimes she dreamed about them; they invaded her world, filling her sleep with whispered taunts: "Wait, wait . . . wait. . . . The terror has not really touched you yet. . . . You must wait for something dreadful to happen to you, and then you shall know what it means to live without hope," and even in sleep her subconscious tried to assert itself with a protest. I need not wait. . . . The worst has touched me. . . . It has. . . . I cannot tell you about it, but it has. . . .

There came a day in mid-April which Frossia would remember for a long time. Hurrying across Nicholas Bridge to her task in Maly Prospect, she met the man she had seen in the train from Kiev. It was a day of high winds, the roar of ice splintering all along the river, and all the lovely, mad secretiveness of a whimsical spring day. The wind came from the southeast, sharp and bitter, and the ice-free islands of clear water in the Neva rippled to the wind and the sudden sun, and offered a gorgeous interplay of color and movement, so that Frossia must needs halt and watch even though she knew she would be late. Then she turned her eyes from the pleasure the river had given her, and saw the man come towards her, and for an instant she thought absurdly: Is he going to Moshkov Lane to ask for me?

Of course, he was not. He hurried on, intent upon his own business. He had, so she surmised, hardly noticed her in the train, and certainly there was no hint of any embarrassed recognition in his face as he came towards her, and Frossia looked at him hard. His hands she could not see, they were hidden in the pockets of a short and shabby brown overcoat. All about him seemed worn and drab. His face was something at one with his clothes. It was neither ugly nor handsome, the ordinary face of an ordinary man, indeterminate of bone and coloring, commonly shaped lips and nose, quiet hazel eyes, little to be read in the outline of either forehead or chin. Yet she recognized him unmistakably. It was as though she and he were no longer on a bridge but again in the airless, overcrowded cattle-truck, and a soiled handkerchief was once again fluttering down to cover a stilled face at their feet, and so real did it all appear that Frossia almost stopped as if there were no more room to move about in. "You said something then . . . I wish I could remember what you said—about a curtain going up," but the man had gone on his way, and she hurried forward to Vasilyev Island, guiltily conscious of several misspent moments.

Nikita was out, but Cherny, an unfamiliar black coat over his shabby khaki, was standing by the table when Frossia came in, murmuring a brief apology for her lateness.

She had met Cherny often enough. Always would he bring the tumult of thunder and swollen waters into the bleak office, taunt her and mock her with his sudden rasping laughter, or else weary her with his endless dissertations on communistic doctrines, and Frossia was not certain which she disliked most, his mockery or his party fervor. The former disturbed her innate sense of separateness, breaching the walls of her severely private garden. The other usually ended by giving her a faint nausea with its flow of loud-sounding verbiage apparently divorced from such stark matters as the dwindling bread ration and the disgraceful drainage in the city. But she knew that Cherny, in common with all his kind, talked endlessly and passionately. Brevity was not given much of a room in their house. If they worked hard, they must talk harder.

Of himself Cherny never spoke. She had met him often, but she knew nothing of his earlier background and his present environment. Nikita kept telling her that Cherny was clever and enjoyed an important position at the Tcheka headquarters in Gorokhovaya Street. What Cherny did in Nikita's office remained a mystery to Frossia, but life seemed to be crowded with apparently insoluble puzzles, and she was learning to curb her curiosity. She knew nothing of Cherny except what he chose to tell her, and so far he had chosen to tell her nothing.

That April morning she was annoyed to see him. She wanted neither homilies nor badinage. She had had her hour of reverie on Nicholas Bridge. All of her was still held in a dream, and Cherny had little use for such unsubstantial stuff.

He never acknowledged her greeting. Instead he flung some direly bethumbed papers on the table, turned his back on her, and walked to the window. He spoke over his shoulder.

"Wait a few moments. I happened to hear a very curious story yesterday. I want you to listen to it—"

Frossia pushed a ledger closer to her and began fingering the thick heavily inked pages. Cherny went on, his face still to the window.

"It is a story so curious that I could hardly believe it. It is about some people who had a large estate in the Ukraine, near Kiev, to be precise. There was a grandmother, a father, an uncle, and two young people, boy and girl. The elder folk had pinned all their hope on a White victory, and when the last chance had gone the grandmother decided none of them was to face a possible firing squad. As a matter of fact, she and the young people's father might easily have been shot. So the old woman got the whole family and all their household into a room, told them of her decision, and offered them poison. They accepted her judgment—all except the daughter. Now, citizeness, could you tell me why did that daughter refuse to die—so quickly and in such comfort?"

He turned round very slowly. Frossia was sitting at the table. She had her chin cupped in both hands, so afraid was she that he might notice how they were trembling. Her face looked white. Her voice rang steady.

"Because . . . she was—and is—a coward."

He shook his cropped head.

"She might say so. . . . Refusing to die a coward's mean death, citizeness, is not cowardice. . . . It is brave, it is fine—"

Frossia got up slowly as if she were not quite certain of her next step. She walked round the table towards him, and in an instant her right arm shot through the air.

"This for my grandmother," she cried, and hit him on the right cheek. "And this for my father, and this for my brother." Her arm fell down, she saw astonishment rather than fury in his eyes, and she drew back.

"And now take me away. You have tortured me enough for today, for the rest of my life. Yes, please take me away. I would not join my people because I was a coward, and I have paid you back for calling them cowards. . . . Take me now, do what you like with me, I am a child of counter-revolutionaries, and it need not matter to you what my own opinions are. I should not be here if I were not a coward. Well, I was the youngest among them. I just wanted to live. But I am sick of it all now. I told you, did I not? that I hate all labels. You said your Party was not a label. You were right. It is not. It is something much more loathsome and hateful. No—you must wait," she cried even though he stood silent, his cheek flaming where she had hit him. "You must wait, I have more to say. I was not ready to condemn when you began all this business, I said to myself: 'Wait and see, it may be the birthpangs of something big and clean and lovely,' and now I wonder if it could ever be. People's bodies are dying of hunger, and you give them meetings, resolutions, red banners, decrees. People's souls are in anguish, and you offer them slogans about religion being an opium—"

He moved, but Frossia could not stop.

"Equality! Equality! And again equality! Do you imagine all human nature is just like a fallow field ready for the leveling? Do you imagine all of human spirit could be poured into one solitary bottle of your precious doctrine? Yes, yes," she exulted, "I know—you will tell me I am ignorant of its beginnings. So I am—but I can see it at work, and in a few years it shall cease—cease," she repeated, "not because of any foreign intervention or blockade or civil war, but because mankind is human and diverse and could not be treated like a tramcar. . . . Well, then, I have said enough. . . . Oh, I don't know what I have been saying, and now it is all over. . . . You can take me. . . . I am really tired and frightened, and I hate it all." She ended on a curiously flat note, all her passion gone to ashes.

Cherny said, his brown eyes on her face: "Sit down."

Frossia did not move. He said again:

"Sit down. I am not used to such behavior. I should not know what to do with you if you fell in a faint. You look white enough for anything. Will you have some water?"

She sat down and shook her head. He moved away from the window and stood so that she could see his face, one scarred cheek still unevenly crimson where her furious hands had hit him. He stood there, both hands in the pockets of that odd black coat.

"Well, you are more of a puzzle than a whole shelf of difficult books. I call you fine, and you slap my face. You say you hate us, and I know that you hated the things which are gone. You are no anarchist. You ask me to arrest you and have you shot. Citizeness, you are a puzzle. Now it is your turn to listen, and listen you shall. Your own voice has left you. You can just croak. . . . Your work can wait. You shall listen. I am much older than you are. I have had no proper education. I am peasant born, I come from Simbirsk where the soil is rich. My family were what you might call kulaks today, because they were well-to-do, only my father was just and he did not oppress the lesser fry in the neighborhood. I went to the village school and learnt my letters. I went to the village church, and sang in the choir on Saturday evenings and Sunday mornings, in a clean red shirt, my hair plastered down with sunflower oil. I wished to help my father on the land, to marry one of our neighbors' girls, to breed healthy children, to stay on the land. I had a happy childhood, happy boyhood, happy youth. I had no ambitions beyond the land. Simbirsk is a happy country. The landowners round us were kind, enlightened people. Whenever distress, famine or flood or fire came near us, they always organized immediate effective relief. I was a boy. I never remembered the trouble of 1905. I had never been in a train until 1914. By that time I was twenty-one, married, had my own *izba*, owned my own livestock, tilled the land I rented from my father. And I had a son.

"I was uneducated. My desires were few and simple. My village schooling had given me my bare letters and a little arithmetic, but I used to get our parish clerk or the deacon to write what few letters I needed to send to livestock breeders, to corn merchants and suchlike. I tell you I was happy. Nobody had ever dealt unkindly with me—not even the local police.

"But I was a peasant. In 1914 I went to join up. My brothers came, too. There were five brothers, all of us were married. By the end of three years there were four widows and one widower. It all began in the army—the trouble and doubt and distress, until I saw how wrong everything had been for most people even if I had led a quiet happy life. The Germans were in front of us, and behind lay treason. Treason—I tell you. We fell in our hundreds and thousands, we froze in our dugouts, we had no boots, our valenki were made of shoddy, our guns had no proper ammunition, our food would have disgraced a prison, and we went on, and we fought sometimes with rusty bayonets, sometimes with bare fists; and behind those lines, in safety, the Technical Department made more muddles, and again plans miscarried, and sometimes a well-padded general would come out of his warm lair in Petrograd or Moscow and review us, and tell us that the Tsar was watching over us and all would be well in the end. Citizeness, I was no mere revolutionary by the middle of the war, I was a staunch communist, the war made me one. And I will tell you something else—I, a soldier, with more wounds on my body than I could ever count—if it should ever happen that the blasted Germans make trouble again, the world will see something different from 1914, they will see men fighting like tigers, and there will be no treason behind—for the people shall fight for their own land. . . .

"So I came back—much later, and I found the village burnt down. The Whites had passed there. I had no wife and no son. I gave the land we had owned to the village soviet, and I came here. No more land for me. They have put me into the Tcheka. Yes, go on looking at my hands—there has been blood on them, there will be more

70

blood on them. We must get the canker out of the country, and it is an ugly job. Now I am going. People like you would speak of feelings, I am a rough man, what do I know of them? I had known love once—my old woman, my land. . . . Now it is all hate and fury. . . . But when I heard your story, I knew I was looking at courage once again. Citizeness Bozert, I salute you—"

He bowed jerkily and was gone. Frossia tottered into the outer room and got herself some water. Her throat burned. Her eyes ached. The water was musty and tepid, but she drank it greedily, and splashed some over her face. She could see no towel, and dried her cheeks with her sleeve. Then she returned to the typewriter. There was a lot of dull copying to be done. She slipped a rough gray sheet into the machine and began the mechanical work. The very monotony brought some strange quietude to her mind. Nikita never came that day, and Frossia went on working until she was free to face the open skies again. But she lingered longer than usual in the bleak little office.

<h2 style="text-align:center">8</h2>

The house had been meant for a glass factory before 1914. It was never finished. Either the owners' funds had failed, or else the architect had got tired of his own design. It stood in one of the slummiest Lines of Vasilyev Island, and however ugly, it could boast of the dignity of open spaces all around it, the humble timbered huts of the immediate neighborhood having gone down in flames in March 1917 when the local police station was set on fire by the mob.

The house reared itself, almost proud of its desolation. Its proportions were ugly, its front wall varied in height, most of its windows had not been given any glass and were now boarded up by unskilled hands. The gaping door stood open about one-third down its untidy sprawling length. It looked as though it had been cut there by sheer mistake. The roof was flat, and parts of it were sheeted with grimy glass—again patchily, as though the architect had realized but late that his erection lacked in light. Part yellow stone, part muddy pink brick, the building stood like an orphan among other houses. Across the several boarded-up windows stretched an enormous sheet of dark gray sacking with huge letters daubed in rain-washed red: The Gospel House.

Frossia did not know how she had wandered to the very edge of the Island that afternoon, but the very ugliness of the house arrested her at once. The door stood open, she observed odd groups of men and women slip inside and, urged my mere impulse, she joined their numbers. The door led into a tiny narrow passage where she could hear people's labored breathing and smell their wet clothes. At the end of the passage a dark curtain flapped to and fro in a draught. A young man on crutches stood there. He smiled and raised the curtain. Frossia went in.

The hall was enormous. The light came down from the skylight. The walls stood innocent of either paper or paint. The well of the hall was cluttered by several roughly carpentered benches. Further on, stood a primitive platform with an army of small deal chairs behind a desk. Men and women pushed past Frossia towards the platform, but she chose a bench nearest the exit. The young man on crutches ambled past her. He looked a boy of about twenty with a thin pale face and rather intense black eyes. Vaguely she wondered whether he was the preacher, but he shuffled past the platform and vanished behind a small door at the other end of the hall. It seemed that his only function lay in welcoming strangers. He does it well enough, thought Frossia, remembering his quiet little smile.

Presently all the chairs on the platform were occupied by a motley crowd, women in shawls and shabby mantles, men in cloth caps, here and there a tattered khaki tunic. Then a girl, wrapped in a big blue-green shawl, took the place immediately behind the desk. Frossia heard a pleasant deep voice.

"Now, friends and strangers, let us come to life," and there followed something of the groaning of a full tide as the oddly assorted audience scrambled to their feet, and they all began singing an interminable hymn with a refrain about the wings of a dove. Sing Frossia could not, she did not know the words, but she stood up with the rest, suddenly conscious of her own isolation among the benches in the body of the hall, but nobody appeared to notice her and nobody seemed to mind what their neighbors were doing. Some of the women on the platform, having stood up, sat down again and turned to books or knitting in their lap. Others seemed to pray on their own. The rest went on chanting, led by the girl behind the desk.

Frossia kept standing. The bitter cold in the spacious and draughty hall, the extraordinarily quiet but tense mood of the gathering were suddenly acceptable, comfortable, reassuring. She was not at home among those people, she had no wish to be, but somehow it was soothing to be a mere outsider in such a place.

At last the wings of the dove ceased fluttering above their heads. Several chairs scraped against rough boards, the people sat down, most of the women propping their chins with that small and definite gesture which suggested whole-hearted attention as well as eager expectation. Frossia, too, sat down on her isolated bench and waited. The girl in the blue-green shawl began fumbling with some notes on the desk. The skylight was immediately over the platform, and Frossia could see her clearly. She was a girl about twenty-five, she had a plump peasant face with broad cheek bones, big gray eyes and a full red mouth.

"Last week," she began, looking straight ahead of her, "you and I considered together some interesting things in Gogol's *Dead Souls*. For four days I have been praying to the Lord for guidance in this meeting, and He led me to choose the writings of Fyodor Mikhaylovich Dostoevsky. So today I am able to give you some worthwhile points from the *Brothers Karamazov,* namely, Father Zosima's testament, Mitia's outburst in prison on the eve of his trial, and Aliosha's speech to the boys at the very end of the book. First comes the testament." She bent her shawled head, she was not speaking now but reading slowly, clearly: "Brothers, do not be afraid of sins in men. Love mankind in its sins: this is the height of charity. Love God's creation as a whole and love it in all its parts, and you will reach God's secret in all created things. . . . Humility and love, not pride and hatred, do vanquish the world. Friends, ask God to give you gladness. Much indeed may be hidden from us, but all of us possess some consciousness of our link with other worlds. Our highest thoughts, our noblest feelings, are not rooted in this world. From His many other worlds God took the seeds, and sowed them in this earth, and tended His new garden, and the seeds grew to maturity. But all growing here depends on its contact with other worlds, and this consciousness is alive in us. . . . Judge no one. . . . If you and I were truly righteous, no third person could become a criminal. . . . If the wickedness and cruelty of men stir you to indignation and unspeakable sorrow, even to the desire of revenge, fear this desire above all things. Go and find suffering for yourself as though you were guilty of others' cruelty. Accept your cross, and bear it. Then your heart shall be assuaged, and you will understand your own guilt: your charity might have lit a lamp for the wicked man's dark path, and your charity had slept instead. . . ."

The girl paused. All stayed quiet. Frossia saw the young man on crutches stand in the opened doorway at the other end of the hall. His face was raised, but she could not see it clearly. The voice began again.

"Now we come to Mitia's speech in prison. 'It is possible, even in penal servitude, to find men's true hearts among convicts and so get nearer to them. It will be possible to live there, suffering and loving. . . . Oh, yes, I shall be fettered, robbed of my freedom, but in my great grief I shall rise again unto the joy without which no man can live. Oh, how full is life! Alleluia! Praise be to God and His joy. I love Him,' and, finally, friends, here are Aliosha's words at the very end of the book: 'Dear children, do not be afraid of life. How good is life once you have done something good, once you have been true to the truth within you.'"

The girl folded her notes together and sat still. Frossia expected comment, embroidery, something of an improvised sermon, but the work was done by an artist. The great words were read in all their beauty, and then left alone, unspoiled by a neophyte's clumsy fervor.

That is how Dostoevsky ought to be read aloud, thought Frossia, with a depth so terrible that it searches out your own depths, and yet no outward feeling at all. You might say that girl's voice was sheer ice—for all its warmth and color. How does she do it? I must read him again, find in him the things she sees. And then Frossia remembered that there were no books among her few salvaged belongings, and this made her think about the journey from Kiev, the morning scene with Cherny, and her mind clouded once again.

It proved a fairly long pause. Nobody stirred. Frossia's eyes wandered from one face to another. All of them were intent and quiet as though they now found themselves in a place where they would truly be. Only one or two among them had a wistful look as though they would have liked to hear more. But no more came. The notes were folded away. The girl at the desk spoke again.

"Our next meeting will be on Tuesday, the Lord willing. I have been led to choose Tolstoy's *Resurrection,* and will read such parts as may be pointed out to me. Next Friday the choir will meet here and sing us some new songs they have learned. And now I ask you to join with me in the gift of peace—"

All scrambled to their feet. The crude untutored chanting began again. The hymn was fairly long, and a pause was kept between each four lines. Then all sat down, and the girl said slowly and distinctly:

"We shall bless the Lord for His kindness in throwing light upon the dark places of life, and may His peace stay among us and within us."

The platform became all movement, men and women came down the few steps and made for the curtained-off door. Frossia hesitated. She had been among strangers, heard Dostoevsky read, listened to some songs, and now she felt quieted, and wished she

74

might express her gratitude. The girl on the platform was gathering books and notes together. The young man on crutches appeared again. Frossia came forward.

"May a stranger say Thank you?"

The girl looked up, smiled, and came down the steps. She was peasant-bred, her bones were large and clumsy, her flaxen hair was plaited round her head. She spoke to Frossia in the same voice that she had used for reading Dostoevsky—deep, pleasant, searching.

"There are no strangers in this place. This is a house of friendship. I hope you like it."

"Yes, but I feel rather puzzled. Is yours a church or what?"

"No. We are merely in the hands of the Lord. I am not very well educated. I dare not teach anyone. But our Russian literature has so much to give us all. Others have said wonderful things, and I bring them before these people."

"You never say anything of your own?"

"How could I? I have no words." She blushed deeply. "Well, sometimes a friend will ask for a prayer, and then I try and say something—but I don't do it often, I don't like it. I am too unworthy. I read the Bible, too. We had a flood here about two years ago, the water never came into this house, but things were bad down in Gavan, and we had the place crowded. I had not prepared anything for their comfort. I work in a factory," she explained. "They had some food and something to drink, and we had no light, and I could not read to them. But I know many psalms by heart, we had those, and then we sang. It was comforting, so they said."

"I am sure it must have been. Now about Dostoevsky. I have read *Brothers Karamazov* again and again. . . . But you have opened the book for me. I don't know how to say it," stammered Frossia, "what makes you pick on such things and read them in such a way?"

"It is the Lord," the girl said simply. "I come to a book and I read it, and then I see that certain things are like candles. . . . Well, a great many friends who come here are illiterate—I used to be myself." Her candor pleased Frossia. "And I made them see it all. There is nothing except what the Lord does with it."

"It is your reading." Frossia spoke with conviction, but the girl shook her head.

"It may be my voice, but, friend, the Lord is at work all the time. Here, Grisha." She turned and beckoned the young man on crutches, who came forward, smiled, bowed, and Frossia bowed in return. "This is Grisha," said the girl very simply; "we work together. Grisha will tell you the same. It is always the Lord. He works in light and in darkness, everywhere, at all times. This is not faith. This is a fact. Surely. . . . Have you not felt it?"

"No," Frossia replied curtly. The exalted mood, born of listening to Dostoevsky, was almost dying. The girl's eyes grew intense, so were the boy's. The beauty of the place, decided Frossia, was a fugitive thing. Now they were babbling away in the ordinary jargon of zealous sectarians avid for more fish in their net.

"No," Frossia repeated briefly, and the girl held out a rough calloused hand.

"You shall. Peace stay with you. I am Klava Voronova. I live here," she added simply. "So does Grisha. We will always welcome you."

"Thank you," Frossia said woodenly and left them.

9

She would not tell Anna about the strange encounter, but she told the story to her friends at the studio. They had heard about Klava. Pavel Pavlovich said that she was a *"rabochaya,"* a factory hand at a cloth mill, "also an artist," he added, and Frossia agreed. Klava Voronova, from all one knew about her, was self-taught. "Sometimes she gets her friends together in the evening, gives them music and games, and something to eat. They bring their own things and then, in the middle of all this frolicking Klava will whisk out some notes, begin reading, and all is hushed. I have heard stranger stories. They swear her touch is good. There is an account of a boy with an abscess on his face. Klava is said to have healed him. I don't know about physical ailments, you cannot credit every rumor you hear, but she is unusual. She will help anyone. She is not robust and, of course, very highly strung. Well, a friend of hers married a manager of a chemical supply depôt near the Finnish station. The depôt was housed in a derelict building supposed to be haunted. In the old days even caretakers refused to go near it at night. The manager was sent out of Petrograd. The Chemical Trust wanted him in the Urals for a couple of months. They said: 'Your wife can mind the depôt.' Could she? She went hysterical. The Trust got annoyed. Klava heard about it. She went and slept at the depôt for six weeks. Her friend got calmer. Once I asked Klava, 'Well, you don't believe in ghosts—so that it could not matter much to you, could it?' And she went white all over. 'Believe in them? What is there left to believe in when you know they are there?' But she held on. She never let her friend down. That is Klava for you."

Frossia thought: And I was rude to her. I imagined she was one of those sectarian people—ready to interfere, to probe. . . . I must go back—

She would have gone back soon enough, were it not for a sudden interruption in the Moshkov Lane routine. For days, for weeks now Anna had avoided her, giving her the freedom of hall and kitchen, but always closing other doors to her. One afternoon Frossia came back. The front door was unlocked. The door into the dusty drawing room stood open. Frossia called: "Are you in, Anna?" There came no reply. She went into the room. It seemed emptier than she had last seen it. Some of Anna's most intimate belongings were gone. Also it was tidy. Some furniture had been dusted, the heliotrope curtains were neatly looped up, the iron stove cleaned out. There was no fuel about. Frossia went into the kitchen. Anna was not there. In her own den, propped against Taglioni's portrait, Frossia found a casually scribbled note. "I have gone. I could not bear it any longer. There is some civilization abroad. I will send you a parcel as soon as I can. Please destroy this. You can stay on in the flat. Do what you like with the furniture. There is nothing else. Anna von Packen."

Frossia went to Moyka. Pavel Pavlovich, a saucepan in hand, muttered:

"How very foolish of her. . . ."

"And she had no money."

Paulina Pavlovna shook her head.

"Anna Yosifovna always had something. She was secretive about things, but she was never in want. She knew so many speculators. She must have been making her plans for a long time. She should have given you warning, though. . . . And I wonder how she has managed it. In winter you simply run across the Gulf of Finland, you are dressed all in white, and you have very efficient guides. It costs millions, but it has been done. Now it is far more difficult. The ice has nearly gone, and it is much too early for boats. What a pity," sighed Paulina Pavlovna, "I used to have high hopes for her. I felt so certain that some day she would come out of her fog and darkness. Now once she gets abroad, she will be just the same as ever—clothes and money. She told me the other day she was getting sick of her old beige tweeds, and she had no other clothes. I said: "Dye them black," and she looked so angry. Anna Yosifovna hated black, did she not, Frossia?"

"I could not tell you," Frossia replied wearily.

Anna had been remote, sullen, secretive. Still Anna had been there. Her going away, without the least word or sign, was some-

77

thing of a wound. "Do what you like with the furniture. . . . Use the flat." Even there Anna had been unkind. The flat had three rooms, a small hall, a separate kitchen. Frossia must not enjoy such spaciousness all to herself. She must go to the House Committee and court the peril of unknown lodgers to come and share the flat with her. Anna had indeed lived there all alone, but Frossia knew that Anna had been breaking the law for years. "And I am just afraid of doing it. . . . I could not. . . . Besides, I suppose it is not quite fair. Three rooms are three rooms, and everybody is crowded into landings and cubicles." Reluctantly enough Frossia went to the House Committee.

The Domkom was housed in the cellar of a neighboring house. They never asked what had happened to Anna. But they were interested in the three rooms. They were gruff but not unkind and, certainly, they asked questions about herself. They said:

"You have come from Kiev, citizeness, quite recently? Well, we must get you registered as living in this house. Then it will be in order. We must have things in order, citizeness, and the labor book must have your address written in and attested by your Domkom. Please let us have your labor book, citizeness."

The request was simple and natural. Frossia always had the labor book carefully tucked away in an inner pocket of her coat. She thrust her hand into the pocket. It was empty. She searched in other pockets. The labor book was not there. Wildly she remembered that she had it on her earlier in the day—there had been a picket or something near Nicholas Bridge, people's labor books examined by a sentry. . . . She had then produced hers. . . . So it could not be in the flat. . . . She must have dropped it. . . . She said feebly:

"I have not got it. I must have mislaid it. . . . I must have lost it—"

"You cannot lose it," said the Domkom man, his fat bearded face showing utter bewilderment at such foolishness. "You must have it. You are not a child. Everybody must have their labor books. Surely, you know that." His voice which had the rattle of several bones in it, went on rasping at Frossia. Did she not know? Did she not realize what such a loss meant to her? The labor book, said the Domkom man, was far more important than clothes were to the naked or bread to the hungry.

Frossia knew this too well. The labor book was more or less one's permit to live. Without it, one had nothing. One's very existence was left unacknowledged, and one became a hunted criminal. Just a piece of yellow-gray paper, sewn together anyhow, cut into so many leaves, bound in black American cloth. Was it more than that to look at? Yet labor books were lords and masters of their possessors.

"I must have lost it," stammered Frossia for the second time.

The man was not unkind. Slowly, carefully, he explained that all lost labor books were taken to the nearest commissariat and later forwarded to König House on Viborg Side.

"You know—the old sugar factory. You will most likely pay a fine. The book might be endorsed. I should not lose it again if I were you."

"About the flat," Frossia began. "Shall I be allowed to stay on there?"

"Well, yes, but you must first retrieve your labor book. Then we shall find other tenants. How many rooms? Three? And a hall? Well, four or five people might go in with you. The kitchen will, of course, remain communal."

So she went to Viborg Side, a long weary tramp from Moshkov Lane. The rain came down, her thin shoes hurt her, and she imagined that every passer-by noticed her helplessness and mocked at it. "Here goes the foolish girl who has lost her labor book. She might find it or again she might not, might not, might not," and the imagined negative echoes pursued Frossia across quays and bridges and avenues.

She did not know the whereabouts of König House. Viborg Side was a huge wilderness of waste patches and mean streets. Someone directed her wrongly, and she misspent an hour in trying to find the right way to König House, and at last reached it, her feet aching and her mouth dry.

The place had been a factory. Now it looked what it was—a prison. The few ground floor windows were barred, an armed sentry paced up and down in front of its enormous gates. He was young, pink-cheeked, proud of his uniform and rifle. He stopped, heard Frossia's nervous murmur, stepped aside and flung over his bony shoulder: "Yes, that is right. Room 45."

Within she found nothing but dimness and a heaving human wall. It was so dim that she could barely pick out a uniform or two in the thick mass of civilian-clad flesh. Room 45 was two floors up. She climbed the wide staircase, innocent of banisters. She found the right door, and faced a tired, hostile girl in a badly patched khaki tunic. Her face had a crimson gash for a mouth, her small green eyes looked weary. Yet Frossia must rein in her desire to fall upon that thick dirty neck. The girl sat at a table crowded with piles of labor books.

79

You—lovely, lovely things, sang Frossia's heart. All the saints in God's heaven, make mine be among them—

But the girl said in a surly voice, an untidily rolled cigarette hanging, crimson-tipped and wispy, between her full, moist lips: "They should not have sent you up here. I stop seeing people after twelve. I have real work to do," she added.

Frossia pleaded in a small broken stammer. She was in a job, she explained rather brokenly, and it would be difficult for her to come all this long way again. She spoke humbly and slowly, and hated herself for the servility, but it served its purpose because the girl became interested.

"Working, are you? Well, that is certainly different. You should have said so at once. Everybody who comes here looks so idle that I have no patience with them. What is your name? And the number of the book?"

Frossia gave both breathlessly. In a few instants she saw her labor book held between two broad misshapen hands. She heard the slow purposeful rustling of pages, and the machine gun bullet of a question was shot at her:

"In a job, are you?"

"Why, yes—"

The girl rose, went to a door, and shouted something. Frossia wished she might ask a question, but her tongue had nothing to do with her will, there was just a ball of thick worsted in her throat, and her hands went clammy. A man came into the room. He wore a black Russian blouse and dirty khaki breeches. He had a fat rosy face. He was smiling genially. Frossia looked at him in horror.

"You are in a job," he said, licking his lips and beaming at her. "Yes—"

"Yet you are not registered. The labor book page is such a nice blank. Is it a private job then?" He came closer. Frossia could see the reddish brown hair above his thick upper lip and, fascinated, she watched that smile ripple all over the fat pink face.

"It is not private," and she stammered out all the necessary details.

"I see," smiled the man, and rubbed his hands as though the information given by Frossia were a birthday present.

Dumbly she waited. The crimson-mouthed girl shrugged and lit another of her loosely-rolled cigarettes.

"Well, Comrade Punin, what are we to do?" she drawled, ignoring Frossia altogether. "We have quite a number of such people below—"

"Wait a second." He checked her and turned to Frossia. "Well,

80

you know you have broken the law. And we don't like people breaking the law. We have had enough anarchy. Things must be put into decent order. I should say you have no great love for our proletarian laws, have you?" he asked, smiling genially.

The girl laughed, her green eyes peering at Frossia, who kept silent.

"Why do you not answer me?" asked the man in the same agreeable voice, his chin almost shaking with laughter, and Frossia stood silent.

The man shrugged and looked at the girl.

"Downstairs," he smiled. "There is quite enough room. Sorry, Citizeness Bozert, but you will have to become our guest. I shall have to find out a few things about you. It is not healthy to have an unregistered job, you should have known that—"

They led Frossia down the staircase. For about an hour she was left all alone in a tiny cubicle, its door opening into a larger room. There was a chair, and she sat down and watched, her door having a lattice. She saw a large florid woman in a magenta feather boa flung over a mussed gray silk dress, come and argue feverishly with a uniformed man at the door.

"I keep telling you I will stand surety for the girl. She never meant to annoy anyone. Seriously, Comrade Commissar, as one intelligent person to another, you must see what a mistake has been made—"

"I am not a commissar," rapped the small man with a thin pox-pitted face.

"Well, comrade, then. We are all comrades now. I am telling you I am an honest citizeness, I want to serve the republic as best I can, and I will have things done decently and quietly. There has never been a brawl at my place. Ask anyone—they all know me, Madame—I mean—Citizeness Touras. . . . I want to go bail for that girl. She never meant any harm. How was she to know about the curfew? It was ten o'clock last week, eleven the week before, and how was she to guess it had been changed to half-past ten? I ask you, comrade? Such things are impossible. My girls are well-bred and quiet—"

"Your bail is not accepted, citizeness. The case will be heard next Friday, and I think you have misunderstood the summons. She is not being indicted for any brawl, nor for breaking the curfew—merely for having neglected to sweep the snow." He consulted a gray slip of paper in his hand. "Yes, exactly, the snow in front of No. 39 Sergievskaya Street, in the morning of 25th February—"

"Snow? But it is nearly two months ago, comrade. The snow is

81

gone. . . . Why, we are at the end of April, and who can be think-ing of any snow—I should like to know?"

"Such is the indictment." He spoke wearily. "I cannot help it. The case will be heard next Friday. There is nothing else to be done."

"Next Friday?" Madame Touras stood islanded in the middle of the bleak empty room, her magenta feathers and gray dress all the tawdrier in the sullen shaft of sunlight. "Next Friday?" she repeated vacantly and pulled at her boa. "And what-is-his-name from Rostov wants her and nobody else. What very bad fortune! And all snow is gone." She sighed and moved away, and Frossia tried to efface herself against the wall of the cubicle. Her effort was unnecessary; Madame Touras was too absorbed by the injustice meted out to her to take notice of anyone else at König House.

Frossia spent two nights at the old sugar factory. König House, she soon discovered, was a clearance station where a motley crowd of people were detained whilst varied inquiries were being made about them. Arrangements were casual, not to say makeshift. In the room where she was presently brought by two garrulous, not unkindly soldiers, she found about fifty men, women, and even children. The place was spacious and light, but its only door was padlocked on each new arrival, and the great windows were all barred. Some indeterminate bedding was lumped along the four walls. Women and children were given the use of it. The men, both gently bred and others, huddled together in the middle of the room. Three electric lamps still swung on dusty flexes from the muddy gray ceiling, but there were no bulbs in them, and twilight ended in unrelieved darkness. The padlocked door swung open several times a day: guards either ushered in new inmates, or else shouted names, and someone would get up and fumble their way to the door. Those once summoned did not return. Three times a day the door opened for a more inviting purpose. Food came in, bread of a kind, gruel, soup, even brick tea in large tin mugs. Food was surprisingly good, almost plentiful, and it might have been enjoyed wholeheartedly, were it not for the stench in the room.

The stillness was incredible. Here and there a child might break into a whimper. From one corner or another a plaintive mutter might be heard for the space of a few instants, and then die. Those were isolated, widely scattered sounds. There were no others. All curiosity seemed asleep among those people. New arrivals were met by searching, vaguely compassionate glances, but hardly a word was spoken to mark their coming. People's departure was accompanied by the rapped orders of sentries but by no farewells.

From her own niche by the wall Frossia watched the guards come in and out. They seemed gruff and grim enough, but not inhuman. The inmates were neither gruff nor grim, but something marked them apart from the rest of their kind.

Frossia dared not intrude upon that scene. A middle-aged woman, with a seamed tanned face, made room for her by a wall, and muttered something inaudibly. The rest observed Frossia's coming in as though it were of no concern to them. She came soon after midday when bowls of thin gruel were being carried through the briefly opened door, and the people in the room were soon absorbed in their meal. No portion was as yet allotted to Frossia; she did not feel hungry, but her taciturn neighbor offered her a share of both gruel and bread, and Frossia accepted them. She said "Thank you," in her ordinary voice, but the room was suddenly tenanted by echoes, and nobody else spoke. Then she knew that silence was preferable to those echoes.

Yet the very stillness had an eloquence all its own. Incessantly, monotonously, it hammered out its hidden gray theme: "We have come here because we had not been careful enough—by descent, by habit, by behavior. We are all strangers. We know nothing of one another, and now we must learn the uses of extreme caution."

The first night, troubled by nausea, anxiety, and the discomfort of bare boards (she had decided not to lie on what bedding came her way), Frossia could not sleep. It was hard for her to imagine that the room of that huge barracky place was in Viborg Side, and that Viborg Side was bone of Petrograd's bone. She kept trying to trace the way from Viborg Side to Vasilyev Island, imagining great bridges and little bridges, splashes of young green in gardens and parks, familiar landmarks, running waters, but all those efforts lacked both strength and color, and gave her little comfort. At length she fell asleep, dreaming about Petrograd being separated from her by a cascading wall of madly swirling waters.

In a different sense those two days at König House proved to be a respite. Frossia refused to imagine herself detained there indefinitely, nor would she contemplate any other possibility than that of being released as soon as their inquiries were completed. Her job was not a private one, both Cherny and Nikita Fyodorov had engaged her, and she certainly had not transgressed the law. Now that she had so much time on her hands, she found she could think—and was herself surprised at being able to think—with a clarity which had not come near her for months. She had almost vowed not to go near Maly Prospect again. Now, in the stillness of that dreadfully crowded room, she re-lived the brief tempest of that morning with Cherny. He had hurt her. She had insulted him. Now Frossia admitted that, after all, she had behaved in such a melodramatic manner that her own defenses must have been crippled. She had hit him several times, and he had repaid her by narrating the story of his own life. Somehow this left her doubly in his debt, and Frossia knew she disliked him more than ever. But she must not be foolish. Jobs were difficult to find, she had no resources, and it was necessary for her to cling to the slender foothold the office in Maly Prospect offered her. Unless, she reflected, unless Cherny has told Fyodorov all about it—

Conjectures were useless. She must wait. She had to wait till the third morning when her name was called out by a very young and pink sentry who, obviously, was unfamiliar with his rifle. As he led her along passages and stairs, the rifle kept clattering against the cobbles. It was really too big for him! Frossia decided. He could not be more than seventeen.

In a room below, the man in the black Russian blouse smiled again as he handed her the labor book.

"We have not endorsed it this once, citizeness, but please take care not to lose it again."

"Am I free then?" asked Frossia.

"Of course you are free. You have done nothing wrong. Sign here—"

His smile was more oily than ever. Frossia hurriedly signed an ill-typed receipt and left König House. The scurrying clouds were good to look at, the air was good to breathe. She ran along as fast as she could. The first glimpse of the river made her halt and stand still for a few seconds—so incredibly lovely it looked, all but free of ice-floes.

"And I am free . . . I am free," she sang to herself as she hurried on and on, away from Viborg Side and König House.

10

"That is how it stands," Comrade Nikita was saying; "I cannot have you come here again. You should never have mentioned me at König House. I could tell you some pretty things about that row, but I think you might not like to hear such ugly language. Really, little sister, you should have had more sense than lose your labor book. Did I not tell you time and again that I had no right to employ anyone out of the blue, as it were, without a proper labor permit, and a real *burzhuyka* into the bargain? You would say Comrade Cherny knew about it, and did not object, but he changes his mind from one day to another, it is no good relying on him," said Nikita. "Nikolashka brought you along. I trusted him. I trusted you. Pfui." He spat on the paper-strewn floor.

"A row?" echoed Frossia. "So you got into trouble. I am sorry. . . . But how did you get out of it? Something must have happened. They let me go free. . . . And are they going to take this job away from you? I could not bear it—"

The dwarf's face went blotchily red.

"No. The trouble is over. Since you ask me. . . . Well, I told them it was more or less a family affair." Frossia stared, so patently at a loss to read his meaning that he added hurriedly: "I said you were living with me. They understood that all right—but all the same it would be safer for you to keep away. You never know—"

Frossia leant against the damp wall, her shoulders trembling with laughter. Then she looked at him, saw the strangely wounded look in his eyes, and tried to curb her laughter. He spoke brusquely:

"Is it really funny? Well, it is human nature, little sister. No, no, what am I saying? Of course, you are right to laugh at me. It is funny. Why, how could you notice me in that way? A verminous dwarf that I am, and you such a beauty, and never a louse have I seen crawling on you. Yes, go on laughing. I don't mind. I don't blame you. But it would not do to go on lying to them, they might find out, and go you must, little sister—"

Then Frossia knew that she had always liked him, and now she tried to ease his hurt by her gratitude.

"Comrade Fyodorov, I quite understand. I must go. But I want to thank you. This place has been like sunlight in the fog to me. You made it possible for me to eat solid food for nearly six weeks, and you gave me work. Work is better than dreams—sometimes. Well, all gorgeous things come to an end, and yet, ending, they go on somehow," she cried, closing her eyes as though looking at something within and also without her. "They can't really end. Gorgeousness, kindness, truthfulness . . . Why they all get grafted into you somewhere, and they stay. But is it themselves—or is it us—or is it something quite different? I cannot tell. Can anyone? Oh, what am I saying?" She opened her eyes, and stared at Nikita, and gestured as though she wished to ward off something lovely, and also terrifying because it drew her out of her depths, and she was not ready for it, "Oh, please, Comrade Nikita, what have I been saying?"

"I don't know," he said awkwardly, "and I don't think you do either. Get your feet down on the ground, little sister. It is safer than any pink cloud overhead. And that is also nonsense." He tugged at his neat little beard almost savagely. "That is what you do to me," he cried like a child faced with an arithmetical tangle it might not unravel. "You talk nonsense, and I repeat it. And I have never been a fool, mark you. A gray man, an illiterate man, an unnoticed man, but never a stupid man. Now we have talked quite enough." He sighed, stopped, pulled out a drawer, and flung a multitude of things at Frossia—a pair of gray silk stockings, some dark yellow soap with Swedish lettering on the label, biscuits in a thin pink carton, some chocolate, and a tin of sardines. Out of his left tunic pocket came a thick wad of pale green paper. "That is not bounty," he muttered sheepishly. "You have earned it, and more—but go you must—"

She took the wad. The things she would not take. A vaguely promised wage had indeed been mentioned at the beginning. Some money she must have, but Cherny had really engaged her. She had struck him and had often laughed at Nikita. Presents she could accept from neither of them.

"I thank you—but I could not. I shall now go to the labor exchange, get myself properly registered, and there will come a job. So it is good-by, Comrade Nikita."

The dwarf touched her hand as though it were a piece of some rare porcelain.

"I like you," he said childishly. "Things must be hard for you. You are a *baryshnia*, nobly born, are you not?"

"Not officially," she replied, "not—in any other sense . . . I am a human being, and you are another—"

"You talk much nonsense, but you think right. That is what Cherny said."

"Cherny said . . ."

"Yes." Nikita's face went a mottled red. "You see, he happened to go to König House. He heard it all. That is where I blundered so badly. Cherny did not believe what I told them. He just stood there, took no part in anything, and then, later, when he and I were alone, we went into the communal kitchen across the road from König House, and we were eating our dinner—it was not a good dinner, there was too much salt in the gruel." Nikita broke off. "Those cooks will spoil the best gruel."

"And—"

"Well, what do you think? Cherny said I was a fool to tell them such a thing, and they were greater fools to believe it; he said you were not that sort and anyone could see it, he said, and it was then he said that you thought right."

"How nice of him," Frossia said dryly, shook his enormous grubby hand, and went away.

She was going back to Moshkov Lane. New tenants had not yet been installed, and she felt glad to be going back to stilled rooms and her own thoughts. "I would not even go to Moyka—just yet," she thought almost fiercely. She had been away for almost three days, and they would shower questions at her, and she knew she would resent them. Her brief experience at König House might not be communicated so soon. Her own world would interpret it each according to his or her views, and Frossia wished for no such interpretations. She could imagine Lilian titter and scold her for lack of caution. The Parnikovs would murmur: "Well, did we not warn you?" Nikolashka could hardly be told anything. . . . There remained the girl who had read Dostoevsky, but she was a stranger; and Paulina who would say: "Anyway, there was quiet there. Were you able to think, to contemplate?"

She should have accepted Nikita's bounty. She had not left much food in the flat. She should have remembered stark facts, and swallowed her uncomfortable pride to dine off sardines and biscuits and a chocolate slab.

Frossia came to a corner and turned into the yet unleafed Bolshoy Prospect. There she saw a young man sitting on a bench. He was bareheaded, he looked shamefaced, tears were trickling down his cheeks. People cried in the streets often enough, it was wiser not to notice their tears, but Frossia could not be wise that morning.

"What is the matter?" She sat down by him.

"I am an artist, and they have pushed me out of the Academy—"

"But why are you crying? Academy or none, nothing could stop you from being an artist."

"I am frightened—"

Frossia spoke in a gentler key.

"We all are—sometimes. But why cry? It makes your fear grow and grow."

"I cannot bear any of it much longer. I am doomed. I wish I were like water, rid of the burden of consciousness. . . . I wish I were like the soil—"

"You are not telling me anything." She was firm now. "You are reciting poetry. It is rather bad. I don't like it."

"Because you can't understand it. I used to write. I wrote well. I wrote the wedding of Venice. I had words, I used them, I saw dreams. . . . Now I am a hungry, dirty body, a battered dustbin, and you come along and tell me I should not cry—"

"Battered dustbins have no tears in them."

"My body is crying," he said savagely. "Can you not understand that I am hungry? I have lost my ration cards, my identity papers, I am a lost body." He choked. "I am hungry . . . I don't want words now. Something to eat—" He turned his thin dirty face away from her.

Frossia said very slowly as if she meant each word to be graven on his feeble, untidy consciousness:

"You shall stay here. You shall wait for me. All will be well." She repeated solemnly: "You shall wait for me," and then as fast as her tired feet could carry her, she ran back to Maly Prospect and to Nikita. She explained nothing. Breathlessly she claimed the earlier refused tokens of his generosity. He pushed the things towards her. She cried: "Thank you, oh, thank you!" She bore her precious cargo back to the bench in Bolshoy Prospect. The boy raised his tousled head, and Frossia thought: "What a scared and battered child he is," and aloud she said, "Now you must eat a little, but very slowly."

"You have invented these things. . . . They are just air," he muttered, but his incredibly dirty hands fumbled among the packages. Soon enough Frossia had to check him. He leant back, wiping his mouth on a frayed coat sleeve. He never thanked her.

"How old are you?"

"Twenty-two."

"Three years younger than I am—"

He made no comment.

"And I—" Frossia went on, "am all alone in the world."

"So am I." He shrugged feebly. "It means nothing to me. I shall not let you pester me. I have eaten the food. I feel better. You must go. I know I ought to say thank you, but gratitude is so common." His voice was almost shrill now. "Why, I feel certain you fed me out of mere curiosity—just to see how I would react to it."

"You have not even looked at me," said Frossia.

He had not. Nor had she seen him properly. She had found him crouching against the back of the bench, small, thin, crushed by grief and by hunger. He had fed stooping over the food on the bench, eating very much in the manner of a ravenous animal. She had seen little except the tousled fair hair, sharp bones of forehead and temple, and thin grimy hands. Now he lifted his head, and Frossia saw a face as flawlessly chiseled as any she had ever imagined, skin and muscle clothing perfect bone work of chin, cheek and forehead. The straight thin nose, the large sherry-colored eyes, a perfectly stenciled mouth, all suggested breeding. Yet the mouth hung loosely, the eyes were twin pools of despair, and now that they were looking at her, something like a sneer crept into them.

"My God, have you ever been painted? You are incredible. . . . You are beautiful—"

"So are you," Frossia said dryly.

"I have always known it." Somehow she disliked the way he tossed his head. "And I am also a poet. Listen, I know French, Italian, English. They have a place in Nevsky Prospect where they call themselves poets. I went there. I had heard they wanted translators. I saw a dreadful man—all dirt, sweat and gray knobbly flesh. He said: 'Yes, we want *In Memoriam* put into Russian. You will get paid so much a line. You must put the literal meaning of each word in pencil—but legibly.' I said: 'But you wanted translators?' He replied: 'Well, is that not what you want? Our poets know little English. They might miss the meaning of some words, but you must write legibly—otherwise it is no use your trying to do it.' Can you imagine it? Me—doing hack work! I swore at him and ran away."

"Life is more important than vanity." Frossia began scooping up biscuit crumbs. "Do you not want to live?"

"They will not let me—"

She let it pass. "What is your name?"

"Michael—"

"Michael what?"

He did not answer. She shrugged.

"Listen to me. Life is worth more than poetry. No, I am wrong— life *is* poetry. . . . It is all imagination."

"They live without imagination in this bedlam country."

"Will you listen to me—"

"I might if you were ugly. You will make me fall in love with you in the end. . . . No, I am wrong . . . I am not sure whether you have a mind. If you had none, you would not matter in the least. . . . Anyhow, it would all be so boring." Suddenly he stood up and swayed on his legs, a piteously thin figure in a patched fawn overcoat and frayed brown trousers. The overcoat lacked buttons. She saw he was wearing it next his skin, and pity smote her.

"I rather think I should like to sleep now," he said huskily.

"So you shall. You can come along—unless your own home is nearer."

He smiled thinly.

"Beautiful, I have had no home for a year. I have slept on benches, in cemetery vaults, in ruined houses. . . . I should have gone to sleep in the Neva—but I am a coward."

"You are coming with me. It is some distance, over the bridge, right down Palace Quay, but I will help you, and we can rest on the way as often as you like."

He swayed again, and this time Frossia caught his arm. Under the worn filthy coat sleeve she felt the sharp impact of bone. All feeling left her. She no longer pitied. She was merely glad of being needed and used.

"Now please try and remember that you are going to a place with a bed and clean sheets, and I will heat some water as soon as we are there. Hot water is such a comfort." Frossia went on chattering about the various immediate needs of his all but broken, spent flesh. She did not know if he was listening, and his attention or otherwise was a thing of no moment to her. Hers was the harder physical business of shepherding him along Bolshoy Prospect, across the bridge, down the wide reach of the quay. They must halt at frequent intervals to make him regain what pitiful shreds of strength were still his. Sometimes they were fortunate to find a bench. Sometimes Frossia made him lean against a wall, a parapet, a lamp-post. Passers-by flung fleeting glances at them, but nobody stopped to watch them on their slow, broken journey. Down the quay Frossia grew oblivious of her own Herculean task; her shoulders throbbed, her hands ached, and her feet moved because she meant them to. Had he fallen by the way, she would have carried him on her back.

All the time she must talk to prevent him from speaking. Words sapped him, and stay silent he would not. So she must talk swiftly, incessantly. She described the tiny flat left to her as a legacy, she flung a wealth of detail into her narrative, mentioning the dusty photographs and the heliotrope curtains. She said they would have an iron stove for the winter. She thought there was enough fuel in the flat. She mentioned the kindly, if gruff, chairman of Domkom. "Other tenants might be put in, but that is not very important. The house is strongly built, the walls are thick for privacy, and the doors close properly, and you shall have the drawing room all to yourself."

And so they came to Moshkov Lane.

CHAPTER THREE

THEY SOUGHT A COUNTRY

In an airless, over-furnished room in her flat in Sergievskaya Street, Madame Touras sat staring out of the window. The window gave out into the yard, and she could see nothing but a limited expanse of smooth glistening cobbles, a blind wall to the left of her, a row of dirtily curtained windows in the small *fligel* to the right, the humble annex of a great mansion. A lean tabby cat sat on an upturned barrel in the middle of the yard. Madame Touras was not looking at the cat, nor did she take much notice of the spring sun generously, almost recklessly gilding the gray cobbles. Madame Touras was not looking at anything in particular. She chose the window to sit by because she had no wish to stare at the dingily papered walls. The bedraggled astrakhan coat, a fawn shawl over her head, her hands thrust into a huge, moth-eaten musquash muff, all suggested that she had made up her mind to go out. But she never went out in the mornings, and she had put on those clothes—the coat was worn over her nightgown—merely because it was cold in the room, the April wind was still as sharp as a well-whetted blade, and Madame Touras's slender supply of fuel would not allow the stoves to be stoked at so early an hour.

She had awakened that morning to see a spider by the side of her bed. It was a very small and shy spider, and Madame Touras was big, but, on awakening, she had somehow imagined herself small and shrunken, and the spider grown to gigantic proportions. She forgot all her deeply-rooted superstitions, searched for a duster, and flicked off the spider.

Now she sat strangely bemused as though her life were not a flat field any longer but a terrifying ravine. She could not have explained it in any such words. She merely felt hemmed-in, dissatisfied, uneasy.

Business was good. She had been right when declaring her brief creed in the train between Kiev and Petrograd: "No revolution has ever changed human nature." There were difficulties, but she knew

91

how to cope with all of them. Instead of police, there were commissariats. Some comrades were surprisingly stern, unflinching men whom she would not have dreamt to bribe. Others were ordinary men, amenable, pleasant, and ready to accept her persuasive alms. Taken by and large, Madame Touras reflected, bribery was slightly more difficult than it had been in the past—she had never met a police sergeant whose hand was not ready to open for a furtively offered present—but, none the less, it was not impossible, and the heaving sea of speculation was certainly to her advantage. Some of her clients came from those ranks. Life meant a continuous uncertainty to them. Because life was insecure, they never cared what they spent. They had money. They lavished it right and left. Madame Touras's cashbox was crammed with old imperial gold and silver, with sterling notes and queer German marks, with French currency and Danish, with untidy "Kerensky" notes of twenty and forty roubles, and with the actual currency expressed not in hundreds but in thousands and in millions. These latter notes she despised. American dollars and pounds sterling alone were held in respect. She might be paid in them. She never disbursed them. They were kept in a special place, a small brass box which had a good lock to it. The box was never opened unless Madame Touras were alone. Into that box she poured all her hopes about a vague but certainly quiet future when she could retire, smoke her cheroots in peace, and cease from daubing rouge and mascara over her worn skin.

Yet she could not retire now. She did not feel old enough.

They had made her angry at König House. All about the snow vanished so long ago. . . . The girl had been detained for a week, the case heard, and dismissed for lack of evidence. They should not have done it, thought Madame Touras. They treated me like mud, and I went there ready to help. . . . I went there because I am an honest citizeness. . . . They should have appreciated it. She went on nursing that small grievance because she could not determine the larger unease which kept troubling her.

She was sitting in her own private sanctuary. It held a huge bed, sofas, armchairs, tables, all littered with greasy pink satin cushions and covers. Straight opposite her chair stood an ambitious bamboo erection of several, all equally flimsy tiers, with a cracked oval mirror at the very top. The absurd little shelves carried a conglomeration of equally absurd white china ornaments, from a flower basket to a parrot. These looked yellow-gray with their coating of fine dust. Madame Touras slept and sometimes meditated in that room. The brass box was hidden in one of its dusty corners. But she never had time to keep things tidy, to clean, or to dust. Whenever she tumbled into bed or sat by the window, she felt either weary or uneasy, and she disliked domestic work. But now the dust reproached her. She loved the bamboo erection. She had had it since her earliest, hardest days. It had traveled with her from one townlet to another, from one city to another. It had been the property of her mother. And the white china ornaments, so absurd, useless, and ugly, were all given her by friends. When Madame Touras looked at her white china ornaments she forgot money, wine, and her soiled business, and she remembered that there were things like friendship.

"They do look dusty," she murmured, pulled off a soiled pillowcase, and prepared to flick it all over the bamboo whatnot. Her hands were untutored in the simplest domestic tasks, they slid clumsily over the lowest shelf, and a small white china elephant lay at her feet, its fat rounded body broken into fragments.

Madame Touras flung away the duster. She had no further use for it. She threw the fawn shawl off her head, knelt by the broken knick-knack, and wept vulgarly, noisily, wiping her nose on the rough astrakhan sleeve, according to the fashion of her kind. Presently she stopped crying, her red-rimmed eyes looked at the deep rose carpet, her fat grimy forehead was knit hard, and she picked up the dropped pillowcase. Briefly it fluttered in her hands, and then she laid it neatly all over the pieces of broken white china.

"Good-by, Sashenka," she said huskily—not to the elephant, she had not enough imagination to christen inanimate things, and then she stood up, remembering that two new clients were coming later in the afternoon. Now it was time to ring a bell, have her girls wakened, to rouge her sunken cheeks, to daub mascara under her tired eyes. A fresh-looking child of eighteen came into the room in answer to her summons. She noticed the pillowcase on the carpet and made as if to pick it up when Madame Touras checked her.

"I don't want it moved," she said succinctly. "It must remain where it is."

2

The unfinished glass factory in one of the slummiest Lines of Vasilyev Island was one enormous hall, but a thin strip of it was partitioned from the main body, and its two young tenants called it their home. One of its flimsily timbered walls was lined with books. There were two narrow *koykas*, campbeds, covered by torn gray army blankets, a table, a few cane chairs, and such domestic necessities as saucepans and mugs. There was also the everlasting iron stove, its slightly drunken funnel thrust into a hole made in the wall. In the winter the stove warmed the room and filled it with smoke. In the summer they must needs light the stove to cook their meals, and then the heat became unbearable, and sometimes Klava dragged the *koykas* into the main body of the hall. Grisha followed with pillows and blankets. He could not have carried a single *koyka*. He walked on crutches.

Klava was a factory hand, peasant-born, country bred. Grisha was different. His people were school teachers of some importance. His father had taught Latin and Greek at one of the best private schools in Petrograd, St. Peter's School, where the sons of land-owners and merchants were taught various subjects in more or less perfect German. Grisha's father was a Russian, he knew no German, and refused to learn it. But he was a scholar, his Latin and Greek were excellent, and the school let him have his way. Grisha's mother had taught history and geography at one of the best girls' schools. Grisha had been meant for law; he had already started at Pravovednoe College, worn a black tricorne with a minute green motif, and a tunic with a stiff green collar. Then he met with an accident. He did not tell Klava much about it. It was one winter, in a sleigh somewhere in the suburbs round Petrograd, Duderhof or some such place. His parents were killed instantaneously. His own limbs were shattered. His left foot had to go. His right leg was badly twisted. He never went back to Pravovednoe College. There was something about an aunt, a small house in the country. . . . Klava never disturbed him with questions.

She met him one evening when she was hurrying home from the factory. He was crouching under the wall of a half-ruined house. It was in the summer, but he shivered. She had to carry him to her own home, he had no crutches then. Later she heard that a dreadful old woman had stolen his crutches from him. "For kindling," she had said and run away. Klava had nursed him back to comparative health, told him a little about herself, asked few questions, and then went and managed to get a second *koyka*.

"This is deep and true," she was saying, her hand on an opened volume of Gogol's. "Grisha dear, you go on reading it, you always teach me how to pronounce those difficult words. Ach—if only I were as educated as you are."

Grisha said seriously:

"Klava, I am not at all well educated. I have no understanding of things. You are like a match to a kindling with books. But I had better go on," and he read, "'There are whole centuries in the world's history which should be blotted out.'"

He stopped hastily, seeing her sudden frown.

"Grisha, I cannot understand it. It is all dark and muddled. No, this is not true. You cannot blot out time. Time—well, have we not made it? What is Gogol after? Besides, the good and the bad together will go into the Lord's loaf in the end. . . . That is all knotted up, but you had better read on—"

" 'Mankind has always chosen crooked, remote, difficult paths, distant from the high road . . . choosing such in its striving after eternal truths. . . . And all the time the straight way has lain open before all men, a straight highway leading to the King's own house, a way wider and easier than any other, lit by the sun through the day and by stars through the night—' "

Klava shook her head.

"I cannot read it," she said slowly. "This will not do, Grisha. It is beautiful, but it is a dream. Gogol has seen a vision, he has never walked that highway himself. And a vision is a dangerous thing— no two men will ever see the same thing in the same way. And again why does he say: 'the highway is wider and easier—' It may be wider, I don't rightly know, but easier it is not."

Grisha closed the book.

"We must not read any more. It is late. You are always up at dawn . . ." he hesitated, "but you are happy, Klava, you are happy."

"Happy? I am at home, dear heart. I am sort of cozy, wrapped in swansdown, within and without. Nothing could hurt me that way. It is those outside, Grisha. I sometimes wonder if I am at home because I cannot easily speak about it. Here I have started this place, and I give them all a bit of quiet now and again, we have a nice choir, and we come together and sing, and they listen to my reading, and they go away comforted, so they tell me, but it is 'home-ness' I want to give them, not mere comfort. When you are at home, Grisha, you need no comfort. Grief comes to you, and you are glad of it. But this is not everything, Grishenka—"

"You have brought me home," he said, and his face changed. The thin cheeks burned with faint color, the enormous brown eyes grew starry, and his poor bony hands clenched together as if trying to enclose some treasure within. She smiled at his eagerness.

"I could bring you home indeed, Grishenka, because you love me."

He said stubbornly: "Those who come here love you, too."

"They do, Grisha, but differently. Their love is sometimes born from within, sometimes it comes from without. Sometimes they will listen to all the nonsense you say about me. . . . You should

95

never do it, Grishenka. . . . Now it is your loving me that makes me say so. Listen, do you remember once, last winter, when we had no candles, and it was some poetry I read them—from memory, yes, it was Lermontov, and there came a strange girl with a very long nose and strange green eyes. She wore a red blouse and a big black *bashlik* over her head. Do you remember how she sat there and laughed at us. . . . 'You just give yourself pleasure with your voice . . . You do read magnificently,' she said. Well, she was rude, she meant it unkindly, but I have often thought of it. They come here because they have no money for picture theaters—"

"Klava," he repeated rather mournfully, "you are wrong. They love you."

"Well, it is true, Grishenka."

"What is true?"

"I do pleasure myself by these readings."

"This is nonsense, Klava."

"It is sense. You know when I was a child in the country, I used to think they shut God up in our small wooden church. One summer day it was burnt down. For three whole years I went about believing that God had perished in the flames. And that is what is happening all over the country today, and what do I do? Get them together, and have a choir, and read to them. And nothing is happening to them, and yet I go on getting richer and richer. It is unfair, Grisha, unfair to be so much at home when so many are miserable vagabonds, starved beggars wandering far from God's barns. I tell you I feel it deepest when strangers come here. The other day that girl—do you remember her? Talk about beauty! She nearly took my breath away. Well, even from my desk on the platform I could feel her inward stillness, and she was at the other end of the hall. It was a strange stillness, Grisha, the kind which falls before a storm. . . . Sometimes it is just a breath of stillness between two storms. . . . I could not tell. . . . I spoke to her. . . . You spoke to her. . . . And neither of us could get anywhere near her. . . ." Klava added: "She must have thought me a humbug telling her that all things lay in the hands of the Lord. . . . Well, they do—for me. . . . I, myself, am between those hands. . . . But I could not convince her. . . ."

"You saw her only for a few instants."

"It would not have mattered if I had been talking to her for hours. Now listen, I once read a bit from the Gospels to them, and all within me was singing as I read, but would they have heard that singing? Why is it, Grishenka, that when the loveliest thing happens to you, you just can't put it into words? Suppose I were

96

to stand up in this very hall and say to them all: 'Dear people, we go to sea once we are born, and no sea is without its shore even though we cannot always see it from our boat?' Well, they would listen, they would go away comforted, but that is not a beginning even. That leads you nowhere—"

"You began with me in the same way, Klava," he said softly. "It has led me—it has brought me somewhere."

"Because you love me, *golubchik*. You and I are all in all to each other. That makes a difference. It is not your flesh merely that is precious to me, but your spirit that has seen truths and touched them and lived near them. . . . And it is the same about me with you. . . . And then you are different, Grisha. . . . Your father was Russian, but your mother a German, and I am all Russian, and that is what happens to pure-bred Russians always—"

"What happens to them?"

"Why, once we have seen, we cry for blindness, and once we are blind, we must cry for the light."

Grisha closed the volume of Gogol. Klava began getting their evening meal ready. They talked no more. He loved her. He asked for nothing else.

3

Nikolashka stopped outside the Parnikovs' door, bent his enormous head, and listened. He could hear the murmur of voices, a drawer being opened and shut, and he knocked. All sound ceased. Nobody went near the door. Nikolashka knocked again more loudly and urgently. He heard Maria Nikolaevna whisper: "Vanichka, they never come by daytime. It must be all right. Open the door," and Nikolashka sighed, "Oh, dear, half their trouble is always that fear . . ." and waited for Captain Parnikov to open the door.

He opened it, but, on seeing Nikolashka, he stood dry and stiff in the manner of people reluctant to let anyone cross their threshold. Captain Parnikov did not even say: "How are you, Nikolai Pafnutievich?" He merely stood, in his shabby coat, scarf and cap, and behind him Maria Nikolaevna also kept still, and Nikolashka must begin explaining his strange visit, standing there, outside the unwillingly opened door. He threw a pleading glance at the Captain; "man to man," that look insisted, "you must help me. I find it difficult, and there is a lady, your wife . . ." But the Captain stared past Nikolashka at the dirty ocher-painted wall of the narrow landing.

So Nikolashka began mumbling:

"I have no opinions, and I said so to her. I knew Euphrosynia

Pavlovna was poor—in a manner of speaking, and who is not today? But there were her opinions, and now she has gone, and Comrade Nikita says there had been trouble, and there is Comrade Cherny, too—"

Maria Nikolaevna gathered her tattered shawl closer round her.

"We are not acquainted with—comrades, Nikolai Pafnutievich."

"No, my dear madam, my dear sir, you would not know Comrade Cherny, but it does not do to quarrel with people like Cherny. You see, Russia is made in such a way that it never pays to quarrel with important people, no matter what their opinions may be. I mean important people are like hobnailed boots, and unimportant people are not much more than worms, yes, worms, and as I was saying, there has been such trouble." He looked from the husband to the wife, his small currant eyes ran about from one face to the other, but neither the man nor the woman appeared to wish to understand him. Maria Nikolaevna turned away, folding together a few things on the table behind her. Captain Parnikov cleared his throat.

"We are going out," he spoke peevishly. "We are going across the river. Well, Nikolai Pafnutievich, I said we are going out—"

"I apologize most humbly, but the day is young, days are longer now at the end of April, are they not? I am here because Irina Nikolaevna is still in the country, and I feel lost without her. My dear sir, my dear madame, think of it, a gently bred *baryshnia*, surely, Euphrosynia Pavlovna is a gently bred *baryshnia*, and I find her in this house, and I also find her a job, and now what am I to do about it? Yes, I know they have dismissed her, but this is not the end. I beg of you, Maria Nikolaevna, dear madame, as a mother—" Nikolashka faltered because Maria Nikolaevna would not turn round and face him, and he found it difficult to go on pleading, his eyes on her unbending back.

Captain Parnikov went on in a peevish voice:

"If you have come about Euphrosynia Pavlovna, she has gone from here. We—she—well, there was a certain disagreement. . . . Euphrosynia Pavlovna is not in the least inclined to continue her friendship. It has all been very odd. She left here some time ago. Surely, you knew of it. . . . Yes, you must have known," he said accusingly, "she left her belongings in your care. Well, there is absolutely nothing else, and we are just going out—"

Here Maria Nikolaevna said, without turning round:

"Ivan Petrovich is perfectly right. She does not want people like us. She and I and he differ too deeply. And I am sorry, but we must be going at once—"

Now Nikolashka grasped his momentary advantage. They had not asked him in, he was still standing in the doorway, and it was too narrow; so long as he stood there, they could not pass him. Nikolashka continued standing in the doorway.

"That is it." He spoke vehemently. "Yes, sir and madam, she wants everybody. It is her nature. The moment I met her in the back yard, I said to myself: 'She wants me for a friend.' I have tried to be a friend to her. I shall go on being a friend, but I am troubled now. She wants you, sir, and, you, too, madame, she wants anyone, anything, any lame dog or bedraggled chicken, or books, or pictures. . . . What can I say? I am a clumsy miller . . . I don't understand delicate situations, and I have no opinions, but I do know this about her—she cannot have too many people about her, and she is alone, and I had thought you might help me. . . . Goodness," he said almost helplessly, "have you not been young and in the dark yourselves? Can you not see? She has run away, you see. She will go on running away from all she needs most—"

They looked at each other. The Captain said: "We shall be quite civil to her when she comes here again." And Nikolashka shrugged in a weary defeated manner and clumped his heavy way down the stairs.

4

The city, Frossia knew well, was full of people with neither roof nor belongings of their own; one of such was the city's sudden gift to her. He lay asleep on a sofa in Anna's dusty drawing room.

Frossia's hands were busy enough. She must wash up, and no washing up was possible without water being fetched from outside. She must also mend and darn odds and ends of things, being always careful of needle and thread; and, in brief, produce something like orderliness in the small place she still hesitated to call her very own. But, busy, she thought hard.

"Michael—" Michael what? He never answered. His hands, his accent, above all, that piteously unanchored look, had already sketched for her a broad outline of his beginnings, and she did not want to know more. Most likely he was a well-bred nobody, and that labored reluctance to mention surnames was due to a pose. He seemed full of attitudes. He even managed to clothe his purely animal hunger in something like fierce grandeur. The chocolate offered by Frossia had answered a double need; it filled his stomach and pleased his vanity. A bowl of common gruel would have been swallowed greedily enough—but with a difference.

Frossia spoke to a saucepan simmering on the stove:

"When he wakes up, we had better start explaining ourselves to each other." She went into her own cubicle and stared at the slim crimson-bound book by Taglioni's portrait. "The legend of Euphrosynia. . . . He has very likely never heard of Taglioni," she mused, "and the legend might bore him. . . . All the same, he looks rather inquisitive. . . . He might listen just because of that."

An hour later Michael woke up. Disheveled, slightly bewildered, he sat up on the sofa and muttered something. Frossia shook her head.

"You are trying to be grateful. You don't have to thank me for anything. There is no room for inanely civil gestures in such a topsy-turvy world—"

"What very odd candor—"

"Well, it is just me."

She fed him again on soup and carefully doled out rusks. The chocolate, biscuits, and sardines lay on the table. She did not offer them. Michael drank his soup slowly. In the end he remembered his manners, helped clear the table and stack their few crocks in the tiny kitchen. He would have done more, but Frossia stayed him.

"You must not get tired again. Here is just one cigarette. Would you like to sleep again, or shall we talk?"

"We had better talk. . . . Why, you saved my life—"

Frossia lit the cigarette for him and observed his face. Yesterday they had not met. Today she had him in her flat. Tomorrow she might have to explain him to her acquaintances. She shrugged.

"Yes, I shall talk," her voice rang grim, "and you must be patient. I daresay my talk will sound clumsy to you," and his brief nod annoyed her. The beautiful, though unkempt head moved in such graceless condescension. The very air between them was heavy with unspoken words—"I know you cannot help being clumsy. How else? You will give me a rough stone, and it is for me to chisel it, give it facets, make it acceptable and beautiful—"

"I shall not bore you," she began, her eyes purposely away from his face, "with chunks of autobiography. I was in the Ukraine in 1917. I came back here because I belong here. Some places do that to you. This city is a glass bowl, and I am the water poured into it. Well, these days are like so many question marks. . . . Of course, life is grim and edgy and hard. It may be worse later on, but it need never be impossible—even for you and me. Life need not be lived in and on queues. Something like real thought still drifts about. . . . Why, you yourself mentioned that place in Nevsky Prospect. . . . Well, the Conservatoire is still open, and the

Academies, and the University, too. Some of the theaters do go on. Why should people like you and me behave like flies caught into proletarian amber? There would be no sense in it. People still dance, hear good music, study, go to see plays. . . . Never mind if some among them do spit on the floor, keep their caps on, and carry mud on their boots. Most of them had never before sat in a decent chair. . . . No wonder they feel loose and giddy. What do clothes, manners, governments matter?" She must pause and subdue her vehemence. "Now you have given me an impression that all is over. That is stupid." His sherry-colored eyes smoldered; she took no notice of his anger, and grew bolder. "You have an exaggerated idea of your own importance. You would not mention your surname. I am not asking questions, but you might give me confidence in return for bread—"

He did not reply. His mouth was curved in a childishly sullen line.

"I am not asking questions," Frossia said again, "but, after all, you are my guest," and his pallor gave way to deep crimson.

"You are unkind."

She cut short the piteous preface.

"Pretenses are rather like millstones in these stark days, are they not?"

"Well, what do you want to know?"

"What are your assets then? I don't mean clothes and things—but—"

"Yes," he said bitterly. "I understand you. Well, I can draw, I can write, once I could think, and now it is too difficult. . . . And not worthwhile. . . . It is so much easier not to think—"

"That is just it," Frossia cried. "Surely, you can see how much a mind is strengthened when all effort is difficult? Listen, you say you are a poet. I am not. I have merely day-dreamed all my life, and there has been one particular dream, I have always wanted to give it a shape, and make other people see what it has meant to me. It is a very odd dream. It has kept me alive for years, but it has really been asleep. You know, it is all like a stormy red dawn, and if you look at it hard enough, you can almost see the deep calm behind every madly speeding cloud—"

"That sounds like poetry," he said slowly. "I have written some. You seem to have lived it—"

"I have not." She grew impatient at his lack of understanding. "I am a fumbler. I cannot merge with anyone or anything. But I was not talking about myself. It is that other thing. I shall tell you all about it—some day," she added hurriedly, noting his obvious

101

weariness. "You might see a poem in it. . . . It has always seemed movement to me—like a ballet."

His weariness left him suddenly. He stared at her in anger.

"That is how you mean me to pay for the food and everything? You are unkind, and worse than unkind. Whatever life has done to you, you are mad. Talk about ideas, intellectual life . . . There is none. There has been a ghastly civil war, and now we have a Tcheka, and famine, and decrees, and the International, and endless speeches about the rebuilding of national foundations. Only they will never be national. They are communistic, utilitarian, drab. There can be no room for art."

"Now you have made a speech. And a silly one . . . They are still working at the Mariinsky Theater. I have heard about their evening classes. There is a good ballet school. It is stupid to nurse such violence against a mere outward expression. It is bound to be temporary. But you are so Russian that you cannot get away from politics. All right, have it your way, but you could not deny that Lunacharsky is an artist."

"Proletarian art . . . Concerts at the local Proletcult Club . . . Propaganda on execrable posters done by third-rate men at the Academy! Red faces, brown biceps, red hammers, green and violet sickles . . . Art . . ." Michael's thin left arm swung out and swept a mug off the table.

"There is only one left now," Frossia commented coolly. "Proletarian art? Can you not forget the adjective? It is as vulgar as anything in the middle-class psychology—" She stopped and stared at the tears in his eyes. "I did not mean it," she faltered, but he turned away his face.

"It is not that. Only you look lovely when you are angry. All right, we shall go to the Mariinsky, we shall try anything. . . . Perhaps you are right, I am just an undeveloped weakling. . . . But I cannot follow you. Why this wish to do anything? Why try and climb heights? There might be some nice soft moss in an abyss to lie on. . . ."

"There is nothing exalted in it. It is merely that I want to live. I should hate to grow into a queue sheep with a mouth and a stomach. I should also hate to become a platform parrot."

"No," he agreed wearily, "but one must eat to live—"

He had eaten all the food on the table, she would have to go to bed without much supper; nearly all her treasures were stolen, she had no job and but slender prospects of getting one, but the weather was warmer, she still had a roof, and a companion, however uncertain of moods. He had beauty, an easy flow of exaggerated words, casual manners, and not much else. She knew that he had no identity papers, there would be trouble with the Dom-kom and the food control people, and she wondered how any people of her own small world would receive him. Yet, as she was falling asleep that evening, Frossia thought: Tomorrow I shall tell him more. Tomorrow I shall struggle again. There must be a job somewhere. There is the little Proletcult Club round the corner. The fat woman there looked pleasant enough when I went to see *Coppelia*. Why, I can always tinker with the piano. . . . And to-morrow surely, the sun will rise again.

She slept.

5

Bi-Ba-Bo was a café in Nevsky Prospect. Its battered half-painted door had no name except just the few letters daubed in faint pink over the lintel. Inside you found a brief dim staircase which led to a landing made all the gloomier by a heavy brown curtain. Beyond, lay an enormous room littered with dirty imitation marble tables and rusty iron chairs. Red velvet sofas were arranged along the dusty green walls. Some forty odd electric bulbs were surrounded by silly pink silk shades, all shirred, beaded, and dirty.

It was said that some people came to Bi-Ba-Bo simply because they forgot where they had meant to go in the first place. Bi-Ba-Bo offered few visible inducements. Its chairs lacked comfort, its air smelt of soapsuds, dust, and unwashed human flesh. Its windows were never opened, their drab brown curtains screened off much daylight, but the light was rationed, and the bulbs burnt low. There was no music. Those with money could get their drinks at all hours, but every drink must be paid for in advance. The humbler clients were offered oddly-colored liquids in small white cups. The bored waiters said nimbly enough: "Tea? Coffee? Cocoa?"—but which-ever you chose, you always got the same strangely tasting concoc-tion. Sometimes hard little biscuits were carried round on chipped white plates. More often there was nothing to eat.

Bi-Ba-Bo was hardly ever empty. Girls from places like Madame Touras's drifted there on their off-days, hungry-looking students from universities and academies came and sat at the dingy tables. Bi-Ba-Bo was always well heated, and it was pleasant to sit at a table and to feel your hands thawing, even though it meant paying some few thousands for a cup of dark brown brew smelling of soap and tasting of acorns. Vaguely dressed remnants of intelligentsia, men and women in khaki, obvious Tchekists, well clad and always armed, not so obvious speculators, and, finally, a sprinkling of those

103

people whose social business status could not have been easily identified even by a detective. There were many such—men and women with faces and legs and arms. They moved slowly. They spoke little. They never looked round them. They sat at their tables, sipped their brew, spilled it a little, traced odd circles and squares on the imitation marble under their slow, purposeless hands. Then they stopped sipping and tracing, got up, and moved away, and you could see them going anywhere, slowly, vacantly, the loveliest, most confident spring day incapable of piercing through their fog of mind and body.

There was never any hurry at Bi-Ba-Bo. This was an added pleasure. Even the few white-coated comrades, who served food and drink, moved about the flimsy tables very much at their leisure. Outside in the streets everybody ran about and hurried as though swift movement alone was a preventive against some unspecified criminal charge being leveled against them. But at Bi-Ba-Bo people sat still, sipped and munched, talked in quiet, unhurried voices. Everybody spoke quietly. There was not much space left between the tables, and nobody cared to be overheard by anyone else.

That early May morning Bi-Ba-Bo was nearly empty. At one of the tables Lilian sat alone, in full view of the brown-curtained door. She was tidy, though her thin face might have done with less rouge and powder. She looked brittle and alert. Her dress was made of an old linen sheet, but it fitted her surprisingly well, and her small green cap had once seen the skies over Paris. She had already had one modest drink, and dared not order another because her tarnished silver purse was nearly empty. However, so many tables were vacant that she knew she could keep hers with impunity.

A tall heavy man in suspiciously smart khaki noticed the challenge of the green cap, stopped and stared, but Lilian ignored him.

"Well, citizeness—" he began genially.

"I am here on my own business."

"Why, I can see that."

Her green eyes went narrow.

"And my business does not concern anyone."

He merely pulled out a chair and sat down facing her. Her over-painted mouth trembled a little.

"Well, I know who you are," he began conversationally. "You are Garonne's wife. You are waiting for a woman to come and see you here. Take my warning, the woman is not coming, and you had better go—"

104

Lilian clenched the small silver purse so hard that her knuckles went white.

"I never imagined that any responsible comrade could talk such nonsense."

"Is it nonsense? I had better make it sense. I know who you are waiting for. A woman called Packen. You wrote to her. You were meeting her here on business, and I know all about that business. It is all off. She is not coming. Now you believe me, do you not?"

"No . . . That is untrue. It is someone else. A girl, a friend of mine . . . Someone I have known from childhood, and my husband—"

"Go," the man said so roughly that Lilian must rise, forgetting all about the empty purse on the table. She moved away, then turned back, and snatched at the purse with limp, shaking fingers.

"But I don't understand," she murmured, distressed, genuinely in the dark, it all seemed a tangle with her own self caught into it and held so tight that she could not even struggle. "I don't understand—on my honor—it is a mystery."

The man said brusquely: "All right. Sit down. Wait."

He pulled out a fat notebook, and Lilian watched him, a small piteous fly observing a nonchalant spider. Thick spatulate fingers licked over the pages; he was muttering odds and ends of phrases all to himself, and Lilian made to get up again. His head bent, he murmured almost politely: "Are you in a hurry? Please wait . . . You have plenty of time. Wait." And now Lilian was frightened. She had known thick animal fear before, and could not mistake it. Under the slovenly thick layers of rouge, pallor streaked her thin face. The saucer-like depths of her mind were fretted with perplexity. Of course, this meant that Serge had got himself into trouble. She had not seen him for five days. He had transgressed some law, and now they were choosing her as a scapegoat. Serge was so clever, he knew how to escape their suspicion, their vigilance. Serge could never be caught. Dimly she thought of all the luxuries tossed by him on the roughly tumbled bed. Bottles of wine and spirits, good English and German cigarettes, pound notes and dollar notes, a suit from Berlin, gloves from Paris, some delicately scented soap. Frightened, perplexed, Lilian suddenly remembered that tablet of soap he had brought last time, a generous tablet, pale violet in color, "lilac soap," it called itself, and it breathed of lilac, it came from Germany, it had a spray of lilac painted on the wrapper. She wanted to hoard it for a little time, its scent was so pleasing. . . . Lilac soap . . . Somewhere, long ago, far away, she had seen a white lilac tree in full bloom. . . .

Yes, flowers were good in cakes of soap and bottles of scent. . . .
Cut flowers in a room meant trouble, the water to change, a mug
or vase to find. . . . They died quickly. . . . She was suddenly
taut. Was Serge dead? Did they kill him? For nearly five days she
had not seen him. For about a month she had seen so little of him.
Understanding nothing of his ways, Lilian feared everything. Now
—for nearly a week—she had had no money, that was why she had
written to Frossia. The man had mentioned Anna von Packen, that
was absurd, she had not written to Anna since the winter, she
thought Anna had gone away or something. Frossia was kind,
Frossia had some substance of her own, she might help. Nobody
else would help her, Lilian knew that. Pavel Pavlovich had twice
refused her, all other acquaintances were equally hard, but Frossia
was different, Frossia would help anyone, whether she cared for
them or not. . . . The man's brusque voice cut across Lilian's fears.

"See this." He whipped a piece of paper and dangled it before
Lilian's clouded eyes. "You dare tell me that this letter is not to
Packen. . . . Oh, no . . . And you call her your dear friend—"

"It is someone else," Lilian whimpered, "Euphrosynia Bozert. . . .
She lives there. It is all my absent-mindedness. . . . I forgot to put
the name on the envelope. Surely, I begin it: 'My dear Frossia—' "

"You do not," he said grimly. "You begin: 'My very dear friend—'
and you go on asking for help. Now Citizeness Bozert is poor, we
know she is, she has nothing, she has been working at a place we
know, she could not help anyone, and Packen is different. Packen—"

"I would not dream of asking anyone like her." Lilian spoke
shrilly, her eyes staring at the hostile face across the table, and she
stared so intently that she never noticed the brown curtains move,
the door open, and her husband come in, and a tall dark man, his
face scarred, behind him. Only when Serge was half-way down the
room, did Lilian notice him, and she smothered a little shriek. She
must not appear surprised at seeing him, she must let everybody
imagine that she had left her husband earlier in the morning, and
most people met sooner or later at Bi-Ba-Bo. Lilian managed to
shape her mouth into a smile, to arrange her hair under the green
cap, and to say: "Oh, Serge, at last," as though she had been expecting him, "this is so absurd and unusual," she went on and on,
recounting the fantastic story until she broke off, stared at Serge,
and realized that three, and not two, strangers were near her table.

"What? Who? Why, I know nothing whatever about it," Serge
said in his thin voice. "If she has written to No. 10 Moshkov Lane
and if a Packen woman lives there, why, she must know her. I
don't know her friends. Of course," he glanced at the big man

106

opposite Lilian and smiled, baring his bad uneven teeth, "of course, she will tell you any story. She is very good at them. Well, she has got herself into a scrape, and now she will have to get out of it. This is an enlightened community, and a husband need not be responsible for his wife's behavior." He smiled again and walked off to the other end of the room.

"But he knows her," Lilian said hoarsely. "I am asleep. . . . I am drunk. . . . How can I prove it to you? He knows her, he has met her, Euphrosynia Bozert. . . . Why, he said he had known her people. . . . It is to Euphrosynia Bozert I wrote, I assure you."

The big man shrugged. But the other with a deeply scarred face sat down abruptly.

"I shall deal with it." He spoke briefly, weightily, so that the other man must perforce get up and say:

"It may be a bad case, Comrade. . . . You see—"

"I shall deal with it," he repeated, and waited until he and Lilian were alone, then he asked:

"Do you know Bozert?"

"Why, of course—"

"What made you write to her?"

"To ask for help—"

"She is out of a job."

"She does not need one. She has got rubies, diamonds, she is very generous, though, of course, I meant to pay her back." Fear still kept breaking out in Lilian's voice, but some reassurance now came back to her, and her lips were steady. "I know she is not one of us—perhaps, I should not say so. That is why—no, what am I saying? Of course, she is proud and strange—but she is generous. . . . I meant no harm—"

He measured her with an odd searching look.

"Do you want another drink?" He tossed a small green note across the table. A waiter ambled along. Lilian gave her order and waited.

"You are not a very good liar," said the man with a scarred face, "and yet you could deceive anyone—"

"This is fortuitous. . . . You have asked me questions, I answered them. Is there any more to say?"

"Yes. Keep your mouth shut about that girl."

"She is my friend—"

"You don't say it very convincingly. Here is your drink. Have it. You might like another. There is no food here today, but let us imagine there are pickled herrings coming, and a cucumber, and balyk, and a nice well-peppered sausage, and mushrooms, of

107

course, there must be mushrooms. One's mouth was made for a mushroom—in a manner of speaking. Have a pickled herring which is not there. And taste this cucumber—delicately in your imagination. What, you cannot imagine a cucumber? You—a liar, and no imagination? That is a unique combination! Sister, I must take you to St. Mary Magdalene's Hospital and ask them to open your skull. I shall say, please examine this rarity of a liar who cannot imagine a cucumber. . . . Drink this stuff," he said, pushing the small tumbler towards her. "Drink it. I have not done talking yet—"

Lilian's fingers took to shaking again. She could barely grasp the stem of the glass. Suddenly she let it go, the muddy yellow liquor trickled down, staining her white skirt. Her mouth curved in an abrupt ugly way. The tip of her long nose reddened. She cried, staring at the soiled white linen. At the man she dared not look.

"What waste," he said mockingly. "Shall I buy you another? What are you crying for? That rag of yours? Why, anyone would buy you another, or a knitted suit, or a brocade gown. . . . You are a rotter. Who were you before you married your man? A daughter of some old régime family, at home in French, with good table manners. . . . Why did you marry him? You could not tell me the truth. You are so honestly proletarian that you would not accept luxuries from anyone except a proletarian, and you are convinced he is one."

"I must go. It is late—"

"Bi-Ba-Bo is not the Kresty Prison. I cannot keep you here by force. You said you were in need of help. Why?"

She tittered.

"Why, I have not got the price of a cup of coffee on me—"

"You have always been bankrupt. . . . Well, I may be a stranger to you, but you would accept money from a gorilla." He threw a fat wad of multi-colored paper across the table and got up, measuring her with his huge brown eyes.

"They will never shoot you, sister. If you ever get taken to the Tcheka, you will scream the *International* at the top of your voice, and you will tell every tchekist you meet that communism is the salvation of Russia, and, damn your eyes, they will all believe you. If you ever escape abroad, you will join the ranks of tearful émigrés, you will speak French like a native, and bewail the grandeur gone from the Russian sky. . . . You are a chameleon—and you will never get hurt. . . . But keep away from that girl in Moshkov Lane, and you will not get me to tell you why this would be better for you." He walked away as abruptly as he had come.

She looked round. She could not see Serge anywhere. He had

108

behaved in a degrading fashion, but that was not unusual. The other man, the first to bully her, had also vanished. Lilian composed her face. Now she had some money, an apparent madman had tossed it to her, but money was always money no matter what hands gave it to you. Now she had enough to pay that tiresome backyard shoemaker in Gogol Street, and she would have those beautiful boots with gray suède tops, and there would be enough left for a supper somewhere.

She beckoned to a waiter to bring her a rag to wipe the stains off her skirt. Then she asked casually:

"Who was that comrade? Just gone out . . . With a scarred face . . . I have forgotten. . . . Fancy, one does forget so many things. . . ."

The man said indifferently: "Comrade Cherny—"

"Of course," Lilian said hurriedly.

6

Frossia had fallen asleep, dreaming of a day rich in adventure and narrative, but nothing of the kind could be brought to the bedside of an unconscious boy. She looked at him helplessly. She could, of course, guess at the inevitable results of exposure and probable inanition, but his definite surrender to the demands of enfeebled flesh irritated her. She stood, observing the grimy, sunken cheeks, the matted hair, the black-rimmed nails, the bony, bared chest. She got hold of one emaciated hand, brought her ear closer to his face, called his name, but he did not hear her. His blackened mouth continued moving. She bent down and heard a child's broken, muted patter—the young man on Anna's sofa was back in the nursery, afraid of dark corners and curtained windows, and, listening, Frossia was ashamed of her earlier hardness.

She left him. She ran to the House Committee. She grew at once pathetic and bold, and won their sympathy, and also a chit for the nearest state drug depôt, and a vague promise of a doctor's visit. At the depôt they flung at her some gray cottonwool, a bottle of liquid quinine, a packet of mustard, and a large flagon of cod liver oil. She ran here and there, got some milk and a bag of rye flour in exchange for her ring from a casual speculator down in Millionnaya Street and, running back, flushed with the pleasure of several accomplished things, Frossia must needs halt at the door, her temples beaded with fine sweat. She stood, listening for a sound. None came. She opened the door, tiptoed into the heliotrope-curtained room. Michael's eyes were wide open.

109

"A doctor?" he echoed huskily. "Certainly not. A doctor would turn me into a corpse or a lunatic. And I would rather die or rave here." Exhausted by the brief speech, he said no more.

Frossia never answered him. She tidied, boiled the milk, heated some water, combed his hair, fed him, washed him, and waited. Presently the doctor came, a middle-aged German from the Baltic provinces, clean, cold, dry, and laconic.

"The patient? Yes—"

Frossia motioned to the door. He went in. She remained on the landing. The door closed. She must wait. It was cold on the landing. The narrow cobweb-curtained window gave a blurred view of a back alley, blind walls to the left of it, blind walls to the right of it. Dull gray walls, gray skies, gray pebbles . . . She must wait. This is my job. . . . If only they had not burgled the flat. But things must come—like the sun in the summer. I shall not stand still. I mean to live and find work. He must live.

The doctor was outside.

"Nothing is the matter. It is mere exhaustion. Feed him. Keep him warm and quiet. . . ." His pink tongue licked his thin pink lips. "There are thousands like him in the city. He is lucky. He has a home." Suddenly he saw Frossia. "How long have you known him?"

"Since yesterday."

"Well, this is Russia." He really said that any madness could always find permanent lodgment in Russia, but Frossia was not listening.

"Yes." She watched his straight spare back vanish down the staircase. "He shall live. That is my job now."

Michael had come to Frossia in May. Now it was high summer. For Frossia those three months had slipped by, each of them crowded with a succession of varied jobs. "He must live," she repeated to herself every morning, and the resolve branched out into a host of endless activities, each making a separate demand on her will, her initiative, and, sometimes, her cunning. "To live he must eat. I must work to get him food." She hurried off to the nearest labor exchange, passed the faintly inimical scrutiny of several clerks, and now various casual jobs began drifting her way. She must accept them all. She was a duly registered worker now, and she might not refuse the least of those offers. She had no wish to refuse any. She swept Moshkov Lane for one sultry hot week. She cut bread at a communal store, deputized for an absentee nurse, answered the telephone at a Proletcult, even did scavenging

110

work for two days and one night. Her very body seemed charged with an energy she had never imagined to exist. She got up every morning to face an interminable sequence of tasks. Michael must be kept clean, fed, and cared for. Anna's flat must be kept moderately free from dust and dirt. There was no leisure for day-dreams, discussion, arguments. Frossia was neither happy nor miserable: she felt she had been divided into so many tidy pigeon holes. Her brain was wholly occupied with food, nursing, barter possibilities, her feet were there to carry her about, her hands were ready to chore from sunrise to sundown, her tongue could shape a series of clear and trivial questions, remarks, comments—"Is this gruel cooked enough? I think you ought to have a clean shirt. I mean to go to Sennaya Market tomorrow. Goodness, we are quite out of salt. Yes, there are five cigarettes left. I am going to ration them. They are getting terribly scarce now. Please try and go to sleep. . . . Have you had a good night? Drink your tea while it is hot. . . ."

The doctor had been right. Food and the sense of security, however strangely framed, soon worked on Michael. He got better, the sunken cheeks and thin arms began clothing themselves with flesh, and the care Frossia expended on him came to lose some of its earlier, feverish urgency. An occasional spell of leisure was now hers. Sometimes she went to Moyka and spent a happy enough hour among her friends. She had mentioned Michael in a brief fashion, and left him unexplained. She met Nikolashka, and was able to allay his fears about herself. "Nothing is ever likely to happen. There had not been a real row with Comrade Nikita, and I am a fully registered member of the working community," she assured Nikolashka. "Please don't look so troubled." To Nikolashka she had said little about Michael, conscious that a casual meeting would explain more than necessarily fumbling explanations. The Parnikovs she had not seen for many a day, nor had any news about Lilian come her way.

There were evenings when she wandered down Millionnaya Street, crossed the huge, silent Palace Square, and meandered on, always westwards until she reached the end of her desultory pilgrimage at the mouth of the spacious Mariinsky Square, and could look at the huge pale building of the theater, and her memory was free to steal into the days when she had understood the ballet and needed it. But the walk back home was not disturbed by any such flights of fact and fancy intermingled. She knew she was walking back to Moshkov Lane where a thin, wasted body still demanded attentions which no chase after beautiful phantoms could have satisfied.

Michael no longer discussed either poetry or painting. He began showing rather heavy gratitude, and this descent to admittedly normal levels of behavior at once pleased and annoyed her. The newly developed housewife in her could not but welcome the relief of ordinary approaches to ordinary tasks of the day. Her other self nursed a vague repugnance at Michael's novel absorption in cups, plates, basins, and their contents.

"What really divine gruel," he murmured one evening when she gave him boiled millet for supper, and the extravagant word slashed at her so that she stood, platter in hand, looking at him hard.

"It will be cold," he cried piteously. "Frossia, please don't let it get cold."

"What a glutton you are!" She spoke sharply, and at once reproached herself for the cruelty, but she need not have so disturbed herself. The sharp edge of her words glanced off his understanding. With the return of physical strength, Michael's appetites became largely animal.

"I am a glutton." He rubbed his hands over the heaped plate. "Frossia, it does taste so good. And I shall not hurry over it. I shall eat it very slowly. Watch me—"

Frossia could not. Her mind was indeed capable of devising means for finding food. Her hands could prepare it and carry it to the table. She could make herself plunge wholeheartedly into the market business, into her casual jobs, keep her attention in a dim speculator's den, but she felt she could not maintain that temporarily needed absorption in things. She wanted a respite, and did not know where to look for one. She thought of the disused glass factory in the slummy street of Vasilyev Island; she had not met that girl—Klava Voronova, was that her name?—since their first encounter. Should she go there again? She had no wish to. Suddenly she knew she wanted nobody's company. Even the kindly people in Moyka would have to stay unvisited for many a day. "I am waiting for something to happen, and there are so many intrusions every day. . . ." And aloud she said to Michael:

"Yes, I am going out this evening. Just for a walk—"

She roamed as far as Vasilyev Island, vaguely wondering about Nikolashka and the Parnikovs. In the end she decided to keep away from them all, and turned homewards. On the quay, close to Nicholas Bridge, she passed a woman, caste and age both indeterminate, drab, drawn, tattered and pale except for the fire in her sunken black eyes. Frossia stopped and asked:

"What is your name?"

They were alone on the wide granite pavement. Far down the quay, past the bridge, someone was addressing a thin cluster of men and women. But Frossia and the stranger were alone.

"They call me Nikitishna," she replied simply, and without the least hesitation as though she accepted Frossia's right to question her, "I was going to Warsaw Station," she added, touching a bulging string bag. "I have my ticket and permit, and food, too—"

"You were going—"

"Yes, I reckon there is no sense in my getting there." The woman spoke pleasantly, and Frossia had a feeling that to the woman the river at their feet was no river at all, but something like an empty cradle.

"But you just cannot do it," she said gently. "Have you anyone in the country?"

"Yes, near Vitebsk," mumbled the woman. "A niece. She is expecting me. She has a heart of gold. She wrote, saying they still had a cow and some poultry. . . . There would be milk and eggs, too. . . . Just imagine—eggs. . . ."

"I can." Frossia smiled. "I can all too easily. Eggs—fried with rye bread in a nice deep frying pan. . . . All yellow and golden . . . A lovely dish for a summer evening . . . And then potatoes boiled in milk . . . Must you just imagine such riches? You are going there—"

"I was going," amended the woman, "and then it came all over me . . . like a cloud of dust—"

"What came over you?"

"Well, that kind of feeling—as though there were no need to go on carrying every burden. . . . I have had many in my life." Her brief confession rang with the chiseled quality of truth.

"I know," said Frossia. "Why put another burden on your niece's shoulders? You say she has a heart of gold. She would be so miserable—"

"She is waiting for me. But if I came to her, all my burdens would be hers. Mine are heavy. Eggs and milk could not lighten them, dear soul—"

"No—but it is not like that—ever. The other would be worse for her, and that for always, and then you could not do anything for her. Just think about your niece. . . . What is her name?"

"Irinushka—"

"Well, Irinushka might say to herself: 'If I had been there, it would not have happened. I should have gone to Petrograd to fetch my aunt,' and Irinushka would go on thinking so all her days—"

"She might . . . again she might not—"

Frossia took the large calloused brown hand into her own. Her breath went hot and jerky.

"No . . . I know. . . . Before God's face I can tell you it does happen. It will not be Irinushka's fault, it never is, but she will not think so. I know life is horrid and bitter, but when it is—you see—we don't sort of belong to our own selves, we are all together—oh, what am I saying?" she muttered under her breath. "It is all so clear, and I cannot say it. . . ."

But Nikitishna was tugging at her sleeve.

"Say it again, dear soul. Please, say it slowly. I want to understand it. It is not your words—it is the feeling behind them. Say it again," and Frossia must fumble once more through the broken misty phrases, and Nikitishna listened, then bowed in the peasant fashion—from the hips, and made to move away.

"I shall go to Warsaw Station. I don't know what I shall do when I get there. No, dear soul, you can come with me if it is on your way, not otherwise. I shall be thinking—"

Frossia watched her vanish down Nicholas Bridge. Then she walked home, and she was angry with herself. "I was a fool. . . . That niece might not need her at all. Why did I meddle? Why do I talk such rubbish? Trying to help, and, perhaps, Nikitishna might have saved herself from all trouble, all burdens—" Frossia reached Moshkov Lane, flung her oddly assorted bundles on the table, and was curt with Michael. His sudden laughter made her wince.

"What is the matter with you? It is lovely and warm, and I am getting well, and your face is full of vinegar."

"I rather like being a vinegar bottle sometimes. Come and eat. But don't talk to me, my mind is full—"

"What—ideas in this churchyard of a place?"

She looked at him in despair. She had had enough time to study his variant moods. A churchyard? That was all he thought of life in the city. He could not understand that things were happening all the time, and happening so swiftly that one could hardly pigeon-hole one before another came along. True that people looked afraid, whispered about horrors in underground places and in shadowy corners, avoided one another, but most of them remained stubbornly alive. "Except such as the poor Parnikovs. . . . But Michael is young. . . . He should not be like the Parnikovs. . . . Things were strange, sometimes revolting, usually chaotic. Peaked caps and khaki tunics and khaki minds ruled the city. Markets were raided, shots fired in the dark, trains stopped running, electric light was rationed so strictly that she must provide stumpy stearine candles bought furtively at a well-nigh prohibitive price; but life was lived none the less, and Michael, his sense of loftiness now almost completely abandoned, either made moan over the administrative chaos or else behaved like a maniac over a plate of thin gruel. Frossia must remind herself that it was a passing phase, his mind would surely be its own self again, and hers would be the pleasure of shared dream and rapture.

Away from the shallow calix of the purely economic vortex, other more important things were slowly taking their shape. For all the undeniable chaos in high places and in low, the country was being governed, and so was the city. Decrees plastered charred walls and tumble-down hoardings. Their usual burden was that of threat and prohibition, more threat and more prohibition, and Frossia scanned them but lightly. She had neither time nor wit to cope with their appallingly knotty verbiage. She knew that she transgressed the law about twenty times a day, and she continued doing so. She broke the law in keeping on Anna's flat, in giving shelter to one who had no identity papers, in buying eggs and meat from greasy cheats and thieves of speculators. But life was not that only, and she soon discovered that with Michael she could exchange nothing except purely negative impressions. He was ready to join her in any outburst against tyrannical officialdom or some fresh and petty prohibition issued from the Smolny. But one afternoon Frossia brought home a different tale. Near the Admiralty Gardens she had seen an improvised street meeting, a man from the Goelro haranguing a surprisingly attentive crowd about the gigantic electrification of the country in the future.

"It will take years, citizens," he thundered. "Our generation may not see it, but done it shall be. Electricity in every hamlet. Imagine it. . . . No more dirty corners . . . Dirt and disease thrive in the dark—"

He had spoken simply and burningly, his own voice rather like a sword of dazzling light, and Frossia had listened, reluctantly aware of her pleasure. But Michael mocked at her.

"Electrify Russia . . . One chimera after another . . . Words, words, and more words . . . They have not got one idea among them."

"That is untrue." She stamped her foot.

"Did I not say you were a Red?"

"I am not." In her wrath Frossia could not see the fatuity of such arguments. "I hate them. . . . I hate all these systems. . . . But one must be fair," and she tried to check her anger. "Michael, must we go on boring each other with politics?"

115

"You brought it in," he reminded her sullenly.

Yet, unaccountably, he could be different. Some of his moods were as lovely as an unexpected birthday present would be to an orphan. There were times when he was quiet, courteous, considerate, and sat, watching her, his own hands busy over some pedestrian chore. He would dust, sweep, wash up, and then surprise and please her by a sudden recital of some classic poetry. He read it well, and Frossia listened enraptured. At those moments she indeed felt that the day might yet come when mind would touch mind.

7

Paulina Pavlovna opened her eyes and listened. She had neither watch nor clock in her cubicle, and she could only tell the time by sounds from her brother's studio. Now everything was still. "Asleep . . . It is not seven yet," she murmured, folded her thin blue-veined hands, and began her prayers.

Paulina Pavlovna considered herself a mature initiate in most mysteries; the russet-gowned vagabond at Ochta had often assured her of that, but anyone seeing her on the narrow bed, in a tidily patched nightgown, her mousy hair tumbled about the pillow, her eyes closed, and her mouth slightly expectant, anyone seeing her so still, confident, and defenseless, would have known her for the child she was. To Paulina Pavlovna her very adventures into the occult were so many brightly colored toys. She delighted in them, she spent her best hours among them, and they offered her a serenity she might not seek elsewhere.

Her lips were moving almost inaudibly. Sometimes she forgot caution, and Pavel Pavlovich would poke his enormous head through the improvised partition, and stare at her until she broke off in confusion, provoking him to a sally. "The light vanished again? Well, I had better withdraw my sinful shadow. But you ought to hurry, little heart, otherwise the sinner might eat the saint's breakfast." And on such mornings Paulina Pavlovna felt thwarted and dwarfed, and got up to face a slow and leaden day.

But now she had woken early, and could afford a widely scoped meditation on truths as she saw them reflected in the mind of the Ochta giant. In the studio Paulina Pavlovna must not mention his name too often. Pavel Pavlovich must not be unduly annoyed, it was bad for his heart, she knew that, and he said it was bad for his work, though she could never understand why it should be.

She could not understand many things in life, and her dimness of perception, rather than any other quality, left her happy, even

116

if slightly bewildered at times, to cope with circumstances which had always been unusual. From a cultured home, being beautiful and always a child at heart, she had married her princeling. The German emperor having refused to recognize the marriage, Paulina Pavlovna's days abroad were largely spent in hotels and bleak country houses, the palaces being closed to her. The princeling supped unwisely off roast pork and died, and Paulina Pavlovna made a long journey to Bavaria to meet his mother and to mourn with her. The dowager, a ruined body in a ruined castle, kissed her sourly. "What a blessing that you never had a child," she mumbled in badly accented French, and Paulina Pavlovna said yes, she would have found it very hard to bring up a child in the Lutheran religion. The dowager looked annoyed. At last, one night, over a meager supper of smoked fish and thin white wine, she said:

"The Russians are thick-skinned, stupid, savage. . . . They are dirty. . . . They cannot even bake good bread. All the bakers in Russia are German—"

This time Paulina Pavlovna did not agree. She left her food and drink unfinished, stood up, bowed to the dowager, and went up the spiral staircase to her bleak room, not to weep but to pack. She left early in the morning.

"Those words scalded me," she later remarked to a friend.

She stayed on abroad. Her passport described her as belonging to the Russian Orthodox Church. Various foreign-bred heresies had already begun to attract her, and she could not have indulged in any such excursions, had she gone to Russia. She came back early in 1917, and wept with joy. "Freedom of all things . . . Freedom of spirit . . ." She clapped her hands at every scarlet rag she saw in the streets, and tried to preach her own views of the highway to heaven. Kerensky's Government left her alone. Some communists frowned, and once she was cautioned in rather sharp terms. She left off itinerant preaching, and soon found her way to Ochta. People like Lilian jeered. They had never seen the flame-clothed prophet, but Paulina Pavlovna's enthusiasm led them to imagine some uneasy flowering of autumnal passion. Paulina Pavlovna did not mind their mockery, but she observed proprieties, and kept house for her brother in Moyka. He often outraged her sense of decencies—by his frankness on canvas and his casual intrigues. But she forgave him. She forgave everybody, dimly sensing her own shortcomings. In her own *monde passé* Paulina Pavlovna was no heroine; she could join neither the Parnikovs nor the powers that were. Children loved her, animals took to her; she would have been the whole world's friend, had it not been for her fervor. It always overflowed, it ran across other people's paths, and it annoyed them. "If you could only see," she would say simply and earnestly, "it is all so obvious—" And once a bitter-lipped *déclassée* retorted: "Perhaps we would see if you got out of our way—" "Perhaps, I ought to," said Paulina Pavlovna. "I shall say nothing more—but I mean to keep you in my mind. . . ."

She kept a crowd of faces and names in her mind, and this morning she thought of Frossia. Often enough Paulina Pavlovna contrived meetings in the studio. She had hopes of everyone she met. They came, ate of what provender she could provide, and argued about themselves, their world, pictures, books, some mild current scandal. Sometimes Paulina Pavlovna snatched at a pause, and spoke her well-prepared words, and they listened and laughed: "Dear Paulina is off again," but she parried their rudeness with a smile which left them unaccountably ashamed of themselves.

Frossia had never been rude, she reflected. "Such a pity that Anna should have gone. . . . But Frossia is so different from them all."

It startled her to realize that she had not given much thought to Frossia of late. Frossia had come in and gone out almost casually. They said—Paulina Pavlovna could not remember where she had heard it—that she was giving sanctuary to a mysterious young man in Moshkov Lane, a boy whom she had rescued from an equally mysterious violent death. They said that she was working off and on. She had been seen at market places and in queues. But she had kept remote, uncommunicative, and Paulina Pavlovna remembered that she, Frossia, and a few others, were coming to the studio that day.

The place would have to be cleaned. Paulina Pavlovna ended her meditations with stray thoughts of dusters, brooms, and pails of water. Pavel Pavlovich had to swallow a hurried breakfast. She sent him out for a walk and started battling with her several chores. When he returned, he found her in the thick of it. The tidiness of the place annoyed him at once.

"What is the matter with these cups?" he thundered. "They are clean enough—"

They stood in an odd array, blue and pink and orange, all chipped, some without handles, most of them cracked. The sudden shout made Paulina Pavlovna drop the one she held in her hands. "Another gone," she mourned. "Only eight left. We shall have to take to jam jars like the Parnikovs do. Paul, you must not shout at me." She spoke mildly. "Why, you have forgotten—it is my saint's day, we have guests coming. I told you in the morning. That was why you went out. And you might wash the gamboge off your left cheek. It has been there for a week—the gamboge, I mean, not the cheek. . . . Of course, you have always had your left cheek. Yes, Paul, I have baked some nice *oladiy*, but we cannot serve apple sauce with them. Who are coming? Oh, the Captain and Maria Nikolaevna, and I have asked Klava and her poor Grisha. . . . Also Nikolashka, and Frossia." Her cheeks reddened. "And then I met Lilian yesterday, she looked rather miserable. So I invited her, and also that man—I cannot remember his name—the one who tells stories to people. . . ."

"Is this a gunpowder factory then?" bellowed Pavel Pavlovich. "Have we not got enough trouble that you must needs go and—"

"Nonsense, Paul. In a properly balanced world there would be none of this. It is my aim to do away with all the jealousy and rivalry. They are stupid. I know the Captain will not speak to his daughter, and they all despise Nikolashka, and all of you detest poor Grisha—and that is precisely the reason why I want them all here together—that is my work in life, Paul, to make people see the evenness in all things. This is truth—"

Pavel Pavlovich swore and went out. But he knew that he would not miss that motley party. It might provide him with a scheme for a sketch, if not for a picture. He would see them all there in the huge room, made all the bleaker by Paulina Pavlovna's frenzied housemaiding. They would come, observe brief civilities, and gradually become themselves, and he could then enjoy his great pastime of inventing situations; he would make his mind take in the color, movement, texture of anger, self-control, meanness, bewilderment, fear, spite, disgust, and faked indifference. He would see them thus, he could read them all—with one exception. He could never decipher Frossia. He had heard a highly colored story from Lilian. Frossia had had some trouble with the Tcheka, lost her job, and now was nursing some princeling or other she had salvaged from the wreck. . . . Lilian had told the story, smiling, and Lilian's smiles always hinted at muddy corners. For weeks Pavel Pavlovich would say to himself: "This very day I must go and see her. I must go. Anna introduced her to us. Anna is gone. Surely, we should feel concerned about her," but each day brought its own burden of tasks and duties. Once Pavel Pavlovich went out and made towards Millionnaya Street, but a large tortoiseshell cat crossed the pavement in front of him, and Pavel Pavlovich knew he must turn back immediately. There was no sense in his going on. The cat had turned a casual friendly visit into something like a hostile intrusion. Pavel Pavlovich sighed and went back to his easel. Such things happened to him, he reminded himself, and he could not help it. Apart from his work, the tiniest decision poured something like poison into him. Once, a young man, very ardent and poor, he bought a large expensive bunch of lilies of the valley from a florist's near St. Isaac's Cathedral. He just liked the flowers. He brought them home and stuck them into a vase with no water. "I must give them some water," he said to himself several times, but this meant taking a can, going down two flights, filling the can from a filthy little tap in a rat-riddled cubbyhole below the stairs. He did not do it. The lilies of the valley blackened and shriveled. On the third day he went for a walk, the sad dead things in his hands; he came to the quay and flung them into the Neva, and cried.

"And Frossia is coming?" he flung sullenly at his sister. "Why, she has been here quite a few times. She is not looking well."

"She is tired. I saw her the other day—we were at the fish depôt together. . . . She has no job at present." Paulina Pavlovna tried to remember where she had hidden the few remaining teaspoons. The next moment she forgot the teaspoons, her small seamed face went warm and alive with a generous smile, and she said: "Yes, Frossia. She will be all right. . . . Without nonsense and without art . . . I know you could never paint her, Paul. You cannot read her—"

"Can you?"

"But I never want to read people. If people want me to know them, they read themselves aloud. If not, I know the book is closed, I never try to open it, I merely hope they may do so themselves, and come out of their darkness. . . ."

"Yes, yes." Pavel Pavlovich hurried out of the room.

Late in the afternoon they came—all with tiny smiles and warm kisses and carefully premeditated gifts. Captain Parnikov clicked his heels, kissed Paulina Pavlovna's hand, and presented a pound of salt in a rough blue paper bag, and Maria Nikolaevna pressed a small and exquisite Dresden plate into her hostess's hands. Niko-lashka, freshly washed, his huge red beard finely combed, put a bag of flour in a corner and winked at the company. There were some strawberries from Grisha and a white linen face towel from Klava, and Paulina Pavlovna, happy and moved, kissed, smiled, and thanked them, and Pavel Pavlovich bustled about with cups and plates when the door opened once again, and they all became stiff as though several wires had suddenly taken possession of their bodies.

It was Lilian. Lilian had not chosen to come alone. Maria Niko-laevna looked at the floor, coughed, and then got up almost too suddenly. The Captain cleared his throat. Nikolashka tugged at his beard and mumbled: "Now was this necessary? Oh, dear!" But Paulina Pavlovna rushed forward, kissed Lilian's thickly rouged cheek, and shook hands with Serge.

Lilian also brought presents—a pair of brown kid gloves, a pound of chocolate, a flask of real Scotch whisky, and a box of German cigarettes. The presents were all on the table, the gloves, the chocolate, and the whisky, and Paulina Pavlovna, stammering her thanks, heard carefully concerted movement behind her. The provocation had been too great. The whole room heard Nikolashka's heavy mutter: "Leave it alone, Maria Nikolaevna, Madame. . . . All of us are made of the same clay. . . ." And Maria Nikolaevna's trembling reply: "I cannot . . . I cannot. . . . This is not to be suffered. . . . Vania, we must go," and Paulina Pavlovna, her large child's eyes still on Lilian and Serge, wondered about the coming catastrophe—when the door opened for the third time, and Frossia stood there, in a thin green dress they had not seen before, and a thick cluster of wallflowers pressed to her throat.

"My warmest congratulations, Paulina Pavlovna. Am I late? Forgive me, please—I am a stranger, and you must take me in and forgive me." Her quick glance journeyed all over the tension in the room, she saw the fury, despair, and insolence, she noted Pavel Pavlovich's detached curious eyes, Maria Nikolaevna's shaking hands trying to fasten her old-fashioned black lace mantle, the Captain's tired face crimson with anger, and the mockery in Serge's narrow unkind eyes. She saw Paulina who stood like a child before a broken toy, and Frossia thought: Shameful. . . . I could drive Lilian and Serge away . . . but Paulina Pavlovna's little festival will be spoilt, and for a few seconds she stood still, the smell of wallflowers close to her, her lips almost buried in their velvet coolness.

"We are going, Vania," said Maria Nikolaevna in a wounded voice when someone else stood among them, and Frossia heard Paulina Pavlovna say loudly enough to drown Lilian's snigger: "Nobody could go . . . Igor Vladimirovich, you will tell us a story, and, of course, nobody could go in the middle of a story," and Frossia wished she might add her own plea; it would have sounded extraordinary, but nobody round her was saying ordinary things, and she wished she might say: "Yes, a story . . . And have you got another handkerchief to cover it all up again?" But, of course, she did not, and the newcomer bowed to Paulina Pavlovna and said in his faintly peasant voice: "But this is a party, Paulina Pavlovna, and I have only just come. Please allow me to congratulate you."

He moved towards the center of the room, an ordinary middle-sized, middle-aged man with a very ordinarily shaped face and that peasant touch in his deep voice. He shook hands with his hostess, bowed to the others, and stood, his head a little on one side, his eyes full of interest, and Frossia never knew how it happened, but the Captain and Maria Nikolaevna sat down again. Serge and Lilian were quiet on a bench by the door, Nikolashka beamed, and Klava and Frossia began fetching and carrying for their hostess. Above the clatter of chipped cups and plates rose a few sounds of unstinted praise. There was no apple sauce, but Paulina Pavlovna's thin, nicely browned *oladiy* were excellent, the tea was hot, the chocolate slab, free of its wrappings, was carefully broken up, and the pieces handed down the table.

"And have you heard about Anutka?" said the man they addressed as Igor Vladimirovich. "She was a fifteen-year-old peasant girl from Archangel—with a sick mother and a father gone mad in one night. He was blind, and he started breaking what furniture they had; their hut was worlds away from anywhere, and he wanted *kvas* to drink, and Anutka had no *kvas*. So she said: 'Stay here, *batka*, and look after mother.' But he would not stay. It was in winter. Anutka harnessed the mare, put her mother in. He was raving. 'You are coming, *batka*,' she said. 'There will be warmth and *kvas* in Archangel, and they will give mother good medicine. I must take her there,' she said. He said: 'I will kill you and the mare.' She replied: 'Kill me. Spare the mare. She has been a pal. She can take mother to Archangel.' She took him by the shoulders and looked at him hard. 'Listen, if you kill me, you will hurt me, and you will be punished because I have a soul. But if you kill the mare, you will go unpunished, a mare has no soul, and it will be beastly and mean.' He said: 'All right, you drive to Archangel. Take your mother, they will kill her with their medicines.' She made him come, too. He kept quiet. She drove to Archangel. They took her mother in and him, too. They looked at her. 'You must come in also,' they said. Anutka was ill herself, and they saw it. But she asked, 'Is there a spare bed?' They told her there was not. They also said: 'But we have an old woman here, she is not long for this world, it does not matter where she dies—in bed or on straw.' Anutka said: 'I can wait. The old have so little left to them, nothing must be taken away from the old.' She went away. The old woman lingered for a week. Anutka came back. They took her in. But her trouble was too far gone."

122

"What a fool," said Lilian crisply. "She was young, more important. The old should not matter—"

"That is Russia," said Captain Parnikov, looking away from his daughter. "You will never find an Anutka anywhere else—"

"Why should you say that?" bellowed Pavel Pavlovich. "You are like Anna Yosifovna. She had money, and she had traveled, and that was all she could say: 'The French are mean, the English are snobbish, the Italians—dishonest. Certain things can be found only in Russia.' My God, what awful waste of one's days. . . . Always, always we in Russia are on top of a tree. . . . Always this harping on other nations' shortcomings. . . . One war barely over, I tell you we shall see another before we are dead. Yes, to you, to Anna Yosifovna, to millions of others, other countries are just so many sieves, and you love counting holes in them. An Anutka might have been a German girl, or Japanese, or Norwegian. . . . Why should charity live in Russia alone? Now I," and Pavel Pavlovich stretched out his huge arms, all but upsetting another of his sister's precious cups, "now I belong to art, and I can never say that the Flemish school is better than the Spanish, or the French superior to the Italian. I prefer to say—this is excellent in Flemish, that is great in Spanish, and something else is lovely in Italian. The world is a jig-saw puzzle and every piece of it is indispensable. Do people admit it? No. They go to Karlsbad, and Mentone, and Florence, and they come back, and they tell you about bad ventilation here, and a waiter's rudeness there, and a shopkeeper's dishonesty at some other place. They may, perhaps, enthuse over a bridge or a ceiling or a statue, and sometimes they add: 'Oh, if we could have it . . .' But when I look at a bridge in Venice, its beauty catches me, and it is mine in a way. I take people as God meant them to be," roared Pavel Pavlovich. "I have felt at home everywhere—in Madrid and Bruges, Florence and London, Dresden and Paris. . . . It is all a point of view."

"It has nothing to do with Anutka," smirked Lilian, "and, anyhow, you have always been an internationalist."

"There you go again! What does the word mean? I want something more living in life and in art. That is why I have never cared much about politics—let a Tsar, or Lenin, or an ordinary Petrov sit and rule there—"

Maria Nikolaevna pursed her lips.

"They have left you in peace," she reminded him acidly.

"Exactly. And why? I am no peasant by birth, I have never worked at a factory, my people were well-moneyed, well-educated. My sister married into a royal family. My old passport described

123

me as 'dvorianin', gentleman. I should have been shot. Why was I not? Nobody could call me a nonentity. My work is known, my work is good. Why did they not come here and say: 'Citizen Ratov, you have no proletarian blood in you, to the wall with you.' Why did they not? Just because I am ready to believe there is something good hidden in the worst of them."

"You might say so about the devil," rasped Maria Nikolaevna.

"I do not believe in him, but I do believe there must be a grain of commonsense in them, or else they would have broken up within two or three years. You see," thundered Pavel Pavlovich, "I believe in man." Suddenly he veered to Frossia. "And so do you—"

They all looked at her. She went crimson and pulled at the belt of her green dress. Serge smiled in a slow unkindly manner.

"Euphrosynia Pavlovna believes in mankind. I think Comrade Nikita Fyodorov might know best, or else Comrade Cherny, if not that mysterious young man she has saved from getting drowned in the Neva—"

Someone giggled. Someone else looked bewildered. Frossia heard Nikolashka give one short jerky gasp. The man they called Igor Vladimirovich sat still examining the flowered pattern of the tablecloth. And Frossia thought summer had gone. She was back in the arms of winter, huddled against the cold marble of a bench in a tumbledown summerhouse. She was shriveling to a handful of small frozen bones. She was flung out on to a heap of hard, merciless snow. Her grandmother used to say: "Frossia's temper is like a Polar wind." Her cold hands were clenched hard. She knew she must not speak yet, she must gather herself up, escape the iciness which kept touching her lips. She must wait. She waited, and she saw Serge's small eyes almost closed on his cruel face, and she noted the fleeting shadow of revulsion steal across Maria Nikolaevna's small shriveled features, and she also heard Nikolashka's voice.

"Nikita Fyodorov?" he echoed. "Why, he is a pal of mine. A nice man he is, and Euphrosynia Pavlovna had a job there—"

"She had," agreed Serge.

"And why should we ask him—and the others?"

"Well," sneered Serge, "need I be obvious?"

The studio was a battlefield. Frossia could not tell which of them might be counted as her allies. The girl who had read Dostoevsky and the crippled youth, what did she, Frossia, know of them? The man who sat there, examining the flowered tablecloth? He was a stranger—met once in an alien land between Kiev and Petrograd. The Parnikovs had grown into strangers. . . . There was always

124

Nikolashka, but even he feared the suddenness and obstinacy of her opinions. . . .

"Obvious?" roared Pavel Pavlovich. "You are not being obvious at all. You are talking in riddles—"

"Well," Serge said slowly, "you said you were left in peace because you were ready to believe the best of them. I have good reasons to think that Euphrosynia Pavlovna will never be molested. Why? Go to a house in Maly Prospect, and ask Comrade Fyodorov of the Special Provkom Commission, and—"

"I knew it would be a gunpowder factory," said Pavel Pavlovich very quietly, rose from his chair, his enormous arm clove the air, and the huge hairy hand struck across Serge's face. Lilian screamed. Maria Nikolaevna whimpered. Paulina Pavlovna ran to her brother. "Paul . . . Paul . . . He is our guest. . . . This is not honorable. . . ."

Pavel Pavlovich sat down heavily.

"Honorable? No, it is not. Let him get out! He can summon me—or fight me—whichever he prefers, but I will not have mud flung at my guests—"

Serge clutched at his wife's arm.

"I could not fight you." He tried to speak calmly but he could not help spluttering. "People like me can fight their equals only—"

"True—" Pavel Pavlovich wiped his face. "I am not your equal. There was a Ratov who fell at Kulikovo in 1380, and another who helped in the first Romanov election in 1613. We have been quiet, undistinguished people, but we have walked through history. No, I am not your equal."

"Serge, please let us go—"

"Vania, we should never have come—"

"Oh, dear, Paul, you must remember they are our guests—"

"If only dear Irina Nikolaevna were here. . . . She would have put everything right—"

They all babbled, whimpered, gestured. Pieces of uneaten chocolate lay on the bright pink cloth. Nobody wanted them. Paulina Pavlovna's eyes were closed, her mouth looked unhappy. Klava's face was wet with tears. Frossia no longer felt cold and isolated. Her cheeks were flaming. Her voice was furious.

"Wait—" she said suddenly. "Please, you must all wait." She had not wanted to speak, but Pavel Pavlovich had hit Serge, and now she must explain if only by way of showing her gratitude for the chivalry shown so unexpectedly. "Comrade Fyodorov gave me a job. I was not registered then. There was some trouble at König House because I had lost my labor book. Comrade Fyodorov got me out of it by saying it was all a family affair, and he apologized to me for the lie. . . . Comrade Cherny knew of it," she finished coldly. "The rest does not concern anyone." She paused, measuring Lilian's husband with a look. "Yes, you mentioned Comrade Cherny. You may, of course, know him, but I don't think you know that you are not fit to lick his boots—" She got up, bowed to Paulina Pavlovna and the others, and left the room so that the vehemence of her last words was left with them.

CHAPTER FOUR

DANSE MACABRE

One naked bulb hung from a fly-blown flex. In its sharp light all the various stains on pea-green walls gained in depth and intensity. One of the two barred windows was left open. The June breeze danced now and again into the small soulless room, and the flex trembled slightly, and the stains changed color and shape. So Anna thought, sitting upright on a wooden chair. Outside, the wide cobbled Gorokhovaya Street lay fairly quiet. From a distance rang the discordant sounds of an ancient accordion, and a husky voice croaked the familiar refrain of someone's bewitching black eyes.

Anna sat upright though she felt weary, and her body felt as though all bone and muscle were taken from it and moist sawdust put in instead. In front of her was a square table littered with papers, an inkstand, a loaf of queerly colored bread, a piece of green blotting paper, and a huge pickled cucumber in a pink saucer with a thin gilt rim.

That is a good saucer, thought Anna, Sèvres, I believe—

She thought of china, and of the shadows flung by the wall across the stained, uninviting walls. She thought of the prickly stubble in the field not far from the Finnish frontier where they had caught her, and she also thought of the odd tapping pain somewhere near her heart. There seemed nothing else to think about, and she knew she was bored as well as tired.

Cherny felt bored also. She was but a case, simple and rather foolish. There were so few things he could get out of her, and for nearly two months they could not make her answer any questions. Anna neither lied nor evaded. She would say: "Give me time. You see, I am not young. I am very tired. I want time." And they gave her time.

Now Cherny said: "You can have some tea if you are thirsty."

She shook her head and reached for the cucumber.

"We have now come to a point." He examined a paper. "We have accounted for all the things found on you—except those three: the

127

cabochon ruby set in pearls with a platinum chain, the sapphire cross with a pearl chain, and that anchor of rubies. It has a chain of smaller stones, I believe. . . . Now they are important. They are mentioned in the inventory of the Bozert shop. Did you then steal them from the man?"

"No—" Anna never added that she was not a thief.

"How did you get them?"

Cherny expected no reply, but Anna surprised him by saying:

"Paul Bozert gave them to me himself."

"When?"

"Perhaps, ten years ago. . . ."

"That is untrue. Bozert's graded their pieces. Those marked "A" were never repeated. The three are mentioned in the inventory of 1916, not earlier."

"Well, it may have been four or five years ago. . . . How can I remember dates? I am so tired."

"How did you get them?"

She bit at the cucumber and said nothing.

"You asked for time," said Cherny. "You have had almost two months. You will not have much more. You would have been shot two months ago . . . Now I want you to tell me how you came to possess those three things."

"You have heard me—"

"I have heard a story—"

"There is nothing else to tell. Perhaps it is all a story, birth and life and death, and food and clothes and jewelry—"

She tried to speak lightly, but Cherny saw her wince. He thought: What an actress. . . . Life must have been a fairy tale to her, and now we have changed the theme, and she wants to die, and he watched her intently. Anna stopped eating, the cucumber was back in the dish, her hand had fallen limp by her side, there was no movement about her at all, none to see, and yet Cherny realized that she was withdrawing herself from him. "You must not go to sleep yet." He spoke fiercely. "Those things of Bozert's are of national importance. You may sleep when you have told me," and, even when speaking to her, he knew the distance between them was widening. Anna no longer sat upright, her back and shoulders sagged, her neck lolled a bit, her eyes stayed half-open but they appeared vacant and astray as though space and objects dotting it were of no further concern to her. Her lips remained a tight-drawn line. Cherny stood up and leaned across the table. This brought him no nearer to her. Still he said in a deep urgent voice:

"Bozert never gave them to you, did he?"

128

Slowly, as if held by pain, she shook her head. Her eyes battled with the heavy lids and opened widely. They seemed to be asking questions from the fly-blown flex, from the stains on the wall, the barred window, and from Cherny's intent face. The tiresome tapping against her ribs now turned to a hammering. Anna felt that she must get up, beat the air with her hands, ward off something she might not name even in her clouded thought. Her eyes kept on asking their question. But she could not speak, and with a final, dreadfully slow sag her head fell on one side.

Cherny's left hand sought and found a handbell. Two khaki-clothed men came in. He gestured at Anna and turned away to the window. It was a dark, limpid green summer evening. The other side of the wide street suggested a dim engraving done in gray and in sepia brown. To the right the massive shadows of Admiralty Gardens lay deep in sleep, and someone's raucous voice asserted an undying passion for a pair of bewitching black eyes. Behind him Cherny heard the stertorous breathing of the men, the sharp rap of their hobnailed boots on the stone floor. He also heard a brief question, and replied just as briefly. Presently, all sound ceased in the room, he flung the other window open, then turned back and rummaged for a blank form on the desk. For a few seconds he sat, chewing the pen, then abruptly he filled in the chit and rang the bell. "I shall be waiting here," he snapped at the man, handing him the chit.

He had waited for nearly two months. Now he could wait no longer, and he must harden himself to question, to shed civility, to be ruthless. . . . He wished he might think, but instead he frittered his time away in trivial little activities. He got up, straightened the untidy papers, took the bread and cucumber and hid them in a locker, pushed away the hard wooden chair into a corner, and moved another behind the table, and, doing those things, Cherny knew he was being weak and foolish.

At last he heard steps behind the door. It opened. He kept his eyes on a paper which told him that electric light would be strictly rationed from the 16th of August. "16th of August," he repeated under his breath and said aloud, "Here is a chair. Sit down." And he thought, Now I must get to the point, hammer it out of her somehow, and how can I do it?

Frossia sat down quietly. He began: "Your friend, Anna von Packen, died in this room half an hour ago," and he waited, watching her face go a strange gray white.

"But she got away—she escaped—"

"She tried to. We caught her. She was ill. She got worse. It was heart failure—in the end, I believe. In her possession we found three things—" he described them minutely—"a cabochon ruby, set in pearls with a platinum chain, a sapphire cross with a pearl chain, and an anchor of rubies with a chain of smaller stones. She said they had been given to her by your father. Is this true?"

"No . . . I suppose—well—they were mine—"

"You gave them to her—"

Frossia said nothing.

"She told me a story." Cherny was trying to speak patiently. "I sent for you because I knew you would rather say nothing or else tell the truth—"

She kept silent.

"You gave them to her—"

Frossia raised her face. She looked past him, at the dark blue shadows outside the barred windows.

"Is this not foolish? We know who you are. Well, then, if they were yours, how did you come to have them?"

"I took them. My grandmother had some of our valuables when we left here four years ago. I helped her draw up the inventory. When—I made up my mind to come back here, I took those three things. I supposed they were mine. I had no clear idea of their value. I knew they were good because they were graded 'A.'"

"You knew you were breaking the law?"

"Everybody is breaking some law or other, Comrade Cherny—"

"Well, you brought them here, and you gave them to Packen, did you not? I am beginning to understand—she knew a great many speculators, and you thought she might help you."

"No—"

"Did you then hand them over to her?" he asked, waited a second, and then said bluntly: "You need say nothing more. She stole them from you."

"She was a friend of my people's, Comrade Cherny."

"Well," he pushed a chair away, "you have answered me at last."

"I have not—"

Cherny ignored the proud interruption, and went on:

"What happened to the rest of the things?"

"I cannot say. I heard they were looted—"

"Have you got any more?"

"I have one or two lesser trinkets, not of our own make. Also a dressing-case with gold fittings. It belonged to my mother. I have few other belongings. A few clothes . . . a few books."

He said nothing. She thought: It is an act in a play. And it hurts as though it were real. That burglary and Anna . . . Anna . . .

130

It would hurt more if she had been a real friend. And she is dead. He said it was heart failure— Suddenly she heard him say briefly and coldly: "You can go, Citizeness Bozert."

"Have I not broken a law?"

"You have broken several. But you can go."

Frossia remained in her chair.

"You can go," he said for the third time.

"And suppose I did not want to go? Suppose I were to admit that I was in the wrong—in my wanting to live? Suppose I were to ask you to kill me. . . . One dream ended, another might begin. You get me to come here and ask questions, and then you say: 'You can go,' as though this were a dentist's and you had just pulled a tooth out. . . . It is not out, Comrade Cherny—"

"We are very busy here, Citizeness Bozert. You have answered my question. I thank you."

Frossia's cheeks flowered wild crimson, and she walked out of the huge, ugly, terrible building. A squint-eyed sentry at the door looked at her idly. Her pass seemed in order. She slipped through the dim vestibule, weary and afraid and at variance with all things in life because the story about Anna was a cup full of poison, and Frossia's lips were pressed against it, and she must drink of it. Anna had lied and cheated and stolen, and Anna was dead. All the riches from Bozert's strongrooms could not have helped her across the Finnish frontier. All the riches of the Urals would not now guide her back across a different frontier. Anna had died in that same room, tired out, robbed of all hope, her strangely perverted heart failing her in the end, and she had died, tainted and twisted, defeated by a surge of circumstance her narrowly economical perspective could not confront. The banks closed down, and one like Anna must steal from a defenseless refugee, and indulge in her melodramatic passion by narrating a richly imagined burglary. This was sordid, grotesque, incredible, and Frossia knew that people like the Parnikovs would mutter darkly: "Well, what can you expect? This dreadful chaos ruins even decent people—it perverts them, it shatters all their sense of morality," and for some time, stumbling in among the green-lit shadows of that June evening, Frossia herself felt uprooted, a stranger to all earlier known and respected standards, until she must stand still, a shadow herself lost in the thicker shadows of Alexander Gardens, and whisper in her fear, her overwhelming sense of lostness: "Oh, please make me remember that there are other, stronger people. . . . Please make me remember—"

Anna had cheated her, and now was dead. The Parnikovs remained faintly hostile. Lilian became an enemy. Pavel Pavlovich and his sister alone stayed friendly. But Petrograd was still there, still waiting to receive the homage Frossia deferred to give it. She had accepted its scars, having once discerned a deeper life below the easily accessible levels of stone and timber and mortar. She had come back because she belonged there, and she felt she must in a sense belong to its people also, belong to them simply, directly. The glittering tissue of fancy could no longer sustain anyone. Frossia had groped, and blundered, and been hurt. She had nursed a feeble starveling back to life, and hit an important communist, and recoiled from a procuress, and stayed perplexed by people like the Parnikovs because of their muted passion for shattered walls. . . . And sometimes in her impotent fury Frossia imagined all of them to be exactly like Anna; she assured herself she could not trust any of them, and wondered if she should start creating a new circle of acquaintances, made after a casual fashion and kept at a distance which would allow of no deep exchange of feeling and outlook.

That would be better. . . . That would mean keeping to the surface. . . . Nothing would then be painted in exaggerated colors . . . she thought and then checked herself. Life could not be lived like that. People should not allow themselves to drift even when they are all splintered inside, she thought, accusing herself of such drifting, and she stopped under the General Staff Arch as if uncertain which direction she was to take, and then heard a man's voice at her very elbow, a tentative, apologetic voice, asking whether he was anywhere near Palace Square.

"You are there." Frossia turned round and peered at a fairly tall shadow beside her. "Where do you want to go? It must be hard on a stranger to get lost in this city, but then they say there will be no street lamps at all next year. . . . Why, you can't say it is really dark yet."

"I am sorry." The pleasant voice rang the same faintly apologetic note. "It is always dark for me. I am such a nuisance. I am not yet used to it—"

She thought swiftly. Michael would be waiting for her and his supper. He could wait a little longer. She asked:

"Where do you want to go?"

"Home," he stammered. "It is across Palace Bridge, and then across Exchange Bridge. It is in Sobornaya, Petrograd Side—"

"I know," said Frossia. "Well, here is my arm."

"You were not going there," he asserted.

"No—"

"You are kind."

Frossia said nothing. They crossed the square.

"Blindness is not really a curse except when you lose yourself, but people never let you drift."

"Did it happen here?"

"No, outside Vitebsk. . . . Then I came back. My wife is here. She is not always well—"

"How can you bear it?"

"You must be very young. I am thirty-seven, my name is Anton Nachimov, I am an engineer. Bear it? Why, you do not stop seeing when you go blind. Only it takes time to learn. At first it all went blank, then I began to see—"

"See what?" Frossia asked almost fiercely.

"Well, whatever I could remember—a Rembrandt at the Hermitage, or a bridge . . . or falling water. . . . I did hydraulics. Also a sunset over the Gulf of Peterhof, a child's face. . . . My little girl is five. Well, you go on remembering, and then you invent shades and colors and shapes. . . . Life is so full. An old man in Alexeevskaya Street is teaching me to make baskets. I have just been there. Usually, his son takes me home. But he has a cold. I said I could manage—"

"Were you not afraid?"

"No. . . . Once only someone told me to get out of their way. I said I could not see. The man said: 'More fool you for getting yourself blinded.' I did not feel scared then. I was just sorry for him. It happened once only. Usually I get so much kindness that I am ashamed of myself. My little daughter said that my voice caught at people. . . . I don't think so. I believe it is the people themselves. Kindness comes naturally to them. Cruelty means something else—but I cannot put it into words. . . ."

"What about the people?"

"Well, take them in this city, they are nearly all miserable and cold and hungry, and sometimes they go to pieces, and they cheat, and they also hurt one another, and still they make it their business to go on living, and that is good. Our landlady stole a shabby small scarf from my wife and sold it for a loaf of bread. It was on a day when we had no food. We did not know she had stolen the scarf. We thought her honest. My wife said nothing to me, but she went to the landlady: 'Anisia Ivanovna, please could you spare me a slice of bread?' she said. 'Not for myself, but my husband had no dinner, and I have a bad cold, I cannot go to the market, and what is the

133

use him going alone?' she said, and the loaf was there on the table, and Anisia Ivanovna covered her face with the apron and cried her eyes out. 'Take me to the Commissariat, take me to the Commissariat, I am a thief. I stole that scarf of yours, with him in the room. I had come in to do a bit of dusting, and I stole it because I knew he could not see me, and I cannot bear it,' she cried."

"Well?" Frossia caught her breath.

"My wife kissed her. We all shared that loaf." He added: "Anisia Ivanovna will never again steal—from us. And that is what I meant —all of us are at something or other. Living is a grand business in happiness, grander still in misery, no matter how often you stumble—"

They were at the corner of Sobornaya Street. He described the house, and they came to the doorway. "Can you find your way up?" Frossia asked. "Are you sure?" He nodded and began thanking her, but Frossia stooped, snatched at a roughened hand, kissed it, and ran away.

And she ran nearly all the way home across the deserted creaking timbers of Palace Bridge and down the quays. She ran fast because something was suddenly singing within her. She flung an unusual smile at Michael, fed him, drew his chair to the window, and ran to fetch her crimson bound book.

"You will not be too tired to listen?"

He had caught her strangely exultant mood. He smiled back.

"Oh, no," and hoped she would not detect the thin indifference in his voice. Frossia never noticed it. She cupped her chin with her left hand. The book lay in her lap. She began to read. She read well since the theme of the story had lived in her all through her days. It had once been a slight inconsequential game to while away the lonely hours inevitable in most sheltered childhood. From the narrow field of a game, a pastime, it crossed a stile, and lost itself in a faëry wood. She wondered if sometime it would emerge, all finely washed in the pale clear light of a morning. Living was a grand business, and she must attend to it, she who had sight and wit and that strange deep passion for sound blended with movement. She read well, aware that, for once, Michael's attention had wandered away from the small-scaled demands of his tired, hungry flesh. He was listening:

" 'The Legend of Princess Euphrosynia, God rest her turmoiled soul and cleanse her from all sin, and bring her to the place where the Holy Light abides eternally. The word of Euphrosynia as told by me, Macarius, unworthy monk of St. Sabba his abbey.

" 'In the days of Tsar Michael there dwelt in Moscow an illustrious Boyarin, Stepan, Prince Martov, whose soul may rest upon the bosom of the Saints. His dwelling was rich, and he had much substance, and was esteemed among his friends, and feared by his enemies.

" 'And the mother of the Boyarin was an infidel, a Pole, who refused to relinquish the Latin idolatry. The Boyarin came to the age of reason and, moved by the spirit of wisdom, he banished his mother into the country, where she lived in a humble manor house under the supervision of two pious Orthodox nuns.

" 'Now the Boyarin had one daughter baptized in the name of Euphrosynia, and brought up in the tenets of our holy faith. Many words were spoken in Moscow concerning the beauty of the maiden, but none had ever seen her except the trusted acquaintance of her father's. The maiden lived in her *terem*, its windows strictly latticed, and she employed her time in prayer and needlework. In due time the good Boyarin made it known that her dowry would be:

" 'The manor of Tishin,

" 'The manor of Gradost,

" 'The manor of Pelotz,

" 'Five hundred souls, all under the age of fifty,

" 'Twenty horses, five coaches, three chests of foreign linen, ten silver cups, one small coffer of pearls and emeralds, a miraculous ikon of St. Sabba, also a suitable array of such clothing as a maiden of her station would require.

" 'The maiden grew in stature, beauty, and piety. But it had been better if she had a wart on each cheek or some such disfigurement, because the hand of the Unclean One would then not have rested upon her shoulder. Yet the Unclean One will choose for himself the most beauteous fruits of the earth, as was well known of the ancients, and our blessed fathers, Anthony and Sabba, were not tempted by harridans with withered faces and pallid lips, but by splendidly arrayed damsels as beautiful as the Father of Lies could make them. Therefore doth it behove a pious orthodox maiden to keep her soul and body unspotted from the world, and to veil herself decently when abroad so that none but her close kin may be acquainted with her lineaments.

" 'Now it fell one summer that a strange sickness visited the city of Moscow, a veritable visitation of the Evil One. The sickness fell in this manner: first, the eyes of the stricken one welled with tears as though onions were pressed against the eyeballs, then the body began to wax hot, and the skin to be covered with red spots, the size of a cherry. The heat of the body entered the mind, whereupon

135

wild words came from the mouth, and vehement and unseemly gestures distorted the limbs. By reason of this vehemence none might approach the unfortunates who died unshriven and unanointed. It was said that the dreadful plague was brought in by the infidels in the German Quarter who drank milk on fast days, and thereby polluted the sanctity of Moscow, which might well be true, and may the Evil One take everlasting care of them in the place where fires are never quenched, nor is there any refreshment for the soul's weariness.

"'So it came to pass that the prudent Boyarin commanded his wife and daughter to depart from the city and to bide a while at one of his manors. This was done. Yet by an error, most certainly inspired by Beelzebub, the coachman and outriders brought the Boyarina and the maiden to the manor where the Boyarin's mother lived in penance and exile.

"'It was a matter of three weeks or more before the Boyarin learnt of the grievous error, and in his righteous wrath he commanded his servants to be hanged forthwith. The maiden and her mother were sent to a neighboring manor, and a strict watch was kept to prevent them from venturing near the forbidden grounds.

"'But the Devil had already made an assault on the soul of the maiden. She had greatly delighted in the intercourse with her exiled infidel grandmother, and many strange and unfortunate notions had entered her mind and distracted her from devoirs of meek piety and profitable needlework. In the land of Polonia women have no lowly station such as befits the fallen daughters of Eve. Their faces they veil not, nor are they kept in any salutary seclusion. A monk's pen must needs tremble as it writes of such horrible practices as dancing, playing on musical instruments, and singing abroad. I hear that in all foreign countries men and women gather together and break bread in common, to the grief of God's angels and the great pleasure of the Devil's hirelings. But my vows forbid me to dwell on such loathsome practices whereby what little virtue there be left in a woman is speedily destroyed.

"'Albeit but a brief while did the maiden pass under the forbidden roof, yet the poison of those horrible and unseemly discourses had so worked upon her that her nurse soon observed a lamentable lack of modesty in her demeanor. Thereupon the faithful servant carried her knowledge to the Boyarin who forthwith summoned his wife and daughter to Moscow, the plague having left the city on the fervent prayers of the holy Patriarch. There was the maiden chastised and severely admonished to keep the strict observance of modesty, meekness, and piety within the walls of her *terem* until such time when the Tsar and her father would appoint a husband unto her. And the Boyarin commanded that the maiden was not to appear abroad between the months of October and May except when she followed her mother to church in a coach with its curtains drawn and the maiden wearing a thick woolen shawl over her face.

"'The Boyarin thereupon began searching for a man who would best be pleased with the maiden's dowry. There came into his mind the name of a nobly born man of his acquaintance, of seventy years of age, a widower, of wholesome substance, and great strictness in dealing with his womenfolk. To him did the Boyarin repair, but the matter could not be concluded forthwith by reason of a sickness of the Tsar.

"'Now it came to pass that the nurse often observed her charge sitting silent and bemused as though she had no ears to hear anything. Her cheeks grew pallid, and she walked like one held in an unholy dream. And the nurse took to watching her diligently.

"'In those days there lived a multitude of infidel Germans in holy Moscow. They were gathered together from all nations. Of their ways and customs it befitteth one ill to speak at all, so evil they were and so contrary to the precepts of our blessed fathers. They abode in Moscow for the pleasure of the Tsar and his boyars, building and painting, but never were they suffered within any pious household. They lived in the German Quarter, separated by strong walls and stout gates lest their vile ways were to pollute our sanctuaries. All the God-fearing people held them in contempt (and would it had so continued), albeit the cunning of their crafts made their presence pleasurable to the Tsar, and banish them he would not, to the grief of some among his subjects.

"'Now there lived in the German Quarter a man of the English nation, a fellow whose countenance might have been esteemed pleasant, were it not for his infidelity. He was some thirty years of age, clever in the use of oils and other colors, and much esteemed by the Tsar who had promised him a rich manor, were he but to enter the bosom of true Orthodoxy. But the infidel preferred to continue in the worship of his English Luther.

"'It so happened that the Tsar commanded him to paint the walls of the ancient church of St. Barbara, and, she, being the patron and guardian of the Boyarin's spouse, the Boyarina and her daughter frequently repaired thither of a morning to offer their supplications to the saint with numerous bows and prostrations. According to custom, the maiden bared her face in the presence of God and

His saints. Little recked her pious mother that the Unclean One had chosen those same walls for his habitation.

" 'It so happened that the man of the English nation, looking up from his labors, perceived the maiden at prayer, her face unveiled. He, by reason of his race and infidelity, had no respect for maidenly modesty, and continued looking at her until the maiden, herself forgetting the presence of God, turned her face him-wards, and the Devil rejoiced in a victory as easy as it was shameful.

" 'Now the Englishman, not wholly ignorant of our customs, knew that the maiden had grievously transgressed in returning his insolent look, and it greatly pleased him.

" 'Now the mansion of the noble Boyarin had a back wall facing a dim and unsavory lane, and in that wall was a gate, and a little beyond the gate in a back yard stood a great barn shunned by all the household by reason of it being haunted by noisy evil spirits which took upon themselves the semblance of bats.

" 'And it fell on the eve of the Thrice Holy Epiphany that the maiden was tempted, and she bribed one of her attendants with a pearl, and secured the key to the gate, and ventured alone in the lane, and here my pen must needs fail me since the Devil had seen to the nefarious arrangements and the man of the English nation met her in the lane.

" 'What need is there to defile this parchment any further? Not the Englishman, but Satan himself took possession of the maiden's heart, and she, remembering the unseemly precepts taught her by her ungodly grandmother, now purchased her utter damnation in this world and in eternity, foreswearing modesty, piety, and her rank in a manner befitting a creature of no account before God and man.

" 'Seeing the frightful change which thus came upon her, the nurse charged her to answer openly as to the reason of it, and the maiden was obstinate in her silence until the attendant, bribed by a larger pearl, betrayed the secret of the key to the little gate, and the noble Boyarin rode forthwith to the Tsar's majesty, begging for justice, but the Tsar, loth to cause a disturbance in the city, deemed it prudent to ordain that justice be done privily, and that nothing were to be said to the maiden as to the unveiling of her terrible secret.

" 'So it happened that the maiden, sinfully longing for her infidel lover, stole through the gate by night, and she found him in the haunted barn, a dagger thrust through his heart and, seeing him thus, her wit forsook her. She got hold of his body, and dragged it outside, and lay close by, her face to his cheek, and it being

138

February, snow took to falling, and speedily it covered them both, and thus were they found when dawn broke in the city, and—'"

3

"Unfinished? It would be. . . . And the Unclean One danced at the funeral," said Michael. "Oh, probably, there was no funeral. I say, there is a ballad in it. . . . Your own ancestress, and you bear her name, but there is no Englishman on the scene. Frossia, I wonder—"

"That I am her. Oh, no. . . . I have always thought that the mere idea of reincarnation is such a slur on the wideness of God— just as though He had not got enough in Him and must needs repeat a type. . . . You say it is a ballad. Well, do make a poem of it if you like. . . . I have always seen it as a ballet."

"Why? Why?" And suddenly he lost all interest in the surface value of the old manuscript, and stared hard at her. "What does this mean to you? You read it as if you had lived in it time and time again. Of course, it is a family story, you would know every word of it, but, all the same, you seem to have an intimacy with the theme."

"You are imagining things." Frossia shook her head, secretly pleased that, for a time at least, she had succeeded in weaning Michael from the tiresome preoccupation with creaturely comforts. "I have never lived in it. It certainly touches a chord in me. Euphrosynia is one big adventure. I have always thought that her love for the Englishman was not the main thing. She longed for the open, and she won it—even though the open meant a dim haunted barn, and brought her death in the end. That girl is a prototype of a Russian woman. She may flaunt tradition and every contemporary custom of her sex, and she remains purely womanly. She is satisfying."

"Yes, she may be, but why think of a ballet?"

"Well, her scene was so deadly static, and she is all movement against it. Think of that ending. . . . Snowflakes whirling all round, she joins in the dance to escape and then to come back—" She halted, wondering whether Michael would ever understand that life at its very hardest would still keep some beauty in it precisely because it had movement. She waited, trying to marshal more words, but his brief interest was ebbing. There was one more potato left in the brown earthenware dish on the table. They had long since finished supper, they had had nine potatoes, and he

139

had eaten five of them. Now he reached for the last one. Frossia pushed the dish towards him.

"Are you still hungry?"

"I am always hungry," he said sullenly and dug his teeth in the silvery flesh of the potato. "Well, if you are so interested in it, we might perhaps go and see Zerst at the Mariinsky Theater. My uncle used to know him." And Frossia forbore to say that her own people had known Zerst all their lives.

She had no wish to go with Michael to the Mariinsky and, having read Euphrosynia's legend, she felt flat and disappointed. Michael had listened to the words, their beauty could not be escaped, and some day he might try and turn the story into a ballad, though Frossia was uncertain about it. Michael's accomplishments were largely oral. What verse of his own he had recited, always struck Frossia as being blurred, wooden, lacking in clarity and depth.

Yet the newly remembered narrative led her along other paths than furtive barter and makeshift housekeeping. A few days later she found her way to an open door at the back of Mariinsky Theater. There was a narrow dim staircase beyond; she mounted it, wondering whether they would turn her out. But she came to a large well-lit room with several rows of chairs and a desk at one end. Some chairs were already occupied. Young men and women kept their heads bent to books and papers, and barely noticed her coming in. Nobody seemed to be in official charge of the gathering, and Frossia, even though quite uncertain of her bearings, was bold enough to take the nearest chair. For all she knew, this might prove to be a lecture on drainage or Australasian flora. True she was at the Mariinsky, but buildings were being put to very odd uses at the time. She remembered Pavel Pavlovich telling her once about his having strayed into one of the halls at the School of Mosaics close by the Academy of Arts in Vasilyev Island. "I had been told there would be a talk on the work of Vasnezov. I was interested. And would you believe it—a little dark fellow came in and orated about the Zulu marriage customs. It was quite attractive in a way, but I wanted mosaics. . . ." And Frossia felt the same. They might tell her things about Hottentots or forestry in Canada. . . . She did not greatly care. She had come in to learn anything, to listen, above all to sit quiet, to escape the innumerable tiny irritations of Moshkov Lane.

Presently she saw a face smile at her, a thin hand beckon to her. It was the girl who had read Dostoevsky. Frossia remembered —she had been at the party in the studio, but they had not noticed

140

each other much. She smiled back a little uncertainly. The girl, still wearing her blue-green shawl, left her seat and took the chair next to Frossia's.

"You are Klava Voronova," said Frossia.

"Yes," Klava smiled, "and I know who you are now."

Frossia could not help her bitterness.

"Yes, we met again at that studio—and—"

"Well, dreadful words did fly about then, but the sun loses nothing by shining into a puddle—"

"How is Dostoevsky?"

"Oh, we are doing Tolstoy now. It will be *Resurrection* next Tuesday. Will you come?"

"I might not be free," said Frossia a little curtly, and made a confession. "I just wandered here. I don't know what is going to happen."

"It is a lecture—on the history of ballet. I come here to learn things. It is good to sit still and just listen."

Young men and women stirred in their chairs. Notebooks rustled, pencils were chewed. Frossia saw a door open, and a thin brown man, with an untidy crop of hair and enormous horn glasses on the tip of his nose, came in and sat down at the desk. He had neither notes nor books by him. He looked at his motley audience, smiled, and pushed the thick-framed spectacles further down so that Frossia wondered how he could keep them there. He did not. He took them off. She liked the candor of his large brown eyes. He was a stranger, but she felt warm and friendly. When he smiled at the audience, she knew she was being included in the smile. She waited luxuriously. The thin brown man folded his hands together and began. His voice was clear, easy to listen to, though it had no particular beauty of color. The man spoke, and everything about him remained motionless, even the hands clasped together on the desk. That stillness was like a magnet.

"As you know, this is going to be a brief series of lectures on the History of Ballet. Today I mean to give you a few preliminary points. Taken broadly, all ballet should be considered as visual music. Remember that ballet is articulate and definite just like speech—"

He noticed that some of them were busily scribbling, and his pause was kindly.

"Now will you please imagine the framework of any ballet. This is important. First, we have the idea, the story which of necessity belongs to poetry. Next there is the visual background, called décor, its purpose being to give a frame to the story. Thirdly, there

141

is the music which again retells the story and, finally, we come to the actual dancing which must be at once itself and the other three together. In brief, it is a harmony with a fourfold expression."

Frossia began wishing she had brought some paper. The words were falling into her mind like so many drops of gratefully clear water. There was a drought within her she had not realized before.

"You will remember," went on the pleasant even voice, "that there are three factors in all creative expression—the artist, his material, and the creative power. These three must come together if any fruition is to be reached. Now I have said that in ballet the harmony has a fourfold expression, and no ballet justifies itself unless there is a deep affinity between the four. The least discord between music and décor, or music and story, will ruin the loveliest ballet phrase. Idea, sound, shape, and movement must be in complete harmony, but never really identical. Is this rather obscure?" He paused for a moment, his brown eyes sympathetic over their notebooks, and he repeated the statement until one or two among them answered him eagerly and gratefully. "Now from our childhood onwards we live to express. All life, human, animal, vegetable, is always moving towards some expression. Think of a tulip bulb. Its expression, certain processes completed, will be both leaves and flower."

Frossia glanced at Klava's face. It looked quiet, rapt, so much at home with the words which were being spoken.

"Now whatever is inside the mind passes through several crucibles, and is finally translated into thought, mood, action. The least expression insists on a framework of its own—else it might lose itself in thin air. . . . An idea must be communicable to be of any real value. . . . And here is another point." He broke off, and his eyes wandered to the opposite wall. "Some people might say to you: 'Why this interest in one particular form of art? At the moment, at least, it has no relation to the urgent problems of today? Is it not then pure waste of time and mental energy?' What would you say to them? You cannot argue that ballet is pre-eminent among arts because no single branch of art enjoys any pre-eminence. Yet there is one detail which you might bear in mind as you continue your studies. It is the close relation of ballet to life. Now I should like you to remember that even any unco-ordinated movement is life. Dancing is movement carried within the very gates of harmony, and dancing is life all the more urgent because of its close affinity to all essential life-processes."

There came a lengthier pause.

"Now please, all of you, don't despair if a ballet, seen for the first time, leaves you lost in a maze of impressions and reactions. Ballet's variety of mood and phrase is almost infinite, and such a feeling of lostness is well-nigh inevitable. Every detail of any ballet must be learned before the core is reached. I should say that the most difficult—and certainly one of the most important—ballets is *Petrushka*. There you have an outwardly pathetic puppet come to life, striving to express an infinitesimal fragment of that lovely, brooding discontent which should be alive in us all. You have two other puppets—the Moor and the Ballerina, but they dwindle into insignificance by the side of Petrushka, who is a prisoner, a madman, and a fool—but is always alive. He is raised far above the puppet state when he recognizes his hopeless love for the Ballerina. She, as you know, prefers the Moor who might not satisfy her but does not perplex her. Cast your mind back to the scene of Petrushka's bridal with his grief. Remember those phrases in Stravinsky's score. The Ballerina is all neat and open, no dim corners in her movements for anyone to wonder at and explore. The Moor strikes Petrushka with a wooden sword, and he dies. He was but a puppet, but the sawdust shows red. Petrushka is truly dead. . . ."

He stopped and waited for a few seconds.

"I am sorry that a meeting prevents me from answering any questions. But we come here again on Wednesday. Beginners please attend the practice class tomorrow at nine. Citizen Maxim will give the instruction." He bowed briefly and vanished through the slit of a door behind the desk, and Frossia leaned back in her chair, eyes closed, hands folded.

"You will come on Wednesday," urged Klava.

"No," Frossia whispered back. "That was enough—for days, for weeks, for months."

"Nothing is ever enough for me," sighed Klava. "I go on and on. I am greedy. I sometimes think that the mind has a hole in it, no matter how much you put in, there is always room for more and more and more. Anyhow, pure Russians are made like that. Insatiable . . ."

They left the great building together, and crossed the huge square towards Moyka river. Late afternoon sun flushed all the roofs with crimson and orange, a little gray bridge to the left of them looked as though dipped in copper; the solemn ruins of Litovsky Castle, once a prison, suggested something from a medieval fairy tale. Almost, thought Frossia, a face might appear in that broken window, a pale thin hand flutter, a wilted flower fall down into the quiet silver green Moyka. Then she knew herself to have been discourteous to Klava, and turned round with something of a forced smile on her face.

"Yes," Klava was saying. "We are mere acquaintances, but I reckon this life is too fierce for acquaintanceship. Either you are a friend or a foe."

"That is much too definite," fenced Frossia, and now they had gone down Galernaya and were turning towards Nicholas Bridge, and she glanced at the people hurrying towards Vasilyev Island. "Now take any of these people. If you were to jostle past one of them you would say you were sorry, and they would smile and say something, and you would have been in touch with them . . . but this is not necessarily friendship—"

"Why not?" parried Klava. "A smile is worth ten rubies."

Frossia had forgotten her own way was not across the bridge, but Klava walked on, and Frossia followed her. Suddenly they heard the rasping noise of winches at the farthest end of the bridge, and saw two spans poised in mid-air. The sun flooded the dark iron with glory, but Klava sighed. "Well, I shall not get home for hours. . . . The Lord be praised for a warm summer night."

"Do you mean the bridge stays up?"

"Yes, for barges and steamers. It always did. But now they have taken to raising it at such odd times that one is never certain of getting home."

"And all these people are stranded?"

"Yes, but they have the Arabian Night with them."

"What?"

"You have met him," explained Klava. "He came to the studio. The little man. . . . The one who told the story of Anutka. Igor Vladimirovich."

"Why is he called Arabian Night?"

"Well, he tells stories. It makes the time pass. People love him."

"Who is he?"

"Just a man. There are few like him about. He has a job at Warsaw Station—travel permit inspector, I think. It must be a hard job for him."

"Why?"

"Because you should be hard when you are there, and he is not."

"Who is he?" insisted Frossia. "I mean who was he?"

"I don't know. A grocer—someone said, or a schoolmaster, or else a railway man. I don't know. It does not matter. He is so ordinary— and yet I say there are few like him. Come on, you might hear him tell some story."

Frossia stood hesitant.

"Come along. He is good at it. It is mostly from books. Hamlet he gave once, and Othello. Also Dickens—I remember Oliver Twist and Copperfield. . . . Usually, it is something Russian, Turgenev, or Pushkin and Lermontov."

Reluctant, Frossia came along and stopped at the fringe of the crowd. Now dark green shadows had almost swamped the scene. Someone was busily lighting a lantern. A lorry with a load of timber had overturned there earlier in the day. The lorry had been towed away, but the timber remained, and all of them had the unexpected luxury of improvised benches. They sat in small groups and untidy clusters, men, women, children, all tired, mostly tattered, all burdened with various sacks and bundles. They sat so still that Frossia wondered if they were about to fall asleep. But as she drew nearer and nearer she knew that their stillness was born of suspense, excitement, interest. Igor Vladimirovich she could not see at first, and then caught a glimpse of him crouching behind an enormous log, the fitful light of the lantern catching his face into its dancing web. Frossia heard Klava's labored breathing, and then she caught the first accents of a deep voice which was like an embrace in that it held the heterogeneous crowd together, gave them one common focus, kept them within a place where neither fatigue, nor darkness, nor hunger, nor even fear mattered greatly.

She stood and listened. She had been listening all day—to Michael's thin whimpering, to the professor's exposition of basic laws in ballet. The former had wearied her, the latter had given her pleasure blended with nostalgia. Here, in the broken shadows of the bridge, she had forgotten both weariness and discontent. She listened. Igor Vladimirovich was telling them about Tolstoy's *Resurrection*. He was telling it in his own abrupt, direct way, engraving one separate episode after another in the mind of the crowd. Frossia heard him sketch the dreadful, unforgettable scene of the convicts' pilgrimage through the parched streets of Moscow.

"There was a private carriage about to cross the road. The convicts' procession made it stop. The carriage held an ordinary wealthy family father, mother, and two children, a boy and a girl. They were probably going to enjoy a picnic on Sparrow Hills. The father got angry at the delay, the mother remained indifferent, the little girl felt frightened at the sight of so many manacled men and women, and she was relieved when the last of them slipped out of sight. But the boy knew that the convicts were the same people as themselves, and the boy wept. Tolstoy says: 'He knew it from God directly, clearly, indubitably.'"

145

He told them about Prince Nekhludov following Katia Maslova and the convicts on the terrible journey to the Siberian mines.

"Now, comrades and friends, why had he done it? Katia had no love for him. But he had done her a great wrong, and this was his idea of making it up to her. She never understood his generosity, she never thanked him, she ended by choosing another man for her husband. But Nekhludov had his reward. Away from important drawing rooms, we see him discovering what the French call the great world among the workmen, the convicts, the peasants. There is a man called Simonson, whose soul is like a clear-running river. Simonson says to us all: 'Everything in the world is alive. . . .' The timber we sit on, comrades, the bread we eat, and all in your minds and mine, and all we do is a service to the living. Now Tolstoy leaves us with Nekhludov alone. He comes to the parable of the unjust steward. Mankind has set itself an impossible task: evil in themselves, they try and get ready to fight evil. There is no guiltless man in the world, and only such can punish—Tolstoy says so through the lips of Nekhludov. That is the great theme of *Resurrection*. But you could not speak freely in the days when that book was written. It could not be printed as it stood. They punished Tolstoy for writing it. There were foreign editions of the book."

And, listening, Frossia remembered her daring Aunt Alina and the Russian book published in Essex, England. Suddenly she wanted to cry. The scene made her think of the loveliness to be born some day. There is something indestructible in us, she told herself, and heard Klava draw in a breath. A woman sighed and belched. The man's voice had ceased, all kept quiet, and Frossia knew she was afraid. She flung a hurried good-by at Klava and ran back to Moshkov Lane. In the morning Michael drawled at her:

"I don't think there is much in your story—but we might go and see Zerst about it."

"No," said Frossia, herself astonished at this new-born decision. "No," she repeated, "it is no use—"

"I think you are right." Michael yawned. "I say—what is there to eat? We had such a poor supper last night."

There was little enough except a few small rye rusks at the bottom of a bag, and Frossia moved about, silent, perplexed. She knew she saw Michael as a vain, tarnished popinjay, all his earlier trappings now irrevocably soiled, and she also knew that she could not yet say to him "Go," because she was still sorry for him, but her very pity had something stained in it.

In the tiny cubicle partitioned off the bleak big hall of the un-used glass factory in Vasilyev Island, Klava sat at a table littered with books. Grisha lay fast asleep on his narrow *koyka*. It was past midnight, and Klava had to be at her factory at six in the morn-ing. Her body was limp with fatigue, but her mind refused the idea of a rest. A tattered exercise book lay open before her. The green ink gleamed wet in the lamplight. She had just written:

"If I cannot learn to read His will in the light, let Him make it dark for me, thicken the shadows till I cannot see the shape of my fingers. . . . And I will walk through a shadowed valley, my hands will grope for His, and not find them, and my soul thirst for the living water, and wander on through a dry desert, and the light of His stars will be to me for a dark night, yet I shall go on cleaving to His presence even when He seems absent, until the dark around be to me for a candle in His tabernacle, and the silence live with His voice, and until I learn that neither dark nor light, as my soul experiences them, can determine Him. . . ." She had written it, impelled by her constant need to express herself. Now she read it again, and wondered if she had really been conscious of the mean-ing in the words. . . . They rang pure, exalted notes. Within her nothing seemed in harmony with either purity or exaltation. "Shall I ever truly learn it?" she whispered and fingered the thick rough leaves until she came to a quotation from the *Brothers Karamazov,* embodying Father Zosima's testament to his friends: "Russia's sal-vation is in her people. . . . And the Lord will save His people be-cause Russia is great in her humility. . . . I can see into the future: it shall come that the rich man be ashamed of his riches, and the poor man respond with joy and caress to the splendid shame of the rich man. Believe me, this shall come. Equality is nowhere ex-cept in spiritual dignity of man, acknowledged by all alike. We shall keep the image of Christ, and it shall shine like a precious dia-mond before the whole world. . . ."

"But how can we?" she marveled, and then blamed herself for the seed of an unworthy doubt, and remembered the lateness of the night. Her factory day began early. She sat there on a low stool, pushing a small steel handle in and out, and the handle came towards her, and then disappeared, and, unseen, accomplished its work of joining one cotton thread to another. Downstairs, in the yards, Klava would come across huge fawn-colored bales, and guess that her small steel gadget had been at some of them, and yet she knew nothing of the detailed process. The foreman had tried to explain it to her several times. "You might become a skilled hand, Klavdia Ivanovna." He would frown at her clumsy efforts and shake his capped head. "Are you not interested in the machinery?" Klava could not be. Steel had no soul for her. Sometimes a man would come and drop a few drops of oil into her gadget, and she kept it clean and shining with a rag, but she could not pretend to grasp its intricacies, and had to ask for help whenever the small steel needle refused to run its appointed course.

They liked her at the factory. They teased her, and were proud of her. She helped at their own tiny Proletcult with her songs and stories and readings. She had had a poem printed in the *Red Gazette,* a small poem about some soldiers seen marching down Nevsky Prospect, a few tidily rhymed lines written because Klava had seen a perplexed, wounded, turmoiled, and none the less triumphant Russia in those bodies clothed in verminous, tattered khaki. At the factory they kept telling her how proud they were of her. She was a peasant, unlettered except by her own effort, unaccomplished except through her own zeal. They teased her about her readings and meetings, about the tiny candles she bought to light at an ikon in the Kiev chapel off Nicholas Quay. They teased her but they never condemned her. She was the only one among hundreds and hundreds who could sing proletarian songs and church anthems. It puzzled them. She would go to their own meetings and speak freely, and she never alluded to the shadowed manacled past, nor would she refer to the obvious sadness of the day. Nearly always would Klava speak of the future. There was no bitterness in her about the dim years the locusts had eaten. There lay no hatred in her. An important communist met her and said later: "She is too rare to be dangerous."

But Klava was in danger now—in danger from herself, and she knew it. Less and less did she delight in her own meetings, in her hours spent among an eager, listening crowd. She had tried to approach Frossia to save herself from looking too closely at an abyss. More and more did she begin to love privacy, rare secluded moments, the walls of her cubicle at those times when Grisha must be away on his own business.

"This is dreadful," she said to herself, closing her untidy scrapbook, "I must not indulge in it," but she knew that virtue was slowly trickling out of her.

She snuffed out the evil-smelling lamp, lay down in her clothes, and could not sleep. The summer dawn found her awake. She looked at Grisha, asleep, defenseless, and clean. She would not wake him. Cautiously, on tiptoe, she slipped out, slightly comforted by a sip of cold water and a boiled potato. She came out and turned her face to the river. It was one of those mornings when the beauty of buildings, water and air made her wish for words she had never had leisure to learn. The houses on the English Quay across the river had their scars drowned in a sea of amber-rose light. The wide street before her, running to the generous arms of the river, was stippled with faint gold, and the faces of those Klava passed wore an air of expectancy as though all the souls had been reborn in the night. Later on, the day would age, and its texture of worry, uncertainty and, possibly, anxiety, spread its dust over the buoyancy and the pleasure. But the morning had youth and songs in it, and Klava braced herself to meet the city's brave mood, and she smiled at the passersby, all her comrades, as they turned away from the light-washed quays, and pressed towards the great red mouth of the factory gates.

"It makes you glad to be alive," shouted a middle-aged man, his face pitted with smallpox, his right sleeve pinned to a gray linen coat, and Klava nodded.

"Comrade Klava," whimpered a spindle-legged girl in her late teens, who wore blue trousers and a resplendent scarlet blouse. "Comrade Klava"—she hugged a dirty textbook—"I cannot get this word at all. What does it mean?" She spelt it slowly, "collectivism—"

"Well, that is easy. Getting together, several people working at several things."

"Why such a word for it?" said the girl peevishly. "If only they printed Russian words. They will find another word for 'bread' soon, but that will not stop the famine. . . . And anyhow this working together does not seem to do much—"

Klava smiled, suddenly. The red-bloused girl said impatiently: "What are you smiling for? I am asking you a question. . . . What is the matter with you? You look mad to me."

"It is the morning," said Klava; "there is always something mad in a summer morning—"

The girl shrugged her scarlet shoulders, closed the book with an angry snap, and passed on.

Klava had not smiled at her but at Igor Vladimirovich whom she had seen running past the gates. They had smiled at each other, sharing the morning and the sky above them. Klava's somber mood of midnight fled, and Igor Vladimirovich hurried on. He had a great distance to cover—all the way from Vasilyev Island to Warsaw Station where one tiny room, its outer walls bulging on to a platform, belonged to him for twelve hours out of twenty-four. Igor Vladimirovich was an inspector of travel permits. A friend of his

149

had held the post, and was leaving, and said to Igor Vladimirovich: "Would you like to take it?" "I could not do a clerk's job," said Igor Vladimirovich. "It is people," replied the friend, and Igor Vladimirovich applied for the vacancy without any further questions. They appointed him soon enough.

His work meant scrutinizing travel permits, issued by house committees, various health commissions, and commissariats. Permits were small drab oddments of gray paper, smudged with the violet ink of the ubiquitous seal. "Watch those seals," warned the friend, "that is where they always cheat you. A mere smudge the seal is . . . . Well, you can imagine—"

Igor could well imagine. He merely glanced at the seals. He watched the people.

From morning till late afternoon they queued up before his little door, men, women, young people, mere children, precious permits housed in their often shaking hands. That little office was their Mecca. Igor's hand would presently affix the second violet seal to the document, and that second seal would open the platform gate to them, make it possible for them to board a train, give them the free road, carry them to Viazma, Orel, Tula, the Crimea, Perm, Tobolsk, anywhere over the length and the breadth of the great Republic, bring them to their relations, assuage hunger of body and soul, slay space, draw families together. Their papers said that their holders were going to visit the sick, no other pretext was allowed, a cousin, a grandmother, a father, a sister, a wife. They all came pleading, adding the urgency of their voices to the efficacy of the violet seals.

The tiny room was all the smaller because of mountains of papers, and Igor, behind his plain deal desk, felt that some day he must bestir himself, dust the grimy shelves, destroy most of the litter, and conjure tidiness into the bleak little warren. But papers and dirt were inanimate and therefore unimportant. His main business lay with people, and it never ceased.

This morning he found a queue of about a dozen people, and the first was a smiling woman in a black print skirt and a white shawl with bright orange flowers on it, a comfortable, middle-aged woman, who was planning to see an aunt in the Poltava Government. He scanned her dirty permit and sighed. He scanned her plump self-satisfied face, noted her pride in the flowered shawl, and the peacocky way in which she strode into the office, and sighed again.

"Why did you do it?"

The smile stole away from the full mouth. The woman looked

ugly. She was no longer middle-aged but old and fretted with worry. She did not answer. Igor said patiently:

"And I believe you have paid money for it, too. You must have. These things never get done for nothing." He scanned the permit and now noticed the clumsy erasures of dates and place-names. The permit had been used once before. He could see the faint outline of the second seal probably stamped by his predecessor. The woman tugged feebly at the fringe of her shawl. Igor could see her fear. He used a quieter, gentler voice: "What is the good of doing it?"

"Hunger, little father. And they would not give me a permit—"

"How much did you pay?"

The woman stared past him. After a pause she muttered:

"They all said to me: 'You will get a ticket all right. You must not go to Nicholas Station,' they said, 'the man there is very unkind . . . but the man at Warsaw Station,' they said, 'he is kind, he will give you the manna from heaven,' they said."

"But I have nothing to do with it." He spoke patiently. "I am only your servant, you are not cheating me, you are cheating the country, and that is yourself. Listen," he leaned forward, an earnest note in his voice, "it is not impossible to get genuine permits, but it is difficult. There is little fuel in the country, the rolling stock is worn out, we have few new trains in the making. So they say to you: 'Travel less. Travel when you must. Don't cheat. Cheating hurts your own self, *grajdanka*.'" He looked at her carefully, but her face was closed-in and indifferent. "Do you understand?" he asked, and she shook her brightly shawled head, and Igor slipped the clumsily faked permit under a paperweight. "Go." He raised his voice. "I must keep this. You go—"

The woman sucked in her lips.

"Why keep the permit if it is no good?" she asked, her voice no longer timid but swollen with something Igor interpreted as challenge and mockery, and he got up.

"Next," he shouted in a voice which did not quite belong to him, the voice of a disappointed, wounded man. The woman shrugged her plump shoulders, drew the flowered shawl closer round her, cursed him with her eyes, and slunk out of the room.

5

Gosizdat, the State Publishing Company, was housed on Catherine Quay. There Frossia went by chance one morning, and was not turned away. A spare middle-aged man gave her an interview on

151

the staircase. "Your qualifications?" he rapped, steel-rimmed glasses dangling in one dirty hand. Frossia explained them just as briefly. "Ah, you know French and German. . . . Good . . . Your labor book? All in order . . . Come tomorrow, ask for Comrade Bokina." He dropped his spectacles, picked them up, and vanished up the stairs. Frossia could hear his voice—"Elena Petrovna, Elena Petrovna, where is my hot milk? Elena Petrovna, my milk. . . . Yes, at once, please—"

She returned the next morning. Comrade Bokina proved to be a girl in the late thirties, a university student, thin, intense, dark, untidy. She ushered Frossia into a small dim room, spoke rather indifferent French to her, and left her alone at a table crowded with pamphlets bound in orange and green and red paper.

"You need not read them all through. We want the best translated. Just scribble your opinion on the fly-leaf." She pursed her narrow mouth a little scornfully: "The real work, of course, will be done elsewhere—"

The pamphlets were not all French or German. Some were English, Spanish, and Italian, and once an Arabic sheet found its way into the mass. They were all on political economy, communism, various aspects of social endeavor. Frossia conscientiously read the French and the German ones; such as seemed good purely from the literary point of view, she approved by penciled notes on the margin. Later she might recognize a familiar quotation in a well-trimmed Russian dress as it appeared on a poster or in a decree. The subject matter was far too technical for her. But nobody ever came into the office. Occasionally she met the man dropping his steel-rimmed spectacles on the stairs or in a passage. He no longer recognized her. Comrade Bokina hardly ever came near her. But this was work, some money came Frossia's way, her hours were fruitfully occupied, and she asked for no more.

From Catherine Quay she would often stray back to Moyka or even Vasilyev Island. The flat in Moshkov Lane was becoming airless in every sense. Michael continued drifting about from day to day as though no single issue of life were of any concern to him. He had talked about escaping abroad, and Frossia did not spare him a luridly detailed narrative about Anna's adventure. Then he stopped alluding to the plan.

At the house in Moyka Frossia felt happy. Now Pavel Pavlovich was working hard at an exhibition picture of a miner in the sun, and though inwardly Frossia deplored the faintly propagandist handling of the theme, yet the thing absorbed her in its very vastness, its pagan abandon; the miner was the son and heir of the

152

sun, his hands clenched in fury at the light all but blinding him, but the outward thrust of the enormous, sharply muscled shoulders, the poise of the neck, the upraised face, all had in them a joy which was almost akin to wrath, and somehow made it sublime. The miner was no imitation of a Greek athlete: he was pure Slav, Russian, he stood in the fields, the implements of his calling around him, steel gleaming in the wet green grass under his feet. Pavel Pavlovich broke the tall grass with budding cornflowers. Looking at the all but finished canvas, Frossia thought of a sea and plentiful harvests.

"He ought to have made his sky blue," complained Paulina Pavlovna.

"No—"

"But there is the sunlight—"

"Yes"—Frossia went back to her country days—"but you will remember, Paulina Pavlovna, a typical day—with the sunlight over the grass, and the sky gray rather than blue, gray with a faint violet in it—"

Paulina Pavlovna turned her back on the easel.

"I am glad we are alone, my little pigeon," she said suddenly, "I know what is wrong with you. You will keep out of harmony with the great source. You must really listen for once." She hurried on though Frossia kept silent and still. "You are all like little mice in a very big cage, running all over the place. You must stop it. My own way is so simple. Every morning when I wake, I just lose myself, I become nothing, and the source pours into me. See how simple it is. Try it—"

"How do you do it?"

"It is so simple," repeated Paulina. She never explained things. She could not. She merely added: "It is the most precious time of the day."

Frossia said nothing. It would have been unkind to point out that Paulina Pavlovna's most precious hours were in the afternoon when she tramped, her ill-shod feet hurting her, to the Gutuevsky Works crèche, and there tended, nursed, and comforted squalling babies whose mothers were at work.

"You see," went on Paulina Pavlovna, "as soon as it happens to you, you know what to do, you are no longer astray."

"Why do you not get hold of the Parnikovs or Lilian?"

"I have tried to. But there is too much fear in Maria Nikolaevna, it is like a tall hedge all round her. And the Captain is the same. Lilian is too shallow. You could not pour anything into her. Dear Pavel is a genius, but he is so stupid about these things. . . . And

153

that dreadful Serge—heaven forgive me—is a badly painted marionette. Imagine anyone inventing a pedigree which goes back to Charlemagne! Why, it is more than five centuries ago."

"Eleven—"

"What does it matter—five or eleven? Does it matter to anyone when Charlemagne lived? Time is like the sea."

Frossia asked patiently: "Paulina Pavlovna, I am also stupid, and you must forgive me—but what is it that you call your source?"

"Your questions are like dried peas. Why? Why? What? Who? You want an answer to all things. The source is just something behind and above everything. Some will say 'God' and leave it at that word. But words don't explain all living, my dear. Words do muddle one so. Well, the source is in the air, to begin with. The air is sacred. I never, never eat game. A chicken is not the same thing. Never a partridge or woodcock. I know a woman in Moscow who says that the source is also in the water. She will not eat fish. I don't argue though I can't agree. These are such minor things. I would not condemn anyone for enjoying a partridge," and she looked so wistful that Frossia knew Paulina Pavlovna was imagining a nice plump partridge, red wine sauce, and cranberry jelly, set before her.

"Tell me more," she urged, genuinely interested.

"You are smiling, Frossia. I think you are laughing at me—"

"I never laugh at anyone."

Paulina Pavlovna stared hard at Frossia as if she were a stranger in a strangely furnished room.

"No, you never do." Suddenly she leaned forward, no longer a devotee of the occult, but merely a simple, warm-hearted woman. "Child, do you ever laugh at life?" she asked, and Frossia drew back into a room, its walls dim and blue, the fire dancing in the open English grate: they had so many *kamini* in that house near Kiev. She winced and answered in a voice as natural as taut wire: "Why, yes, sometimes. There is Nikolashka and his incomparable Irina Nikolaevna whom none of us are likely to meet. And the man in Rumiantsev Gardens with his tarnished Petrushka show. . . . Why, there are so many things—"

"There are," said Paulina Pavlovna.

CHAPTER FIVE

ASHES FOR BEAUTY

The Zabalkansky Club was nowhere near the street of that name. It was housed in the back yard of a ramshackle building at the end of Galernaya Street behind the English Quay. The house had been partly burnt down early in 1917, and its windows and the front door were blackened, gaping holes. The gates into the back yard were nearly down, and you had to step across an untidy pile of half-charred timber. In the summer when Frossia came to know the Zabalkansky, young grass grew, bold and beautiful, in between the ebony-colored planks. Facing the gates stood a door, and there, in a three-roomed flat, was Elena Ivanovna, two canaries in a tarnished brass cage, a good deal of heavy shabby furniture, and the Zabalkansky. The door had neither bell nor knocker. The key was missing from its hole.

Elena Ivanovna was a priest's widow. Her husband, a military chaplain, had been killed early in 1914. So she still wore black, but the mourning ended with her clothes. She came from Vitebsk, in western Russia, and drifted to Petrograd having once fallen in love with a view of the Neva on a picture postcard. She had done some rough nursing at a military training hospital. When Frossia first met her at the house in Moyka, the huge ungainly woman looked at her carefully, kissed her on both cheeks, and said in her deep voice:

"One more for the Zabalkansky—"

"For what?"

"Come and see," invited Elena Ivanovna. "Why, we have been waiting for you."

They said the Zabalkansky had started that March evening in 1917 when angry fires flung blood-red shadows across the dark green skies over Petrograd, when a frightened woman and a wailing child found themselves in Galernaya Street, and could go no further, and Elena Ivanovna dragged them in, and gave them sanctuary, counsel, tea, and potatoes.

Potatoes were no longer dispensed there by the time Frossia found her way to its door, and oddly colored syrup was offered in lieu of tea. They all paid for the syrup, Elena Ivanovna being poor. But she asked no fees for either sanctuary or sympathy or advice, and all were found there.

Paulina went seldom enough. Lilian tittered whenever she heard the name mentioned. There were no adventures to seek at the Zabalkansky. But Nikolashka went any evening he could spare, telling Frossia that just being there made him feel cheerful for several days. The other habitués were a necessarily motley crowd, some *ci-devants* among them, also workmen from the Gutuevsky, Putilovsky, and Baltiysky Works, scavengers, students, ex-army officers, pallid women who drifted in and out, silent and timid. They had two rooms for their use. Elena Ivanovna and the canaries had the third. Elena Ivanovna had pushed all the bulkier furniture into her own warren. The club premises had chairs, sofas, and armchairs. There was no electric light, and the hostess was sparing with her candles, allowing but one for each room.

They went there to relax after their day's varied experiences. Some were so poor that they could not afford any syrup. Some sat so tense as though they were waiting for urgent hostile steps to thump across the cobbled yard. The Tcheka had indeed once visited Elena Ivanovna, and they left satisfied that no counter-revolutionary schemes were being hammered out on her humble anvil. "They were quite polite," narrated Elena Ivanovna, "but they left the place so untidy. They looked for bombs and literature. They found nothing really. But they took away twenty volumes of the *Lives of the Saints*. I was not sorry to see them go. Big books take so much room."

Elena Ivanovna still conformed to ancient usages. She bought oil and candles, and burned a lampad in front of Our Lady of Kazan. Sometimes she would be found deep in prayer, but she went to church seldom and spasmodically. Altogether she was an oddity. Round-shouldered, ungainly, with her pale broad face and peering blue eyes, she outwardly suggested a typical *"popadia,"* priest's wife, placid, somnolent, and afraid of the least activity. You could imagine her seated in front of a copper samovar, slowly pouring amber tea into big glass tumblers, sucking a piece of sugar, and listening to some pointless and interminable story brought in by an ecclesiastical neighbor. "I should never have married a priest," she confessed to Frossia once. "I did grow fat. I could do nothing else to resemble the rest of them."

The club had merely happened. It lived on by shared thought.

Tumblers and mugs of pink-colored liquid in their hands, men and women and young people sprawled on chairs and on the thinly carpeted floor, and talked of animals, flowers, weather, mankind, shoeleather, and even metaphysics. They also loved discussing foreign countries, theater, music, pictures, and books. Most often they talked of Russia, and sometimes their talk reminded Frossia of a mosaic fresco by Vasnezov, an ancient theme in a modern framework.

There she went one rainy autumn evening—on slow, aching feet. It had been a thorny summer. She still had Michael in the flat, and the earlier joy in him had grown so thin that she no longer could believe its erstwhile substance. She would say to him: "Yes, we are all becoming stomachs, enormous, greedy, insatiable stomachs," and he would retort sullenly: "Have you got anything to put into mine?"

So often Frossia had nothing. Marketing had grown more precarious. Speculation dealt in staples and in luxuries, but the prices left her dazzled. She had hardly anything left to sell. Her work at the *Gosizdat* ended with the cessation of foreign pamphlets. She had tried one casual job after another, offering the skill of her hands rather than her mind. Sometimes she made enough to ward off hunger for a few days. Sometimes she did not. Michael whimpered, complained, and murmured odd inconsequential hints about trying to earn his own livelihood. But he stayed on at the flat, sullen and idle, and Frossia strove to cut down her leisure hours. Hunger was worst when she had nothing to do. To the Zabalkansky she went that evening to escape Michael. The club had no attractions for him. But she walked slowly: she had had no food that day.

She went past Nicholas Bridge. The evening was closing in, a soft spun cloak round the tired, silent city. In the doorway of Clark House on the English Quay Frossia saw something sprawling, bent down, and saw a young girl fast asleep, her bare head against the carven door. In her lap lay an uncovered wooden tray with a few buns on it. Frossia understood. Bun-selling was a perilous business, it also seemed incongruous: queues of hungry people patterned the city streets, and yet some had enough food to sell to others, and suddenly she felt furious, and stretched her hand towards the tray. Then the girl woke, yawned, and jerked her head.

She was a young slim thing, no more than fourteen or thereabouts. She had a well-shaped face, lovely for all its griminess, but Frossia staggered back when she saw the look in those dark eyes. They asked: "Are you a friend?" They said: "Please don't hurt me if you are not." They said: "Please, I have not done you any harm." And Frossia stood still, her own hunger nearly forgotten.

The girl shivered and said in a thin voice, her dirty hands clutching at the rim of the wooden tray:

"Would you like to buy one?"

"I would like them all—"

The girl scrambled to her feet.

"All? Is this not good? They are only one thousand each, and they are good. It is real flour—wholemeal, not rye. There are nine left—"

"I have not got the price of even one." Frossia spoke through her teeth. "You should not be out selling such things. Not in the streets. . . . Don't you know so many of us are hungry." And she added slowly, "I have not eaten today." She raised her voice. "Please run away. . . . Why, I meant to steal them when you were asleep. Then you woke up. Why did you wake?" and she shrank back, feeling a soft bun thrust into her fingers. "No. . . . I can't accept alms—"

The girl said in a voice of a solemn middle-aged woman who had seen too many suns set in her life:

"This is not alms. You give alms to beggars and strangers. None of us are that to one another. At least, we should not be. My grandmother says that. I try to believe it. Please eat. I must see you eat, and I will tell you something: flour is scarce and dear, butter and oil are scarcer and dearer. And I have someone at home—never mind who," she hurried on almost angrily though Frossia, her mouth full, was far from asking questions, "someone with a rotten lung. You can help with butter, and if you turn flour into buns, you can get butter if you are clever enough. Now you understand. . . . But it is all wearisome, difficult." She sighed. "Here is another bun for you. I can spare you another, and no more. Otherwise there may not be enough money for the butter." She almost threw the bun at Frossia and screamed, "Don't come near me. . . . I shall not let you have any more," and, tray in her arms, she ran off towards Nicholas Bridge, and Frossia ate her second bun slowly and carefully, mindful of the tiniest crumb.

As she was opening the door of the Zabalkansky, she heard the deep voice of Pavel Pavlovich:

"Yes, that is just what I think also. Years later, when all of this will have simmered down, people will write profound books about the civil war, and the economic upheaval, and this and that and the other, vast, grand topics all of those, and few will ever know that the absolutely unimportant people had their lives to live, and

158

lived them somehow, anyhow, and did some work, too, and never really cursed anyone or anything."

"Perhaps some would like to," murmured a woman's voice from a dim corner. "Pavel Pavlovich, I am fifty-eight. I have no feet left. I stood in that queue for five hours, and not a morsel of bread was left when my turn came—"

From the room beyond boomed Elena Ivanovna's comfortable fat voice:

"Poor dear soul. . . . Don't we all know them—those queues? Never you mind, Anna Vasilievna, I have put aside a piece of horseflesh for you, nicely broiled, too. And here is your syrup, dear soul. I am sorry I could not fill your glass tonight, but there is not very much, and Pavel Pavlovich will pay for it, the Lord bless him. And now"—she came nearer and stood in candlelight, shapeless, heavy and kindly—"*dobrye ludi*, good people, what do you say to a song? We have talked enough, and the talk ended in those infernal queues, the Devil twist them. A good song, Semyon Antonovich, think of one . . ." She paused. "What about 'Haz Bulat'?"

> "*Haz Bulat udaloy,*
> *Bedna saklia tvoya,*
> *Zolotoyu kaznoy*
> *Ya osypliu tebia* . . .
> I shall give you my horse,
> I shall give you my dirk,
> I shall give you my gun,
> And you give me your wife.
> You are old, white of hair,
> What is her life with you?
> At the dawn of her years
> You will mar all her joy . . .
> She has promised herself
> Unto me evermore,
> And she swore by Allah
> That she has no love for you—"
> "Prince, your story is clear,
> But in vain it is told . . .
> Go inside and admire her,
> Your beloved of a day . . .
> See her sleep in my hut,
> With my dirk in her breast . . .
> Yes, I killed her, my prince,
> I, half-blinded by tears,
> And my kiss came to die
> On her lips . . ."

The conventional Caucasian ballad with its motif of treachery, murder and passion as wild as the storm and as gentle as almond blossom on the slopes of Kazbek, spilled its plaintive notes all over the dim rooms. It died, and they sang another, a cheerful Volga song, about ripening wheat and cornflowers and skylarks and a beautiful girl, and Elena Ivanovna went round, trimming her candles very carefully. She came on Frossia and peered at her hard.

"I thought I heard your voice—"

Someone found a chair for her. Through the uncurtained square windows the September evening looked in, wet and murky, but gratefully mild. Pavel Pavlovich would not have another song, and Elena Ivanovna could not silence his thundering voice.

"Yes," he insisted, "it is among such unimportant people that life goes on."

"Why," began a different voice, not so much plaintive as obstinately sour, "in a queue today—" But Elena Ivanovna said firmly: "No more about queues. Tell me—any of you—what has happened to Klava Voronova?"

"She is still working at her factory. Why?"

"She looks shriveled," said Elena Ivanovna, "and I feel troubled about her. Grisha's hip must be worse. He ought to go to the south somewhere. Igor Vladimirovich." She raised her voice. "Ah, Igor Vladimirovich, Grisha should go down to the south. Would he get a permit?"

"Any day," answered a voice now familiar to Frossia. "Yes, Elena Ivanovna, you need not feel troubled. I shall explain to Klava about going to the Health Commission. It is quite simple. They are not hard people, they will understand the position."

Someone said: "No, they are not hard people. I had some internal trouble. They examined me most kindly. They gave me a chit. Would you believe me—I got a permit for half a pound of sugar for five months. They said I needed sugar. . . . Yes, they are kindly people—"

Elena Ivanovna spoke almost roughly: "Now there you go again, Peter Semenovich. I said no more food was to be discussed—"

"I heard something interesting today," piped a shrill young voice from the dimmest corner, "from Nikolashka. About a man, a Tchekist, a name like Cherny, I think. He is a peasant really, not a soldier at all. He is a queer man. Nikolashka said Cherny had one hundred children out with him one Sunday, took them to the Summer Gardens, and explained to them all about lime trees. Nikolashka says he knows all about trees. Is it not strange?" Frossia heard a smothered titter. "A Tchekist and a peasant, and so fond of trees. Almost incredible—"

"He is a strange man," offered someone else. "I have heard about him."

"He is real," said Frossia, and was silent, herself astonished at her remark.

Elena Ivanovna had finished trimming the candles. Now she arranged her heavy bulk in an armchair and said dreamily:

"Well, I have a new job. At the Gutuevsky Orphanage. There are sixty children there. But the house has no roof. All burnt away. So I went to the Domkom. He said: 'Of course, children can't sleep there, you must have another house.' He gave me a chit for a count's mansion in Morskaya Street. I went there this morning. The roof is all right, but the stairs have no banisters, and the house is three stories high. I went back to the Domkom. He said: 'Keep to the ground floor. It is big enough for sixty children.' I said: 'How can I keep them from scrambling up the stairs and tumbling off?' A woman stood there. She said: 'What would it matter? There will be fewer to live, fewer to feed.' The Domkom said: 'Do you think so? We must save every child. When we get tired and useless, they will be there, fresh and strong. . . . And we are getting tired, all of us.' Well, he gave his orders. Now they are making new banisters for the house."

They talked about children, and the Cossacks, and Finland, and the coming disarmament in Europe. The candles began burning low. Elena Ivanovna yawned, stood up, and said: "Good night, *dobrye ludi*," and the Zabalkansky dispersed.

2

Since the party at Moyka, Maria Nikolaevna had not been herself. It had hurt her to meet Lilian and Serge. The dramatic climax of the gathering had frightened her more than any raids had ever done. She felt that the least activity on her part would now lay her open to perils she might not analyze or name. So she did nothing. She would get up, put on her shabbily quilted dressing gown, and sit by the window, her eyes on the narrow grimy sill. It was cold in the flat, the Captain could not get any logs for the iron stove, and Maria Nikolaevna sat shivering, huddled in her dressing gown, her feet thrust into valenki with many holes in them. She had an old astrakhan muff, and she kept her hands in it. Sometimes she took them out, blew on them, and laid the muff on the window sill as though she had no further use for its warmth. Her fingers

161

would then go numb and purple, but for hours she would leave the shabby muff on the window sill, and sit, her poor cold hands idle in her lap. Sometimes, her back to the room, she talked to the Captain. But he could not always understand her. Maria Nikolaevna no longer spoke in phrases. Separate words seemed adequate for her, and the Captain at first tried to understand what she said, but he soon had to give it up. There seemed no imaginable links between lilac and herrings, ivory cardcases and soap, mothers-in-law and cowbells. The words were all nouns. Maria Nikolaevna had no further use for the other parts of speech. "Have your gruel, my love," pleaded the Captain, and she replied: "Necklace, waterfall, snow, agates, Wiborg pretzeln, nightmare, nightmare." This last word she repeated so often that the Captain came to guess she was now living in a nightmare he might not penetrate, and he devoted himself to the tasks she could no longer do, tiring out his sapped flesh so that at the end of the day he might go to sleep for sheer exhaustion. He now dressed and washed Maria Nikolaevna, he bought and bartered, cooked and swept and mended. He conquered his earlier aversion and mistrust, and often called on Nikolashka for the loan of a saucepan, a spoon, or a match. But he would have nobody come to the flat. When friends and acquaintances inquired after Maria Nikolaevna, the Captain looked troubled enough, but answered politely and briefly: "Well, well, she is very tired, very tired. . . ." He would not have anyone see her by the window sill, remote and lost to all things, muttering her strange chaplet of separate words.

Captain Parnikov had no adroitness in him. He lost matches and needles, he broke their few pieces of crockery, he often forgot things, he dusted the room most inadequately. He sometimes went to the market and, having got there, realized that he was empty-handed, so that he must tramp all the way home again and collect whatever he had decided to offer for barter. It was getting more and more difficult for Captain Parnikov to think about anything since his entire mind was focused on Maria Nikolaevna. Sometimes, having washed her, however sketchily, and dressed her in the old purple dressing gown, he would take hold of her thin hand and say with deep feeling: "My love, my little pigeon, I have had a dream about out honeymoon. Do you remember putting salt into your lemonade at Ymatra?" He would repeat his words and try not to wince when Maria Nikolaevna spoke, her clouded eyes fixed on the window sill: "Silk, black cat, spoons, sofa, gloves, nightmare, nightmare . . ."

Then Captain Parnikov would let go her hand, and remember

the duster and the broom. Diligently he swept the dust from one place to another. Maria Nikolaevna kept still in her chair. Captain Parnikov slipped away into the kitchen, came back, and thought of the next task to be done. But never would he keep away for long. He always feared that after a lengthy absence he might come and find a vacant armchair by the window. She was not there really, she hardly noticed him, she barely looked at him, but she was all he had, and he cherished her so much.

3

Frossia, walking down Nevsky Prospect one afternoon, ran into Cherny, and vanquished her pride by asking him:

"Is there a job you think I could do?"

He was in such a hurry that he barely stopped. He measured her with a glance she could not interpret, and said:

"Yes, at the Goelro. . . . Typists are wanted there. Go if you like. Tell them I have sent you," and hurried away before she could murmur her thanks.

So she was working once again, typing endless intricate technical specifications; but in the flat at Moshkov Lane things were just the same. One evening she carried a platter of broiled fish to the table and said briefly: "Come and eat," and Michael came and ate, and then produced a crumpled cigarette. She stared at the gold tip in silence. He lit it very leisurely.

"I am tired," Frossia said, annoyed at not being offered her share of the cigarette. "My eyes hurt. Let us turn the light out, shall we? The Goelro was a bedlam. I never stopped typing from nine till three, nine to three, Michael. And I hurried and spoilt so many sheets of paper, and paper is scarce. . . . I know I can't spell. . . . Those things about electricity are so hard to spell properly—"

He smoked on. He was not listening. "I am talking to a lovely doll," she thought angrily. He smoked and stared at an old coffee stain on the red-checked cloth. She said for the third time: "From nine to three, Michael! Six hours without a stop! They gave me a bowl of rye gruel after two. I ate it an hour later. It was cold and lumpy, but I left the bowl clean. The Goelro is so alive. . . . I like it better than that dim little office at the *Gosizdat*. Nobody talks any sickening propaganda stuff. It is all so real and practical and tremendous, though I find it muddling. I know nothing about electricity."

"Yes," said Michael and then, "I mean no—"

"Shall we turn the light out? I told you my eyes were hurting tonight—"

"Well, you might wait until I have packed—"

"Till you have what?"

"Packed. Sorry, Frossia, but I can't stand much more of it. Now you have got a job. It will end soon, and we will begin all over again. Frossia, you must understand that I simply could not be hungry again—"

Weariness left her for disgust.

"You could always get work. Hack work, donkey work, any work. What does it matter? Do you think I am in love with the Goelro and the infernal typewriter? I would like to sit and dream dreams—but dreams will not give you much of a supper."

He smoked on in silence.

"Where does this cigarette come from?" she challenged him. "Have you earned it?"

He did not answer.

"Well?" and suddenly she glanced at his feet and saw his new shoes, surprising shoes, almost new, of patent leather. "How did you pay for them? You have no money—"

"I did not pay for anything. How could I pay? I merely went to Bi-Ba-Bo, and I met a very intelligent woman, and we had a business talk. Her name is Alina Touras."

"Who believes her husband to have been a Lett—"

"So you know her?"

"I have met her once or twice. You don't forget anyone like Touras once you have met them."

"No," Michael shouted suddenly. "You must not talk so bitterly. What does anything matter? You said so yourself. Well, here is the whole truth for you, and you have wormed it out of me. She has rich clients, I don't know where such women come from, and I don't care much. I just will not go hungry again, and that is all."

She smiled.

"Don't smile." Michael crushed the tiny tip of the cigarette and leapt to his feet. "How can you smile? Curse me, hit me, tell me I am vile, but stop smiling at me—"

"But you don't think yourself vile. . . . And why should I curse you? You had better pack. I am tired—"

He moved away, and she knew he was angry: she had cheated him of a richly emotional scene. There she sat, quiet, almost indifferent.

"I had once thought that you cared," he began huskily, "and you don't seem to mind my going—"

"Why should I? If food and drink alone must be essential to hold you, I have no hold over anything except a husk." She, too, got up. "Please go and pack at once—"

But he hung back.

"This must not be a good-by. There is your lovely old story, Frossia. We have never even been near the Mariinsky Theatre. Madame Touras has friends all over the place, and it might be possible—"

"You are not even a Petrushka." Frossia spoke from a distance. "Poor Petrushka did suffer—in very truth."

He went a dull red. "And this is your manner of saying good-by?"

"This is not a good-by, Michael. Good-bys are clean, final things— usually. . . . Even a vague *au revoir* has something nice and poignant in it. Here." She turned away from him, she found more pleasure in looking at the heliotrope curtains than in considering his face. "Here is nothing to say good-by to. Just a husk. . . . I know people do say good-by to inanimate things, to a house, a wood, a pond or a picture, but differently after they had put a bit of their own spirit into them. You are all flesh, Michael. Beautiful flesh, clean and supple once again, but of less importance than poor Petrushka's sawdust. Madame Touras will doubtless pamper your flesh, bed it in good linen or silk, perhaps. Bed it so softly that all of you will go to sleep all the deeper. . . . Go. . . . Why should I be talking to mere flesh?"

He shrugged. "You are rather insulting. We need not talk any more. Packing will not take me long, but, Frossia, I have no brushes or anything. May I borrow your dressing case for a short time—?"

"Borrow it for its jade and gold." She appraised him scornfully. "It would not much matter if you had it, but it used to belong to my mother, Michael, I could not let it go there."

"I will keep it clean," he pleaded. "Frossia, I feel really famished for beautiful things. Please let me take it."

"No." She stamped her foot. "Go, go at once, will you—"

He slammed the door. Frossia turned out the light. Her temples burned with a dull stubborn ache. She was still looking at a paper she had typed seventeen times over that morning. The word "coefficient" kept dancing before her. Did one spell it with one "f" or two, and a girl at a table next to hers, kept laughing in a brittle unkindly fashion. She was a thin, roughly rouged girl, with clumsy stumpy fingers. "Goodness, *grajdanka*, where were you educated? Dancing and French, I suppose nothing else was ever taught you. Of course, it is spelt with a double 'f,' and don't you dare spoil another sheet, curse you!" She spoke with a heavy Novgorod accent, her o's biting into you like so many hard bullets. Frossia sat in her chair and thought of the Goelro. She heard Michael shuffle outside, and ignored the noise. Presently all sound was stilled. A door opened somewhere and was closed rather furtively, and she sighed as though acknowledging herself free of a nightmare, and spent the night huddled in her chair, but, in the morning, her red-lidded eyes peering about her few possessions in the cubbyhole back of the drawing room, Frossia came on a gap on the shelf. She stroked the wood thoughtfully. She dressed herself and went to the Goelro. In the late afternoon she found her way to Sergievskaya Street. The door of the flat was opened by a lumpy piece of a girl, her face unwashed and her eyes faintly suspicious. Frossia asked for Michael in a loud, hard voice, and was ushered into a room which—for her— was full of ghosts, and sat there, hands clenched. She heard murmurs and steps outside and, presently, Michael came in.

"You are going to give me back my dressing case," she said simply.

"I—I—did not—I mean—"

"Unless I have it back, I shall go straight to Gorokhovaya Street and inform them against you," Frossia said so firmly that his face blanched, and in a few minutes she had the dressing case returned to her, and went out without another look or word.

She reached the Summer Gardens, and sat on a bench not far from the great wrought iron gates, facing the Neva. She sat very still, the slim shagreen case on her knees. Presently she opened it, and caressed one beautifully finished detail after another. Jade, gold, and crystal shone at her, but the brief autumn day was hurrying on, she saw a keeper amble towards the gates, and she knew she must leave the gardens. The quay lay deserted. She crossed it, and leaned against the rough cold granite of the parapet. It was a very still evening of shadow and counter-shadow, and the pale green air lent an other-worldly grace to the half-ruined wharf on the opposite bank. On such an evening Frossia might once have found herself communing with the beloved city, its stones and waters, its strange cold courage, its superbly poised defiance of the spirit of fury in nature and in man. But now she was far away from all such things. She remembered the fussiness of the day now behind her, the busy, noisy day at the Goelro, her own incessant and stupid spelling blunders, the hostility of her neighbor, the crude taunts and roughly worded contempt for her manners and habits. I wonder if Elena Ivanovna might some day find me a job with her babies. I think I could do something with them . . . Frossia thought desultorily.

Then, all suddenly, she remembered what she held in her arms. She raised the lid once again, almost able to imagine her mother's thin, beautifully shaped hands moving among the jade and the gold. Then she closed it down swiftly and bent forward. The next moment an oblong green shape cut through the darkening air. Frossia listened to the splash, and knew that, had Michael kept her company that evening, there might have been a louder splash, and, probably, a shout heard by none except herself. It frightened her to sheer immobility. "Why, I don't hate him enough to kill him, and killing coldly—without any hatred, without any feeling even, is ghastly, unthinkable. . . . Why? Have I ceased to live then? Have I ceased to dream? Do I want to walk in a nightmare?" she asked herself, and knew she could not grope towards any answer. Slowly she moved on past Trinity Bridge where a bored sentry challenged her, and she must fumble in her pocket and produce her sadly bethumbed labor book.

"I am on my way home—"

"Better run for it, *grajdanka*. Listen—" From across Mars Square came a thud, the dry sharp noise of a shot, soon to be swallowed in the louder sound of several running feet. "Convicts," the man explained laconically, "those who escaped from prisons back in 1917. We are rounding them up. Not an evening for a woman to be out," he added severely, and under the dim light of a street lamp Frossia read the rough kindness of his bearded face. "Run for it, *grajdanka*," he counseled once again, and she darted away, past the great curtained face of Marble Palace. For reasons she could not explain, the whole scene grew inimical. In the ever thickening dark, least movement, faintest sound, all hinted at unpredictable dangers, and stories of unlawful depredations, launched by numberless outlaws at large in the city, now crowded into Frossia's mind and tormented her. The air seemed bristling with guns at the ready, gleaming Finnish knives and short Circassian daggers, held by hands which would not stop short at mere wounding. "But all our days are lived in danger—I must not let go, I must not be foolish," Frossia reminded herself, and forced her feet to carry her farther and farther. Behind her, a vague tumult grew and grew always from the direction of Mars Square, and, above the general din, a sharp report flashed its own brief noise here and there. She ran on, halted at the mouth of Moshkov Lane, and found the small narrow street picketed by Red militiamen, gruff but not unkindly. "There is trouble going on up Millionnaya Street," they explained and insisted on her going elsewhere. "I live here," Frossia murmured, and saw them shrug. The fitful light of two lanterns picked out their tired

bearded faces. She realized that fatigue, rather than firearms, pre-
cluded all arguments, and turned away, back into Palace Quay.
The day's turmoiled, uneven scene had wearied her also, and she
thought she might wander on till she could find some temporary
sanctuary beneath the gateway of a palace along the quay, and
there wait for the ceasing of trouble. But Frossia had not walked
another hundred yards when she heard the running of hobnailed
feet behind her. She gasped, did not turn round, and ran.

She had never run so hard in her life, and she could not tell
why she was running. The self-control of years had slipped off her,
her behavior was shaped by nothing except the pounding hot panic
within her. It began to drizzle, the granite pavement grew danger-
ously slippery, but Frossia never missed her footing. Her feet were
wings, and she was a bird flying from one unknown towards another, in the wet glistening dark, along a quay she knew so well,
her face burning, her hands clammy, the roof of her mouth as dry
as a piece of well-tanned leather.

At last she halted, her breath utterly failing her, and listened,
and could hear nothing except the ceaseless plash of water against
the stone girdle of the river. Her face was burning, she laid both
hands on the granite, then pressed them to her hot cheeks, and
moved forward at a normal pace.

Presently she came to Nicholas Bridge and made for the house
where the Parnikovs lived. She was more than uncertain of her
welcome, but she knew that a return to Moshkov Lane would be
unwise.

The street was lost in darkness. Frossia carefully picked her way.
Here, in Vasilyev Island, the road and pavement alike were pitted
with holes, and running would have been impossible. She reached
the house more by guesswork than any sense of real direction. A
tiny lamp was burning in the narrow doorway, and she climbed the
slippery stairs. The door into the Parnikovs' flat was closed, she
knocked once, twice, and then waited, aware that her fingers were
shaking. Nobody answered her. She tried the handle. The door
opened, but all was dark within, and her call: "May I come in?
It is Frossia—" returned to her in a hollow echo from the passage
beyond the hall. She strained her hearing, but no other sound
reached her. Then she was startled by the noise of booted feet
trampling down the stairs. She recognized Nikolashka, and knew
she was ready to throw her trembling arms round his neck.

"I came here. . . . There is something happening off the Summer Gardens. I could not get to Moshkov Lane. I thought Maria
Nikolaevna would not mind my spending the night on the sofa,

but they don't seem to be here. What has happened? Have they gone?"

Nikolashka said awkwardly: "I will tell you, Euphrosynia Pavlovna, but not here, not on the stairs. Come to my place. Why, your coat is soaked all through—"

"It has been raining—"

Upstairs Nikolashka put out the lantern, lit the oil lamp, and produced a generous chunk of bread. Frossia was hungry, but she shook her head at the food.

"You said you would tell me. What has happened?"

All at once she felt dismayed and contrite. The Parnikovs had not been close friends, they had disapproved and kept aloof, they had frowned at her. But they were people, not just names, and in a world where one moved in fear of things known and unknown, least durable links seemed made of purest gold. Frossia repeated impatiently: "You said you would tell me—"

"It is Maria Nikolaevna," began Nikolashka. "She got—so very tired. The Captain could do nothing with her, and he would not tell anyone. Well, this afternoon I came back and told them they had better keep indoors—because of that trouble with the escaped convicts, you know, and she heard what I said." Nikolashka coughed uneasily. "You see, Euphrosynia Pavlovna, for weeks now Maria Nikolaevna had not spoken to anyone, not even to the Captain. She just sat by the window and kept as still as though she were made of stone. But this afternoon she heard what I said, and she spoke. She said it was her business to make peace in the world, she must put an end to all that nightmare, that was what she said, Euphrosynia Pavlovna, and the Captain could not dissuade her. She put on her coat and shawl."

"Well?"

"Of course, I followed them. She made for Palace Bridge, and the Captain walked behind her. There I had to leave them. The Captain asked me to go back. I believe they crossed the bridge. Maria Nikolaevna kept stumbling all the way, she had not been out of the house for weeks, she had no strength in her. I don't think she knew what was happening, and I had to be careful of my own words. You know, Euphrosynia Pavlovna, they never trusted me because of my work at the bread depôt—"

"We must go and find them."

"In the dark? We shall never find them in the dark—"

"No . . . Perhaps not . . . We must wait till the morning. It is no use trying to find anyone in the dark, Nikolashka."

"Will you stay here then?"

"Yes."

The room was bare, untidy, and not too warm. Nikolashka fetched some dirty blankets from an adjoining cubbyhole, apologized for the cold, the chaos, and the dust, and asked if she would mind sitting in the dark. "I have hardly any kerosene left, and winter is round the corner—"

"I don't mind anything," Frossia answered.

She sat huddled in the blankets. They smelt of straw, mildew, and dust. But they were warm enough. Nikolashka blew out the lamp, and the smell of kerosene wafted all over the room.

"It is a queer life—" he sighed. "Are you warm enough, Euphrosynia Pavlovna?"

"Yes. Thank you."

She was to tired that she would have fallen asleep on a wet pavement. She felt that she would not mind a thunderbolt bursting into the room. She remembered that she was due at the Goelro at nine in the morning. She would work from nine to three, and try to make fewer mistakes. "Coefficient has two 'f's' in it," Frossia murmured and slept.

Nikolashka's hand on her shoulder woke her. The dawn had painted the room a dirty, uncertain gray. It was bitterly cold. Frossia shivered and tried to swallow the boiling water Nikolashka brought in a thick yellow mug.

The streets were wet, unfriendly, and almost empty except for an occasional militiaman. Neither mentioned directions to the other, but they made their way to Palace Bridge, turned left, and presently reached the outskirts of Mars Square. At its farthest end, close to Swan Canal, they saw a picket of sentries, and Nikolashka stopped and asked: "What are we to do now, Euphrosynia Pavlovna? I cannot see them anywhere—neither the Captain nor Maria Nikolaevna."

"We will ask the men. Maria Nikolaevna would not have got into any trouble. She meant no harm—"

Mars Square, its cobbles torn up here and there, was a sea of gray-brown mud which in places reached almost to their ankles. Behind them the ocher face of Paul Barracks stood blind and indifferent. Ahead the gaunt lime trees of Summer Gardens swayed in the cold wind. Here and there a gray-white detail of a bridge or statue broke in among the darkly lichened trunks, and the silver-gray winding sash of Swan Canal gleamed dully at a distance when suddenly the gray morning slipped away, the woolen skies turned diffident blue, and pale autumnal sun rose above the stark desolation of the great park so that the bare trees, the dirty gray marble, the sullen waters, each and all were clothed in such loveli-

170

ness that Frossia must needs stand still and look. But Nikolashka urged her to go on.

The sentries questioned them. Their replies were halting enough. They had come searching for two friends. Frossia described them as best she could, Nikolashka supplying various details. One of the sentries nodded. Then Frossia saw something like a mound covered with odds and ends of sacking. The covering was not adequate. Here, a man's hairy hand lay bedded in soft brown mud, there a boot. . . . She looked away. The sentry was saying in the soft sing-song voice of a man from the southern provinces: "Yes, citizens, we got four of them last night, and an old woman was mixed up with them. We don't know whether we got her or they did. Anyway," he added, clumsily trying to be kind, "she is well out of it by the look of her," and he tore off part of the sacking. "The lorry will be here in a few moments—"

Maria Nikolaevna was not lying in mud: they had put some rags under her. Her shabby coat was unbuttoned, and the drab brown shawl across her shoulders was soaked in blood. Her hat was off, and the small face, its unseeing eyes opened to the pale sun, was that of a child gone to sleep in a strange place. She lay, shrunken, defenseless, but no longer bewildered. Gently Frossia put back the roughly improvised pall.

"But was she all alone?" insisted Nikolashka.

"There was an old man also. He saw her. . . . He did not come near. . . . The Square was cordoned off by then. . . . He went off again." The soldier gestured towards Millionnaya Street. "A quiet old man . . . He looked dazed or something. . . . She never spoke to him."

"He may have gone to Moshkov Lane," said Frossia to Niko-lashka. "Let us go."

"The lorries are coming," the sentry reminded them, and Frossia turned back.

"But we are coming back." She spoke very earnestly. "We are her friends. Please wait for us till we come back," and the sentry promised to wait.

In Moshkov Lane they found the front door ajar. In the room with the heliotrope curtains they found Captain Parnikov on the sofa, his face turned towards the wall, and Nikolashka ran up, touched him, and said to Frossia over his shoulder: "He could not leave her behind, could he, Euphrosynia Pavlovna?"

He had not been hit. His clothes, however shabby, looked neat enough. His face looked tired as though he had wandered so far that he just could not go any further, and Frossia sank on the floor by the sofa. You could not offer pity to the living, she said to herself fiercely, but the dead were different, you could give them pity and prayers and love. . . .

"Nikolashka." She would have cried if she had any tears to shed. "Nikolashka," she said so softly that the giant had to bend his head to her face to hear her at all, "he came here—from Mars Square—he knew she was dead, and he came to an empty place, and he could not go anywhere else—and he was all alone, Nikolashka, all alone—"

"We all die alone, Euphrosynia Pavlovna. Death is an important business, nobody can share it with us, except the Lord who made us. . . ." Here he changed his voice: "Now you have a wash, Euphrosynia Pavlovna, and go on to the Goelro. I shall see to everything. I promise to come and fetch you at the Goelro, four o'clock, did you say? and we will come here, and you gather your belongings, and I think I know of a quiet perch for you. You won't mind living in Maly Prospect, not too slummy for you, is it, Euphrosynia Pavlovna? Now off you go, the living must work no matter what happens, that is what my dear Irina Nikolaevna always says. And mind you work hard today, Euphrosynia Pavlovna, don't you be idle for a single moment today." And he bustled about, leading her away from the stilled room.

"I shall work hard, Nikolashka," Frossia promised.

4

Presently a lorry drove to Mars Square and then on to Moshkov Lane, and later deposited some of its burden at a hospital along one of the lesser quays. The wind rose in the afternoon, and the angry plashing of the water came through the small opened windows of a mortuary. Maria Nikolaevna and Captain Parnikov lay side by side, the four convicts at a distance from them. Nikolashka spent a busy day and arranged for the funeral in a double grave at Smolensky cemetery on Vasilyev Island, and paid a Kiev-Pechersky monk for two *panikhida* at the small Abbey chapel off Nicholas Quay, and ran all over the place, buying wreaths of such late flowers as could be found, and two garlands of pine branches, and ordering a coffin wide enough for the two. Then, having arranged everything, he went to wait for Frossia outside the Goelro. Together they went to Moshkov Lane, Frossia's few possessions were soon packed, she handed the key and a brief inventory to the man at the Domkom, and then silent and thoughtful, she followed Nikolashka to a new home and a new life. On the way, Nikolashka explained to her about the *panikhida*. The first was to be sung at five in the after-noon. He looked at her sideways as if uncertain of her decision, and she replied swiftly and warmly: "Of course, I am coming, Nikolashka. I am so glad, so grateful to you for thinking about everything."

The dark tiny chapel was full of candles and the satisfying smell of burning wax. They stood alone for a few moments till a small door opened in the richly painted wall, and seven monks came in to chant the *panikhida*. They prayed for God's servants, Ivan and Maria, that all their sins, witting and unwitting, be forgiven them, and the gentle intimate use of Christian names comforted Frossia. They prayed for light and sunshine for those two in a place remote from all sickness, grief, and disease, and for their entering the company of God's saints, and, finally, they came to the moment when all things temporal and all things eternal were mingled into one, as their deep muted voices chanted *Eternal Memory*. So are we all held together, thought Frossia, kneeling on the stone floor, in God's memory where not a single blade of grass, let alone a human soul, can stay forgotten, and she listened to the two words, filling the chapel, stealing away from its dim walls, and spreading themselves across the river, towards the sea, towards the west, towards the un-seen city of God. Two words only . . . *"Vechnaya pamiat," "vech-naya pamiat."* And when the last echo had gone and the remem-brance of her friends was, as she believed, firmly graven in the gar-den of God, Frossia begged Nikolashka for a scrap of paper and a pencil, drew near a candle, and scribbled several names, heading her list with the words "For the rest of their souls," and handed her paper to the tall monk by the door: "Could these be remembered in this place?"

The monk took the paper, glanced at it, and bowed to Frossia.

"But I have no money," she stammered.

"They shall be prayed for," the monk said kindly before Niko-lashka had had time to whisper a surname in his ear, and the monk bowed again.

"They would have been prayed for, had they been strangers," he said to Frossia.

5

The house was off Maly Prospect in Vasilyev Island. It stood on a narrow dismal quay facing Little Neva. It was a queer timbered house, with clumsily carved balconies, and a perilous outer stair-case. The rooms were small and low-ceilinged, it had no electric light, and the water must, of course, be pumped from a well outside, but the two rooms Nikolashka had secured for Frossia faced west and the river.

She had not lived there a week before she had a guest one evening. It was Cherny.

Cherny lived at the other end of the city, in one of the several Christmas Streets, towards the Zabalkansky Prospect. He worked in Gorokhovaya, and Frossia was astonished to see him. Her world, as she came to learn, knew him well. Nikolashka feared and admired him. Pavel Pavlovich spoke words of unstinted praise about him. Sometimes Frossia heard Cherny's name mentioned at the Zabalkansky, he had talked of trees to some children one Sunday, he had got someone a permit to go into the country, and Igor Vladimirovich thought Cherny could arrange for Grisha to go to the south. Frossia had met him quite casually, asked for a job, and he had sent her to the Goelro where she was still working. They had had a wild encounter, she had struck him, he had humiliated her. He still annoyed her. His sharp sense of caste, his unbounded fanaticism, his very habits, all rebelled against her. He often poured scorn on her accent, her customs, the very shape of her fingers, the way she wore her shabby clothes. . . ."

"Spit . . . Swear . . . Be rude for once. . . . Wipe your nose on your sleeve—"

"Need you be childish?" she wondered, and sometimes he would look dark and menacing.

"Nikolashka says that you are all right, that you are in love with life. But you are like milk and water. You don't like us, you can't like us. . . . All the same, you are no idler."

"No. I sawed wood for an hour last night. My arms are aching. I am too tired to dream—"

"Can you not get back to the real?"

They were walking along the Nevsky, past Kazan Place, with its enormous, over-ornamented statue of Catherine the Great, and Cherny shook his great fist at the granite plinth.

"That is what you are after . . . eighteenth centry, all grace and furbelows and emptiness—except for the French Revolution—"

"Comrade Cherny, could you not get off the platform? I am not clever in your way. I can't argue. But I am sick of propagandist idioms. Russia is neither Tzarist nor communist to me—just a country, the country to love and live for. Ought this not to be enough? I am sorry. I am so dense, but all this talk of yours about internationalism is like Esperanto to me—"

"What do you mean?"

"Is it not clear? I am sorry for some things which are gone. I am

174

human. I am also sorry for some of the things which are happening today, but I could never work myself into a passion about either side. They are all passing expressions, the rest will remain—I mean, the country—"

"Passing expressions! Why, the country is going through birth pangs—" Annoyed, Cherny lectured her long and fiercely. Technical terms flew in the air, and Frossia felt weary after a day at the Goelro. Then as suddenly as he had started, he stopped, and became a tongue-tied peasant aware of a woman's face through a latticed window.

"You have made me late for my meeting," he muttered, strode away, and reappeared at the Little Neva house a few days later.

It was a Sunday. Frossia had used her rare leisure for a few household tasks whose simplicity was now made difficult by several things. The timbered house shared its pump with six of its neighbors, and Frossia possessed but two small jugs. Laundering in cold water with sand soap was a slow business. She bent over the basin, eyes closed, seeing a fat blue and white cake of Zhukov's kitchen soap, and stood up, wringing a woefully patched shift when Cherny appeared in the doorway. She had hoped for an hour at the Zabalkansky, but the brief dole of daylight would be over by the time Cherny had done talking. She hung the shift on two homemade pegs by the window, wiped the chair, and invited him to sit down.

"Have you come to continue the argument about Catherine the Great?"

He would not sit down.

"What are you talking about? Do you not see what you have done to me since the day I met you? Do you want me to go down on my knees before you like any old régime gallant? I am not made of such stuff." And he added somberly, "You would despise me if I were—"

Frossia remembered another article still lying at the bottom of the basin. She pulled out a small blue linen handkerchief and began wringing it out.

"Shall I put an iron on?" he offered.

"You can't iron things when they are wet. Besides, I have no iron. It is superfluous—" She hung the handkerchief, picked up the basin, and went to empty it in a hole in the back yard. When she came back, she found Cherny astride the window sill.

"Frossia—"

"Well? I have heard you. What could I say? It is like a thunderbolt. How could I notice anything? You have always mocked me—

175

except once, and then you were insulting. . . . I thought you saw an enemy in me, and now you come, asking so much—"

"Much? I want all, all."

"And why all?"

"Because it is fair. . . . Because I mean to give you all—"

"You could not," Frossia said with a strangely deep conviction. "You could not. Nobody can give all."

"You have never loved a man. Otherwise you would not talk such nonsense—"

"Nobody can give all or take all—for that matter. All is not ours to give. We think we have given our all, and it is only a bit, and we imagine that bit to be the whole, and we are wounded when the bit gets broken—"

"But I do mean what I say." Now he was shouting at her. "See, I shall give you all—I could not help myself."

Frossia sat down cupping her face in both hands. She must speak slowly, because she was mustering her thoughts all the time. Some of them came to her mind, clothed in a strange fashion. Almost she wondered if it could be her own voice uttering the words. Also she must speak gently—however alien his approach, she could not help seeing his sincerity.

"Forgive me, Cherny, but you have the body in your mind when you talk like that. And love cannot be limited by the body. Dip a pin in poison, prick your flesh with the pin, and the body dies. It is so small, of so little consequence."

"Frossia—"

"I know. . . . I may be tiresome and slow, but I have not done yet. You say you are ready to give me your all. There are so many things in you which will be denied me. Some I cannot take. Others you may neither part with nor share. . . . Your frenzied fear of treason in hidden places, your enthusiasm over a political gospel I cannot understand, your worship of the purely technical in life. Do you remember that exhibition of new tractors in Taurida Park a few months ago? I went to see it, I was glad of them, they meant help for thousands of our Sovkhoz farms; I thought of the coming efficiency in agriculture, our peasants have deserved well of the country, and I hope Sovkhoz will do great things; but it is the land and its corn that I love and understand. Steel leaves me cold, and you are in love with the least piece of machinery. It is part of you, Cherny, you could not give me a million things which are all you."

"Because you will not take them—"

"I could not share them if I took them. And what can I give you? Leave the flesh and its business alone. I know I could give much where I loved, but even then I could not give everything. Why, that is impossible." Frossia halted, searching for fit comparisons. "Well, there you are: some time ago you found me alone, rather bemused, looking at the river, and you asked what my thoughts were. I said I was thinking of a spire caught into moonlight. I gave you but a shred of an idea. I could not tell you what—to me—lay behind the spire, the moonlight, or anything else. If I had the necessary words, they would not have said much to you."

"Wait." Cherny spoke hoarsely. "Would it be the same if you loved me?"

"How could I tell? There would be more freedom, more giving, equally more taking. But you must forgive me—I am in a great muddle—you did it all so suddenly. . . ."

"I think you are afraid of me—"

"Yes," she admitted without the least hesitation. "If you will have it so, I am afraid of your wish to possess all of me. Why, it would be like an invasion—"

He climbed down from the window sill. His lean scarred face looked all the more somber in candlelight.

"I had better go," he said slowly. "If you could only understand one simple thing—I love you."

Then Frossia's heart was moved with strange feelings, and, unaccountably, she found herself able to speak her mind without the least accent of restraint or reluctance.

"You have said it, Cherny, and you were a peasant when you said it. One simple thing. And I feel you have done me great homage by saying it, and I thank you for it. Truly, it is one simple thing. But do you not see that twisted atoms, like myself, are robbed of all simple things? Love, life, death, service of one's country—they are all plain and beautiful to you. You may be tormented, but your agony must always be different from ours. Where was I when you grew in simplicity and great hardihood? I grew after the fashion of my kin and learnt my own dreams. The fashion has gone, the dream may yet become a nightmare unless I stop it. But simplicity . . . Search for it in my past. . . . Perhaps, this is my own hunger, Cherny. Yours is a different one."

A candle was burning on the rough little table. There was twilight outside along the banks of Little Neva, and there was twilight between them.

"But I love you," he repeated stubbornly. "You are unlike all the others. You are beautiful and true, you work hard, and you have neither scorn nor hatred in you."

"I am a Russian! I could neither despise nor hate my people."

He went on without listening to her, without looking at her.

"And you have suffered and not got hardened. You have been buffeted this way and that, and you still seem whole—"

"You must not overwhelm me with such homage," she cried. "At least, you do respect me."

"I could worship you—" And then, as suddenly as he had come, he went. Frossia never heard the door shut, nor his tread on the wooden staircase outside the house. She sat still. Presently she stirred, found a little milk and drank it, standing by the window. It was cold in the room, but she wanted air and wind to be about her, and she pulled at the feeble window frame, and leaned out. Someone was singing, someone was swearing, and a cat miaowed underneath the window.

Frossia sipped the milk. Presently a neighbor's sleek black cat jumped upon the window sill. Frossia turned back towards her candle and carefully measured some milk into a saucer. The cat sniffed, miaowed again, and rubbed his face against her ankles, the plumy tail curved in disdain.

"Vaska, Vaska," chided Frossia. "You won't drink the milk, I have so little left, and I cannot have Cherny, and we are both as difficult as we can be."

"Miaow," said the cat again, jumped on the nearest chair, and curled himself to peace and comfort.

The room was getting colder, but Frossia would not close the window, and, leaning forward, let the sharp air bathe her hot aching eyes.

Cherny had come and gone, and now alone and quieted, Frossia could take her small world one by one, and consider it all from a distance. There was Lilian, poor, battered, tarnished Lilian, her morals worn like a soiled, badly fitting kimono, Lilian of whom now Frossia caught an occasional glimpse in a street, at the Zabalkansky, at some food store, Lilian of whom Nikolashka had a strange story to tell. "I told her about her parents. Her husband was in the room, and she said very coldly: 'Well, you need not have come to tell me, a letter would have done,' and then, Euphrosynia Pavlovna, Serge went out and she wept like a fish, all her coldness melted." I must not lose sight of Lilian, thought Frossia, and she remembered Lilian's people, now safe against all penury and fear and darkness both of flesh and spirit, and again she saw them lying side by side, still and defenseless and somehow lovely, gone in a whirlwind they had not sown. Anna von Packen . . . Frossia dismissed her briefly: it was hard to remember Anna and to school one's self against all bitterness. There was Klava, now a thin wax candle burning on a strange altar dedicated to misgivings and fears. . . . And yet Klava is so utterly at home among the stars, marveled Frossia, and so is Grisha whom I know so little. Paulina Pavlovna, running after the exotic in her leisure moments and ministering to all but neglected babies and forgetting her own weariness among them . . . Madame Touras, extolling prostitution in words as greasy as tepid mutton broth . . . Pavel Pavlovich whom Frossia had begun to love because of his vanquished titan, an autobiography on canvas, beautiful because it was so honest. Of Michael she would not think at all. But she remembered Nikolashka, and her heart lightened. Once a merchant prince, now a humble baker, fearing hunger more than the firing squad, single-minded, large-hearted and lovable, who could never be despised even if his entire idolatry lay in the needs of his stomach . . . And Serge whom one could pity but never condemn, a grotesquely strutting marionette on a tawdrily furnished stage . . .

There was also Igor Vladimirovich, whose face Frossia could not remember clearly. He is like a dissenter, she thought. Faintly smug, and he never looks astonished, and he says such irritating things. But he is alive. They all are—except me. I still want to escape. And I blunder so often, and I feel afraid of so many things. But I am never afraid of this city, she whispered, shivered in the cold air, and so closed her window at last.

CHAPTER SIX

A DESPISED THRESHOLD

Madame Touras was saying in a soft oily voice: "Gentlemen, citizens, comrades, you are welcome to look all over the place, but I have nothing here. I respect every decree that is published. I know my duties. I have no real property. I have never forgotten that all property was nationalized some years ago. All the furniture in this place is not really mine, it belongs to the Domkom, it belongs to the State. You are welcome to everything." She finished and pressed her plump hands together.

But the thin little man in tattered khaki took no notice of her. Eight of his men were already searching the big, tawdrily furnished flat. In the room with pink satin cushions and the collection of white china ornaments, a few girls in loudly colored kimonos, bedroom slippers, and curlers in their hair, were trying not to be hysterical. Against the doorway Michael leaned, his face white. He knew that a staircase lay just beyond the doorway, and the stairs led to the street. But he kept motionless, divided between fear and curiosity.

"No, you have nothing at all," said the little man as a cupboard door swung open, and his bayonet prodded at sacks of flour. "This is nothing, this is sand, you are wise to hoard sand, citizeness." His dark face remained unsmiling.

"It is flour—" Madame Touras spoke shrilly—"but I am a very economical woman, I have always been, these are just two years' rations, citizen. Nothing more—I assure you."

"There has been no issue of flour for more than two years." The little man went on prodding among the sacks. "You may be a peasant or countess, I don't care, but people are hungry all over the place, and you are hoarding."

Michael moved away from the door.

"She is telling lies," he said thickly. "It is not hers. It was planted on her. She did not know . . . Look." He fumbled in a pocket and produced a gold-lidded scent bottle. "Do you see this? I know who had it. A whole case of them . . . She sold the case and bought the flour. She thought it would be safer if it were kept here. She came here, ask any of them. . . ." He turned round, one of the pale whimpering girls nodded, and Michael went on: "It is true. Make your inquiries. I cannot expect you to believe me. It is a girl called Bozert, jeweler's daughter—"

"Not so fast," said the thin little man. He had a notebook in his hands, but he was not sure about his letters and he put things down very slowly, spelling out every word. He had done his duty; having heard about food being hoarded in a certain flat at No. 39 Sergievskaya Street, he had paid his call and had found flour. Now different information was being given him, he must verify all the details, and the flat and its owner could wait. Brusquely he ordered his men to take away the sacks, and left, saying he would be back in an hour. The room was still. The girls stopped whimpering. Michael sat down and chafed his hands. He felt hungry, cold, and slightly frightened. He had thought those men were after him. He smiled at Madame Touras, and found her looking at him, her heavily lidded eyes strangely non-commmittal. It was early in the morning. She stood there in a light shawl and her dressing gown. She had no make-up on her cheeks. She looked very old and puzzled. He thought: She must have been frightened. . . . Otherwise she would have thanked me at once."

She asked slowly: "Bozert? I have heard you mention that name. You spent the summer in her flat, did you not?"

"Yes—"

"She was kind to you. She fed you, did she not? She worked for you, did she not?"

"Why, yes. She liked it—"

"She did not send you away—"

"No. . . . You asked me to come here. But—she laughed at me—"

"I see. She laughed at you—" Madame Touras sat down among a nest of soiled pink satin cushions.

"What are you disturbed about? They will not do her any harm. She has important friends—"

"I am not disturbed about her. I did not tell the man it was all a stupid story about the flour not being mine. That can wait. I wanted to settle it with you. This is my business."

"Of course it is—"

"So she laughed at you. Some day I might laugh at you. You are very beautiful, but you are funny. I might laugh at you, and you will think: 'Ah, she has mocked me, and I must hurt her some day.' Is it not so?"

"Why should you ever laugh at me?"

"Is it not so?"

"I—don't know—"

"But I know. Listen, there is very little food in this city. There is little room also. So many houses have been burnt down. There is little room for reptiles. The Zoological Gardens were closed down a long time ago. One must not waste a single crumb on reptiles, must one? Human beings must be fed first."

"Why are you talking about the Zoological Gardens? Why all these words about reptiles?"

"I am not talking about reptiles." Madame Touras was gentle and patient. "I am talking to one of them." Slowly, quietly, she got up and came towards Michael.

"But I have done you a service," he screamed, and could say no more. Madame Touras stopped in front of him, a small black revolver gleamed in her steady podgy hand, and, swiftly, neatly, she shot him. There were shrieks from the doorway, and several of her inmates came rushing in, but she remained quiet, saying to the girl nearest the door: "Stop that screaming. Go to the Domkom at once. The chairman will be there. Tell him that Alina Touras, Lett, procuress and wanton, has just shot a man. Tell him it is a killing, not a murder. You will go at once. All of you leave me, do you hear?"

Alone Madame Touras pulled Michael's body away from the door, covered the shattered face with a soiled pillowcase, and walked to the window. When the Domkom man arrived, she turned and said quietly:

"There is blood by the door. Don't step into it. I have hardly any wood left for the stove, and I cannot get any hot water—"

The Domkom gasped at her. "So there has been a murder. I thought that girl was inventing a story—"

"There has been no murder. I have shot him. I had to. He was a reptile—"

"First a raid, and now a murder. This is too much for one morning, Citizeness Touras. Why, this house will get a bad name. . . . It is like a chapter from Dostoevsky. And who shot him? You? Goodness, and I have no paper. I have used the last bit in the office. How can I make a proper report? The girl said it was a killing, not a murder, but you cannot get away with a killing."

"I am not trying to get away with it," said Madame Touras. "I have done it. And you must do your duty. It should be easy."

"How can it be easy? I must make my report, call in the militiamen. I have no paper. The telephone is out of order." He sucked

182

"It is in the family," explained one of the men. "His mother was at St. Nicholas's. He understands."

They must wait for the sergeant's return. There were things to be done. They sat quietly. They spoke little. They never looked at a certain corner, and the Domkom man kept his face towards the window.

2

Frossia suddenly discovered that she could sew. Her slender wardrobe was rapidly going the way of everybody else's tatters, even a pair of clumsy white canvas shoes cost so much that her salary at the Goelro made their purchase unthinkable. Yet Frossia had lawfully taken her small rooms and what pieces of furniture they contained. The former owner having disappeared, the Domkom decreed that the things were Frossia's so long as she remained a tenant. The smaller room had a chest, and in it she found treasures: two thin carefully darned sheets, some pillowcases, and two door curtains, one of faded green plush, here and there ravaged by moth, and the other of old rose damask, exquisitely patterned and in perfect condition. Frossia took her treasure trove to the Domkom. "Do what you like with them. They are yours," and the man glanced at her frayed brown skirt and added: "Goodness, *grajdanka*, you might turn them into dresses or something."

Needlework used to scare her. She had hemmed handkerchiefs and embroidered her grandmother's house linen. She had never attempted anything else. She spread the old rose damask on the floor, looked at it, picked up the scissors, and started on the job. At the end of the week she had a dress, straight and flowing, very much after the style of Greek drapery. The plush proved far less tractable: Frossia had hoped for a coat, but the old curtain ended in becoming a somewhat wildly shaped cape, partly left unhemmed, her thread having gone just before the end. Her fingers were needle-pricked and sore, but the results of her efforts left her heartened. It was great to have a new dress. It was still nicer to know that she owed it to her own skill.

The rose damask came most opportunely. The Zabalkansky were going to give a party, a proper *vecherynka* with music, singing, and even supper. Pavel Pavlovich had promised one of his Petrograd water-colors for a raffle, and Frossia hoped she might win it. Elena Ivanovna was going to make *pastila* from frozen cranberries, Klava's contribution would be a reading from Turgenev, and another member had suggested reading his new play on the Decembrist rising in 1825.

Therefore Frossia came back from the Goelro, wasted little time on her scanty supper, and put on the rose damask when suddenly the wooden staircase outside the house shook with the tread of several feet. There came no knock on her door. They merely came in, and it seemed to Frossia that they all were talking together. There was something about flour, and a gold-lidded bottle, and Madame Touras, in labor books. She drew in her breath. Once again she stood in a no man's land, she felt herself shrinking and shrinking, and the men in khaki grew so big that the walls receded behind them to give them the space they demanded. The walls went back for Frossia also, distance and time ceased to carry meaning; she was in a small room of a house not far from Kiev, she could see a rose-colored phial in her grandmother's hand, and hear that inexorable dry voice insist on a cessation she, Frossia, had refused to accept. Yet now she was wondering whether in her imagination, at least, she had not drunk of the phial: her feet and hands were going cold, her lips felt icy, and her mind became a small shriveled October leaf buffeted by the wind. This was a familiar enough experience, and running away from it meant a defeat. She must meet it again—face to face, and she found her voice: "Yes? Labor books? Do you want to see mine? It is in order. I am a typist at the Goelro. I am a fully registered worker."

But none of them listened to her words. They had not come there to listen. They asked for no explanations. They stood there, confronting her with a tangled series of crimes she or somebody else had committed. Once again Frossia tried to speak: "I know nothing about any flour. I have no food hoard in these rooms. I never sold my dressing case, and I don't know anything about anyone being shot."

"The shooting," said one of them, "has nothing to do with you, *grajdanka*. But the dressing case is a different matter. Do you recognize it?" He raised a gold-lidded bottle, and Frossia shrugged.

"Yes, I remember—I think one was missing when I claimed it back. It was never sold. There is nothing for me to say."

One of them sprawled across the table and began scribbling in a dirty notebook. Two men remained by the door. Two others stood idly, a little contemptuous. The man finished writing and pushed the paper towards her.

"Will you sign?"

"I cannot do any such thing."

"It is only your name and your admission that the dressing case did belong to you. Also that you knew the deceased—"

"But who is the deceased?"

186

They told her what little they knew, and Frossia learnt that Michael was dead. In an environment like Madame Touras's even the most sudden and violent death did not seem impossible. The old woman had done it, said the men, but they could not tell Frossia why she had done it, nor could they make it clear what they wanted of her, and she kept refusing to sign a paper. She had scanned those roughly scribbled lines: they were not a mere enumeration of facts, they were a rather involved statement which, if signed, would forge a link between her and a world she had no share in. Frossia kept repeating her refusal, the men kept telling her that this was her duty, when the door opened again, a small swarthy man walked in, and the men stood to attention.

"Have you got a warrant?" he asked one of the men.

"We were sent here, Comrade Glebov." He reeled off a few names, but the newcomer shrugged them away.

"Have you got a warrant?"

"No."

"Then you will go." And he turned to Frossia. "I must apologize, *grajdanka,* these things will happen, and you had no right to give shelter to someone without papers. Now he is dead, and there will be no end of inquiries—" He waited for the men to file out of the room, and said awkwardly: "And I must see your labor book."

She handed it over. He whisked over the pages, handed it back, and said almost sharply:

"You were born in the province of Kiev. Would you like to have a permit to go there?"

"No—"

"It might be better for you to be where people know you so well. And there is more food in the country, *grajdanka.*"

"I don't in the least mind going hungry sometimes."

"I have come from Gorokhovaya Street." Now Frossia knew that Cherny had sent him. "We heard that things were being done illegally, and we try to keep the law. But you are not wanted in Petrograd. Your name has a bad odor. You are not really working—not in the way we understand work. You are a typist. But you would not have been a typist except by sheer compulsion. There is no dearth of typists here. And what else can you do? Paint a picture, do silk embroideries, strum a piano? You have no college degree. We don't want useless people in this city—"

"Of course not. There has been famine and sickness and war, and everyone must be of use, but usefulness is not a chicken, citizen, you cannot just hatch it—"

"They call me Comrade Glebov," he said coldly.

"Comrade Glebov then . . . You mention uselessness. Have you ever heard of people who try to walk? Not infants but grown people? Those who have to learn all over again. They don't start running about all at once. They crawl, they grope, they stumble. . . . That is what has happened to so many people in the country. Give them time. Don't talk of uselessness." And, seeing his swarthy face go angry red, Frossia hurried on, "I am not important enough to be talked to, or about. I have not even begun crawling yet. I might never get a chance to start. Do I matter? I love being here because the city is so much mine, but I would not complain if you sent me to Kiev, or Solovki, or the Urals. I could type in Kiev or saw timber at Solovki. I am strong. . . . But why can you not let me be useful?"

"*Grajdanka—*"

"Well, why do you not? I am young, I want to live. I love Russia. I don't care much about any government. I am a Russian, and Russia matters—till it aches—till it aches—" she cried.

"Your Russia . . ."

"There you go again! Comrade Glebov, we have coined so many new words. 'Red' . . . 'White' . . . 'Green' even . . . Imperial, republican, soviet . . . Short refrains of a great song. Russia is a song neither you nor I could have written. You say contemptuously 'your Russia.' And what do you mean? You have got a few facts out of my labor book, you know that I am a rich merchant's daughter, once cradled in silk. But all those things never molded me. Do you think I would have stayed on here if I had lived by those things? I would have found enough money to run across the Gulf of Finland, I would have gone to Paris, Rome, Mentone, Lausanne, anywhere. Why have I not? Wait—" she cried. "I shall answer you. I have not gone because I would hate to live in exile, because whatever you choose to make of freedom, custom, tradition, you cannot take my country away from me—" Frossia said, glad of having found her way out of no man's land, certain of walking about dear and familiar meadows once again, and because she was so utterly at home among them her words rang with the richness of a conviction no mere pose could have imitated.

The swarthy little man was obviously startled. He fingered a button on his tunic. He sleeked down his dark hair. He cleared his throat.

"Well, *grajdanka,* I don't know much about you, others do, but I should say that if all your kin were like you, the dark people, *cherny lud,* of Russia would have had fewer miseries in the past—"

"That is so sentimental," she retorted, but they shook hands almost amicably.

3

Frossia could not go to the *vecherynka* at the Zabalkansky. The absurdly turmoiled scene had not shaken her very deeply, but she felt that she must give a few moments to Michael. There was no sense of grief or loss in her, she could have neither, but she experienced deep pity that all the earlier undoubted promise should have come to so barren and soiled an end. Michael had come into her life like a bud, and the bud withered before it came to its flowering. She had tried to make him see some of the light and grace she still saw in life, and he would see neither. Now it is nothing but pity. Pity for him, and pity for Anna also, she reflected, but I cannot find any pity for the Parnikovs, there was nothing tarnished about them. Is it only the soiling of people and things that makes them deserving of pity?

But for days his memory seemed to haunt her all the more so because she had no clear, detailed knowledge of any circumstances round his death. She imagined that there must have been a brawl of some kind, something inevitably ugly, but details were not for her to imagine. He haunted her merely because once again Frossia found herself confronted by a misgiving. She had tried to offer help and failed, and had grown impatient because of her own failure. Was it not my own short temper, my frequent taciturnity, my closing of a door which may have sent him away? None of these were responsible; in calmer moments Frossia realized but too well that she could not have held him since he had mattered so little to her and she to him. Yet she continued avoiding the Zabalkansky and all her acquaintance for a time.

Her rooms were surprisingly comfortable. She had made them so with her very few belongings, and kept them neat with an old broom and two patched dusters. The small narrow quay outside gave her for gifts the constant splashing of water, the bitter-edged wind from the sea, and the incredible glory of sunsets. She had two tiny rooms all for herself, and the right-of-way through a passage to a diminutive and primitive kitchen with an old-fashioned stove, a *plita* for communal use. Her neighbors were all rough folk. There was a woman who worked at a paper factory. She had a small crippled daughter. They came from Grodno. There was an elderly lugubrious undertaker who kept a coffin lid as a chief ornament of his room, and regaled all the tenants with endless stories of funerals. And,

189

finally, there was a middle-aged woman from Tula, fat, unkempt, and bulging, garrulous about most topics, her own work excepted. "I am a midwife," she confided once in a sonorous whisper, "but don't let us ever discuss it. It is such a tiresome inevitable business." "I should not like to discuss it," admitted Frossia, "but, surely, it is a grand business?" Olga Semenovna shook her wispy head. "It is not. It might be if there were not so many wars in the world. I heard the other day there is something happening in South America. Another of those wars that nobody knows much about. Now a child born in Russia might grow up and go and get killed in some stupid battle between two South American countries. That is what they mean by internationalism. Is it not sad?" Olga Semenovna remained gloomy, in spite of her cheerful red face, but Parfen Nikitich, the undertaker, occasionally amused all of them by strumming on his ancient accordion and telling slightly unsavory Armenian stories. In Armenian stories most extraordinary things always happened in trains.

"Now, Euphrosynia Pavlovna, there was a very nice lady from Kharkov, a wealthy young lady, traveling first-class, and all her luggage was of good strong leather. She was going on to Kislovodsk. And there was a very fat Armenian wine merchant. You know what they are like. Well, the young lady lost a garter—"

"Parfen Nikitich, your kettle is boiling over." Olga Semenovna spoke severely.

Anna Trofimovna, who worked in paper factory, spent all her rare leisure in laundering her little child's tattered clothes, and telling her fairy tales in a slightly tremulous voice:

"So the goldfish said to the fisherman: 'Go, go home at once, and see what I have done for you.' And the fisherman went and found a nice stone house instead of a tumbledown hut."

On the whole, Frossia's neighbors were kindly enough people. Nikolashka met them all, laughed with them, and approved them. "They love you, Euphrosynia Pavlovna," and Frossia protested: "How can they? They don't know me at all."

She was trying to learn them. On the days when food depôts stood empty, they all met in the narrow passage, wrung their hands, and the two women sobbed noisily, in the manner of hurt and unhappy children. Parfen Nikitich remained stubbornly sullen, and would say to Frossia that weeping never produced a loaf.

Sometimes she went and sat with little Dasha, Anna Trofimovna's child, and told her stories. Dasha had never walked in her life. She was born so, the mother said. Now her arms were getting almost useless, two thin short sticks of blue-veined, pallid flesh. She lay in a wooden box by the window, watching the river and the sky. She was unnaturally quiet for her eight years. Her mother said: "Come spring, they will send her away—to the south. But I know better than they do—Dashenka will never walk. It is not her nature to walk. You see, she was born like that."

Dasha had two toys—a wooden Petrushka theater and a shapeless, eyeless doll with hanks of bright yellow hair. Once Frossia busied herself with Petrushka, set the stage up, and moved the tiny, gaudily painted marionettes. Dasha said suddenly: "What is dancing like, Frossia Pavlovna?"

"Why?"

"Because they are dancing outside, are they not?"

Frossia came nearer, leaned out of the window, and saw four small children pirouette round a lamp-post.

"It is dancing, is it not? But you do get tired once you begin to move. And you can lie still and make believe you are moving, that is what I do, it is all in my head, and I can run, and play and dance, and I sing little songs, and I never get tired."

They came from Grodno, but Dasha could remember neither Grodno nor her father, killed early in the war. But she remembered a scene at some station.

"It was in the night, and they lit a candle in the room, and I felt warm and cozy, and a very nice woman had a big *vatrushka* with the sour cream nicely browned on the top, and such soft, soft pastry. She had no knife, and had to break the pieces off, and I got such a big one, and I waited until it grew light, and I asked a man to carry me out, and I ate my *vatrushka* under the open sky."

"And you were happy?"

"Yes," said Dasha, "the sky was lovely, and that woman so kind. She might have eaten the whole *vatrushka*, and she shared it with all of us. Frossia Pavlovna, why is it that some people are kind and others are not?"

"Most people are kind."

"Some are not," Dasha said with such a deep conviction that Frossia asked no further questions.

On the whole, she found it to be rather a close neighborhood. Small landings, a narrow staircase, and the communal kitchen, all led to an inevitable interchange of small impressions and brief scraps of conversation, till Frossia came to discover that she had not been thrown into the company of queue sheep; those three were not privileged, they led the ordinary, streakily colored lives of the rank and file, and their uttered thought often wore the clumsy dress after the fashion of their kind, but they could and did think.

191

She was rather astonished at their complete indifference to any political matters. They accepted life as a whole. Politics formed but a small part of it.

"You have got your loaf to bake—whether you are white or red," said Parfen Nikitich, the undertaker.

"A broad back can bear any burden," asserted Anna Trofimovna one day when no bread came her way, and she must soak a stony rye rusk for Dasha's supper.

Frossia said to Nikolashka: "When I came first, they wondered so much about me, but now it seems as if I were just at home."

"You are, Euphrosynia Pavlovna, all of us walk under God."

"Things are not easy at the Goelro," she confessed to him. "It is not always my bad spelling. Nikolashka, do you think I should go back to Kiev and try something else there?"

"But you came back here—"

"Oh, I would not go for good. I mean to come back." She knew she wanted to see Kiev once again, but Nikolashka shook his head.

"If Irina Nikolaevna were here, she might advise you. Euphrosynia Pavlovna, there are so many difficulties about a permit, and if you do get one, you might not be allowed to come back." He tugged at his huge beard. "Wait, though, go and see Igor Vladimirovich at Warsaw Station. He is a kindly man, he will give you good counsel."

"And why should I trouble him?" asked Frossia.

4

Yet, her intent dim and uncertain, Frossia made the tedious journey from Maly Prospect to Warsaw Station, and took her place in a long queue outside the door which displayed a slovenly notice—"Travel Permit Inspector."

The queue interested her. Used to the endless chatter of bread queues, Frossia felt outside its uncanny silence. There were old men and old women, people in coats, shawls, capes, and mantillas, middle-aged folk and even little people of Dasha's age. They shuffled their feet, they cleared their throats, but they hardly spoke one to another. Each of them suggested a human island in an oddly inhuman sea. It looked as though they were wholly intent on husbanding their vocal energy till their turn came to pass behind the dirty ocher-painted door where their several fates would be decided favorably or otherwise. All of them clenched various crumpled papers in their hands. Frossia alone had no papers, and she could not bring herself to ask questions of her taciturn neighbors.

Here we are not persons, she mused, we are so many labor books, numbered and labeled. But I must be fair. In the old days we used to be passports, and the police had the right to examine them. To be a folded piece of paper, just a few typewritten lines and a smudgy violet seal in the middle. . . .

She had come late. Nobody stood behind her. She watched the door. There seemed nothing else to do. One by one people came out, still hugging their papers. They appeared more alive when they left the office. At least, there was a comforting obviousness stamped on their reactions. Some turned sharply to the left, their gait lightened, their faces smiling shyly. They vanished behind a spiked barrier. Others came straight down towards the main gates of the station. They wore the leaden look of those denied a sunrise, an apple, or even a quiet hour; these shuffled rather than walked, and the dirty papers in their hands were so crumpled as to suggest utter uselessness.

Frossia thought, watching them:

There is something like a play going on, with a dreamy background melting away in the winter sky. Zhitomir, Viazma, Smolensk, any of those may have been their goal, and now Petrograd will go on holding them, and they want none of it. It is strange the way people can live in a beautiful place and remain untouched by it.

She had been standing for about an hour. It was hot, and her cumbersome clothes irked her. The entrance hall of the station smelt of sunflower seeds, cheap tobacco, coal dust, sweat, and rotten straw. There were no benches, and the walls were too dirty to be leaned against. But, at last, she found herself facing the door. It remained closed, but through the thin, cracked timber she heard a deep kindly voice, and her heart went warm, and she forgot weariness.

"Arabian Night, Igor Vladimirovich," she said, coming in.

He looked at her gravely.

"I am not an Arabian Night in this place. I don't tell stories. I am merely an inspector. Please let me see if your permit is in order. You see, we must not keep other people waiting longer than necessary."

"I am the very last," Frossia said quickly, "and I have no permit—"

"Why are you here?"

"To get one." She hesitated. "Also to ask advice."

He sighed.

"*Grajdanka* Bozert, the Information Bureau is just outside the

193

station. Here my business is to examine your permit, not to issue it—"

"How do I get it?" Frossia ignored the reference to the Information Bureau.

"Your place of work if you have been there long enough." He spoke a little wearily. "Your Domkom, or the Health Commission."

"I have worked at the Goelro for a little more than a year. There is nothing the matter with my health, so there is just the Domkom. . . . Well, I have met them. They seem kind enough."

"This is not my business, Euphrosynia Pavlovna, but no matter how kind they are, they will not issue a permit unless you have a real reason for going."

"What should it be?"

He shrugged and moved some papers on the desk. His hands uncovered a small brown bound book, and Frossia, reading the title, felt reassured: nobody capable of reading Plato in such surroundings could really send her away empty-handed.

"Well, it is generally illness of a near relative or something like that."

"I have no relatives."

"In that case, well, is there anything else? I am afraid I have some work to do, Euphrosynia Pavlovna—"

So her imagination had once again deceived her: he was a rigidly uniformed inspector of railway permits, not a man of richly told stories, laughter, and a widely windowed heart. Also he was a piece of paper, smudged, bethumbed, and crumpled. Frossia moved away from the littered table.

"Some people are like oranges," she said clearly, "all divided into neatly separated segments."

He laid down his pen. "Why did you want to go away?"

"I wanted to see the country again—"

"Euphrosynia Pavlovna," he said earnestly, "I know something about you. You must not mind what I say. Our business is to stay where we are and to do our best wherever we are. You want to see the country. Such a wish is a good thing in normal, peaceful times. Not now . . . If you had rheumatism or a bad lung, you would be sent away to warmer places. But aimless traveling is almost criminal now. Surely, all idle curiosity is out of place during a birth—"

"What birth?"

"The country's."

"Ah," said Frossia, and thought: Life has indeed become a piece of paper, kept in place under a nice heavy paperweight, and this

194

Arabian Night is another piece of paper. And he talks like a badly educated schoolmaster from a village school.

"Why should you say 'Ah' in such a voice, Euphrosynia Pavlovna? You feel the same as I do. Otherwise you would have left long ago—for a foreign country."

"I don't feel the same as you do." She cut him short, bowed briefly, and went out.

Outside, the wide cobbled street melted in the heat. Frossia's shabbily shod feet hurt her. Her hands were hot. Suddenly she stared down at them. They were roughened, red, uncared for, they suddenly appeared clumsy, as though they had never belonged to her earlier self. She went on staring at them, and remembered her long past passion for fresh kid gloves. The Eltz said I was extravagant, and Grandmamma defended me. She said it was my only extravagance. I loved gloves. I used to go to Scipion's, pay five and seven and ten roubles a pair, beautifully cut, pastel-colored kid, pale rose suède. . . . All these hands need now is a pair of thick shapeless gauntlets for the winter, and I have none. . . . She continued thinking about gloves almost all the way back to Vasilyev Island.

5

Paulina Pavlovna put her heavy string bag on the cobbles and wiped her face.

"I am not tired, Frossia," she said lamely, "but it is my thoughts. I am worried about Klava. She has not been near us for several weeks. I went to her factory once, but she said: 'Please excuse me, I must not waste even five minutes of my day's work.' Frossia, I wonder if you could do something. She seemed to like you."

"What is the matter?"

"Well, she has changed. She has given up those meetings of hers. She said to Elena Ivanovna that all her virtue had gone. She just goes to the factory and then back home again. She has sent Grisha away. She is full of brooding. It is all wax candles, incense, ikons, services at the Kiev Abbey chapel, and what not. Last time she came to us, I said: 'Klava, please read us some Tolstoy. A chapter from *Resurrection* now—you can do it so beautifully.' I said that Paul had been rather in low spirits and her reading might hearten him. Frossia, she said: '*Resurrection?* The book ought to be burned.' Now is this like Klava, I ask you?"

"It is not," said Frossia, and went to the Gospel House as soon as she found a spare evening.

The enormous hall was empty, unlived in, dust on the floor and

195

the window sills, all the benches pushed against the walls. Frossia knocked at the partition door. There came no reply. She peered. The cubicle was empty, and she decided to wait. She thought:

There were the Parnikovs, quiet, inoffensive, and the abyss has swept them away. There was Michael, I had meant to help him, and I could not, and I shall never know why Madame Touras shot him. There was Anna, but Frossia knew she could not think about Anna. And there was the man with a handkerchief, and now there is a queerly cut marionette, a cog in a machine. . . . Now Klava has turned into a wax candle . . . And she heard the door open, and saw Klava.

"Why, welcome." Klava spoke in a high dry voice. "I had heard you were going away."

"No. . . . And you are still here. . . . Where is Grisha?" Frossia knew she was being clumsy, and hated herself for it, but apt words would not come to her.

"I sent him away to Pskov. His aunt was ill. She needed him," Klava answered in the same strange voice. "Sit down. Would you like some cold water? I have nothing to offer you except a stale cabbage pasty—"

"Why did Grisha go away?"

Klava kept her back to Frossia.

"I sent him away. Please, don't talk about it. Do you know what it means—to send your man away? What it means to put space between yourself and something that is more than God's very skies to you? If you have not, what good is my explaining it to you? If you have, you could not bear words about it—"

"It is not like that, Klava. Why?"

"I was not worthy of him. That answers you just a little. I could not give a complete answer. Have pity on me, Frossia. I was not worthy of him. He was pure. I made him sin. And he is good. The country needs lads like him, who say so little and live deeply and can work hard, and are clean just like snow. Yes, I sent him away."

"But, surely, you belong to each other. People like you are valuable. Think of the good you can do together. Why, the first time I saw you and heard you, and you wore a blue-green shawl that day, I remember, and you read something of Dostoevsky's, I knew you were unusual because of your strength. You could not be weak, Klava. . . . And Grisha, too, is strong, and he loves you. You say the country needs him. . . . Yes, but why Pskov?"

"Because of the sin," Klava said somberly, "and now we have repented, and I have chosen a different bridegroom."

"Klava," said Frossia, almost ignoring those words. "Once, a year ago, I think, we all went to Peter's Park. In June . . . In bluebell time, and we sat on the grass and ate curd-cakes and drank water from the fountain. Grisha was with us, and I remember thinking how much like a bluebell he looked—in spite of his being a cripple. Slim, cool, clean, and beautiful, yes, beautiful, Klava. But his beauty came from what you had given him, and now you have bruised him out of all comeliness. This is the greater sin."

"You would not understand—"

"I am no pagan, but I cannot see your God. Now you say you have repented, turned to prayer, but your earlier life was a prayer. Klava," Frossia cried, suddenly frightened by her own vehemence, "you cannot shut yourself off. None of us can. I wanted to. I still want to—at times. But don't you see, we—here in Russia—are in the vanguard of the dispossessed, the stricken, and a vanguard carries a banner, Klava, and what use keeping a banner behind a closed door? I know your strength, and I know Grisha's. All of it can be used, all of it is wanted—"

She went on and on, crouching on the floor of that bleak and dusty cubicle. The drab walls were washed with crimson and deep orange from the evening sky. Through the door left ajar Frossia could see the dusty deserted hall stir faintly under the onrush of color and glow through the skylight till the very dust burned with gold and copper and the common deal of the unused benches suggested something rare enough for a king's palace. Her eyes on that color—for Klava sat with her face averted—Frossia went on and on. She could not hear her own words. She was not really speaking but seeing.

"Klava, it may be impertinent of me, and you must silence me if I grieve you too much, but there is a religion that puts one's own soul and its salvation above all else, and it must have a narrow cell all to itself, and this religion is unlovely and grim, and stays barren for evermore. And there is another religion that forgets one's soul and its needs, its very hunger even and, loving the narrow cell, leaves it for the maddening hustle and bustle of a market square. I should not talk like that, I have not your faith, Klava, I sometimes wonder if I have any faith, but, surely, these are great and tragic days, and the narrow cell is not for those who feel anything at all. Klava, don't you see how important it all is? I talked with Cherny once, he said they are out to destroy religion in Russia, and he meant the organized religion, and I told him I did not think they would ever succeed in stamping out the other kind—otherwise there would be no Russia, just an enormous country peopled by moving machines, and I think they know it too. . . .

197

But the heat and the turmoil must pass, and then what? Klava, please, think of what you are doing. . . . This century has begun with the music of guns for us in Russia—first China, then Japan, and the last dreadful war, and there will be others, I know there will, and in a century like that one dare not live for one's own self, one dare not keep to a cell. . . . Please get your friends together again, or else go to Pskov, and start something there. But, Klava, open your arms again—and your heart. . . . Forgive me—I may have trespassed—I could not help myself—"

Her fire had burned itself out. The cubicle went dim. The glory left the hall. And Klava sat still, her face still averted. At last she said in a hollow voice, speaking slowly as if it were difficult for her to move her lips at all:

"I have a mother in the Rostov Government. She lives in a small *uezd* town. There is a market and several churches. She has a house and a small garden. There are many cherry trees, lots of lilac. Relations come to see her in the morning, they drink tea, and she tells their fortunes. She has a will of iron and she feels no joy in her orchard or her lilac. I lived there until I went to work at a factory. She never left me alone. She does not understand anyone's wish to stay alone. She must have people around her, watch them eat and drink, and hear their thin chatter. In her house you must not love the garden overmuch. Cherries are gathered in their season and brought into the kitchen. Lilac is left alone. In her house you must sit in the parlor and you must chatter, too. She hates silence. She is afraid of stillness. She wears wide white muslin blouses. When I lived with her, I had to launder seven blouses a week. In the evenings when I felt tired, when I wanted to think or pray, I must light the oil lamp and fetch the cards, and we had ten patiences, never nine or eleven, but always ten. Then we went to bed. Was that a good life, do you think?"

"No, Klava, it could not be. . . . Barren and rather dark."

"I thought you would say so."

A thin strip of leaden silence now fell between them. Then Klava rummaged under the *koyka,* brought out a wickerwork basket, threaded a needle, and started patching a worn gray shirt with some faint blue embroidery at throat and wrists. Frossia recognized the shirt: she had often seen Grisha wear it. She sat still.

"When I was sixteen, I ran away to a soap factory—far away, near Staraya Russa. Cheap labor was scarce, the foreman said, and they got me a passport, and the police never troubled me. Then I went into the textiles here in Petrograd. A girl from the

University came and read us a story by Chekhov in the evening. We lived in the factory, you understand. We slept in a room which smelt of tallow and grease and copper cauldrons, and there were no windows. Well, I was illiterate then. I begged the girl to teach me. She did. Then I began seeing things differently. In 1915 we all went on strike. We never had enough money to buy decent food, and we had to pay hospital tax and other dues. I was twenty-two then. I could not really speak at all well, but I saw things clearly, and I was for the strike because God helped me to see justice. They gave me a year at the Kresty Prison, heaven forgive them. Then I came out, and the workers were rising everywhere. I had read much by then. I began getting friends together, and reading meant life to me. Grisha came. I found him helpless, you know. . . . An old woman had stolen his crutches for fuel. . . . I was glad of him. You heard me read. . . ."

"Yes—"

"And was that a good life?"

"All giving is good, Klava—"

"I thought you would say so." Klava threaded another needle. "But pretending to be generous when you have nothing left to give, is a crime—" She put in a last stitch, bit the rough thread off with her strong white teeth, put away the shirt, and stood up. "Frossia Pavlovna, don't think me lacking in hospitality, but the evening is drawing in, and I have had a hard day at the factory, and I must be up early."

Frossia stammered: "Of course . . . You have forgiven me. . . . Have you not? But could you tell me—"

Klava bent her shawled head.

"You have made me tell you, Frossia Pavlovna. I have answered you—"

CHAPTER SEVEN

"THERE IS MORE LIGHT THAN THAT SEEN FROM A WINDOW"

"You should have arrested her at once," fussed the fat, purple-faced woman with a peacock feather on an enormous bedraggled black felt hat. "She is mad, I tell you. . . . Anyone with such staring green eyes and that long nose, must be mad. . . . Of course, she may be a witch, but we don't believe in witches any more. Anyway, you should have stopped her. Did you not see—she ran past me, then turned back, as though she did not know her way about Vasilyev Island, yes, she turned back, and pushed me quite violently, and nearly tumbled me into the gutter. . . . After all is said and done, I am a respectable citizeness, I have never been in any trouble, I have no dealings with speculators or such like, and I feel I should get some protection from the militia. She may be dangerous in the city. You should have arrested her, I say."

"But do I have to run after anyone running about the streets? Have some sense, *grajdanka*," protested the bewildered militiaman; "nobody has been whistling about a thief. Anyone can run about if it pleases them. There is no decree published that prohibits running in the streets," said the militiaman, wiping his moist cheeks with a dirty sleeve. "Though why anyone should want to run about in this heat, is beyond me—"

"There is a very clear decree about lunatics," insisted the fat woman. "A man in my block went mad about a month ago, and everything was done in a most orderly manner. They did not leave him at large. Now don't you tell me—" her peacock feather swayed menacingly—"now don't you tell me there is no decree about lunatics, because I know all about it."

"There is one," he soothed her. "And if that woman is properly mad, things will get done. She did not look as though she had no place of her own, she must live somewhere, and her Domkom will have her certified and taken away. But she has done no harm to you, has she? You say she nearly pushed you into the gutter?

200

Even if she had, there would have been no great harm done, *grajdanka,* you must understand that gutters are bone dry in this accursed drought, and a little dust will not hurt anyone—"

"A little dust," sniffed the peacock-feathered woman, and moved away towards Nicholas Quay.

"I would like to stuff your mouth with it," grumbled the militia-man. "Teaching me about decrees. . . . I wish they would publish one about shrieking in the streets. . . . Far worse than mere run-ning. . . . One would have thought she had been knocked down or anything. . . . Pfui!" Disgusted, he strolled along in a different direction.

2

Frossia heard the urgent click of high heels along the rough cobbles of the narrow quay. She leant out and saw Lilian. Lilian was running, her green eyes filmy, her hair unkempt; she wore a loose white linen coat, something like a nightgown underneath, and her hands clutched an untidy bundle of variedly colored cloth-ing. Frossia ran down, brought her into the room, closed the door, and bustled about. Lilian refused all offers of food, drank some cold water, and hoarsely begged for a cigarette.

"I have none," said Frossia, trying to speak gently, but she found it difficult; Lilian in her obvious distress looked rather repulsive. Tears had ravaged the slovenly paint on her face. "You had better have a wash," said Frossia, but Lilian clung to her hands.

"I must first tell you. You will save me. It is Serge. He has gone wild. He is mad. I cannot tell you what it has been like. You know he imagines he is the last descendant of French kings."

"You told me he was—"

"Yes, yes, I did. . . . But now he has come to believe that I must be utterly irreproachable—almost like Caesar's wife. . . . It is a joke—but not at all funny. I have left him. I could not bear it." Her green eyes went mysterious. "There is someone who will help me leave Petrograd. I must run away, to the Crimea, perhaps, or else abroad. . . . I am terrified, Frossia. . . . Could I stay the night? Just tonight only, and tomorrow it is market day, and you are always free on Saturdays, Frossia, will you come with me to the market? I have an opal ring. There is a man who comes on Saturdays, and he is interested in opals—"

"You can stay tonight. Yes, I am free tomorrow, but why do you want me to go with you?"

"I am frightened, Frossia. . . . I am afraid of anyone in the street. Even as I was coming here, a dreadful woman screamed at

201

me because she said I had pushed her. I never did push her. . . .
But I am afraid. . . . She may have been sent by Serge—"

"This is silly."

Lilian pouted, far more sullen than frightened, and Frossia
turned her mind to more immediate problems. She had one mattress and one bed, but she remembered the rugs and the pillow
in the chest. She moved about busily, saying little. Lilian, comforted by temporary sanctuary, sat on the bed, and talked about
gambling, Soviet gin, the so-called *hanja,* about a place in Morskaya Street where you could still buy caviare, and she talked freely
and venomously about corruption in high places, until Frossia,
tired of the verbiage, checked her coldly:

"Can you vouch for any of it?"

"They all say—"

"Yes," mocked Frossia in an icy voice. "They always say. And
the horse also said something before he ran away to fight the wolf,
but the horse never came back."

That evening Frossia discovered that she had run out of candles.
That was an advantage. In the dark she could pretend to be asleep,
and Lilian's chatter died a slow death; but in the morning she
woke dispirited and morose. Her earlier plans seemed to have
faded in the night. She twisted the opal ring round her finger,
looked out of the window, complained of the heat, and suggested
that they had better spend the day indoors. She might be able to
find the speculator at home in the evening. Frossia lost her temper.

"You will have to see him alone then. If you don't want to go,
you need not. But I cannot keep you here another night. You must
go back to your flat or else get the Domkom to give you a tenant's
permit."

Lilian wept.

"I have always wondered if you were hard. Now I know. You
are my friend, and I am in great trouble. I come here, and you
are as cold as a fish. You did not even give me any supper last
night—"

"I had some cod. You refused it. I had nothing else. You will
have to eat it for breakfast."

Over some substitute tea and the fish Lilian, her patchily washed
face now covered with powder, broke into a differently colored
plaint. She would not go to the Crimea after all. She must go
abroad. It was all this beastly revolution, it left no decency in life.
Frossia interrupted the monologue by going out into the yard to
fill another kettle.

They went out. Lilian whimpered about the heat, the dirt, the smells, the cobbled pavements. She kept looking over her shoulder, halted at corners, clutched at Frossia's unresponsive arm, and whispered in her husky voice: "Did you see her? The woman in the pleated white skirt? That was Countess Klohnbach. She bowed to me. Do you think anyone could have seen her bow to me?"

Frossia remained cold.

"I never noticed her. Was it Countess Klohnbach? I had no idea you knew her—"

"But of course, I did." Lilian was indignant. "What is the matter with you, Frossia? You are talking nonsense—"

"We both are—"

But Lilian had wholly forgotten the limited army scene of her past. Her mind, now definitely absorbed on escaping abroad, was living in a world she had never known. She could almost see herself in Paris, Nice, Berlin, her lips were silently shaping the loud-sounding words, "Comtesse de Garonne." The name might do in Germany, but, unfortunately, not in France. . . . In France the name would have to be given a different twist, German or Norwegian, perhaps. . . .

"Of course, we knew the Klohnbachs very well," she repeated. "Why, do you not remember?"

Then Frossia realized that icy remoteness and anger were futile. Nor could she bring herself to laugh at Lilian. Frossia wished she might take that savagely painted face between her hands and say: "Have your dreams if you like. I have mine. But do go away. You cannot live in this country and go on taking from everybody and giving nothing at all. It is dangerous as well as stupid. Perhaps, in some foreign city, life may be really harsh and unkind to you, and you might learn to give," but such things could not be said to Lilian.

"Be careful with your ring," Frossia said instead, having seen one or two militiamen on the fringe of the market square. The day was so hot that the familiar shoddy scene almost lacked movement. The very timber of the few stalls looked warped; people went about slowly, listlessly. Frossia could smell rotten cabbages and something like offal. Huge flies were crawling about as they passed between two rows of stalls. A woman had just bought a bottle of hair lotion with something French on the label. She caught sight of Frossia and pulled at her sleeve.

"Please, what does it say?"

Frossia translated. The woman's face went angrily purple.

"Hair lotion? And that rat told me it was some vegetable oil, good for cooking, he said," and she rushed back to where a man, in an irreproachable khaki tunic, stood selling his bottles. That man was Serge. He turned round, saw Frossia and his wife, apologized to the woman, took back the bottle, and returned the money. Frossia heard his rasping voice: "Just a mistake, citizeness, just a mistake. . . . I apologize most sincerely—" But above his voice rang Lilian's sudden scream, and the scene became grotesque, unreal, exaggerated. Lilian's moist hand still clutched Frossia's cold fingers, and Frossia could hear her mutter: "He will kill me. . . . He will kill me. . . . He said so."

Serge carried a basket with several bottles. He let it fall, his eyes on them both, and from a distance Frossia listened to the plaintive music of splintered glass. Then Serge's right arm shot out and seized Lilian. His left dealt Frossia a blow, and she swayed. Above her head rose an incredible din of several voices, Serge's drowning them all. Frossia knew he was abusing her, and she also knew that she did not care, but Lilian had trusted her, and she must not abandon Lilian who was weeping, paint streaking down her cheeks. Serge was telling the tense gathering of buyers and sellers that his poor misguided wife had been enticed from virtuous paths by her, Frossia, and Lilian sobbed on, and nobody knew what it was about, but a crying girl and an angry husband provided a thrilling chapter from life, and nobody thought of anything except that it was interesting, fraught with violent movement and no less violent abuse. Serge's dark evil face looked almost tragic, they thought, and his raucous voice alive with conviction, and the crowd left off buying and selling, and drew closer watching eagerly. They knew nothing, there was nothing to know, but Lilian wept, Serge shouted, and Frossia's strange cold face reflected disgust rather than bewilderment, and no crowd could ever remain indifferent to disgust. It stirred them to slow anger, but they waited. The scene belonged to Serge for the moment, and they enjoyed listening to him, and the few militiamen kept outside the crowd. Serge continued painting a picture of peaceful and even decorous home, its loveliness and worth shattered by the cunning and perfidy of Frossia. He stopped, and someone muttered in an angry voice, and a big potato was aimed at Frossia's head and hit her on the shoulder. She was no longer cold but furious.

"How dare you? How dare any of you?" Yet her voice did not truly reflect her mood. She kept thinking of Lilian, she must not lose sight of her, and the crowd misread the hesitant note in her voice for cowardice and fear. The first potato was followed by another, and by a third. They were aiming more carefully now, and suddenly a pebble hit Frossia on the lips, and at the same time Serge, his grievance fully avenged, rushed away, dragging Lilian along with him. Frossia made to follow them, but an elderly woman, her face deeply marked by smallpox, held on to her. "You have done your evil work, you—sister of Satan. Don't you dare trouble them any more. . . ."

The crowd stepped back. Frossia was on an island, a small island washed all over by waves of unreasoned fury and malice. She was a stranger to all of them, they knew nothing about her, but this did not matter. They had heard Serge out, and they thought they knew all.

She had forgotten the blood trickling down her chin. She could not feel any pain in her arm though the elderly woman had hurt her. She was merely thinking odd, fragmentary thoughts: Lilian? What is the matter? Queue sheep . . . Queue sheep—nothing but stomachs to them, yet they have fury in them. . . . And the sun is so blinding. . . . There is a tree at the back of the square—"

They came nearer. They were pulling at her harder and harder. Frossia could not find her voice. She closed her eyes. Someone hit her across the face, and she staggered. There was no sense in remaining on her feet. Her legs crumpled under her, her legs were made of tissue paper to go round a green velvet box, with a big opal pendant inside. "Write, Euphrosynia, a necklace of pearls, diamond clasp. Forty-nine pearls. Five diamonds. Grade A. . . ." "Grandmamma, would you mind my writing in red ink? There is so much of it all round." "No, it must always be black or green, Euphrosynia. Open your eyes. Here is the black ink," and dutifully, she opened her eyes, and saw herself swimming in a sea of black, black all around her, black all above her, and a voice saying: "But you could not get your traveling permit that way," and another voice: "Well, what did we know about it?" and then the same Warsaw Station voice murmuring: "They have all gone, and they are ashamed," and her own lips said slowly, brokenly: "Yes, and have you got a handkerchief for my face? I am dead, am I not? Please cover my face because the sun hurts me so much. Grade A in green velvet or black."

When she came back, Frossia was lying in the shade of a tree. She begged for water, she opened her eyes, and was not surprised to see Igor Vladimirovich. They seemed to be alone. Water was brought by someone Frossia could not see, and a clean rag for a towel, and some cold gruel in none too clean a tin. Frossia closed her eyes once more, and felt a man's rough but gentle hands go over her chin and neck, and she knew she was cleaner and strangely stronger. She lay in the shade, and the sun no longer hurt her eyes.

She drank some water and tried to swallow a few lumps of cold gruel.

"I will take you home," Igor said slowly and distinctly. "You must not talk—you are very tired—"

"Am I in anyone's way here?"

"No—"

"Then I would like to stay here for a while," and she said to herself: That is Vasilyev Island. There is an elm behind me, and I know every stone of the island, and the river is not far away, all the rivers, the Neva, the Nevka, the Chernaya. . . . Water . . . Blessed, blessed city— She slept, and awoke to find the breeze brush against her hot swollen cheeks.

"You have been asleep. Now you are going home."

Frossia lifted a hand and touched her head. It did not hurt too much. She could move her limbs, too. She was strong, quiet, herself again, and she must do something and at once. She told Igor Vladimirovich that she was going to the nearest commissariat, to try to get Lilian into safety.

"It is not your business—"

"She has forced it on me. She came to me last night. She was in great distress. I knew her people. He is evil." It was difficult for Frossia to speak, the cut underlip hurt her, the palliasse was hard, and, unaccountably, she shivered in the warm July breeze, but she kept insisting on getting up and going to the commissariat, until Igor broke in:

"There is no need to. . . . Euphrosynia Pavlovna, both of them came here whilst you slept. They wanted to help. He apologized. I think he meant it. He said he had a very bad temper. And she was hanging on his arm, she was not crying nor frightened. She wore different clothes, Euphrosynia Pavlovna, she looked very tidy and composed, and fresh paint all over her face. I took them aside. I did not wish them to wake you. They said it was all a horrible mistake. I did not say much to them. I told them I would look after you. But, Euphrosynia Pavlovna, in all seriousness, I should not be so troubled. There are people who are not worth a broken pin. Why do you distress yourself about them?"

She said slowly: "But nobody can be like that. . . . Not worth a broken pin, I mean. Igor Vladimirovich, thank you very much. . . . I am all right. . . . I am going home. . . ."

"Where do you live?"

"Across the river." Frossia had not meant to tell that lie, but Igor helped her up, and she realized that he had no idea about the house in Maly Prospect. It was getting darker, and she let him

206

take her across Palace Bridge, and she said briefly: "It is Moshkov Lane," wondering what possible tenants were now installed in Anna's old flat. They went down the wide Palace Quay, and Frossia walked, a thick sense of unreality all around her. At the corner of Moshkov Lane she turned. "I must have taken you out of your way," she said formally. "I am sorry. It is only a few yards from here. Please go," and he shrugged and went.

Now she was making towards the marble bench in that old summerhouse. Once she had died there, died to an old world of mildly patterned adventures and softly cushioned certainties. Since that day she had seen cruelty and chaos and insecurity and selfishness, and violence too, and Frossia shivered slightly, remembering all those angry-eyed women pressing round her in the market square. Now once again she was making for that curious sanctuary, to press her hot bloodstained face against the marble she would not see in the dark, since she had no matches on her and the summer day had long since died. She was going there, sternly she reminded herself, for hours of reflection and, possibly, mental agony. She accused herself of being a parasite, battening on odd moments of luxurious self-immolation, giving her help where it was least needed and most harmful to herself and to others. Her very work was unprofitable. The idle stories she sat spinning to a crippled child in Maly Prospect, seemed of weightier import than all the electrification documents, misspelt and invariably smudged, that she had typed at the Goelro. There at the Goelro she was a number, a cog, a robot. She could never rise above those low levels, hers was no mechanical mind, and unbounded lyricism over floodlit towns and villages would hardly be welcomed by the least clear-sighted executive. "I am a parasite," Frossia said again, and halted, guessing at the gate in the wall, and then remembered Klava and their last curious conversation. There was something she, Frossia, had said, something rather arrogant, that had come to her both from within and from without. "We are in the vanguard of the stricken and the dispossessed, and a vanguard carries a banner. . . ." Those had been strange, untimely words, and it was not fitting for one like herself to have spoken them. They were also stupid. The civil war was already flickering out in Russia, only famine and disease remained to be fought; peace had long since been signed in the West, and those four bloody years won't easily be forgotten by either side, thought Frossia, and opened the tiny gate.

Then she knew that she was worn out, and all thought left her. She wore a thin coat, and she folded it and slipped it under her aching head, and closed her eyes only to open them an instant after and see the dark blue-violet sky of the summer night above her head. The city was very near her in that derelict summerhouse, a city which could be both mother and lover to those it had bred, and Frossia slept to the softly phrased lullaby of its several waters.

3

She went to the Goelro, she stayed in the little timbered house in Maly Prospect, she told Dasha old folklore stories, listened to Parfen Nikitich's narratives of most recent funerals, sympathized with Olga Semenovna about the appalling quality of bread, and held conversations with Nikolashka about everything under the sun—from the incomparable Irina Nikolaevna to the sorry state of city drainage. She went to Moyka, and discussed books and pictures with Pavel Pavlovich, and the position of crêches with Paulina Pavlovna, and she also spared odd moments for Elena Ivanovna, but the Zabalkansky Club saw nothing of her for weeks. Frossia knew she would find those two dim rooms crowded, and she took to avoiding the least cluster of people. Sometimes she wondered what would happen, should the Goelro suddenly dispense with her most inadequate services, and then forbade herself so to wonder. Yet Elena Ivanovna met her in the street one September morning, and Elena Ivanovna said in her important voice:

"You may think we are not interesting enough, Frossia, and you have not been for several weeks, but you must come to our proverb party, otherwise I shall never forgive you. It is Pavel Pavlovich's idea," she explained. "All of us will come and quote proverbs, and then we will choose whichever are the most interesting, and have a discussion on them. Now—" she peered into Frossia's flushed face— "have I your promise? After all, it is odd to want to run away from all your friends—"

"I am not running away, Elena Ivanovna."

"Then you will come?"

"Yes," said Frossia, and wished she had not said it, and spent an uncomfortable three days in wondering about any possible excuses, but none seemed to answer, and at last she decided to trample down all misgivings and face the Zabalkansky again.

Once there she knew herself glad of her decision. It was so *uyutno* there, the stormy September evening was shut out, the candlelight was soothing and friendly, and everybody welcomed her. She peered round, and could not see a single hostile face. All were smiling at her as though the candles had been lit specially in her honor. The scene at the market place slipped far into the background, and Frossia took heart, smiled back, and waited for the discussion to begin. A young clean-shaven man from the Academy of Sciences sat in a corner, an open notebook in his hands. He would take down all the proverbs quoted, explained Elena Ivanovna, and then they would all vote for such as invited the best discussion.

Yet the evening opened rather haltingly. Many examples came from men and women, and none of them suggested any possible discussion. Pavel Pavlovich strode across the room, looked at the young man's notes, and thundered:

"I say, ladies and gentlemen, *gospoda*, this is really childish. 'Love is a ring, and a ring has no end.' There is nothing one could say about it—except that love is immortal, and that is boring because it is obvious. And here is another: 'Work is no falcon, it will not fly away. . . .' Now, is there anything in it?"

"There might be," said someone doubtfully, "if we thought hard enough."

"There is not," boomed Pavel Pavlovich. "Arabian Night, you have not done anything. Well? What about a good old proverb with a world of meaning to it?"

"They all have that," protested the man from the Academy, but Pavel Pavlovich silenced him with a gesture, and Igor said:

"I am sorry, *gospoda*. They have all run out of my mind. I can remember one only, and that is useless—'Your elbow is close enough, but you cannot bite it.'"

"Good," commented Elena Ivanovna, "though not quite good enough. But put it down, Alexander Vassilievich."

Silence fell, and then Frossia shyly offered her contribution:

"'There is more light than that seen from a window.'"

"That is what we want," bellowed Pavel Pavlovich. "Elena Ivanovna, we need not waste time on voting. This acorn will grow a sturdy oak. Now, Euphrosynia Pavlovna, we are waiting—"

"Why?" she stammered. "I have spoken—"

"No," they said in an urgent chorus, "now you must explain what you think about it."

Frossia hesitated.

"Well, I don't know. . . . There seems so much meaning, I mean —there are so many meanings, I would not know where to begin."

"Never mind. . . . Say anything you like," Pavel Pavlovich urged her.

"It is not easy." Frossia fumbled for words, but they were all waiting, and they were so friendly she knew it would be discourteous not to make an effort. "I have always loved this old saying. It is a bit like Petrograd in the autumn and winter when all things turn cold and dark and bleak, and yet nothing looks altogether hopeless, or deserted, just as if something kept on shining behind the fog and the darkness. . . . And, perhaps, our window is so small now that we can see but little through it, but the shining is there. That is all. It is so feeble." She folded her hands in a childish fashion. "You see, I am no good with words, they escape me, and I can't run after them—they are faster than anything I know."

"Yes," said Elena Ivanovna, "I remember a clear winter day once, not here, in the country, and there was a brook in the garden and, of course, it was covered with ice, but on a clear day you could see the water running under the ice, and it gave you something like a hope no matter how hard the frost bit into you. You would say: 'Well, here is some running water, and the ice is over it, but it is still running,' and you went home, laughing at the frost. . . ."

They all offered their contributions, and presently the candles began burning low, and people got up, and Igor walked across to Frossia's corner. They had not met since that day in July, and she feared lest he would make a remark, break on her serene mood, and leave her regretting her decision to come to the Zabalkansky in spite of her fear of any assembly. But Igor said:

"I loved your proverb. I had nearly forgotten it. It is late. I think I had better walk back with you, but your home is not in Moshkov Lane. You have not lived there for months, have you?"

"No," Frossia replied humbly. "It is in Maly Prospect—"

They came out, and the evening closed round them like a warm dark cloak. They walked in the middle of the road to avoid the pavement pitted with holes. She stumbled once or twice, and Igor did not offer his arm. They discussed the Zabalkansky and Elena Ivanovna, the menace of the famine, and his work.

"It must be difficult work, Igor Vladimirovich. It is like sitting in front of a mirror which reflects nothing but misery, and you want to be gentle and soft, and yet you must be hard."

"I am hard. It is wrong of me, but I must keep a job. One must work these days."

"Yes, to eat," Frossia said.

"Also to keep your mind alive."

They were crossing Nicholas Bridge, and Frossia remembered how very little she knew of him. His past life was almost a closed book, his present pattern was little more than a blur.

"You are still at the Goelro?"

"Yes, but it is not live work, nothing but typing, and I am a poor typist—"

"You would improve if you had a mind to. All work is important." She made no answer. She disliked his sententiousness.

"Is it true that Klava is going to Pskov?" she asked.

"Yes. I don't know why. Euphrosynia Pavlovna, I want to say something. I like the way you behaved that day. There was no feeling of revenge in you. It should be so with everyone, and it so seldom is. Nobody ought to want to get even with those who have injured them. There should be no punishments in a well-run country, though it must begin in a small way. And you were fine, Euphrosynia Pavlovna."

"What about criminals?" she asked, determined not to let him discuss purely personal topics, since he was so much of a stranger, and she was afraid of committing herself unwisely.

"You mean those who break the law? Well, I could not explain, but I think there is only one real law, and it is not man-made and therefore unbreakable. Man-made laws are different." He halted. "Euphrosynia Pavlovna, you mentioned Klava a few minutes ago. I remember her reading Dostoevsky. You know that passage from Father Zosima's testament in *Brothers Karamazov?*" To her astonishment he quoted it: " 'Fear nothing. Let not your repentance grow less, God will forgive. There is no sin committed by man that can exhaust the love of God. Is there any sin above His love? Once you repent, you love, and, loving, you are wholly God's.' "

"Yes," Frossia said dryly, "Klava read it once."

Igor was silent. They plunged into the broad mouth of the Sixth Line in Vasilyev Island. The wind soughed and moaned in the bare branches of elms, and whistled sharply through many a broken doorway. Here they had to pick their way slowly, carefully. Once or twice he said: "Where is your hand, Euphrosynia Pavlovna?" and she felt rough thick fingers close over hers. At last they came to a corner, and he said abruptly: "Good night. It is not far now," and it was she who stayed him. "I am very unmannerly, Igor Vladimirovich. I have never learned to thank gracefully. And I have never thanked you for all your goodness to me."

"It was not goodness. I felt bound to do it," he corrected her, and vanished in the dark; and Frossia groped towards her home, and toiled up the creaking wooden stairs.

"Well, he is a Tolstoyan," she said to herself. "Self-taught, self-made. I found him reading Plato once. He must have a good memory. He quotes so easily. . . ."

Paulina Pavlovna had been to the house at Ochta, and found it silent and deserted. The tawny-cloaked prophet had gone. A garrulous neighbor regaled Paulina Pavlovna with a detailed description of a midnight arrest. It appeared that the bright clothes had covered a genuine prince, if not a duke. He had been scheming to bring a whole imperialist army into the city. His Tibetan manuscripts were so many coded messages. The woman alluded to an aeroplane, a message falling from the sky, and a smell jeweled scepter found among the prophet's belongings. "The whole street was up half the night," she said excitedly, her arms akimbo. "And the things he said . . . Unfit for Orthodox ears to listen to . . . Well, they took him away in a lorry, and most of the things were gone by the morning. My Sashka swore there were jewels and bombs, but I cannot rightly say—I can only vouch for the scepter, and that is good proof, no commoner would own a scepter, even though Mark Antonich further down the street said it was no scepter at all, just a jewel, but you never know."

Paulina Pavlovna listened, tired and bewildered. She realized that there was nothing she might do, but the once eagerly learned precept of inward serenity now forsook her, and she sat down on the doorstep and wept.

"Go from here," urged the woman. "Why, they might come again and say that you had something to do with princes and that kind—"

"It would be true. My husband was one but he is dead," said Paulina Pavlovna and cried again, but the woman vanished behind a door. It closed with a bang, and Paulina Pavlovna was alone, tired and extremely muddled in her mind. She knew the story was woven of sheer nonsense, but it brought her little comfort. The great prophet was gone, and she might not inquire about him. She must think about Paul, she reminded herself. If she were to get into trouble, Paul would go unfed, Paul could not even boil a kettle properly, and he had no idea what to do with a button once it was off. No, she must sacrifice all her nobler intent and remember Paul.

Paulina Pavlovna got up and wandered away. Presently she came to a pleasant garden behind Sobornaya Street in Petrograd Side. She saw a bench, realized that she was tired, and opened the small gate. The lawns were neglected. There were about twenty children playing. A sturdy red-cheeked girl in a drab brown coat was apparently in charge of them. Paulina Pavlovna looked at her timidly and said she was afraid it was rather cold for little children to be out.

"They are out till dark," snapped the brown coat. "They run about, and it keeps them warm."

"They look rather small to be at school."

"This is not a school. This is the Second Red Orphanage, and I am in charge of it."

"You look very young."

"I am nineteen. I know my job."

But not all the children had the heart to run about. Some huddled under the bare trees, they looked cold and miserable and, on seeing a stranger talk to their nurse, they took to whimpering. The young nurse strode across and comforted them rather clumsily. The whimpering went on. Paulina Pavlovna offered to tell them a story.

"They might like it—"

She sat down on the bench and told them the old, old fairy story about the goldfish and the poor old fisherman. They whimpered no longer. They clustered round the bench, thumbs in mouths, and listened. Paulina Pavlovna told it simply and well. Her voice had beauty and color. She finished, and the young girl said heavily:

"Well, they have stopped crying, but I must see your labor book. You have broken the law. Fairy stories are not allowed here—"

Paulina Pavlovna stared at her.

"Surely, you are young enough to remember it yourself."

"Fairy stories are forbidden," said the girl stubbornly.

"But I can put it right. I will tell them it was not a true story—"

"That is stupid," cut in the girl, and Paulina Pavlovna knew it was. "Would they understand you?"

"Listen," said Paulina Pavlovna, "I am not very clever, but I am old enough to be your grandmother. Why should it hurt the children?"

"Because it is not real, because it is all nonsense."

"But so much of life is absolute nonsense. If life were all dry common sense, it would be unbearable."

"I must have your labor book," repeated the girl. Paulina Pavlovna shook her head and produced the document. The girl took it with an important air. "Now, you are coming with me. I must report it to the Matron," and she shepherded the children out of the garden. They came to a grim dirty house just off Sobornaya Street. In a small room on the ground floor they found the matron, a stout kindly woman with a broad peasant face. The girl reported the incident. The matron looked grave.

"You are perfectly right, comrade. Now go and give the children their milk. I shall deal with the case." She waited for the door to close, for the footsteps to die away, and then laughed. "She did right. I will commend her. You did no wrong either. I don't want to see your labor book, put it back in your bag, and please, promise me not to talk about it to anyone. It might prove awkward for you and for me. Was it the goldfish? I do love the story."

"Is it not rather stupid?"

"Citizeness, I cannot uphold you there. It may be stupid. It may not. Life has become so much of a melting-pot. It will all simmer down in time."

"I merely wanted to amuse the children. They looked cold, their noses were so red, and they were whimpering."

"It is part of the system to make them get used to the cold," said the Matron. "You wanted to amuse them? I quite believe you, though, officially speaking, I may not say: 'Thank you.' You see, this is a state orphanage, and even a melting-pot must have its rules. Good day to you."

More bewildered than ever, Paulina Pavlovna went back to the house in Moyka.

5

Nikolashka brandished his huge breadknife and said:

"And why should I be grumbling? I was once a rich peasant, now I am a poor peasant. I go hungry sometimes. Even a bread store is empty three days a week. But there is air to breathe, the sky to look at, and Irina Nikolaevna's letters to look forward to—"

"Yes," said Frossia, "but others are not like that. Look at some of the girls at the Goelro, they belong to the Party, they are privileged, and they are continually grumbling—"

"Ah, but it is harder on women," explained Nikolashka, "though most of them will endure anything. Just like my Irina Nikolaevna. We men always like to have our apples peeled for us."

She wondered. Cherny did not—but then most likely he would eat his unpeeled. And Igor Vladimirovich . . . What did she know of him? She questioned Nikolashka.

"He comes from Tula. He is a peasant's son. He had a small grocery business. But he has always been after books. The stories he knows!" And Frossia was impatient. She had heard quite enough about the Arabian Night. She knew that Igor knew stories, and she wanted to escape from all further mention of that accomplishment.

She wanted to say: "But there must be more to the man. There is his own personality, and what color and shape does it take?" but Nikolashka was talking, and she must not interrupt him. So Igor came from Tula, and Tula meant certain things: samovars, cutlery, firearms, richly spiced gingerbread, none of these somehow explaining Igor at all. "Not from the city," explained Nikolashka, "the country, I believe," and this made things easier. Frossia could see fields, woods, coppices, golden wheat and richly browned stubble and windblown cornflowers, and silver-scaled fish leaping in clear dark green water, and the damp soil smelling of mushrooms, and a hut odorous of freshly baked rye loaves, singed chicken feathers, and cranberry jelly, *kissel,* and pickled cucumbers lying in a wooden bowl.

"A grocer," she repeated, "a *bakaleychik.*"

"Yes, in a small way—he sold *baranky,* and pickled herrings, and sausage and jam—"

"And he baked *sitny,* Nikolashka, enormous loaves of pale *sitny* with a few currants and a golden crust, and nicely sad in the middle—"

"What do you know of *sitny?*"

"I used to eat it in the kitchen. It tasted far more delicious than any roll in the dining room. Hot *sitny* with cherry jam on it, and a dreadful stomach ache afterwards, but I went on loving it—" And Frossia looked gratefully at Nikolashka. The picture of a small grocer's shop certainly filled one of the many irritating gaps. He would have candles to sell, she remembered, and he would sell few of them: he must have used his candles at night. What other time would he have had for his reading? Grocers' shops did not close till after eleven at night.

"Did he fight in the war?" she probed further.

"But I know so little of him except—"

"Yes, yes, his stories, of course," and Frossia had to stay satisfied with the grocer's shop for a time.

Now that the second winter was drawing in, there were needs, duties, demands, anxieties, and problems to be faced every day. Frossia's employment at the Goelro came to a sudden end with the arrival of five experienced and hardened typists from Moscow. They had their short hair waved, their nails were painted, they brought astonishingly good clothes in their luggage, languid manners, and a crop of stories. For several days the whole secretarial staff listened breathlessly. Moscow was definitely civilized, they said. Moscow teemed with foreigners, and what foreigner ever went to Russia without a fat pocketbook? There were Danes, Ital-

215

ians, English, Germans and, of course, Americans, and Americans were the best of them all. Streets were quite decently lit at night, some shops were open, in fact, a great many shops had reopened since the arrival of foreigners. "Foreigners hate not being able to spend their money," said the young girls from Moscow, "and you must have shops to spend your money in." You could buy anything in Moscow—even a pair of real leather shoes or a fur coat. You could eat an exciting meal at a decent restaurant if you kept your wits about you, and, unless you were a fool, you had not a single dull moment in Moscow. The five typists exhibited their flawlessly manicured hands and high-heeled court shoes. "From Paris," drawled one of them who wore an exotic white muslin blouse, all flounces, tucks, and more flounces, all done in most exquisite picoté, and Frossia disconcerted her by saying:

"We have no central heating here. You will freeze."

"We may go back—"

"Well, we are not having a very dull time here."

The girl in white muslin yawned.

"Here? Why, the place is like a cesspool or a churchyard. I don't know why we have come here. We could not say no. We were sent. But I am sure we never deserved such a punishment. . . . Imagine being sent to Petrograd from Moscow. . . . Why, this is not even an important city any more. It is just dead." And Frossia left the room.

But she had not to endure the ladies from Moscow for more than a few days. She received her dismissal calmly enough. She knew herself inefficient. Yet she had tried hard enough, and now her efforts were finished, and the slim wad of pink notes no longer came her way. Boldly she tried the Commissariat for Education, reminding herself that she knew three languages and could amuse a child by stories. She was interviewed by a fat and kindly woman in a shapeless khaki linen dress.

"Languages?" She looked doubtful. "Well, no, not just yet. But do you think you could teach quite small children?"

"Yes, gladly—"

"Could you go to Ufa and teach Russian to little Tartar children?"

"Why, yes—"

"Well, will you fill in this form and it will be sent on to the Commissar?"

Frossia laboriously filled in the form. The fat woman said not unkindly: "You realize you must have two Party references. Can you get them?"

"I don't know anyone—" Frossia refused even to think of Cherny. "Surely—"

"I don't know anyone. Is it any use your sending on the application?"

"Well, I had better be honest—you are not likely to stand a very good chance, but you can always try again when you have met someone." She smiled, and Frossia politely returned the smile.

Her hopes were thin enough, but stubbornly she went on nursing them. Ufa was thousands of miles away, but Frossia was past caring. Petrograd meant so much to her that a part of it would certainly travel with her. Meanwhile she said to herself repeatedly that she must find a job.

She heard no more about Ufa.

She had little Dasha for hours to herself, and now Frossia began giving her improvised lessons to while away the time. Once Nikolashka asked her to go and look up an old friend of his, a woman of seventy who lived in Vladimirsky Prospect. Frossia found the house empty, its doors open. It had evidently been set on fire early in 1917. Now it was derelict, and there was hardly any furniture left, but in a ground floor room Frossia came on a rare treasure—stacks of picture postcards put away in a chest. She carried away as many as she could, and asked Nikolashka: "Was it looting?" and he parried: "And who would want such trash?"

"I do. It is not trash. These are foreign postcards. Look—England, Italy, France, Germany, Norway, some from Egypt, and India . . ."

"Pretty things," he dismissed them. "But you could not barter them for a grain of wheat."

"I don't mean to barter them."

She began using the postcards with Dasha. She went through her treasure trove, and discovered that she had been to some of the places they showed, gaps in others could easily be filled by her imagination, and for about two hours every day Frossia talked to Dasha about the great cities and buildings in Europe, and the child was happy, and Anna Trofimovna acknowledged her indebtedness by an occasional invitation to a meal.

Yet improvised geography lessons, paid for in terms of an irregularly offered bowl of gruel, could not save Frossia from hunger. She went on trying various avenues, invariably finding a closed door at the other end. Once Parfen Nikitich, the undertaker, met her in the tiny communal kitchen, and muttered:

"Still looking for a job, are you? Well, there is a lot to be done, but jobs are about as plentiful as pearls in a herring."

"Oh, don't speak of herrings, Parfen Nikitich," Frossia implored.

"You are hungry," he said in a strange soft voice, fumbled in his pocket, and pressed an egg into her hand. "It is hard boiled. I had a parcel from the country this morning."

Frossia would have shelled and eaten the egg in a few seconds, but suddenly she looked at the undertaker and saw him for the first time.

"I get parcels from the country often enough," he went on. "You would be welcome."

She laid the egg on the dirty little table.

"You misunderstood me, Parfen Nikitich," she said gravely and quietly. "I asked you not to mention herrings because I cannot really bear them. We have had so many of them lately."

He sneered and shuffled back to his den, having first slipped the egg back into his pocket.

Occasional work drifted Frossia's way, there was plenty to do, and so few ways in which one might get things done, and she took everything, careful to hide her joy at the prospect of a few days' meals. Otherwise there was nothing but the official bread ration, given free—so long as the supplies lasted, and the dinner from the nearest communal kitchen. Its doors opened at noon, and the queue began at nine or even earlier. In sleet and in snow they stood and waited for their portion of tepid fish soup. Those who had a carrot or a potato thrown into their pannikins, were the lucky ones. But the unkempt woman behind the low greasy counter had her favorites, and Frossia was not among them. She carried her pannikin, careful not to spill a single drop and, once at home, she sternly divided the unsavory watery contents into halves and her bread into three portions. A certain amount of fuel was given for the kitchen, and there Frossia heated up the fishy mess, swallowed it hot, unaware of either taste or smell, and broke off tiny pieces of coarse unpalatable bread.

Yet those were red letter days. Often and often a minute portion of vegetable oil was doled out in lieu of bread, and the unchanging fishy mess from the communal kitchen had to be swallowed without any bread. On such days Frossia must avoid Dasha and the whole of her world because hunger made her clumsy and afraid, and, after a spell of panic, she compelled herself to go to the Zabalkansky and to Paulina Pavlovna, talk and listen, and politely refuse what slender provender Paulina Pavlovna had to offer. She sat and talked, her eyes grown enormous in a thin pale face.

Yet Paulina Pavlovna could not be deceived. She spoke to her brother. She spoke to Lilian:

"Frossia is out of a job. You must help her. You owe her so much in the past. You know all kinds of important people today. Frossia has been kind and generous to you. You must do something for her."

Lilian grumbled.

"Things are difficult for everybody. Why, I have not seen Serge for three weeks. He said he was going to Chernigov for flour." Her mouth curved bitterly. "I had a look at his permit, it said Odessa, not Chernigov. You would not go to Odessa for flour, would you?"

"I don't know," said Paulina Pavlovna unhappily. "Odessa is a big place, you might find flour there. I was not speaking of your husband, Lilian, but of Frossia. You go to so many places, you meet people. I know there is much against her, and Paul and I cannot help, we are two uninfluential bits of flotsam, but you are different, Lilian, and you—"

"Yes, what about me? I am an officer's daughter. I have had important connections. I must tread carefully—if only for the sake of Serge. And Frossia is not easy to help, Paulina Pavlovna. She has strange ideas, keeps strange friends. . . . Think of what Anna von Packen did. . . . If it had not been for Cherny, Frossia would have suffered. . . . And then her keeping that boy in Moshkov Lane, a young man with no identity papers. . . . He must have been one of those old régime people—"

"Frossia does not believe in the old régime."

"She says so. Paulina Pavlovna, I do go to many places, and I do meet people. I could say to some of them: Please do something for me. They might or might not. But I don't trust Frossia. . . ."

"You are very foolish, Lilian." Paulina Pavlovna looked unhappier than ever, her eyes welled with tears, her mouth shook, and Lilian was ashamed.

"I might try," she said, but she did not try, and for some time avoided Paulina Pavlovna and the flat in Moyka. This was not difficult. Lilian had her own friends, her own haunts where none among Paulina Pavlovna's world could have penetrated. Also she had her own amusements, and her leisure occupied all her waking hours. Yet once a strange hand touched her thin shoulder so that she shuddered.

In old days, the Islands used to be the fashionable ground of Petrograd. The Point, a narrow tongue of land lapped by two rivers on either side, used to be crowded with carriages and riders. There were elegant bridges joining one island to another. It was a kingdom of bridges, small coppices, spacious parks, and leafy lanes. Apothecaries' Island sheltered many a ruined villa once built in a pseudo-Egyptian style; the dark violet and dull red paint flaked off the flimsy peristyles, and splintered windows hinted at bats and owls. The villas on both Elaguin and Stone Islands had long since lost their dazzling whiteness, few of them were peopled at all, but the trees on all the Islands still kept their deeply leafed loveliness through the summer and a stern naked beauty in the winter, and sunsets could still be enjoyed from the end of The Point where two rivers ran into the leaden gray waters of the Gulf, and where to the west, towards Finland and Sweden, the sky lay washed in swathes of copper, crimson, cobalt, and dim smoky green.

To The Point then Lilian drove from Bi-Ba-Bo one clear, cold October afternoon. She drove in a hired sleigh, the snow having fallen very early that year, and she had a companion whose name she had not caught. He was a slight brown-faced man with a gentleman's manners and a slightly exaggerated accent. She had noticed his wallet at Bi-Ba-Bo, and the thick wad of multi-colored paper had reassured her. Also he wore an army uniform, there were several red stars sewn on the right sleeve of his tunic, and he had a definite air of authority. At some distance from The Point, he paid off the driver and sent him away.

"And how do we get back? There are no trams running near here?"

She was anxious, and his very casual: "Need you worry about that?" made her feel worried. The Islands were deserted. the pleasances looked gloomy in that uncertainly colored hour before twilight, there was nothing in the world around them except silence, thin snow underfoot, thin blue-gray ice on the river, and the sky covered with a pale green mesh in the West, and Lilian shivered.

"There will not be a sunset tonight."

"There is always a sunset."

She glanced at him sideways, and realized she had been a fool. He looked different. "Is it this uncertain light?" she wondered, and knew it was not. He walked warily, glancing to the right and the left, as though his main business was concerned with solitary places. Suddenly, hands in pockets, looking straight ahead of him, he halted and began talking. Lilian learned that he knew of her, and of Serge, also, and of Serge's slimy economical depredations, and her heart quailed within her. She had been mistaken, he was no army man, he was a Tchekist. He had set a trap, she had fallen into it, and now she would have to cringe and plead for mercy, but his thin brown face looked harder than iron.

"Yes, comrade—"

"You need not call me that. Do you not hate it all? You are a lady, your father was in the army. Do you not hate this tyranny?"

She kept silent.

"And you are attractive. That was why we decided to use you. We believe you are clever. Will you work for us? Your husband is so often away. You have leisure and wit. You can easily become intimate with some important commissar. Why, you might be able to go to Moscow, and we have several of our people there. Does it not appeal to you?"

She said nothing. He caught her hand. She wrenched it away. He could hear her jerky, uneasy breathing, and he laughed.

"You need not be afraid of us. We never shoot women—"

"I am going back—"

"So you are afraid—"

"That has nothing to do with it. You were mistaken in my feelings, Monsieur—"

He laughed.

"You need not imagine that I will tell you my name. You say we were mistaken in your feelings? But you were overheard bemoaning your fate, wishing you might escape abroad and live in peace and freedom. Was this just a passing mood, Lilian Ivanovna?"

Lilian never answered. She ran. He did not follow her. She ran down the broad avenue, her slender sense of direction torn to shreds. Twilight fell. She stumbled, slackened her pace, and listened. But she was in a still, lonely world. She moved on and stumbled again. After an hour of aimless roving, she reached a bridge, and somehow, weary and frightened, she came to her flat back of Liteyny Prospect. She met no one on the stairs, she was alone, but the untidy room, with its disheveled beds and dusty furniture, disturbed rather than reassured her. There were four hundred odd people living in the huge house, but in her bedroom Lilian was alone, defenseless, and tormented by fears she might not name. She snatched at a bottle and found it empty. She seized a cracked mirror and examined her face. Then she poured some water into a small basin and rubbed her eyes fiercely as if she were trying to wash all fear out of them. She must not be alone, and she had no acquaintance among the tenants. She locked and barricaded the door, and crouched on the bed, munching a stale crust. But a lodger's rasping cough reached her from the room above, and she shook like a leaf driven by the wind.

Then anger swept over her that anyone should dare to try to entangle her into a vicious, dangerous coil of darkly meshed intrigue, and anger fought with her fear and all but vanquished it. With steadier fingers Lilian painted her thin face, brushed her hair, wrapped herself into a warm coat, and groped down the dark abyss of the staircase.

Presently she stood outside a small unlit house in Kazanskaya Street off Nevsky Prospect. She rapped, and an insignificant middle-aged body let her in. She ran towards the light, a few familiar faces, and a table set with smoked fish, sausage, and some bottles. She drank a whole tumbler of *hanja*, and felt better and braver. Her friends offered a game of cards. They played late into the night. In the small hours Lilian was sitting on the floor, chanting in a cracked voice:

"I have got the queen of clubs, and the ace of hearts, and the king of diamonds. I have got the queen of clubs. . . . Goodness, are there two of them in the pack?" And she fell asleep, the greasy ace of hearts clasped in her thin fingers.

7

One Sunday morning Frossia went to the soup kitchen, got her meager portion, and hurried back. At the corner of Maly Prospect, a semi-derelict house had recently been turned into an elementary school. There was a square yard in front of the house, but the wooden paling had tumbled down in places, and she could see the yard with its two ancient lilac trees in the middle. They will be good to look at in the spring, she thought, halting for a second, when a plump earnest-looking girl of about twenty came out of the door and crossed the yard. She wore a sheepskin coat. Her spectacled face looked troubled, angry, and wistful all at once. Frossia guessed she was the teacher.

"This is a nice life! My section is meeting at 1 o'clock. It is an important meeting, all about dietetics, and I must speak, and my assistant is down with bronchitis. They have taken her to St. Mary Magdalene's Hospital. Just imagine, I cannot go to the meeting because of the children—"

"May I help?"

"Are you a teacher then?" The spectacled eyes swept over Frossia and obviously found her wanting. "You don't somehow look like one—"

"No . . . But I have been—quite well educated . . ." Frossia grew bolder, "and I have been giving lessons to a tenant's daughter—"

"This is not proper lessons—" the girl spoke severely—"but they must be kept amused unless they choose to go to sleep. They are free to do what they like, of course. They are tiny things, the eldest is eight. There are thirty-six of them."

"Let me come," pleaded Frossia, but the teacher looked thoughtful.

"What will you do with them? This is most irregular—"

"Just for this afternoon," said Frossia, and shepherded the hesitating girl back to the front door. There, in a spacious dim room, she found thirty-six children, ranging between three and eight. There were about a dozen cots, a map, some paper flowers, odd boxes of colored bricks, and an enormous quantity of clay in the corner. "This is the new system," said the girl in her best pedagogical voice. "They are free to express themselves, you know." She looked round rather helplessly and vanished.

Frossia drew in her breath. The children stared at her very solemnly. They had had their dinner, they were not hungry, and she was glad to see that they were dressed warmly and decently. But she did not like their quietness. She tried to get near them, but they were shy, most of them turned their faces to the wall, a few cried. The rest went on regarding her with a solemnity she found most disconcerting. However, there were the paper flowers, the bricks, the clay. Wildly, Frossia plunged her hands in the clay, found some water, and began molding an animal no Zoological Gardens had ever seen. She gave it a head, a tail, and four legs. She looked round, discovered a dusty box of colors in a corner, and daubed red and yellow all over the extraordinary body. By the time she was finishing the tail, most of the children were clustered round her. Two of them grew bold enough to demand the creation of yet another animal. Frossia nodded and set to work. A child seized her brush and began dabbing violent yellow all over the clay. By the time the teacher came back, most of the thirty-six were generously bedaubed with wet clay and various paints, and perfectly happy.

"They have taken to you. They usually howl when my assistant tries to do anything," said the girl. "Well, please come tomorrow morning. I shall have to regularize it of course. What is your name? Oh, you live round the corner. You could be on duty in the afternoon sometimes, could you not? You see," she went on importantly, "I am a fully qualified teacher, but my section takes so much of my time."

"I shall come tomorrow," cried Frossia, her heart singing.

This time there was no question of any Party references. The spectacled girl had it all done within a week. Frossia found herself occupied every morning and occasionally in the afternoon. There was a wage of sorts, also a teacher's ration card. She taught them the alphabet, told them animal and flower stories, molded weird shapes out of clay, made paper flowers with them. Sometimes she arrived, armed with a few postcards, gathered the eldest infants around her, and gave them a highly colored geography lesson.

It was in those days that Igor Vladimirovich found his way to the balconied house in Maly Prospect. The first time he came one late afternoon, bowed awkwardly, and played with the fringe of Frossia's shabby tablecloth. She told him about her occupation.

"That is good."

She stopped her sewing.

"Tell me something about yourself?"

"There is nothing to tell, Euphrosynia Pavlovna. I come from Tula. My father had a small grocery business—"

"And there you learnt to read Plato?"

"I don't understand you," he said unhurriedly. "It happened this way. One day a carriage broke down outside my shop. It belonged to wealthy people, the woman wore silks and ostrich feathers, she had a sickly, bad-tempered boy with her. It took the man some time to repair the wheel. So they came in. I dusted two chairs for them. They did not thank me. I offered them sweets and plain gingerbread. They would not have any. They just talked as though I were not there. Well, could you blame them? What was there to talk to a grocer about? The boy was going to an expensive school, he hated it, and the mother was trying to make him see that education was worthwhile. He got angry: 'Being learned is all right for the poor. We are rich. Why should I waste my time over those silly books?' Well, the wheel was repaired, they drove away, and I never saw them again, but I never forgot them. I could just read and write, that was all. Few books then came my way. There were no libraries I could use. But I had a kind customer. I talked to him. He lent me Kluchevsky's *History of Russia*."

"What did you get out of it?"

"Pride in my country, Euphrosynia Pavlovna, but Russia alone did not seem enough. You cannot be of much use anywhere if you know a lot about your own land and nothing of any others. So I took to burning candles out of the shop. . . ." And Igor went on in the manner of his countrymen, earnestly, unhurriedly, and at great length, telling Frossia about the varied nature of his reading.

224

It grew dark, she left off sewing, and would not light her tiny oil lamp.

"What happened afterwards?"

"My father died. The war came. My mother went to live with a sister at Byalostok. My brother and I went out to join her. We kept another small shop. My sister died. They would not conscript me, they said I had something wrong with my eyes. My brother was a hunchback." He paused. "Euphrosynia Pavlovna, this is a hard subject. Have you ever lived with real cruelty?"

"Never—"

"My brother was cruel. I always tried to think it was his infirmity. . . . But he was cruel to my mother, and I loved her. Then she died, and the Germans came, and I fled from Byalostok, and went to Kiev, and stayed there till the Revolution. That is my whole story, Euphrosynia Pavlovna. I had the railway job given me at Kiev. Then they sent me here. It is a hard job, it is making a hard man of me, but you cannot choose your work nowadays, and they say I am good at it."

She lit the lamp, and offered him tea and some rye rusks. He drank his tea in true peasant fashion from the saucer, slowly puffing at it, holding the saucer carefully with the five fingers of his right hand.

"Yes," Frossia echoed, "I know you are good at your job. You do love people."

"And who would not? Especially our people. . . . Dirty they are, and slow, and idle sometimes, but worthwhile. Why, a Chinaman came to me the other day. He had been robbed in a street in Moscow. An old woman took him into her house, fed him, and gave him a coat. 'I cannot pay you for the coat,' he said. 'And do you take me for an infidel?' said the woman. The Chinaman said to me: 'If there had been a Russia all those thousands of years ago, Confucius might have been a Russian.' I did not agree with him. I have read something about their Confucius. I don't think our people are like that. They have charity, and they can be cruel. It is said this is the Tartar leaven in us, Euphrosynia Pavlovna. But we are not pure Tartar. We are Scythian and Norse, too. And there is much evil in us, but do you know—" he got agitated, almost there burnt a fire in his quiet eyes—"I have never found it in any book on philosophy—I have just felt it in myself. The mere knowledge of evil does not defile anyone. Indeed, Euphrosynia Pavlovna, a man who knows evil and is able to say 'no,' is purer, stronger, than he who ignores the very nature of evil. I am putting it badly, you will understand—"

225

"I do . . . No, I have never read about it."

He finished his tea and wiped his mouth on the palm of his hand. She found herself watching him. Certainly, he was didactic, rough, and the peasant in him would never disappear. And why should he behave any differently? she thought, and heard herself asking:

"All you know, Igor Vladimirovich, has not come to you from books only?"

He put his head on one side.

"Now that you are asking it, no. Take immortality, for instance. That was not reading, but experience. I had a great friend once. He was a teacher in a private school, Euphrosynia Pavlovna, a very well educated man. He taught me to read Plato and Marcus Aurelius. He lived in Kazan. I knew much about him. I owed him much. But I never met him. I never saw his photograph. I could not even imagine what he looked like. But his mind, his spirit, both were an open book to me, and I knew that both were fine and rare. Then he died. I heard about it some time later. I just had his letters, but I had nothing in my memory—neither face nor voice could I remember because I had never met him. When I heard he was dead, I knew he had not gone altogether. I am not clever, Euphrosynia Pavlovna, I may have read much, but it is difficult for me to explain things clearly. I just knew he had not vanished, and that was all—"

"I think I understand," said Frossia.

8

One sleety November morning the chairman of the Domkom made his sporadic inspection of the house, poked his head into Frossia's rooms, and said gruffly:

"Housing shortage is getting worse, *grajdanka*. You must have a lodger."

The inner room had no other door. Frossia's heart sank, but argument would have been futile, and she said:

"Well, send me a lodger."

Varvara had once worked at a shoe factory. Her only job was clipping the metal tags to shoe-laces. She used to be paid one kopek for a hundred laces.

"But how many did you do in a day?" asked Frossia.

"Thousands! The foreman counted them. His last thousand always had two hundred in it, not ten. But we were not allowed to count them."

"How much did you make in a day?"

"Sometimes twenty-five, sometimes forty kopeks."

"And you lived on it?"

"Yes, and I kept my mother and paid the hospital tax. It was not so bad," laughed Varvara, "but we were not allowed to learn any other jobs. You were taught one job, and you stayed on, you never moved—"

Now Varvava was nursing at the Exchange Hospital down Bolshoy Prospect. She found the work hard and exacting, the hours were long, the food occasionally scarce and nearly always bad, but she liked it none the less.

She arrived with a small hamper, a coat over her arm, a kettle and a saucepan. The first evening they shared a lamp for the sake of economy. Varvara sat with her hands folded. Frossia offered her a book.

"I cannot read," said Varvara.

"Would you like to learn?"

"I ought to . . . I might . . . If it is not too much for you. I am not very bright, you know—"

Varvara was clean, grateful, and exhausting. When she did not talk, she sang. She snored when she slept. But her sense of gratitude was that of a child, and Frossia tried to endure both singing and chatter. Pavel Pavlovich called and offered to make a sketch of Varvara. She was beautiful in the generous Russian way—big gray eyes, brown hair, good modeling of chin, cheek, and forehead. But she did not want to be sketched; she put her hands to her mouth, went deep crimson, and rushed out of the room. One evening she danced. Frossia left the door open. Olga Semenovna, Dasha's mother, and the undertaker, all left their saucepans and came to watch. The undertaker rubbed his hands and smiled. Later Frossia said:

"Varvara, you are not a fool, you will understand me: don't joke too much with Parfen Nikitich—"

"I understand," Varvara said gravely. "I want to marry a proper man. I would not spoil my life with anyone so old. I want to have children," she explained, her gray eyes shining. "Several children, Euphrosynia Pavlovna. Why, you look at it now—we may starve and go in tatters, but they do much for the children. If I had a son, he would go into the army. If he were clever, they would make him an officer. If I had a daughter, she would go into a factory, and if she had brains, she would end high. It is worthwhile having a child today, Euphrosynia Pavlovna. In the old days a *fabrichnaya* lass never had one if she could help it. Well," she added, "it may

227

all be muddle and hunger and dirt now. But these must pass, and a morning is always wiser than an evening."

"When you have learnt your alphabet, Varvara," said Frossia, "there won't be much left for me to teach you."

But Varvara was insatiable, as ambitious as she was talkative. Within three months she passed her examinations for a trained nurse, and left for Kazan.

"I am sorry for you," she told Frossia before leaving, "we have everything to look forward to, but I reckon your world is shattered."

"No," Frossia said very firmly, but Varvara's gray eyes doubted the denial.

CHAPTER EIGHT

"CHARRED WORLDS"

Varvara was gone. Frossia's inner room stood empty. The Domkom suddenly sent along an old carpenter. A hole was made in a wall, a door was made to communicate with the outer passage, and the other was bricked up. Frossia's floor and things were thickly coated with dust and rubble. She questioned the carpenter. He knew no more than she did. A new lodger would be installed, Frossia could not doubt that, and she did not rebel. So many houses on the Island were uninhabitable. Frossia decided to go and see the Domkom chairman. In his cubbyhole of an office she saw a stocky small man, whose Russian savored of a grammar learned too laboriously. The chairman was saying slowly, taking care to enunciate every word:

"Now do you understand, Comrade Zolperich? I have a room for you, in the house next door, a small room, but you will not mind—"

"No." The stocky man turned round, and Frossia's eyes met his. She could not tell much from his appearance. He was just small and dark and slightly furtive. His drab brown coat was carefully buttoned up, and so was his lean face. His eyes peered, his mouth opened into a very thin line.

"Here you are," said the chairman to Frossia, "Comrade Zolperich from Essen, Germany, a technician, working at the Baltiysky Works—"

Zolperich bowed. Frossia bowed.

"You have been here before?"

"Oh, yes. I have spent many years in Russia," he said politely. "It was my business to be in Russia. Now I am back."

She looked at his small well-shaped hands. The right thumb was missing. The fingernails were clean, well-kept. His hands were closed in, secretive in all their gestures. His thin lips kept smiling.

"So—I am to go."

"I had better show you the way—"

The chairman said importantly: "Comrade Zolperich is also joining the State Planning Commission."

"Yes, the Gosplan," added Zolperich.

"Ah," said Frossia, and led the way to the balconied house. She showed the room, pointed to the tiny communal kitchen, and left him alone.

Within a few days Zolperich was at home. He carved a doll for Dasha. He fetched water for Anna Trofimovna and the midwife. He loaned his magnificent pocket knife to the undertaker. He volunteered to get the rations for Dasha's mother. Paulina Pavlovna met him, and he enchanted her. Nikolashka came and asked if Zolperich could bake rolls in the German fashion. Zolperich immediately lighted the kitchen stove, mixed flour in a tin basin, vanished into his room for other ingredients and, within an hour, the tenants were regaled with hot gold-brown rolls.

"If I had sugar, saffron, candied peel . . . Ah . . . *Zutaten—*" he sighed, and Nikolashka roared with laughter.

"Candied peel? What is it?"

Zolperich noticed Frossia's downtrodden heels, purloined her shoes one evening, and cobbled them. She found it an effort to have to thank him.

"Ah—but it is nothing. Just a bit of thread and a bit of leather and a bit of time—"

Pavel Pavlovich passed his verdict. Zolperich, according to him, was not real. He suggested a stuffed angel, or one of those characters from a German fairy tale. "The man cannot be what he is. A technician! Goodness, Euphrosynia Pavlovna, I heard Igor Vladimirovich say that he could not be a real German. For my part, I think one day he will vanish in a spiral of blue smoke—"

Elena Ivanovna was much more vehement.

"Stuffed angel, you say! Well, I would prefer to make another comparison. . . . That night Zolperich came to the Zabalkansky. . . . He did not come empty-handed. He brought gifts—cigarettes, two bottles of lemonade, matches, a pack of cards. He talked so slowly. . . . And I felt all the time that his words were one thing, his mind quite another. He never answers a question, he never really asks one, and he gets told everything."

"He never talks about Germany," boomed Pavel Pavlovich. "He just said: 'Germany is tired. I am not now interested in Germany. I want the world to be one place, now it is a chest of drawers, all locked. . . .'"

"He knows Russia," said Frossia. "He has been to Odessa, Moscow, Kharkov, many other places. He has traveled East of the Urals

230

with the Goelro people. He has seen Sovkhozes and Kolkhozes. . . .
But you can never tell what he thinks of anything. . . . Elena
Ivanovna is right—he tells one thing and thinks another—"

She did not invite Zolperich to the Zabalkansky again. He had
not been a success there. But he came unasked, brought a few more
gifts, sat, listened, and talked in his careful, buttoned-up way.

He was not one of them, and some people at the Zabalkansky
showed this in no uncertain manner by refusing his lavishly offered cigarettes, but Zolperich appeared to have no resentment in
him. He went on smiling. It happened to be one of those evenings
when Pavel Pavlovich occupied the stage almost by himself. The
others were tired. They were content to stay in the shadows, to
listen, and to sip their syrup. Pavel Pavlovich was holding forth
about the idea of good, when Zolperich leaned forward and said
politely:

"But it does not exist. Things happen—it is all cause and effect.
If you are strong, you are everywhere. If you are weak, your place
is in a dim corner. Goodness does not come in at all."

"I was not talking about that," said Pavel Pavlovich. "I was not
talking about things at all, but ideas—"

Zolperich remained very polite.

"But everything is always determined by strength. A thinker with
marvelous ideas could not enforce them if he had not the strength
to do so."

Pavel Pavlovich looked annoyed. His thread was broken, his horizon temporarily clouded. Elena Ivanovna acidly said that there
were two ways of arguing—the Russian way and the German way,
and, "We don't understand your way," she added. But Zolperich
merely said that he was not arguing at all.

They disliked him more than ever at the Zabalkansky. But Frossia was uncertain. Is it just his very tiresome kindness? she wondered to herself. We, too, are kind, but again in a different way.
Zolperich bakes you a roll or offers you a cigarette, and both the
roll and the cigarette seem superior as it were, he makes them so,
and one feels cheated and annoyed—

Igor was non-committal.

"He is a German. They were defeated in the war. He may feel
awkward."

"We did not defeat them," argued Frossia.

Zolperich wanted to see Petrograd. Frossia asked Igor to come.
She could not see herself wandering about streets and quays alone
with that strange, buttoned-up, embarrassingly generous man. They
took Zolperich down the quays, past the Senate, the Admiralty Gar-

dens, the Winter Palace. They showed him the exquisite Stroganov Palace, Rastrelli's masterpiece. Frossia told him about Rinaldi's work in girdling the Neva with dark purple granite. They showed him the State Bank in Fontanka Street, the Kazan Cathedral, the incredibly lovely Falconet horses on the Nevsky. They took him across several bridges and led him to the Fortress where so many Romanov men and women slept under their heavy white marble sarcophagi. It was almost spring when Frossia and Igor were trying to teach the story of Petrograd to a man they barely knew and rather disliked, and that story was all lettered in pale green, tawny gold and faintly powdered red. They gave Zolperich a whole morning at the Hermitage, leading him up the gorgeous staircase between its canyon walls of yellow-veined marble. At the Hermitage Igor showed him the Rembrandts, and Frossia snatched a few moments to ponder alone over the delicate lavender and gray theme of Fra Angelico's "Virgin and Child"; but even to the Hermitage Zolperich went with a notebook and a well-sharpened pencil, and marked the number of the Rembrandts before he as much as glanced at them.

"What it is to be a German!" marveled Frossia when alone with Igor. "Just listen. . . . There are three Nevas in the city, Big, Middle, Little, three canals, Obukhov, Catherine, Fontanka, twenty-three smaller streams, and 150 bridges in all! Igor Vladimirovich, I never knew Petrograd had 150 bridges. . . . Can you get much from a city by learning the number of its bridges? I don't think I know more than fifteen, twenty, perhaps, but they are all familiar friends—not just things in stone, timber, and steel. . . ."

"It is the German way," said Igor.

Zolperich noticed Taglioni's portrait.

"So you like ballet?" She was surprised.

"I am a mathematician. . . . Ah, I see. . . . You are astonished at my words. A mathematical idea is endless. So is ballet. There is an appearance of finality in any movement. You might say that the multiplication table is final. It, too, suggests finality, and is none the less endless. And ballet is a mathematical fact. . . . But let me fill your kettle." Zolperich seized it when she stayed him.

"Facts and things and strength . . . Always strength, Comrade Zolperich—"

His eyes never opened widely. He spoke just as politely as ever: "That is a strange tone of voice. How sadly wasted you are! You have Taglioni on your table, you teach little children little things—hemming a handkerchief, singing a small song, showing them pictures of the Alps and building houses of painted bricks. . . . You probably tell them stories. And you know so few facts. You could not even remember there were one hundred and fifty bridges in this city, and you have lived here all your life. You showed me Falconet's horses, and you did not know his dates. I asked you whether there had been a city here before 1703, and you did not know. Yet you are a teacher. This is very interesting and astonishing—"

Stuffed angel, thought Frossia, and spoke hotly. "What does it matter? What do dates matter? I love Falconet's horses, I have loved them all my life, I love their fluidity of limb and mane. I don't care when Falconet was born." Viciously she added: "You see, I am a pure barbarian, I am no German pigeon-hole—"

Zolperich said quietly:

"Is it not stupid to try to hurt those who will not be hurt?"

But Frossia pretended not to hear, and went on:

"But you would not really like anyone to become a pigeon-hole. You have been here some time, and you have asked questions, but you tell us nothing. We live in an enclosed garden, some of us are hungry and thirsty. You have traveled widely. Also you have traveled recently. Do you know what this means to some among us? Yes, you have baked us some nice scones and you have been generous with tobacco. But kindness is not everything. . . . You tell us nothing. Pavel Pavlovich asked you about modern painters in Germany. You said: 'Germany is tired.' His sister wanted to know if there were any new books on philosophy. You said: 'Germany is tired.' I suppose you say the same thing at your Gosplan committees—or, perhaps, you say nothing at all. Yes, yes, you are very kind, but I would much rather you did not fill my kettle again—"

He repeated: "Is it not stupid to try to hurt those who will not be hurt?" bowed briefly, and left her.

He had angered Frossia. He had also disturbed her. "You are a teacher. You know so little. . . ." She could not help brooding over the words, and the next day winter was back among them; it was so cold that at the school the children had to be smothered under blankets and mattresses. At noon the milk was a huge iced cake in the can. Frossia had to chip it, and she filled mugs and tumblers with milky splinters. "Hold it between your hands, children. Don't drink it before it melts," but suddenly the eldest among them wanted to know why the milk had frozen. Because of the cold in the room, she told them, and explained the freezing of the milk as best she knew, and felt she had done it very haltingly. Zolperich was right about her: she knew so little that she had no right to teach anything. The children needed clear and solid beginnings.

233

"And I am really ignorant about the simplest things," she said to herself, and decided to spend an evening with Elena Ivanovna.

At the corner of Annunciation Square Frossia heard a thin pitiful wail, stooped, and felt her hands touching a bundle left on the pavement. The wailing turned to a queer sucking noise. She gathered the bundle closer in her arms, and ran into Galernaya Street. She came in crying: "Milk, please, Elena Ivanovna, some warm milk for a guest."

Elena Ivanovna asked no questions. She pushed an armchair nearer the stove, took the bundle from Frossia, and struggled with cumbersome folds of an enormous dirty gray shawl. Presently the tiny thing lay naked before them. Its gray eyes were open. It cried piteously. Elena Ivanovna tried to give it milk, it refused, and went on crying, its voice getting thinner and thinner. Elena Ivanovna put the milk aside, warmed her own hands at the stove, picked up the tiny body, chafed and rubbed, and crooned a soft song all the time, and her face was full of a light which came neither from the stove nor from the candle.

Frossia watched, fascinated and yet repelled. She had never before seen anything so thin, tiny, and helpless, so dirty and ravaged by hunger and disease. But Elena Ivanovna's movements were service and worship together. She got water, clean rags, a towel, she warmed a blanket, and all the time her face was bent over that tiny piece of helplessness on her knees. Presently the small body was clean, warm, comfortable, the tiny mouth opened, a few drops of milk were poured in, and Elena Ivanovna wrapped the poor ravaged thing into clean linen rags, and Frossia said:

"Zolperich would have said, 'I found it at 8.50 this evening at the corner of Annunciation Square. Clothes: a gray shawl and some dirty rags. Sex—male. Age—about five months. Condition: emaciated, skin covered with sores,' and Zolperich—"

But Elena Ivanovna was not listening.

"I will take him to Mavra Grigorievna tomorrow morning. She is clever. I think these sores are nothing but dirt. Poor little mite. . . . He must have been dropped a few moments before you came along."

"Why?"

"Else you might have found him dead," she explained calmly. "Now I will look after him till the morning and then hand him over to Mavra Grigorievna. Thank goodness they don't worry about birth certificates, but you and I are going to christen him, Frossia, and I want him to be called Bogdan—given by God," and Elena Ivanovna dipped her right hand into a basin of water and made

234

the sign of the cross over the small puckered forehead. "I baptize thee, Bogdan, in the name of the Father, and of the Son, and of the Holy Ghost." She picked him up and rocked him gently. "What was it you were saying about Zolperich?"

"He has dug a pit under my feet," sighed Frossia. "Elena Ivanovna, I am very ignorant, am I not?"

But Elena Ivanovna carefully laid Bogdan on a pillow along a wide sofa, listened to his quietened breathing, and spoke without turning round:

"I have not had my supper yet. You must have it with me. It is late, it is cold, and you are not going to cross the bridge again tonight—"

There was some millet, a few pickled onions, and a very diminutive piece of bread. Elena Ivanovna carefully divided the bread. Frossia refused her share.

"Nobody has ever said 'no' at my table," said her hostess so solemnly that Frossia must needs accept the gift.

They had eaten, and leaned back in their chairs drawn close to the iron stove. The room was in half-darkness except for the island of light round the candle. Bogdan slept peacefully on his pillow, Elena Ivanovna picked up a blanket she was mending, and waited.

"Why has Zolperich come here, Elena Ivanovna?"

"To work, I reckon," shrugged the elder woman. "Someone said things in Germany were hard enough for everybody."

"He never mentions Germany—except the fatigue there. He never does talk much. He listens and asks questions."

"Well, he is a foreigner, all foreigners are eaten up by curiosity. What pit has he dug under your feet?"

"I must leave my school," said Frossia dully, and told Elena Ivanovna about Falconet's horses and the 150 bridges and the frozen milk and her inability to give adequate explanations. Elena Ivanovna sat listening. But Frossia paused, and Elena Ivanovna said nothing. She knew that Frossia had not done, and then Frossia understood why people came to Zabalkansky, went away, and came back again: Elena Ivanovna was a haven in herself, a quiet room in a sadly turmoiled house. So, strangely encouraged by the hostess's silence, Frossia went on. She went past Zolperich and his irritating intrusion, she went past Cherny and Michael and Anna, she even went past the train from Kiev, back to a hushed room in her people's house. In the end she said:

"People can live. People can also die. Or else they can fall asleep in spirit and in mind, asleep so fast that thunder would not waken them. I have not had the pluck to die. I fear death, Elena Ivanovna.

But I cannot live either. I think I have fallen asleep or else I may have wandered into a burnt-down house, and it is nothing but charred walls all around me—"

Elena Ivanovna put down her needle, leaned forward, and glanced at Bogdan.

"Still asleep, bless him," she murmured. "No, Frossia, that foreigner is wrong. You may be ignorant—who am I to judge—or you may not, but I reckon that book-learning alone will not carry anyone far on this road. There is Sofia Efimovna for one. You don't know her, do you? She is a general's daughter, had a grand life in the past, and then went to the university. She has studied law, I think. She is learned enough, but I don't think it is the law that is bearing her along. The other day I met her in Alexeevskaya Street, shabby as shabby can be, helping some little guttersnipes to build a snowman. Just imagine—all of them filthy, verminous. . . . And Sofia Efimovna as happy as a lark among them. . . . It is not her books. It is the deeply human in her. . . . Just knowing that all of us together are one flesh, whether we be clean or dirty, and not knowing it from a distance—but closely—right within your heart. That is the secret—

"Now you say you have gone to sleep. And that is much more important than anything else. But is this true? Dear heart, you cannot suffer and not change. And we are all suffering today, however much we grin and joke about it. My father—the Saints rest him—used to say in his old age that he had had a dream given him about the next century being drenched in suffering. He died in 1893. Well, what was I saying? You cannot stand still under suffering—either it warps you or it widens you. And the warping is so much easier for you. You just sit and gather the hurt into yourself, and it turns into sourness, and there is no effort in it. It never hurts anyone to get smaller than God meant them to be. The other is different. The other means bearing your own hurt, and your neighbor's hurt in you, and so you bear both, and you heal both, and you grow and deepen in them both. But that is not like eating a pickled cucumber, *golubushka*," she said with so much tenderness that Frossia went tense, "only it is good in the end. And why it should be good, I cannot tell you. Christ knew on the Cross."

She paused for quite a while in the manner of people unused to long speeches.

"Words would not make a fur coat," she yawned, "but the other day I met a deacon's widow just about to go back to Tula where she came from, and I brought her in here for warmth, frozen she looked to me, and she burst into such tears that I thought her world was broken. 'What has happened to you?' I asked. Well, she had been to have her travel permit examined at Warsaw Station, and so met Igor Vladimirovich whom she had known well in the old days in Tula. '*Matushka*,' she wailed to me, 'he used to go to Vespers every Saturday and to mass every holy day, and there he sits with the heathens, himself as hard as any unbeliever.' 'Was your permit in order?' I asked her. 'Oh, yes, that was all right, but imagine him . . .' And I was hard on her, *golubushka*. 'What does it matter where he sits?' I said to her. 'An angel in hell will not be turned into a devil, and I know Igor Vladimirovich, and he is a grand man.' Well, dear heart, the deacon's widow stood up, spat on the floor, and out she walked, and I never called her back. What good is it showing a red ribbon to a blind man? Now she is gone, thinking me a hard unbeliever. I may be mad, *golubushka*, but I know somehow that burnt-down churches and martyred priests will never dig a grave for Russia's faith—" Elena Ivanovna stood up. "It is time we spread our blankets. I will just make Bogdan comfortable for the night," and suddenly she turned round and laughed her deep clear laughter. "I wonder if that Zolperich of yours is such a pigeon-hole after all. . . ."

2

The affair of the frozen milk continued disturbing Frossia. She avoided Zolperich, but this did not make it easier for her to forget his oddly delivered strictures. She confessed herself ignorant, and Elena Ivanovna's philosophy—for all the solace it had brought her at the moment—made her see her various shortcomings. She sought to remedy a few of them by paying a call at the nearest public library, and choosing a book on elementary physics. She began reading it in the bread queue. When her turn came to be served with her ration, Nikolashka fingered the thin gray volume, grinned, and said: "This will give you more opinions." But it did not. It left her more than ever bewildered. Later on, at the school, all alone in the spacious dim room, Frossia put her forefinger on the nearest electric switch. I don't even understand how it works. . . . When the lights fused a week ago, Sofia Nikolaevna knew how to put them right. She is only twenty, she is not a very good teacher, but she does know so much.

That day Frossia returned to Maly Prospect to find the balconied house seething in a turmoil. Olga Semenovna, the midwife, had quarreled with Dasha's mother about a saucepan. The saucepan belonged to the midwife. Anna Trofimovna had borrowed it and left it too long on the *plita*. Now the saucepan was ruined, and the midwife cried: "Next winter I shall have to eat my millet uncooked because of your stupidity—"

Dasha's mother offered no excuses. She merely wept in the noisy peasant fashion, covering her face with a dirty darned apron. It was a dreadful catastrophe, and she fully admitted her guilt. You could not get a new saucepan in those days. You could not even get the hole soldered. She was a criminal, and she did not resent Olga Semenovna shouting louder and louder. Parfen Nikitich, the undertaker, stood in the doorway, thumbs in his waistcoat pockets, and he was laughing because even a quarrel meant something interesting so long as you did not have to take sides in it. But his laughter annoyed the women. Both of them forgot the saucepan and turned on the man. How dared he laugh? Was it funny? They screamed at him, shook their fists, he vanished into his room, and they were at it again. The midwife threatened Dasha's mother with the Domkom, a summons, and at least a year at a labor camp. Anna Trofimovna wept all the more noisily.

"This is worse than theft. . . . This is slow murder. You die if you can't eat, and what can I eat now you have taken my saucepan away?" Olga Semenovna was shouting just when Frossia mounted the stairs. She stood, listened, and said that Olga Semenovna might use her saucepan.

Anna Trofimovna wiped her eyes and looked grateful, but the midwife bridled up. She was in need of no charity, she shrieked, she merely wanted her rights.

Dasha's mother whimpered: "Need you go on like that? Euphrosynia Pavlovna spoke out of the goodness of her heart. And I did not do it on purpose. Who would spoil a good saucepan on purpose?"

"You should have stayed to watch it. What am I to do now? I come home, tired and broken-hearted, and I have no supper to comfort me—"

Frossia went past into the kitchen and rummaged on the shelf behind the *plita*.

"Here you are, Olga Semenovna. Please. I am not lending it to you. I am giving it. Please. I have a pannikin, I can do without a saucepan—"

The midwife grumbled: "This is very small. Its quality is not as good as mine, but I will take it. . . . Oh, these are hard days when your happiness depends on an old saucepan—"

Anna Trofimovna managed to smile, Frossia felt happier, and Olga Semenovna continued examining the despised gift when Zolperich stood in his doorway, a real aluminum saucepan in his hands.

It looked so new and shining that the two women eyed it suspiciously.

"This is from Berlin. You are welcome to it." He spoke politely and handed it over to Olga Semenovna, and Dasha's mother murmured: "Now the world is not without kindly folk, is it?" when a terrible thing happened: Olga Semenovna seized the saucepan, flung it against the opposite wall, and shouted:

"Made in Berlin, was it? I would not cook a dog's dinner in it!" She shook her fist at Zolperich and ran to her own room, and Dasha's mother explained in a frightened halting voice that Zolperich should never have said the saucepan was made in Berlin. "Olga Semenovna lost all her sons in the war—"

"Ah," said Zolperich in the same polite voice. He did not seem annoyed in the least. He picked up the rejected present and examined the dents. "It is a great pity," he said, but Frossia felt she could not stay in the kitchen any longer. She dared greatly and knocked at Olga Semenovna's door. She had never been inside before. She found that the room was small and stuffy, all rags and various smells. There was a bed or a sofa, littered with several cushions covered with dirty and faded print. On a rickety table by the wall stood a crimson glass vase holding a few pink paper roses, and above it hung a cheap enlargement of a young man's photograph. Above it again were several other portraits—all showing young men, almost boys, in the uniform of some infantry regiment, and a motto embroidered in bright blue wool on pale buff canvas:

> "Say not with anguish, 'They are no more,'
> But say with gratitude, 'They were.'"

The midwife sprawled on her sofa, and she was sobbing. Frossia closed the door behind her.

"He does say wrong things so often, but he did not mean to hurt you." She spoke slowly, she was not in the least certain whether she was right or not: Zolperich confessed himself to be invulnerable, but she doubted whether he ever thought other people could be as impregnable as himself. Yet those were deeps she could not invite Olga Semenovna to enter.

"He should have known," sniffed the elder woman. "I liked him well enough at first—until I took to brooding somehow. Maybe it was he who killed my sons. He should not have come among us with his oily ways and his kindnesses that nobody wants. I want none of him. Let him choke with his saucepans made in Berlin."

Frossia let her continue. After a while she walked up to the ugly bamboo table and touched the pink roses.

"How very cleverly they are made." She hoped she might be forgiven her insincerity. "I quite thought they were real at first—"

"What else can I give my darlings?" sobbed Olga Semenovna. "Not even a grave for me to cry by. I had seven sons, Euphrosynia Pavlovna. Three died from cholera when they were small. My eldest son worked at the Baltiysky till 1912. Then they sent him to Siberia, they said he was a revolutionary. He may have been. He never talked much to me. Well, his chest was weak, and he died in Siberia. They told me about it a year later. . . . And the other three went to the war. The youngest was eighteen when he died. I have nobody now. I have my work, Euphrosynia Pavlovna, and the work is hard enough. I don't often complain, but when a weary day ends with one saucepan ruined and another coming from Berlin—well—what would you do?" She sat up on the bed, pushed the hair off her forehead, and wiped her face. "It is nice of you, Euphrosynia Pavlovna. I should not have been so ungracious about your gift. Forgive me." Suddenly she leaned forward and pressed a heavy moist kiss on Frossia's cheek, and Frossia kissed her back.

"Yes," ruminated Olga Semenovna, "mine is hard work, and I sometimes wonder about it. I had seven, but you could not blame them now for not having any. It is a hard job to give life when you are tired and despairing. . . . And yet it is cruel not to. . . . I don't understand it. . . . I think that kindness and cruelty are kind of two horses harnessed together in Russia."

"It is not two horses," Frossia said. "It is a troyka, two of kindness and one of cruelty." She sat down on the untidy lumpy sofa, and Olga Semenovna gave her a little more autobiography interlaid with pieces of crude philosophy. But she had dried her tears, and appeared grateful, and Frossia was satisfied when a timid knock came on the door, and Dasha's mother peered in. The saucepan from Berlin had at least succeeded in mending an all but broken friendship: Olga Semenovna wept again and kissed Anna Trofimovna and accused herself of hardness and injustice, and both were happily sobbing on each other's shoulders when Anna Trofimovna suddenly turned to Frossia.

"Why, I had almost forgotten. There is a visitor for you, Euphrosynia Pavlovna, a lady." Dasha's mother used the long since forgotten word, "*barynia.*" "She is in your room, and she does not seem to know what she has come for, but she asked for you most distinctly."

Frossia found it hard to recognize her guest. She looked thin and shabby, her face was unpainted, there were no loud ostrich feathers in her small dingy felt hat.

"Will you give me shelter for tonight?" she asked quietly. "Please

. . . We have met before. I am Alina Touras. My husband was a Lett. We met in a train. Now I come from Pskov. I have a letter for you."

The letter was from Klava, four long, hurriedly scribbled sheets. Frossia lit a candle, offered a chair and food. Madame Touras sat down at once, but she refused food. She said she was not very often hungry nowadays. Frossia read Klava's letter:

Greatly respected Euphrosynia Pavlovna, I am now at Pskov, nursing at a mental hospital, and Grisha and I were married last month. All goes well, and we are both very busy. He is a schoolmaster. The summer was very hot, and the water got bad, and I had dysentery. But I recovered. Truly the Lord is kind. . . . [There followed various details about her home and a new reading circle she had apparently started in Pskov.] Your words never fell on stony ground . . . Alina Karlovna Touras came to us from the Sanatorium by Narva Gate in Petrograd. Now she is being sent back to Petrograd. I shall give your address to her and send her to you. Please give her welcome. She said she had killed someone, but they could not prove it, her mind is too clouded, and nobody can believe much of what she says. She has done some good dressmaking whilst she stayed with us, and, perhaps, she might get some other work. But she must not be left alone, Euphrosynia Pavlovna. Once she did keep a house of bad repute, but all of it is over, and her talk is clean even when her mind wanders. Please be kind to her—for Christ's sake. I shake your hand and remain with deep respects, Klavdia Voronova.

Frossia folded away the sheets. Madame Touras said shyly, her eyes fixed on the floor:

"You must tell me if you mind my coming here. I told that nice nurse at Pskov that I knew you and that I am afraid of the snow. It gets into my head, and I can't think then. I must tell you that I have neither furniture nor money. You understand—I am a real pauper. But I can promise to look after you and make your clothes, and I eat very, very little—nothing but my strict rations, and they don't cost money. Please, you will not make me lie down outside in the snow." Her shrunken face flushed, she was pleading now, and Frossia said hurriedly:

"Of course, you are to stay here. I shall find another mattress."

She did find a mattress, but Alina Karlovna, made warm and comfortable, could not go to sleep. She talked, and Frossia knew she must listen and not appear bored. Alina Karlovna said that nobody would listen to her either at the Commissariat or at the hospital.

"He had no identity papers. He was a *burzhuy*, of course, and

241

they all said he had shot himself, and nobody minded his being gone, and they just would not believe me. But I did do it. He came to me because he was bored and hungry. I liked him. He looked so beautiful. But I disliked his talk from the beginning. He said you had first saved his life and later starved him—both mind and body. How could you have starved anyone? He also said you were silly about a story—something with the snow falling and a girl dying because her lover was dead. I cannot remember much of it. It happened a long time ago in Moscow, Michael said. I did not like the way he talked. It showed so much ingratitude. I could not trust him. He said you were hard and proud. Well, he talked to me, I did not mind it so much, but the militiamen came to raid the place, and then he gave you away. It is horrible when a man gives a woman away. . . . My husband did it once—he gave me away at Kharkov. I got into trouble with the police, and gave a fat bribe to a sergeant, and all was well, but my husband found it out, and gave a bigger bribe to an inspector, and they jailed me for a year, and this harmed my business. Gentlemen do not like visiting a house with a jailbird in it. I could do nothing to my husband: he was wicked but strong, and it was like putting a stopper to a petrol bottle—my doing nothing about my husband. It made me want to get even with someone some day. Then he died. . . . And this beautiful reptile of a boy gave you away and laughed at you, and it all came back to me, and I shot him, and my husband as well through him—though Touras was not in the room—he could not be— he was dead then. You will understand about that stopper coming off—petrol is so inflammable. That was why I had to shoot, and they would not believe me, and all the girls later swore they had seen him pulling the trigger. Now it is all finished, wine and palms in pots and parrots and scent and cosmetics and frilled pillowcases, and I am a pauper. I am here, and I shall be safe. I shall eat so little you would never notice it, and I promise to mend your clothes for you."

In the morning Frossia took Klava's letter to the Domkom. The chairman spelt it out with great interest, and asked quite casually: "Is she well again? Why, she must be if she is discharged. Well, you will have to share your room with her—"

"I mean to," said Frossia.

But the other tenants were skeptical.

"Those who once lost their wits, often take to thieving when they get better," grumbled the undertaker.

"Back to the asylum she goes once she starts any of her tricks again," threatened Olga Semenovna, easily forgetting both saucepan and sympathy.

Even the timid Anna Trofimovna rang an uncertain note:

"Euphrosynia Pavlovna, do you think it quite safe? Supposing she were to harm Dasha." But little Dasha herself answered her mother: "You said God took care of those whose wits were shaky, Mam—"

Alina Touras settled down quietly enough. She had brought little luggage except an enormous workbasket. She mended, patched, darned, washed, dusted and swept Frossia's room. She sat by the window, observing the small scene before her. She stayed indoors. She mended Frossia's ancient oil stove and cooked their frugal meals in the room. She showed herself reluctant to appear in the passage, the kitchen, the stairs. After that bout of garrulousness on her arrival, she lapsed into taciturnity. She kept to one corner of the room, watching Frossia intently, adoration in her deeply sunken eyes. Once in the middle of the night Frossia woke to find Alina Karlovna moving about the room. The steam from a saucepan spiraled in the dim light of the candle. Frossia coughed, and Alina Karlovna whispered: "I have just boiled some water. Please let me wash your feet. They will be so much more comfortable. I know you have had a tiring day."

After about a fortnight indoors, Alina Karlovna ventured into the streets, stood in a queue, brought back the day's thin rations, and a swollen underlip. It had bled, dry blood was caked all over her chin, and Frossia looked aghast.

"It was the old man here," said Madame Touras calmly. "I met him at the foot of the stairs. They call him Parfen Nikitich. I should call him Lucifer's nephew—or grandfather—he is too old to be anyone's nephew. Well, he said you were proud and hungry. . . . I knew what he meant, and I hit him with my right hand. He hit back with a stone. It did not hurt much. But I must wash my face, and that is a nuisance. You cannot wash off blood with cold water, can you?"

"You must not go out without me." Frossia was firm. "Some people cannot help being unkind—"

"He is not a person. He is a snake. I have my ways of dealing with snakes." And Frossia said: "Keep to our room if you want to please me, Alina Karlovna," and Madame Touras wept.

"If I want to please you . . . Need you ask if I want to please you? I would kiss that reptile if you wanted me to."

Nonetheless the situation was beginning to be difficult. Frossia felt that she was virtually tethered to the room in the small balconied house. She had not seen Igor or any other friends for some time, she needed counsel, and knew that she could find it at Elena Ivanovna's, but Galernaya Street lay too far from Maly Prospect, and Frossia dared not leave Alina Karlovna alone for long. The school was not far off, Frossia knew that someone would come and fetch her whilst she was there, should her presence be necessary to cope with any possible trouble, but all her other haunts lay at a distance. "I suppose I shall have to take her along . . ." Frossia reflected.

That night Madame Touras was once again in a talkative mood. She told Frossia all about her early days in Odessa.

"I was sixteen. There happened a ghastly pogrom. The police, as usual, were at the back of it. They had baited the people for weeks. There were some cases of cholera, and the police said it was all the fault of the Jews. The Jews, they said, were dirty enough to start any disease under the sun. Then it began. They even attacked little children. I could never forget the wailing which went on all through the night. My mother said: 'What is the matter with you, Alina? We are not Jews, we are Baltic Germans, we are safe enough.' But I said: 'Nobody could be safe in such a cruel, ugly world.' And soon after that I ran away. A fat painted woman said I was pretty, and she found me a job. It was also cruel and ugly, but then the whole world was the same. What good complaining about anything? From Odessa I went to Rostov, then to Kharkov, then to Riga and Moscow. I was on my own soon enough, I made money. But it was an expensive business. You had to bribe all along—policemen, inspectors, dvorniks, police doctors, lawyers, magistrates, even judges sometimes. I paid. They kept quiet. Then I ran into great trouble in Moscow. A young Georgian prince came. He had money He looked miserable. He drank some poison in the night. They said one of my girls had given it to him. Where was the sense, I ask you? He was a wealthy client. But bribing was no good there. His people were too important. They sent the girl up for trial. The judge was a Baltic German, cold and stern. He gave her fifteen years in Siberia. That finished me for a time. I just drifted about, and then began again until my husband got me jailed. Then the war broke out. You could do anything in wartime. The country was like a house haunted by those jumping ghosts—what is their name? —and now it is finished again—for good. They said so in Pskov when they let me go. Life is like that. Little beginnings, little endings. But I am wearying you—" Madame Touras said suddenly, lay down on her mattress, and was silent.

She kept her promise faithfully and stayed in the room. Gradually Frossia's small world heard of her. Elena Ivanovna smiled and said nothing. Paulina Pavlovna's comment was that nobody could really be called mad in such a mad world. Pavel Pavlovich roared that things were all right so long as Alina Karlovna did not prowl about with a knife in her hand, and Igor Vladimirovich said quietly: "You have been reading Dostoevsky, surely you have, Euphrosynia Pavlovna." Frossia had not, and the remark annoyed her so much that she almost turned her back on him.

Nikolashka called one evening, brought some bread and a jar of pickled mushrooms. He glanced at Alina Karlovna, who took no notice of him and went on putting a patch on a thin gray blanket. Nikolashka muttered:

"Surely, Euphrosynia Pavlovna, this room is not big enough for two people—"

"You have forgotten the overcrowding," she reminded him in a cautious whisper. "Besides, she looks after me like a nurse. I could not do without her—truly I could not."

Nikolashka stroked his red beard.

"I had a garden all round my big house in Krestovsky Island. There was a queer weed in a tulip bed, I have forgotten its name, but the devil's own stubbornness was in that weed. You dug it out, root and all, and you put stuff into the ground, and every spring it came up again as though it had married the tulips good and hard. You are like that weed, Euphrosynia Pavlovna, except that you are no weed at all—but a flower. . . ."

"And what nonsense is this?" cried Frossia. "April is not round the corner yet, Nikolashka. . . . Alina Karlovna, leave off sewing. Look, we have real pickled mushrooms for supper—"

3

It was her third winter in the city, and now it had gone, and Frossia was happy whenever she thought about the waters freed from the heavy imprisonment of ice. Trams were running spasmodically, drainage was a disgrace, but the little *pristani* all along the quays were being repainted dark blue and shining white, and flat-bottomed blue steamers appeared on the Neva once again. From the Island it was possible to go right down to Ochta, stopping at Rumiantsev Square, Alexander Gardens, Finland Station, and on to the Islands once again leafed in pale green so generously that the sad ruins of their houses looked almost enchanting. Down at the corner of Maly Prospect bulbs were struggling up in the school courtyard, all round the old lilac trees, red tulips and pink, a surprising mass of them, and the ancient limes along Bolshoy Prospect were sheathed in silvery-green. In Galernaya Street Elena Ivanovna carried her geranium pots into the open, and walked far afield to get great plumy branches of pussy willow for her ikon corner on Palm Sunday. In Moyka Pavel Pavlovich spent many hours over a huge canvas for an agricultural poster they wanted at the Narkomprom. In his small room, behind a noisy platform of Warsaw Station, Igor sat reading Platonov's history of Russia and examining endless travel permits. Their number increased from day to day. Spring in the city brought a poignant reminder of the country where you sowed in the spring and reaped in the summer.

At the school some of the older children were puzzled, and they carried their bewilderment to Frossia. They were town-bred children, they had never seen a weeping willow pattern a brook with its narrow tapering leaves, nor heard a thrush pour out its love song, nor yet watched a grass blade push out of the ground, turn green and wave in the wind. And because they were town-bred children, used to little else except the ways of timber and stone, they were puzzled; they had planted such ugly misshapen bulbs in the autumn, they said, and now they pointed at the budding tulips. Were texture and color of the flower hidden in the bulb they had planted?

"No," answered Frossia a little lamely. "Only a beginning. The soil fed it, and it grew—"

"But the red must have been in the bulb all the time," insisted a child of about nine or ten, "and I could not see it. I remember breaking a bulb, the teacher said I was clumsy. The bulb fell all in small flakes and pieces, but there was nothing colored in any of them."

"The color came with the growing," replied Frossia, and was glad to hear a bell ring in the house.

That same afternoon the teacher, Sofia Nikolaevna, brought her the news. The school was going to be evacuated to the South almost immediately.

"I might arrange for you to come with us. You have been quite good with the little ones."

"No," answered Frossia. "It is kind of you, and I have loved the work, but I could not come."

The removal was a matter of days. Within a week Frossia had no work again. She was paid for the last term and paid generously, also Sofia Nikolaevna left her a bunch of pamphlets on modern education.

The spring came very suddenly. Before they knew where they were, it was really warm. Alina Karlovna said the sudden warmth turned her hands into jelly which would never set. Brooms and brushes no longer obeyed her. The needle kept falling out of her fingers. Now she stayed in her corner. She seldom burst into lengthy reminiscences. Once she said in a child's frightened voice: "Your school has gone. That means there will be less food, and I am quite useless. But please don't turn me out. I promise to eat less and less. I need very little food," and she would divide her own portion of bread into six or seven pieces, swallow one of them, put the rest into the locker, and produce her treasure trove on a day when the larder was wholly empty. She smiled triumphantly, Frossia got angry and refused to touch the bread, and Alina Karlovna reproached her—"You could do that to an enemy—but never to a friend," so that Frossia must repent and eat and be grateful.

One evening Frossia met Zolperich outside the wooden staircase. He bowed briefly and said he thought she had gone away with her school. She shook her head.

"No. . . . They asked me to go, but I could not leave."

"That was wise of you. You will never make a teacher. But I have news. I have worked out my contract. I am going back to Essen."

"How nice for you," she said mechanically and went up the stairs.

Igor heard about her school leaving, and he came to see her. This once he did not mention Dostoevsky.

"These things are not good for you." He spoke in a low voice in the passage, and Frossia chose to misunderstand him, knowing well he alluded to Alina Karlovna sharing her room.

"Oh, there is more work coming. Olga Semenovna says the matron at St. Mary Magdalene's is looking for a clerk, and I mean to apply—"

"I am free next Saturday," he said suddenly. "Perhaps Elena Ivanovna will look after Alina Karlovna, and you and I could take a train at Baltiysky Station and go to Peterhof for the day."

Frossia was grateful.

"Yes, Peterhof. . . . I want to see the fountains, Samson, and Niobe, and the Chessboard. I have not been there for years."

"They are still there," he said gravely.

So Frossia took Alina Karlovna and a parcel of food to Galernaya, and Elena Ivanovna settled her guest in a chair with an old sheet to darn, and Frossia took a tram to Baltiysky Station. The tram was crowded, she found herself wedged in between a soldier and a fisherwoman, the windows were closed, she could hardly breathe, and someone trod on her feet, but she forgot all discomfort because it was a spring day and she was going to see the Peterhof fountains once again.

They came to Peterhof. They had four hours: the last train for Petrograd left late in the afternoon, and they spent half their time in the magic kingdom of running water. They ate their food not far from Niobe, under the fragrant shade of a great lilac tree in full bloom. It was white lilac, plumy and gorgeous, and Igor got up on the rickety bench, broke off a richly covered branch, and tossed it in Frossia's lap.

"That is forbidden," she protested, and a keeper sauntered past them, and then turned back.

"You must not pick lilac, citizens," he said severely. "It is a stupid thing to do—taking what is yours—in a manner of speaking. The park belongs to all of you." And he stretched out a bony, gnarled hand: "I must take it, if anyone were to see you, there would be trouble—"

Frossia buried her face in the cool white clusters. The flowers were not merely fragrant, they had eloquence as well. They had so much to tell her of happier, quieter days, she could almost see half-forgotten rooms made lovely with enormous branches and boughs of lilac, see vanished faces bending over them, hear that old song about the beauty of lilac and the pleasure of lovers in its fragrance. . . .

"Just to remember it," she said to the keeper. " We are very sorry. We had forgotten. I have no garden in the place where I live—"

The keeper's hand drew back, though he spoke gruffly:

"Well, you look young enough, both of you, and they say lilac belongs to lovers. Keep it, but please hide it under your coat or something. After all, what should I do with it? And you cannot graft a branch back on the tree, can you?"

Frossia had not heard the last words. Her face burnt crimson.

"They say lilac belongs to lovers." The gorgeous cluster lay in her lap. Igor sat beside her. His eyes, were she to look at him, would tell her nothing. She knew it. But none the less, she turned her head and watched him. He was staring at a small statue of Aphrodite across the wide path. She broke the silence.

"What a lot of nonsense—"

"What? Hiding the lilac? Why, Euphrosynia Pavlovna, he meant to be so very kind."

He was looking at her. She could read no embarrassment in his face. Her own was crimson, her eyes looked troubled, questioning. She forced herself to say: "Yes, he was kind."

Silence fell between them. Dimly, Frossia felt that something was coming near her, but it was as fugitive as pale March sunlight, and she could not capture it. She felt tethered in her own awkwardness and shyness. But Igor had forgotten the keeper. Igor, his eyes intent upon Aphrodite, said something about Hellas. Frossia did not want to embark on any discussion of art. She leapt to her feet, the lilac in her arms.

"We had better see something of the park—"

"You are not tired, Euphrosynia Pavlovna?"

"Why should I be tired?" she retorted, and he said nothing and followed her.

Laden with lilac, they came to the fringe of the park, and Frossia looked round.

"I had somehow imagined to find it all desolate. It is merely still and not too tidy, but it has not changed."

"We are not a tidy nation, Euphrosynia Pavlovna. We try to be, and it is always an effort, and it does not last long. We like tumbling things about, tossing flowers and trees and thoughts and everything. . . . Why does it surprise you?" he asked, catching her astonished look. "If it does, you do not know your Russia."

"No, I don't," she said, herself taken aback by her confession.

"And you will have to learn it, commissar and peasant, fishmonger and baker, textile worker and electrician, yes, and professor and doctor and lawyer, all of them together. There is more to it than just people. I do know a little. That is why I am neither frightened nor puzzled. Plenty comes on the stage, and then famine, too, dawn and dark, one government and another government, and what of it? The country is still there, and a Russian back is broad enough for any burden."

"I do believe in it," she cried. "The Russian scene is wide enough for any setting—even for a dream."

"Yes." Once again he dropped into the didactic tone she disliked so much, but this time she compelled herself to forgive him because of the spring day and the lilac in her arms. "Yes, dreams we must have, there is loveliness in them, but a dream must have some reality at the back of it—however faint and remote. A dream on its own is of no value whatever. Such a dream merely beggars you, Euphrosynia Pavlovna, it thins both mind and soul out."

They had left the park behind them, and were almost on their way to the station; there was time for a rest, and they found a bench under an old oak in the street. She sat down and told him the story of that dim Euphrosynia and her English lover. She told it simply and briefly. He listened, his head a little on one side, his eyes on the lilac she held.

"That is no silly dream, Euphrosynia Pavlovna. There is some sense in it. Your Euphrosynia was in prison, and death opened a door for her. Others are in prison, and life gets them out of it. . . . As to that story being turned into a ballet—" he shook his head—"I could not tell you, I don't know enough about such things."

"I don't feel the same about it. I used to think that, unless I succeeded in translating that dream into something real—a poem or a ballet—I could not live. I think differently now. But I still want to live."

"And that is everything in these days. Some lose their desire, and it is better for them to die. You must love life fiercely—like a lover—to live at all today. But, Euphrosynia Pavlovna, your school is gone, and you said something about a clerk's job. Do you not want to teach?"

"How can I? I am so ignorant." She told him about the frozen milk, the tulip bulbs. "A child's simplest question leaves me frightened. I know nothing. Even Klava knew more than that. . . . And I have tried to read—I got a book on elementary physics." She smiled wanly. "I never understood a page of it."

"We must go." He got up. "It is some distance from the station. Please hide the lilac, Euphrosynia Pavlovna."

In the train they were silent. Igor opened a book and began reading. Frossia watched the dying day from the window. They had to walk from the station to Galernaya Street, and Elena Ivanovna said:

"Well, yes, Alina Karlovna has been quiet enough but she went out two hours ago. I tried to stop her, but she said she had not swept the room in the morning, and she did not want you to find anything untidy. I gave her some milk, and she borrowed a broom."

They raced back across Nicholas Bridge. Down at the bottom of Nicholas Square they saw a small crowd of people, heard splinters of loud laughter. They came nearer. In the middle of the crowd stood Alina Karlovna, sweeping the cobbles with the borrowed broom. She was softly singing to herself. Frossia seized her hand. "Alina Karlovna, it is late, and we have come back. It is time to go home. See, I have brought you some flowers—"

Madame Touras smiled happily.

"*Golubushka*, you must not come in until I have finished. You could not sit down here for the dust. . . . And there are still cobwebs—"

Igor whispered to Frossia: "There is a militiaman at the other end of the bridge. I shall fetch him. They can take her to a home."

Frossia whispered back fiercely: "She is coming with me. I will not have her taken anywhere."

"Euphrosynia Pavlovna, this is most foolish."

"This is my concern, Igor Vladimirovich," and she turned and smiled at Madame Touras. "You have finished. How beautiful it all looks, and we are going straight in." She took the other's arm, the crowd gave way before them, and Igor shrugged.

"Euphrosynia Pavlovna, this is even worse than foolishness. You cannot do anything for her. They will take care of her. They have done it before. This is not good for you," and Frossia heard, turned, and flung her lilac into his arms.

"I have no wish to remember this day. Leave us alone, Igor Vladimirovich, she needs me and she shall have me. I have nothing further to say."

He turned away.

Alina Karlovna wore high-heeled shoes, and could not walk fast. Frossia did not wish to hurry her. They reached the corner of Maly Prospect and came to the balconied house. It looked empty and oddly still. They mounted the wooden staircase. The front door stood closed. Frossia tried the handle. It would not yield. Suddenly a window flew open.

"You are not coming in with her, Euphrosynia Pavlovna," said the midwife. "We are sorry, we have no wish to be unkind, but you must take her to a hospital. We will not have her here any more." She closed the window, Frossia looked up in bewilderment and, presently, Dasha's mother fumbled with the latch of another window, and her small scared voice explained that Madame Touras had come back to the house about an hour ago, fetched all the basins and jugs out of Frossia's room, filled them with water from the tap in the yard, and poured the water all over the kitchen *plita*. "She ruined all our food, and we had no kindling left to light another fire."

Frossia pleaded. But even Anna Trofimovna would not waver. The windows were shut. The door remained locked. Alina Karlovna sat down on one of the steps, and began drinking the milk given her by Elena Ivanovna. Frossia raised her voice:

"I am very sorry. But I have come back with her. I promise to look after her. Please let us in. She is rather tired and she is not young."

Then the undertaker's window flew open. He spoke thickly: "You shall not come in. It is not winter, the streets are there," and dead silence fell on the house.

Frossia might have gone to Nikolashka who lived close by or

back to Galernaya where Elena Ivanovna would not have refused her shelter, or even to Moyka where Paulina Pavlovna would have been kind in her own fussy manner, but the locked door and the abuse from the windows filled Frossia with fury against all her kind. She had no money left, what food she had remained in a locker in an inaccessible room, her throat burned, and her feet hurt her. She seized Alina Karlovna's arm and led her away, saying that they were very tired, and she took her to the deserted summer-house in Moshkov Lane, but Alina Karlovna, usually amenable, did not accept the marble bench. She lay on the hard ground and complained about the pain in her back.

"A pillow," she groaned. "Yes, just a small pillow—for my back."

Frossia took off her coat, folded it, and persuaded Madame Touras to lie on the bench. Presently Alina Karlovna left off whimpering and slept. But Frossia stayed awake. Cold and fury would not let her sleep.

In the morning Alina Karlovna awoke limp and feverish. Her eyes were filmy. She murmured to Frossia:

"A hospital . . . Please take me to a hospital. . . . They always have pillows—"

Frossia must needs leave her alone. She ran to the commissariat in Millionnaya Street. It was early enough, but she found someone to listen to her story. They told her what she had to do. Within an hour a horse cart came to fetch Madame Touras. They took her to the Obukhovsky Hospital in Fontanka. And Frossia, weary and alone, tramped back to Maly Prospect. She found the front door open. She knew that she might have lodged a complaint with the Domkom, but she felt too spent for any further trouble.

Three days later Alina Karlovna died of pneumonia. When Frossia heard, she went back to Maly Prospect to the yard of the deserted schoolhouse. Red tulips were burning in the sun. She went in and picked a great bunch of them, and took her gift to the Obukhovsky mortuary.

CHAPTER NINE

THE MIND SHALL LIVE

Frossia was alone in her room, with the sun, the humble furniture, the dust on the furniture, and in the dust she could see Madame Touras sweeping, mending, washing, darning, dusting, and sweeping again. Her ungainly carpet bag, her huge workbasket, were still there, and the mattress she had used, and the two pillows. The lid of the workbasket was closed. Frossia lifted it and looked at the valuable legacy of reels of cotton, balls of darning wool, and needles. A half-darned stocking of Frossia's lay on the top. It was strange to imagine the woman of the astrakhan coat, oily manners, and dreadful speech, the woman Frossia had first met in the train, in that broken and shrunken body who came to find peace in housework chores. . . . Somehow the idea was unbearable, and Frossia could not sit in the room.

In the shadowy passage she met Zolperich.

"I am going away very soon," he said politely, "but I was sorry to hear about your friend—though it is much better she should have gone. Times are bad here, they will get worse. . . ."

"Why did you come here at all?"

"I came to work. Also I was curious. I wanted to see the strength of a people under such a test."

"Have you seen it?"

"No. . . . They have none. They go on crumbling to pieces."

"You know nothing of them," Frossia said passionately. "Steel can never crumble—"

"There is no steel in them."

She was angry, and anger denied her articulacy, and Zolperich went on in his smooth voice:

"Nothing matters but steel. In spiritual and in physical matters also. These people have none. They are queue sheep. The party is full of hardy men, fanatics, but the party is not the nation. Listen, when I was a small boy at Graulitz, my mother used to take me to kirk. I grew up and knew it was all rot. There was one thing

253

the pastor said, 'The meek shall inherit the earth.' I say the meek shall inherit the gutter. The strong shall inherit the earth, the physically fit. Look at the crippled child in this flat . . . I am sorry for her. I carved her a few dolls; it did not mean much of an effort. What good will she ever be? Yet her mother says: 'I have been to the Health Commission, they are sending her to a sanatorium near Feodosia in the Crimea.' Their trains are few, their sanatoria are overcrowded, yet they will waste a place in a railway carriage, a bed in a sanatorium on the useless crippled body of a small girl who will never be of any value to the state. You talk of steel . . . I call it sodden cotton wool."

Frossia leaned against the wall.

"This is—almost interesting. What would you do with the child?"

"Use a grain of a certain drug on her. That would be kind to her and to the community. Look at yourself. You are young and beautiful, and you are a wastrel. You should be in a factory, you are strong enough for really hard work, or else you should marry one of your peasants—I believe that away from the cities you can still find some healthy stock—"

"Steel shall inherit the earth," Frossia echoed. Zolperich was so far away from her that his personal abusive remarks glanced off her consciousness. "Well, go back to the forge and make more steel, but don't discuss things you will never understand. Yes, we live in dirt, hunger, dark. . . . We wear tatters. Often we feel dumb. . . . We muddle everything. . . . We are slovenly, slow. . . . I can quite understand that our present inefficiency has driven your tidy little mind to frenzy. . . . But we still have a mind, and one day that mind shall live again—"

"The Russian mind," smiled Zolperich, *"Die russische Seele. . . .* Yes, samovar, troykas, gypsy songs, and endless discussions about stars and the final destiny of man . . . Also the eternal maddening *nichevo, nichevo* yesterday, today, and tomorrow . . . *Nichevo—* nothing matters—"

Frossia went back into her room and slammed the door. Zolperich left the next morning. She never met him again.

2

Igor Vladimirovich was writing to Klava. It had been a comparatively slack afternoon at Warsaw Station, he had an hour of leisure, and he wrote his letter in a crabbed small hand.

. . . The woman you sent to Euphrosynia Pavlovna is dead. I am very sorry, Klavdia Petrovna, but I disagreed with Euphrosynia Pav-

lovna about her. Alina Karlovna would have been much happier in a
home or a hospital, but Euphrosynia Pavlovna must always go her own
way. Perhaps she is wise—I cannot tell. Also her infants' school left
Petrograd some time ago, and she is without work at the moment, and
this must be attended to. We are all hoping next winter may pass without mishaps, but I am afraid it will not. Almost every day I hear accounts of bad sowings everywhere. The spring came late, and the southern provinces had those disastrous floods. We do not see much bread
here. Now I must stop, but I thought you would like to know that in
spite of the disagreement I am going to visit Euphrosynia Pavlovna
though she may not want to talk to me. I trust she may find work before
winter.

Igor Vladimirovich finished his letter with inquiries after Klava
and Grisha. Then he came out, looked at the great station clock,
turned back again, tidied some of the papers on his desk, and
looked at a slip of paper with a familiar address written on it. Anna
Trofimovna had been to see him, he had to countersign the travel
permit for Dasha, and it could not be done by proxy. So it will
not look as though I were determined to molest Euphrosynia Pavlovna, he thought.

Yet he would not go straight to Maly Prospect from the station.
He made a big détour, came to Peter's Park, and a keeper he knew
allowed him to pick an enormous bunch of bluebells. "They are
for a child," said Igor Vladimirovich, and he said it sincerely, but
Dasha, on seeing the bluebells, cried at once: "There are too many
of them. Far too many . . . Frossia Pavlovna loves bluebells.
Please, divide them"—and Igor Vladimirovich divided the flowers
and countersigned the permit.

"You are going away for two years," he said to Dasha. "It is a
long journey, but you will go to a nice large house near the sea,
with tall trees at the back—I am not telling you a story, I have seen
some photographs, and you will eat oranges and drink good creamy
milk."

"There will be the sun, too," said Anna Trofimovna, her eyes full
of tears. "Euphrosynia Pavlovna says the sun can cure her if nothing else will."

He had the bluebells in his arms. They said Frossia was in, and
he must go and knock at her door. They had not met since the
scene in Nicholas Square some days ago when she had thrown the
lilac back at him. Now she opened the door, looked at the bluebells,
and said at once:

"I should have written or come to see you. I was rude, hasty,
bad mannered. You must forgive me," she added. "They locked us

255

out that night. I could not be angry with them now. . . . But poor Alina Karlovna died. . . ."

"I have heard about it. But there is nothing to apologize for, Euphrosynia Pavlovna. I have not come about such a trifle. I want to ask you if you have heard anything of the Rabfaks?"

She invited him in, offered him a chair, and busied herself with the bluebells. She wore white, a blouse and a skirt obviously made of old linen sheets, and a string of deep rose beads round her throat. The flowers in her hands made one forget the dingy walls all round. She was in a wood, with the sun glinting on her copper brown hair. Igor Vladimirovich remembered a small poem by Apukhtin about youth in spring. . . .

"Rabfaks?" she asked. "Oh, yes, I have heard of them. Workers' Faculties, are they not?"

"Euphrosynia Pavlovna, you know French?"

"As well as Russian, I think. That sounds conceited, but it is not. I have spoken it since my childhood, and Grandmamma was a good linguist. Also she was particular. She would have neither Belgians nor Swiss to teach us, we had French people always." She laughed, remembering something: "Grandmamma used to say that grammatical lapses were pardonable, but an imperfect accent was a mortal sin. . . ."

"Do you know any other languages?"

"Well, yes, German. I had a very good German governess. She stayed on and became a friend. And I know some Italian and a little English—I mean I could read an English book without a dictionary."

"Now listen, Euphrosynia Pavlovna. At the third Rabfak they badly need foreign languages. I think you ought to try. It will be dull at first. It will mean teaching them 'le' and 'la,' and not minding their accent, and talking about an aunt's garden and an uncle's pen—you know—purely elementary stuff. That Rabfak is in Kamennostrovsky Prospect in Petrograd Side. I know the head of the chancery, Comrade Golubev. He has just gone on leave to Kaluga. He will be back in a week. He told me they had nobody to teach French. Now it is a big place. You may have to live in a teacher's hostel or some such place. There is a wage of sorts and also a very handsome *payok*. But it will mean working hard. There are over four hundred students at that Rabfak, and he said quite fifty of them want to begin French. You see, they all feel they are 'dark' people—without languages. It will mean teaching about eight or nine hours a day, and then correcting their homework. And some of them are very rough folk."

256

Frossia said slowly:

"I am not afraid of hard work—but am I not too ignorant?"

"Well, you know the language. But it will be hard. I had better explain. You cannot teach such people from a distance. Their minds would not catch whispering—as it were. . . . You must win an intimacy with them, then only will their minds be near enough for you to handle and mold. It is like starting a garden in a place where a rough grass field had been, Euphrosynia Pavlovna, it is back-breaking work, but the soil is rich, and it repays the backache in time."

"Yes, that will be hard." She spoke slowly, minting every syllable. "But which end of Kamennostrovsky is it? The prospect goes on for miles—"

"I don't know," Igor Vladimirovich answered dryly. "Anyway, you must wait a week before Gleb Semenovich Golubev is back from Kaluga. I will tell you when the time comes."

"This is very kind of you." She spoke so formally that he got up and muttered: "Why talk of kindness, Euphrosynia Pavlovna?" and went out, and Frossia was left alone with the bluebells and her own thoughts. The flowers she would have enjoyed whole-heartedly, she did not feel so certain about her thoughts, and was glad to see Nikolashka come in, waving a letter in his huge hands.

"From Irina Nikolaevna," he shouted. "Euphrosynia Pavlovna, I don't care if the house is on fire or you are busy, but I must read it to you."

Frossia would have read the letter in less than five minutes; Nikolashka fumbled over every word, sometimes spelling out the difficult ones, but she would not have denied him that pleasure for the world, and sat, listening and smiling.

"My very dear Papashenka," read Nikolashka, "the crops are doing badly, but folk here hope for good sun to dry the soil, and I agree with them. Aunt Akulina has sold a pig; she sold half of it to a Jew at a fair, and we shall have ham and bacon; she is so pleased and so am I. They say the Americans are coming to sow wheat and barley in the South, the Starosta says not, but Aunt Akulina agrees, and I think she is right. Varvara, Mitia, and Nadia have joined the nearest Kolkhoz. Oberdiaev, who is a *kulak*, says it is all nonsense, you cannot run a farm like that, all together, they will all quarrel, it is human nature, and animals, too, he said to me, and I could not agree, so I said nothing at all, and he went away pleased. A German came here some time ago with the Gosplan people. He gave men cigarettes and brought real silk ribbons for the girls, but everybody could see he was laughing at our ways all

257

the time, and nobody liked him, and Aunt Akulina said any German is as much good as a forgiven thief, and I think she is right. Now I will send you some lard and a pair of woolen socks, but kindly lock them up somewhere when you are not wearing them, Aunt Akulina says there is no wool left in the country. I kiss you hard. Your loving daughter Irina," and Nikolashka finished and beamed. "Is she not a marvel, my Irinushka?"

"Yes, she is," said Frossia. The letter had unaccountably pleased her. The parcel of lard meant that Nikolashka would soon give another of his parties, and the news about the country, the visit of Zolperich (who else could that German have been?), the crudely worded agricultural philosophy, each and all made a link between her friends in Petrograd and all those she did not know in the country. Irina Nikolaevna would probably never come to Petrograd, her aunt seemed in need of her, and Nikolashka had to endure loneliness for some time before he would make up his own mind and leave the city, but such dispersals did not matter—in spite of sporadic correspondence and poor means of transport. "That is what Zolperich would never understand," Frossia suddenly rejoiced. "Politically, we may never agree with one another, but deep down somewhere we are always united," and she smiled at Nikolashka's naïve question:

"Did Igor Vladimirovich bring you these bluebells?"

"Yes."

"They never live in water," said Nikolashka, and Frossia almost disliked him for an instant.

3

It had been an *osobniak*, a private mansion, standing well away from the dusty hubbub of Kamennostrovsky. There was a garden, a short semicircular drive, fringed with lilac trees in full bloom. The lawns looked sad in their neglect, but nobody could interfere with the lilac trees, and they made the place proud, lovely, and gracious. The pale yellow house had two wings. Its front door was widely opened. Frossia went in, found herself in an enormous sunlit hall, innocent of all furniture. There were several doors. A young man in a soiled white shirt came forward.

"I have come to see Comrade Golubev, Gleb Semenovich Golubev."

"Many people come to see him." The young man appraised her shrewdly. "Have you an appointment—or is it just nonsense?"

"I have. I have come from Comrade Titov of Zheldorkom."

"Ah, well," the young man seemed to lose all interest in her, "you had better go in." He gestured to a door on the left and cried after her: "You need not knock—if you have an appointment."

Frossia opened the door. "Comrade Golubev?"

"Yes, I am busy. There are chairs. Please wait," said a deep unhurried voice.

Frossia found a chair. The room was pleasant, sunlit, surprisingly tidy. It was furnished like an office with a desk, a typewriter, telephone, file cabinets. Everything was clean, everything said, "I am in my place. If you want to use me, you must put me back where I belong"—even the file of papers on top of a cabinet. Comrade Golubev sat at his desk. He looked a peasant, with an open bearded face, deeply tanned and roughly chiseled. His khaki clothes suited him badly. On the desk, dangling high-booted legs, sat a young man in a loud yellow shirt and faded khaki breeches. Comrade Golubev was busy with him. The man in the yellow shirt was angry.

"This is a Rabfak, Comrade Golubev. Not an old régime ladies' school. What do you say to that?"

"There is nothing to say to a fact. But you want to learn Italian. It is very hard to find teachers, Comrade Zolotov—"

"Surely, you might have appointed someone different. We may finish by going on strike, I warn you. Anyhow, I mean to summon the students' committee. I have the right, have I not?"

"Yes, you are the chairman."

"And we shall pass a resolution, I warn you, we shall have to make new arrangements. This is a Rabfak, Comrade Golubev." He leapt down and strode out of the room. He never looked at Frossia.

"Yes, citizeness?" She was called to the desk and offered another chair. Comrade Golubev looked at her. She knew he had heard about her, Igor said he had discussed her with him, but Comrade Golubev sat and waited, and she must explain. He listened. His brown forehead knit into a frown.

"Comrade Zolotov will be summoning another of his committees. Oh, dear, this is difficult. We want them to be taught foreign languages. They are very keen on learning. Just recently I found them an Italian teacher. Well, she used to be maid of honor to one of the Romanov women, and they have discovered it. Of course, she is harmless, otherwise she would not be here, but Comrade Zolotov will not agree"—he smiled wryly—"and how am I to explain you? Now please be honest, Citizeness Bozert, you are no proletarian?"

"No—"

"Have you ever wanted to join the Party?"

"No," she answered so swiftly that he smiled.

"Have you ever tried to escape from the country?"

"No—"

"Why not?"

"Because I want to stay on here—"

"Where are your people?"

"I have none left here." Frossia thought for a moment. "I may have a cousin or two abroad, I am not sure. They are strangers to me—"

"Igor Vladimirovich—Comrade Titov, I mean—said that French was your second mother tongue, but have you ever taught before?"

"Only in a children's school. They were very small. No, I have had no other experience—"

Gleb Semenovich rubbed his nose. He looked very much like an embarrassed sheepdog.

"It will be difficult. . . . You see, our students will ask you the same questions over and over again, and you must not mind, and you must stay patient and grave. Our students are factory hands, sailors, soldiers, peasantry—ordinary people you know, mostly rough and raw, and also clumsy. They are sharp, too. They will not spare you at first. Even your hands will annoy them. Your accent will probably grate on them. Well?"

Frossia thought for a few instants.

"I don't expect I am likely to fall in love with them, but I know I am not going to find it difficult to respect them—"

"Why?"

"Because—" she made a wide gesture with her hands—"why, just because they are here to learn, and learning cannot come easily to some of them."

"Euphrosynia Pavlovna"—he leaned towards her, his small neat beard cupped in his hands—"there is something else . . . I would ask you to imagine the hammer and sickle gone from that wall and the double eagle put back. Suppose it were so—what would you think of it?"

"That is not clever," she parried. "Even if I preferred the double eagle to the hammer and sickle I would not say so because I want my job here. . . . Comrade Golubev, I am sorry—I am no half-baked communist. I know nothing of political doctrines. . . . I am like so many of our people . . . I hate ruthlessness, of course, and I often disagree and want to protest. . . . But I have no passion for the double eagle and all your hammers and sickles mean just as little to me. You see, I am being—or trying to be honest. The country does matter. There had been a lot of rottenness in the earlier days, treachery, cruelty, indifference. . . . There are dreadful things happening today. . . . Don't dislike my outspokenness," she said in a curiously heightened voice; "perhaps your people will change views and systems, how am I to tell? But if a factory hand wants to learn French, well, I think I could do it—"

Gleb Semenovich got up.

"You talk quite well." He pushed a form towards her. "I think you will do . . . but that is what *I* think—I cannot vouch for the students."

4

The house in Kamennostrovsky had belonged to a rich merchant. One of the ground-floor rooms had its walls painted all over with most extraordinarily tinted lilies. The room may have been decorated to please a casual whim of a wife or a daughter. It was extravagant, irritating, and stupid. Against a bleakly buff background the lilies rose up from a startling green dado, and reached to the ceiling, vermilion, cobalt, orange, blue, and deep violet lilies. The pale gray ceiling was lavishly bespattered with rose petals in deep red. The truly graceful proportions of that long room were lost among the disorder of shape and color on the walls and the ceiling. You might have used the room as a stage for a circus, thought Frossia. She knew she would always try and look away from the walls, and also knew this would be difficult. Yet one wall was pierced by French windows, giving out on a neglected lawn, and the incongruity of it all was still further enhanced by a sepia reproduction of Leonardo's St. Anne, sparingly framed in dusty mahogany, which hung in the space between two windows. Otherwise there was nothing in the room except painted lilies and roses, rows of empty benches, a chair and a desk. The desk had a direly frayed blotter on it and a dark green inkstand filled with something like glue.

It was just striking nine in the distance. Frossia had been told by Golubev that lectures were to begin punctually, and she was not late, but the extravagant room was wholly empty when she came. She sat and waited. Presently the door was flung open. Students trooped in, their rough-shod feet loud on the bare parquet floor, about forty of them, young men and girls, middle-aged folk, and even a man with an enormous flowing white beard. From the desk at her end of the long room Frossia caught an impression of white, blue, and black shirts, all open at the throat, faded print dresses, unkempt hair, and rather studiedly indifferent faces. But they came in quietly, whatever their secret intent may have been.

They sat down as quietly as they knew how. A fly buzzed against a grimy windowpane, and Frossia heard some of them breathing in a slow laborious way, and a woman sneezed. Otherwise the room would have been perfectly still.

Frossia did not welcome them. Somehow she knew that the least gesture of friendliness would not have been well received at this stage. She folded her hands, looked over their faces at a peculiarly luxuriant purple-petaled lily, and began:

"The French alphabet consists of twenty-six letters," and she stopped. From the well of the room a plump, squint-eyed woman in a faded green print dress and a white kerchief thrown anyhow over her disheveled head, shouted throatily:

"And that is a good lie to begin with. You have left out ten. Don't you start forgetting that we know our own letters. None of us here are illiterate."

"You have spoken truly, Glafira Antonovna, thirty-six letters there are." A discordant chorus supported the interruption.

Frossia remembered there was a small blackboard on an easel just behind her. She found a piece of chalk, got up, and began tracing neat huge capitals on the board.

"We had better do it together," she said calmly, but with the second capital letter chalked, her audience took to muted hissing.

"Are you a teacher? How can a 'B' be a 'V'? You don't know your own letters."

Some were furious, others were laughing. A fair freckled youth of about twenty sat astride his desk and bellowed that he, for one, would not be taught by an illiterate girl, but Frossia kept her back to them and went on with her chalking.

"She is wasting our time, comrades," shouted the woman in green print. "Let us go and find Zolotov. We are here to learn French—not to look at her back."

Frossia traced "X, Y, Z," and faced her class. The horrible lilies were mocking her. The very buzzing of the fly was taunting her. The rose petals on the dirty ceiling were unkind to her. The forty-odd upturned faces were full of malice and contempt. Suddenly, Frossia yearned for Elena Ivanovna's comforting voice, for Igor's bluntly worded counsel, even for Paulina Pavlovna's plaintive murmur. But she was alone, and she knew it. The forty-odd students were hissing at her:

"You have never done any honest factory work, have you? Just look at her hands, comrades. . . . Out with you . . . Out with you. . . . This is a Rabfak," they went on shouting, using words Frossia could not quite understand, and she sat at her desk, and wondered how in the world she could have imagined herself capable of coping with such a task. Somewhere down the room, the lily painted walls were broken by a door painted a loud pink. Frossia knew she would cover that ugly pink paint with kisses, could she but get near the door. But the door remained at a distance. Between the door and her frightened, furious self stood her fear and forty-odd occupied desks, and her fear made her suddenly bang her hand on the desk.

"Quiet, please . . . Will you be quiet, please—" But she should not have added that "please," *pojaluista*. The class screamed all the harder:

"Please . . . Please. . . . You listen to her, comrades—"

"We are so polite . . . We dress in silk . . . Our hands are snow-white . . . We have never soiled them by work . . . Ah, no . . . No. . . ."

Frossia sat, chin cupped in both hands. She stopped listening. She just heard a volume of din all round her. There came a momentary lull as though their voices were spent, and the white-bearded man raised his face and mumbled to her:

"Why do you not go now?"

"Yes," the squint-eyed Glafira Antonovna caught him up. "Go, and don't you dare come back again. We will have none of you—"

Frossia was angry and, in her anger, she became cold, clear-headed. Her voice rang slow, loud, distinct:

"Why must you be so dishonest?"

For a moment mouths gaped, eyes stared at her. Then the freckled youth shrieked:

"Who is being dishonest?"

"All of you." Frossia could not stop now, and she went on quietly, hoping that neither her voice, nor her face, would give away the fear which still ravaged her: "You are dishonest. The state says to you: 'Come and learn.' The state provides this house and teachers for you. The state asks nothing from you except application and work. You seem determined to waste it all. Why? It is pointless, stupid, above all, dishonest. Nobody compelled you to come here. Nobody compelled me to come and teach you. Let me be frank. I may not be a good teacher, but I want to be of use, and I do know French."

She paused. Some were laughing. The freckled youth turned his back on her and yelled:

"Now it is nice, polite conversation, comrades. . . . She is here to teach us how to converse. . . ." He spat on the floor, and Frossia raised her voice.

"Quiet." This time she did not add "please," and the freckled youth turned round and stared at her, astonished and obviously discomfited. Frossia plunged in:

"You must listen. French is difficult, but it is a beautiful language, and the more languages you know, the wider will your life become. You will travel abroad in time. Do you want to be dumb when traveling? So that any foreigner seeing you, would say contemptuously: 'Of course, what can you expect of savage Russian louts?' Do you want this to happen?" But they were not listening, a bell began clanging in the distance, there came the loud scraping of benches, and they were all on their feet, all scurrying to the door, some amused, others hostile, but all alike contemptuous of her. For some minutes Frossia sat still. Then she went to seek out Comrade Golubev. Her report was weary and brief.

"I am no good. I had better give it up at once."

Gleb Semenovich went on writing something in a ledger before him. He spoke without raising his head.

"Be as punctual tomorrow as you were this morning, Euphrosynia Pavlovna. By the way, Comrade Horst is teaching German here, and he tells me the Berlitz method is by far the best. You can have any books you like—"

"I mean to give it up."

"At nine tomorrow . . . I am sorry. I have a lot of writing to do," said Gleb Semenovich, and Frossia must needs leave the chancery, pass through the hall, on to the sunlit porch with the students scattered all over the place. Some recognized her, she heard a few hisses, and, her face crimson, she waited for the tiny green tram to come along. She strap-hung all the long way across Trinity Bridge to Michael Square, and walked down Nevsky Prospect. A horse cart passed her by. The driver halted.

"I am from the country, dear soul. Which is the way to Warsaw Station?"

"But I am going there." Frossia surprised herself by the reply, clambered in, and gave the necessary directions. The stocky little man in a white shirt and black breeches, who smelt of hay, *hanja*, and sour clothes, was grateful and garrulous.

He came from Ozernovo in Tver Government. Frossia had never heard about Ozernovo. Well, and how could she? Ozernovo was not even a village, *selo*, but a mere *derevnia*, a hamlet, neither church nor school in it, just a handful of small homesteads, and the well had nearly run dry in the last summer's drought, and the crops had suffered. His sister-in-law, Mavra, had left a candle burning on the table, and now they were all *pogoreltsy*, there was neither river nor brook near Ozernovo, and such a wind, the flames ran like lightning. "So many devils on wings . . . One hut after another burnt down like a box of matches."

"So there is no more Ozernovo—"

"No." He sucked in his tongue. "There is no more Ozernovo. We had a *mir*, the Opanchin starosta came along, and a commissar from a town, and Mavra was shot for arson. . . . But there is no more Ozernovo. And there will not be another. Why should there be? There had been a lake, they say, in ancient days, hence the name, *golubushka*, but the Tartars or else the French put poison in it, and it dried up. But I have a grand brother-in-law, Kuzma Kuzmich Muchovkin, and he has land near Pskov, and they have started farming it all together, eighteen men in the community, and I have a hand with potatoes and beetroot, crops always did badly at Ozernovo, and I got the deacon from Opanchin to write to Kuzma, and he said they would be glad of help, so I got my horse and cart and the old woman together, and I went to Moscow first, and they said to me there: 'You are illiterate. How can you study potatoes and beetroot?' and I said: 'You don't have to read books about potatoes.' I said: 'A potato grows,' and they said, 'It is not only about potatoes, it is about everything. You must learn your letters before you join a Kolkhoz.' I said: 'This is enough to make a chicken laugh, I have been a grandfather for ten years, how could I learn my letters? We had no school at Ozernovo, and Opanchin was eight versts away.' 'Yes,' they said, 'we know that, and we are not blaming you, but you can learn at eighty if you want to.' Well, there was I, Artemiy Sorokin, learning my letters, and I liked it, *golubushka*. I spent nine months in Moscow, and I wrote to Kuzma with my own hand, just imagine—"

"It would not have been late at eighty—for you," Frossia murmured. "What is it like in the country now, Comrade Sorokin?"

"Don't you 'comrade' me! Sorokin my name is, christened Artemiy. What is it like? Well, a good furrow, and then a bad furrow, that is what it is like. Men in uniform come down, and they talk a lot, we don't always listen. Some are good. Some are bad. That is human nature. Some are silly. You want good seeds and kindly weather for your harvest. You cannot sow a field with meetings, committees, and resolutions." Frossia barely recognized the Russianized foreign idioms as they tumbled from the thickly bearded lips. "Well, it might be like a stack of hay forked upside down, but it will settle in time, it will settle in time. You just boil your millet long enough and you get your platter of gruel in the end. Take the church now. At Varshino, away back from Opanchin, across the river, the priest was a miser and an idler. Well, stands to reason once the squire and police were gone, the priest went, too. There was not one Christian soul he had ever done anything for. . . . He would not christen a child or bury a corpse without you paid him. Yermola Kabushin's mother died, and they were beggars, and that old anti-Christ took the last hen for the funeral."

"Where did he go to?"

"Why, into the river. They are lucky, the Varshino people, they have a grand river. Now take the Opanchin *batushka*—there is a grand man for you, he would not sell his Christ for a million. He is an old man, he has labored and prayed all his life. His wife's sister married a rich soap merchant from Kazan, and every lean year the Opanchin *batushka* would write to the soap merchant: 'Remember the judgment day,' he said, 'share your gold with my folk. They have not a stale rusk in their larders.' And always would the soap merchant behave properly. Well, when commissars came to Opanchin, they sealed the church door, and *batushka* laughed. 'Close a door to God, and He will come back through a window,' and he said, 'I can praise Him in a field or in a barn.' The commissar got the *mir* together and said they could get rid of the priest, and they asked: 'Why? He has prayed for us, and he has worked for us, and he is the grandest man we know. You go,' they said to the commissar, 'and take those seals off the church door.' So it is in Opanchin to this day. Well, *golubushka*, all corn gets ground into flour in the end. . . . Tru-tru—" he whistled at the horse— "long way, *golubushka*, is it not?"

5

But they got to the station in the end, and Frossia thanked Artemiy Sorokin both for the lift and the narrative, and made her way to Igor's tiny kingdom. She found him alone, reading Pushkin. She looked over his shoulder. She saw it was the Bronze Rider, and her own eyes wandered over the page until Igor said:

"Euphrosynia Pavlovna, you have not come all this long way to read Pushkin. And I thought you would spend the whole day at the Rabfak. Well, it is dinner time. Come on, let us eat at the station *stolovaya*."

"I have no card," she replied, her eyes still scanning Pushkin.

"I will share mine with you. I am rich today. I have had a parcel from Rzhev—millet and rye flour—enough for a whole fortnight, just imagine. . . ."

They threaded their way into the *stolovaya*, once a first-class

266

waiting room, a not too clean and airless place, its old furniture removed and hard benches put in instead. But their gruel was poured into lovely fragile porcelain bowls, faint rose with an exquisitely patterned brim. Frossia whisked her wooden spoon out of a skirt pocket and stared at the bowl, letting her dinner grow cold.

"Why, this is real biscuit china?"

"Is it? Just the same as a tin mug to me. Eat the gruel, Euphrosynia Pavlovna—"

"Igor Vladimirovich." Frossia swallowed a spoonful. The gruel was lumpy and over-salted, but she ate it with pleasure. "I am not going back to the Rabfak—"

"Did Gleb Semenovich say so?"

"No. He said I was to be there at nine tomorrow morning. But what good am I?" And she sketched him her morning's experience.

Igor finished his dinner, wiped the spoon on a piece of newspaper, slipped it back into his pocket, and said solemnly:

"Euphrosynia Pavlovna, you will be very angry—but it is all your own fault—"

"Mine?" Frossia's cheeks burned crimson.

"Yes," he went on calmly, "you are just like a girl in a dream. You go far and not far enough, and you halt in the middle, and it is far worse than not having started at all. You must stop being afraid of them, afraid of new life, afraid of so many things. If you cannot do that, you had better go—try some foreign country, live there, among your own kind, and forget Russia. This is no place for frightened folk, I reckon, because life here can be frightening, and you give way to it. They abused you, they hissed at you, but you spoke to them, and they listened, and that is a beginning, and yet you come away disheartened and miserable—"

"They never listened. A bell rang, and they just walked out—"

"Were they shouting at you all the time you spoke?"

"No," Frossia admitted a little reluctantly.

"Then they did listen. But, if I were you, I would not stress their dishonesty so much the next time you go there—"

"I am not going there again," said Frossia, and wished she had not tramped all the way to Warsaw Station. What is the use of telling the man anything? she thought, annoyed and humiliated, he just goes on in his own way, and it is not mine, and, as though he had read her mind, Igor went on:

"No, I would try a different line next time. Tell them how dreadful it is to be in the dark. Take heart, Euphrosynia Pavlovna, it may be weeks before you can begin teaching them the French alphabet, but just go on talking to them. Don't be weak with them. . . . They would mock at you all the more. Stamp your foot, if you like, bang your fist, don't use too many soft words. Be harsh even . . . There will come proper time for soft speeches. But prove yourself willing, unafraid above all else." His voice deepened in urgency, he went on talking, calmly ignoring the angry crimson on Frossia's cheeks. "Euphrosynia Pavlovna, I come from among them, I know them. They can be bestially cruel in a queer cold way. They can also be kind and gentle like tiny lambs. . . . They used to be full of fears. Days were when they feared drought, fire, hunger, darkness, the police, the church, Siberia . . . people with money. . . . Those fears are still in them—just like bugs in a wall, and if anyone comes along and is afraid of them, all their own fears get knotted together, and something vile comes out of it. I am not much good with words, Euphrosynia Pavlovna, but I hope you will understand—"

"I am not thinking about that Rabfak any more," she told him coldly and rudely. "But you said something about my going away— unless I stopped being frightened. . . . I did hear the other day that they will soon be issuing foreign passports for students and invalids. . . . But I could not go. I don't want to go. I belong here. I want to work—with them, for them. . . . It ought not to matter to anyone that I am not a communist. I shall never be—but I am a Russian, I really have no foreign blood in me. I would be homesick wherever I went to. And where should I go?" She forgot her earlier annoyance and seized his roughened hand, "How could I tell you or anyone what Russia means to me? Perhaps, I would need a thick book to say it all, perhaps, a few words. . . . I get a choked feeling whenever I think of those few words . . ." She glanced around, the huge bleak *stolovoya* was empty, even the gray-coated attendants had gone. "Igor Vladimirovich, my grandmother brought me up. I loved her—in a way. To her, the old régime was the twelfth beatitude. She nearly fainted with rapture at the coronation. It always grieved her that I could not share her enthusiasm. I had always thought things were wrong. . . . But I don't know enough about anything, and mere feelings don't help you much sometimes. I did tell you once that I had no people left. That was true. They did not escape. My grandmother had a will of steel. Her old world gone, she could not stay and watch a new one being made. She made the decision for the whole family. I alone dissented because I wanted to live. . . . I meant to see it through. . . . Some called her a coward. . . . I don't know. . . . I am a coward—now . . . but why should I not be if I want to?"

she cried defiantly, and he began tracing a design on the red checked American cloth and said nothing.

"Every summer we went to Brianskoye near Kiev. There was an orchard, and a field sloping down to a hillocky coppice. There stood a high railing between the orchard and the field. Cattle grazed there, but a silly nurse once told me that wild beasts prowled there. I was afraid of the field, but the coppice drew me. It was such a lovely shape, and there were old oaks and a wild cherry, and I thought I could see the whole world from the top. But I was afraid of the field. Once—I was about seven—I made up my mind and crawled under the railing and crossed the field. I was so frightened that the whole world looked dark green and black. But I did reach the coppice, and I climbed to the top, and sat under the wild cherry tree, and I saw the Dnieper gleam silver-blue in the sun. Igor Vladimirovich, do you know what it means to look at something you had loved before you saw it? I went back home through the field quite quietly, the grass was bright green, nothing was dark or hostile any more. But the Rabfak is so different, oh, don't you see how different it is?" she cried, her lips trembling a little, and she bent her eyes to stare at the rare porcelain bowl before her.

"Yes," Igor said slowly and smiled at her, "I do see it must be different. . . . If I were you, I would get there a little earlier than nine tomorrow morning. You might then see Gleb Semenovich for a few minutes. He is a grand man."

"He has never said much to me—"

"He never does very much. But his outlook is clear enough. You remember that saying, 'peremeletsia—muka budet,' corn does get ground into flour in the end," and the proverb fell from his lips in such a simple, deep way that Frossia forgot the bleak and dirty stolovaya at a crowded terminus in Petrograd. She was back at Brianskoye, crossing a rye field, her eyes feasting on windswept cornflowers, and she almost smelt the earth washed by the summer rain, and all her earlier annoyance died away.

"Igor Vladimirovich, you have often taken me for a fool."

"Why, yes, sometimes, when you were so mysterious about that young boy in Moshkov Lane, and that poor Lettish woman. . . . No, not quite for a fool, Euphrosynia Pavlovna, but for someone asleep in an uneasy way. . . ." Igor got up and looked at their empty bowls. "And you have taken me for a barbarian, have you not? You were struck by this china. And I, an obscure-minded man, have eaten out of such a bowl for months and never noticed anything exceptional in it. Some things are in you. Others in me . . . I

reckon you would say that I speak in a different language. . . .
Well, I am a grocer, and you are a gentlewoman."

"I must go." Frossia rose, too. "Dasha is being sent to the Crimea
tomorrow. . . . I promised to be back early."

"You will give my respects to Gleb Semenovich, will you not?"
he said, and she shrugged and hurried away.

She had presents for Dasha, two lace-edged handkerchiefs, and
an English scarf, gaily woven in blues and greens, bought an eternity ago at the English shop in Nevsky Prospect. She got back to
the house in Maly Prospect, and found both kitchen and passage
swept and garnished for the party in Dasha's honor. Zolperich had
long since gone, and they had forgotten the unpleasant interlude
of Alina Karlovna, and Frossia had likewise forgotten their unkind-
ness to her. They were all together, all resolved to brighten an afternoon for a small and crippled child.

Nikolashka came with a bag of saffron buns and a circumstantial
story about a miraculously found tin of saffron. Paulina Pavlovna
brought a baby necklet of pale pink beads, Pavel Pavlovich con-
tributed an enormous red and blue pencil, and Elena Ivanovna
threw a nice fleecy blanket into Anna Trofimovna's hands. Dasha's
crib was taken into the communal kitchen. Olga Semenovna fried
some fish, and even the undertaker succeeded in looking pleasant.
Paulina Pavlovna asked Dasha to remember all her friends when
she would be eating oranges in the Crimea, and Dasha asked: "But
what are oranges?"

"A bit of the sun to take into your hands and suck," boomed
Pavel Pavlovich.

"But the sun is very far," protested the child, and they told her
how near it would be once she arrived in the Crimea. They joked,
ate and drank, the undertaker brought out his creaking old accordion, and sang the song about the flies and the spider.

> "On the parquet floor,
>   Eight couples of flies were dancing,
>   But they saw a spider,
>   And fainted away."

It was a silly song, but they all laughed. It was good to be silly
for once. Pavel Pavlovich gravely asked the undertaker:

"Parfen Nikitich, have you ever seen a cow drinking red wine?"

"Never," replied the astonished undertaker.

"Nor have I," answered Pavel Pavlovich, and broke into thunder-
ous laughter, and they all joined in, and Nikolashka, his great face
beaming, came forth with a riddle:

"Listen carefully. This is rather difficult. The innocents were massacred by Herod. Well, centuries later, two heaps of bones were discovered on that site. One heap was faintly yellow in color, the other ivory white. Which of the heaps belonged to the bones of little boys and which of little girls?"

Most of them were indignant.

"That is not a riddle . . ." said Paulina Pavlovna. "That is nonsense. You could not tell anything from mere bones—"

"There is no answer to it, is there?" asked Frossia, and Nikolashka looked sly and important and said there was.

"Well," said Olga Semenovna, "it may be nonsense—but the ivory colored bones must have belonged to little girls—"

"Wrong," said Nikolashka, and suddenly Dasha sat up in her crib and clapped her hands.

"I know. . . . I know. . . . There could not have been any bones of little girls. Only boys were massacred. I remember. Frossia Pavlovna told me the story long time ago."

"Right, and you shall have another saffron bun," beamed Nikolashka.

Anna Trofimovna was packing Dasha's few chattels into a frail bast hamper. Proudly she displayed two gingham frocks, one yellow, the other red, new and crisp, and passably well made. She explained: "They offered me two pairs of canvas shoes, but I said: 'My Dashenka cannot walk. What use would the shoes be?' Then they gave me these. She has never had a new dress in her life, she has worn sometimes one rag, sometimes another," sighed Anna Trofimovna. "Mostly old blankets they were that nobody wanted. Bless you, Elena Ivanovna." Carefully she folded Elena Ivanovna's clean new blanket. "This is a magnificent gift. Dashenka, you will be careful with your new things."

Presently both kitchen and passage were quiet. The guests had gone. The tenants were back in their rooms. The evening was warm. Frossia slipped on her coat and stole out of the house. The narrow quay was deserted, but wind and water offered their own music, and from afar a man's deep voice was singing something about a beloved river. Frossia could not catch the words, now and then a fragment of the refrain came to her, a phrase deep blue in color and shot through with passion, and she stood still alone in the warm, friendly dark, listening not to the words but to the theme. Round the bend, past the huddled hovels of Gavan, lay the sea. She could not see it, but it crept into the scene as she could imagine it in the warm enfolding dark. Frossia sighed deeply and turned back.

For a month Frossia continued her struggles at the Rabfak. The forty-odd faces went on crowding the scene, hostility gradually changing into faintly sullen indifference. From nine till one, from three to seven, Frossia went from one extraordinarily painted room to another, the day's several lessons laboriously engraved in her mind. Many a time during that first thorny and unsatisfying month she would pause to doubt and to wonder at the possible futility of all her efforts. Those men and women had come to learn of their own will, nobody compelling them, but would they ever learn from her? True that after something like a fortnight they began taking notice of what elementary material she was ready to offer them. They gradually mastered the alphabet, they brought crude exercise books, they began—however dimly—to grope towards an understanding of very brief and simple sentences, yet they showed no eagerness, asked no questions. Frossia imagined herself an articulate automaton so far as they were concerned.

The lessons had to be extremely limited in content. This she could well understand: minds, unused to the systematic gathering of knowledge, could not be overloaded with impunity. No detailed curriculum had been designed for her, she must improvise from day to day: a few new words learnt laboriously, a new grammatical idea sketched, another simple phrase set before them, and the morning's boundaries were reached, and she might not trespass beyond them.

Gradually, however, they stirred from their sullen neutrality. They were Russians, used to the wealth of declensions in their own speech, and the changelessness of a French noun filled them with bewilderment which, in its turn, led to the first faint stirring of curiosity.

"You mean a cow is always the same cow—whether you speak of a cow or buy a cow or get milk from a cow."

"Yes, the meaning is made different by prepositions. The noun does not change."

The squint-eyed woman scaid scornfully:

"Well, comrades, French must be learnt, I suppose, but it is like a beggar at a church gate. . . ."

Someone tittered. Frossia said:

"I think so too. It is not rich. None the less, it has its own beauty."

Here the bell rang. She wiped the blackboard clean and put her meager notes away. They were watching her in silence, and nobody moved until the squint-eyed woman muttered:

"Well, you put things clearly enough, I must say—"

Apart from lecture halls, there was the common room, its walls painted an incredible bright orange, its furniture expressed in terms of endless sofas, upholstered in stained red leather. There she met her fellow teachers. At first they were shy at comparing impressions. They proved a motley company. A great many were chiefly interested in teachers' generous rations, the famous green *payok* cards. A few deplored the Rabfak system—always in cautious undertones. One was the Italian teacher, almost dismissed by the students' committee and reinstated by higher authority, an angular woman with a bitter thin face and nervous hands, who always wore a long loose garment obviously made from a window curtain. It was deep violet, and the color enhanced all the thinness and bitterness in her. "I don't wish to starve," she confided to Frossia, *"mais tout cela, c'est de la vraie tragédie."* She had chosen a moment when the common room was comparatively empty. *"Et tout cela va finir— je n'en doute guère—"*

"What will you put in its place?" asked Frossia.

"What a strange question from you," marveled the dark violet woman. "What is there except?" She shrugged, and Frossia was cold.

"That shall never be—"

The other shivered and drew back.

"I had never imagined anyone like you—" And with a murmured excuse Frossia hurried off to her next lesson.

But the lady of dark violet draperies was not alone in the field. Frossia had acquaintances among those who had known her Grandmother's kin, Anna von Packen, the Parnikovs. She had studiedly avoided any arranged meetings, but in a queue or in a street she might run across now one, now another of them, all battered, shaken, all too obviously wounded in spirit, incredibly proud, incredibly lonely. There was something in their lives Frossia readily admired. Loyalty made lovely enough furniture for any house, but she could not share that particular loyalty which put class above nation. So they met, and she was greeted with immediate exclamations of pity:

"Paulina has told me about your new work. How very grievous. . . . Are they absolute savages?"

"Well, they were not very friendly at first, but I think they are rather nice now. I don't know, of course, what they may be thinking of me—"

"My dear, whatever do you mean?"

"I am sorry, Ekaterina Konstantinovna, but I am in a hurry," and

Frossia must always be in a hurry at such meetings. She still loved those people, she still admired something in them. She also had her own longings for sheets on her bed, bath water round her body, proper sanitation, silver on the table, underwear next her skin. She still welcomed a well-bred voice, and was glad when anyone happened to open a door for her and gave up his seat in a crowded tram. There were smells, habits, expressions, she could barely tolerate. There was also the continuous, oddly woven uncertainty of both life and employment. Even at her Rabfak apparently innocuous people found themselves dismissed without the least warning. Pavel Pavlovich had two of his best and most appealing poster-pictures condemned by the people in Moscow, and the brother and sister spent a lean enough month before fresh work found its way into the studio. Nikolashka admitted that employment was insecure. "But why spoil a loaf by worrying about the mildew which may never come?" Many a time Frossia met men and women at the Zabalkansky who had flocked to seek counsel as well as help from Elena Ivanovna.

"But at its very best life is insecure. Why pretend that it must be padded?"

Igor said to her:

"Of course it is. How could anyone grow if they were certain of tomorrow? Everybody would be standing stock still like any tethered horse."

But the lady who taught Italian, spoke acidly:

"Of course, you are far too young to realize the vileness of it all."

"Of what?" Frossia was getting impatient of loosely worded generalities.

"The system, the creed, must we use names?"

"There is no vileness," retorted Frossia, "that is stupid. . . . There is a lot of cruelty and injustice. . . ." She paused. "Why talk about it?" But the bitter-mouthed woman shrugged and said acidly: "Well, it is no use talking to you. You must have been born without any feelings."

Frossia found she could not talk to such people. Yet she could and did hold speech with many others, and it fell to her lot to observe the constantly shifting scene around her, and, leaving all sociological and political divagations alone, to remark all hunger and desolation, stubbornness and feebleness, cruelty and pity, kindness and indifference, and behind it all to discern, however dimly, the beauty of something intent upon growing, moving, deepening. And she was it all detachedly, as though its very core were to be considered apart from all criticism or praise.

Also Frossia had her own moments. There was the legend of Euphrosynia and her own urge to recreate the lovely old theme in sound, color, and movement, an urge which, even if left untranslated, had given her much sustenance through a hard and thorny beginning. Something of that enchanting theme stayed with her now even when she no longer yearned for a realization she would have earlier desired to see. She had her moments along the waters and in the gardens of the city which had bred her; she lived deeply and avidly when listening to some such narrative as Artemiy Sorokin's, or else to a calmly worded chapter of Igor's reminiscences from a past which had been so hard, which might easily have led him into the house of bitterness, and had instead brought him on to a highway, a generously spaced country where hedged-in thoughts and ignoble desires had little room, if any at all. Igor's manner was didactic, sometimes peremptory, sometimes aloof. Often he left her annoyed and dissatisfied. Sometimes, even against Frossia's will, the vision of a dim and stuffy grocer's shop stole into the foreground, and she saw a clumsy, ordinary shopkeeper absorbed in the spelling of two-syllabled words, wiping his nose on his sleeve, and eating his supper of pickled cabbage and beetroot with a blunt hornhandled knife and, seeing that scene in her mind, Frossia wondered why she should be feeling so small, until gradually the scene stole away, and she could see him reading Plato and Pushkin and Dostoevsky, watch him continuing to learn the people he belonged to and, finally, her annoyance with all the lesser, inevitably jarring things gave way to something like gratitude that she should have met him at all.

So the city, and Igor, and some students at the Rabfak, Gleb Semenovich, and her small circle of intimates, Anna Trofimovna, glad of those gingham dresses, and Elena Ivanovna, full of concern for all the unblessed folk in her world, even Nikolashka, his huge fat face puckered in laughter as he shared his own bread ration and hid his hunger from those hungrier than himself—in each and all of them Frossia saw life flowing past her own door, and knew that life to be a lovelier river than the Neva in the month of June. But she learnt of it still haphazardly and fleetingly, it came to her in moods to be splintered by the next onrush of hunger, a tiring hour in a queue, or the sullenness of some student at her Rabfak.

At the end of the first month she went to see Gleb Semenovich, and found him staring at a scribbled sheet of rough gray paper.

"The *starshina* of your group has sent in a report about you. Comrade Zolotov has just brought it in."

She halted by the table, still hearing a student's raucous and sulky voice—"Why should I put 'la' instead of 'le'? Is a chair a woman in France?" and her own brief spark of impatience— "Yes, it is feminine. I have told you so scores of times." The raucous voice insisted supinely—"Why?" and she pointed at the nearest window: "Why is a window a window and not a ceiling?" but none of them were in the right mood for a joke, and she could hear them grumbling.

Now they had sent in their report. She knew nothing about such things, and wondered whether she was meant to see the paper, and waited, crimson to the temples and tongue-tied, but Gleb Semenovich pushed the paper towards her and said that she was not to mind the spelling.

Frossia bent her head. She must not smile. But Comrade Golubev had already forgotten her. His telephone rang, he was deep in conversation, and Frossia could read, her immediate reactions unobserved.

The report began with a stilted complaint that the students' committee had never been consulted about her appointment, and went on to quote a verbose and muddled resolution that such elections were to be held invalid for the future. The resolution bristled with platform clichés and rang heavy with class consciousness, proletarian resolve, and infallibility of certain political doctrines. This prefatory burden apart, the report made engrossing reading. They found their lessons interesting but slow, and insisted that the teacher should recognize their ability to cope with more material at one sitting. They also complained of the shortage of textbooks, and Frossia quickly endorsed this grievance. They suggested that oral lessons had best be given during excursions when details of the Petrograd scene might be learnt in French. They wound up with a thumbnail sketch of Frossia:

Her voice is clear and unhurried. Her methods, apart from the slowness, are good. She is never late. She stares at us rather uncomfortably as though we were dolls and not human beings. We would prefer her not to call us *"gospoda"* [ladies and gentlemen]. She has certain habits which we dislike. She is too polite sometimes and she even laughs at us. We don't think she is very clever, but she can teach. Some of us have talked with her; she has traveled much, but is ignorant about many things, including literature. She has told us many interesting things about ballet, but said she could not teach dancing. She was appointed without our knowledge and contrary to all the resolutions. We would like her to stay on.

She finished. Her cheeks still burned crimson. Golubev hung up the receiver.

"How many pupils have you now?"

"Eighty. I have divided them into eight groups. I cannot have more than ten pupils in each group. This means eight lessons a day."

"No," he said slowly, examining a chart. "You could not have more. Pity you could not manage another group—"

"What about the Italian teacher?" Frossia suggested. "She once said she had only six groups, and she certainly does know her French."

"She is gone," said Golubev briefly, not looking at her.

"So the students' committee did dismiss her in the end—"

"The students' committee had nothing whatever to do with it. This is not a commissariat, Euphrosynia Pavlovna. We don't arrest people."

"Ah," was all Frossia said.

The sun had vanished behind a cloud, a blade of sharp wind ran through the room, and she wondered about many things, but Gleb Semenovich was no longer interested in the woman who had taught Italian. Gleb Semenovich wanted to discuss certain things in the report. Was it true that Frossia was as ignorant as it suggested?

"I am," she admitted. "I remember they began talking about the French Revolution and also about political economy. I don't know much. . . . I love poetry, I have read a lot, but history always defeats me."

"I should try to read some," Gleb Semenovich counseled her. "There is a good English history of the French Revolution by Carlyle. I have read it seven times—in Russian, of course. But Comrade Titov says you know some English. Read it. You see, your students will want to read books in a year or so." He paused and looked at her significantly. "You heard what I said—in a year or so. . . . Now I am busy. Good morning, Euphrosynia Pavlovna."

But she dared to linger for an instant.

"Comrade Golubev, about that Italian teacher . . . You have nobody else for the work—"

"Someone will be found," he said harshly. "Euphrosynia Pavlovna, in these days everybody is invaluable and nobody is. You understand. . . ."

Frossia was not quite certain if she understood. But there was little she could say.

Frossia knew she must mend her ignorance and fill in a few gaps left by an expensive and none too profitable education. One evening she found the flat in Galernaya Street almost empty except for Elena Ivanovna and Igor. The club was not going to meet that night, said Elena Ivanovna, there was a good historical film at the Soleil Cinema in Nevsky Prospect, and Lilian, for once unaccountably generous, had provided nearly twenty tickets. "If you had come in earlier, you would have got one," Elena Ivanovna reproved Frossia, who smiled and said she had no desire for an evening at a cinema. She had come to talk. "To Igor Vladimirovich and you also," she added hurriedly.

"Talk to Igor, *golubushka*," said Elena Ivanovna. "I have some laundry to do."

Frossia plunged boldly enough:

"Igor Vladimirovich, have you ever read Carlyle?"

"Why, yes, in Russian. Have you not?"

"Never . . . I could read him in the original. But where am I to find a copy?"

"I have a friend who is clerk at the old Imperial Library. It can be arranged." Suddenly he was interested. "Why, are you going to teach history?"

She laughed.

"Goodness me, how could I? But Gleb Semenovich thinks I had better do some reading," and she told Igor about the students' report. He nodded.

"Gleb Semenovich is a grand man. He is right. Yes, I will get you a Carlyle. But do you know your own history?"

"Don't shame me, Igor Vladimirovich. I know there was a Catherine the Great and Ivan the Terrible and Peter, and that Napoleon burned Moscow, or did we do it? Also I remember the Tartars came once a long time ago—"

"They did, and they stayed more than two hundred years. . . . But, Euphrosynia Pavlovna, history is not merely names and dates—"

"Well, I know something about old Moscow—just before Peter the Great, but that is all family. And, truly, I am not wholly ignorant. I used to make notes of all the ballets I went to." She started rummaging in her satchel for some papers. "I took these along with me today to read in the dinner hour. Listen, they are all disjointed notes, but they might show you that I am not quite a fool," and she read at random. "Best décor should always aim at providing a

single sharp symbol explaining the entire theme of a ballet. . . .
There is a lot here about *pas de deux*," she broke off. "It is the focal
point in all ballet. . . . And here is something rather childish and
quite personal: 'I cried over Petrushka. . . . I think I shall be a
female Petrushka.'" She smiled. "But this must bore you. . . . It
has not got much relation to our present life—"

"No," he agreed gravely, "but it is a bit of you, Euphrosynia Pavlovna. I cannot understand much of it. Your passion for the ballet
reminds me of a toy I saw in one of the old palaces. I think Potem-
kin gave it to Catherine the Great. It was made by some famous
English jeweler, a life-size golden peacock, perched on an oak
bough. It was a clock, really, and every time the hour chimed, the
peacock spread his wings and cried. . . . But they said it was so
valuable that Catherine would never have it wound up, and the
peacock's wings always stayed folded."

"Igor Vladimirovich, that is very unkind of you."

"Well, you shall have your Carlyle, and Soloviev's *History of
Russia*, and a few other books."

She checked him.

"You will never turn me into a bookworm. I have my French to
prepare every other night, and there is mending and washing and
cooking and queues. . . . Yesterday morning the tram for Kamennostrovsky was half an hour late, and it threw my whole day into
confusion. . . . Also one must think of people . . . and letters.
. . . I must write to Klava and Grisha, and now Dasha has gone
away. . . . Goodness me"—Frossia paused suddenly as though she
had never before realized the varied content of her days—"except
in those queues I believe I often forget to think about hunger. . . ."

"It is always an empty day which looks like a cup full to the
brim. . . . You could crowd anything into a full day, Euphrosynia
Pavlovna. But you are a teacher now. . . . You have proved that
you can teach, and no teacher can ever stop learning things. Otherwise you will be drained out."

This once Frossia showed no resentment at the didactic tone, and
said simply:

"All right. But if you bring a whole library to Maly Prospect,
you will have to bring candles as well."

8

Elena Ivanovna was writing a letter. She had been thinking of
it for days, and now she must postpone it no longer, even though
it meant a sequence of tiresome, petty tasks. She had to clear a

table, search for a pen and a bottle of ink, also for a piece of paper. None of those things were near at hand: she needed them so seldom. She must also push the table right under the window, she was writing in the morning, but all the rooms in her flat were always dim—the yard in Galernaya Street had little sunlight in it even on a most dazzling day. Letter-writing had other difficulties as well. It meant turning all the many varied thoughts in Elena Ivanovna's mind into soldiers, marshaling them into tidy ranks, and choosing such as were best fitted for promotion from mind to paper. This was the hardest part of the business. Elena Ivanovna's mind teemed with all sorts of things, but her supply of paper was sadly limited, and so was her time. She always hated correspondence, preferring non-committal post cards to sheets in envelopes. But she loved Klava, and Klava must have a proper letter.

. . . Bogdan is gaining weight again, and Frossia goes to the crèche and plays with him sometimes, and I always remember my own mother and myself under an old lilac tree in the garden at Holmovo. Paulina Pavlovna is well, bows to you, and is very occupied with prayer, needlework, and her children at the welfare center. Since the man at Ochta was arrested she has not tried anything else of the kind. Pavel Pavlovich is busy with another picture, it looks like a stormy sea to me, but there are men in it, only they have no arms and very queer heads, but I am ignorant of art, and I am afraid of asking stupid questions. Poor Nikolashka has had almost half his right thumb chopped off, and his arm is in a sling, but he is as cheerful as ever. Igor Vladimirovich's eyes are bothering him, I say it is the books. Dasha's mother has just gone to another factory near Rostov, I think, and she hopes to be in the Crimea in the autumn. There has been a bad murder in Alexeevskaya Street, a Tartar merchant was killed by a milkman from Narva, they say because of speculation. Bread is getting like bark, and hard to come by. Nikolashka says famine is coming here, but he is wrong: it has come already, and I hear that foreigners from England and America are to come and bring sugar and flour. I always say the world has never been lacking in kindly folk. They say this winter will be the worst, but they have said it many times before. The Zabalkansky is going on, and I have got a small store of wood in the cellar. I reckon most of our friends will be glad of a well-heated stove in the winter. Agrafena Petrovna, a deacon's widow and a friend of mine, writes from Moscow about thousands of homeless orphans wandering in the streets. We have thirty-seven infants at my crèche, but it is hard to feed them, and we have run out of peppermint drops, and there are many cases of dysentery. The doctor says there is no peppermint in the country, so I told him that someone must write to America and say that we would be grateful for peppermint drops as well as for flour and sugar. I have turned my crimson plush curtains into a cloak, and feel very grand in it. Frossia comes often enough. She is thin and very shabby, but one of her students has just given her a good-sized piece of gray peasant linen, and I have promised to make her some underwear—she has had none for years. She is still living in Maly Prospect. That dreadful German has gone, and Dasha's mother also. Now they have a young textile worker, but he looks consumptive, and I don't like his cough. There is also a middle-aged professor, and this reminds me: Frossia says Igor Vladimirovich is always at her for reading more books, and what time has she got? And I have no time left. There is the dinner soup to think of. I kiss you, and I bow to your husband, and please send me some caraway seeds if you can find any at Pskov. I should dearly love to eat a caraway loaf again. Yesterday I baked *"pirozhki"* with cabbage and onions. I made eight, and sixteen people came in the evening, and it meant half a *pirozhok* for each. Never mind: I had the baking of them, a pleasant job. We have had no rain for a month. How is your weather? Your loving friend,

and Elena Ivanovna signed her name with a laborious flourish, and sighed in content. The letter had taken her more than two hours, but it was written at last, and she must take it to the General Post Office in Pochtamskaya Street. There were three or four letter-boxes on the way, but Elena Ivanovna had no faith in letter-boxes. The General Post Office was the only place to send an important letter from, and she made the journey, and walked back satisfied even if tired. Her ill-shod feet hurt her, but the magnificent crimson cloak made her feel happy.

9

"Books again?" said Elena Ivanovna severely. "Well, Frossia, look at Igor Vladimirovich, a young man, and he is having trouble with his eyes. And why? Because he has read far more than is good for him. Books never made a cabbage pie, I tell you."

"But my eyes are not troubling me at all. I like reading, Elena Ivanovna, but I have so little time. Every moment is like a small box crammed full."

"I am glad to hear it."

Indeed Frossia's days were so full that often of an evening her mind refused to cope with any thought. Trams were running badly and erratically that autumn, the Rabfak chancery frequently ran out of free tram tickets, and Frossia must sometimes tramp the long way to Kamennostrovsky from Vasilyev Island, and then back again. Sometimes she returned just in time to swallow whatever food she had in her locker, and then drop asleep. It was a harsh autumn and a bitter winter, few logs could be used in the kitchen, there was no heating whatever in her bedroom. Frossia kept herself clean by boiling a pannikin of water, soaking a rag in it, and rub-

281

bing it all over her body. The rubbing finished, she swathed herself again in all the thick and shapeless garments she wore by daytime. She slept hard. The young textile worker was in the next room. His continuous rasping cough led other tenants to grumble about disturbed nights: Frossia never heard a sound.

The textile worker, pale, shrunken, and shy, was a shadow across the passage, and no more. Mark Alexandrovich Lavrov, the professor, was now in Anna Trofimovna's room. Frossia stumbled on him in the kitchen the very first day he came. Everybody always stumbled on Mark Alexandrovich, so small and slight was he, so very apologetic of having a body at all, and so defenseless with his tiny head, wispy gray hair, and a thin badly shaven face. His very tread sounded like an apology. His voice trembled with the same note. He had once lectured at the Kiev University. He was a layman who had had the chair of Church History. Now he was a clerk at the *Gosizdat*. Occasionally she caught him reading galley proofs in the kitchen. He was about fifty, and looked seventy. She guessed that he had known hunger—and probably worse, and his extraordinary care over the least crumb in his hands rather endeared him to her. One evening they were together in the kitchen. She had had some milk given her by a student, and was now boiling it for her supper, and Mark Alexandrovich stood frying an excessively lean herring. The milk almost boiled over, she saved it in time, and saw his small hands shake as though the roof had been about to fall.

"It would have been such a calamity."

"Well," she reassured him, "I would have had a herring then. But I felt rather thirsty tonight, and so chose milk instead—"

"Yes." He spoke in a far away voice. "Thirst can be terrible. Thirst is far worse than hunger," and he turned to his herring so abruptly that Frossia knew he did not wish her to see his face, and she slipped out of the kitchen at once.

But never again did Mark Alexandrovich so betray himself. Instead he told Frossia odd bits about his work at the *Gosizdat,* and she shared with him her own impressions of the Rabfak. The textile worker never appeared in the kitchen, but Olga Semenovna and the undertaker looked upon the small room as very much their own premises, and Parfen Nikitich began being rather unpleasant, hinting that the kitchen *plita* was far too small for everybody's saucepans to clutter. Mark Alexandrovich heard one of such hints and occasionally supped off what cold provender he could find. Soon enough Parfen Nikitich and Olga Semenovna took to crowding the *plita* with their pots and pans, and one evening Frossia met Mark

Alexandrovich hurrying down the passage, some uncooked potatoes in his pannikin.

"You cannot eat those raw." She stopped him.

"Well, no—but I can wait—I mean—I am not very hungry."

"You cannot wait. There is so little fuel. The *plita* will be cold in less than an hour."

"Well," he admitted apologetically, "this is so unimportant, Euphrosynia Pavlovna, but I don't think there is any room. You see—I came so late. It was very stupid of me. . . ."

"Give me your potatoes," said Frossia, seized the pannikin, and marched into the kitchen. Parfen Nikitich stood, intently looking at his own supper in three large saucepans. The midwife had her meal in two. The five saucepans occupied the whole of the *plita*.

"Your millet is overdone," Frossia said to the undertaker.

"I like it that way. Please, Euphrosynia Pavlovna, there is no need for you to interfere with other people's food."

"I must have room to cook these potatoes—"

"There you are, Olga Semenovna." The undertaker turned to the midwife. "One fighting another's battles. As thick as thieves they are, and it does not matter that poor folk like our two selves are entitled to a quiet meal of an evening. Brewing some plot, they are, I feel certain, always reading and writing and muttering. Honest people"—he raised his own voice—"never talk in whispers. . . ."

The midwife stirred her own gruel in silence.

"Your millet is overdone," said Frossia. "I have said it twice. I shall not say it again. The Domkom office is open, and I shall go and summon the chairman or the commandant—whichever of them is there. This is a communal kitchen, Parfen Nikitich, and nobody's private preserve."

She waited. The undertaker shrugged, stirred his millet, and muttered: "Why pick a quarrel with me, Euphrosynia Pavlovna? Yes, the millet is ready." He went on speaking in a conciliatory voice since the midwife had shown she was not going to join the issue against Frossia, and Parfen Nikitich disliked single combats. So he took off one saucepan, and triumphantly Frossia set her pannikin down when the door opened and Mark Alexandrovich shuffled in.

"But I made a foolish mistake, Euphrosynia Pavlovna. I made such a mistake. Please, please, let these people cook their supper in peace. . . . I have got a big cabbage pasty. I would much rather eat the pasty than boiled potatoes tonight. . . . Yes, yes, much rather." He nearly upset the midwife's saucepan in snatching at his pannikin, and ran away. The undertaker guffawed. Olga Semenovna pursed her lips.

"How could anyone help such a man?" Frossia later complained to Igor. "I suppose every time someone pushes him at the *Gosizdat* he apologizes for being in the way. Why must anyone be so stupid?"

"Well," said Igor. "Perhaps he is afraid of you. . . . Don't you remember you began by being afraid of your pupils at the Rabfak?"

"Yes, but they abused me, they were unkind to me. . . . Have I ever been unkind to Mark Alexandrovich?"

"There are people who cannot help being afraid of kindness even. I should not come near him too often, Euphrosynia Pavlovna—"

"No," she said slowly, "but all the same I cannot understand this being afraid of kindness."

"Why not?" Igor looked astonished. "Have you forgotten Comrade Cherny then? He helped you get your first job, he helped get you out of a scrape, he was kind to you, and yet, by all I have heard, you were certainly afraid of him. . . ."

"But that was different," said Frossia impatiently, and yet could not explain the difference.

In those days she often remembered Cherny. Cherny was now working far away, somewhere in the south. He had completely vanished from her life, he never wrote, and she hardly ever met anyone who mentioned him, but she remembered his strangely attractive fanaticism, his abrupt passion, and her own equally abrupt refusal. Nikita, the dwarf, might know something of Cherny, but Nikita's own job had been shifted to a different and distant part of the city, and Frossia never met Nikita now. I should not have been so brusque with Cherny now, she reflected. I would have worded it all differently. She had indeed learnt much since that dim and tedious day when she had sat in the train, watching a man's kerchief flutter over a dead face and, as she thought of the distance covered by her mind, she began reflecting on Igor's face. It had neither breeding nor beauty. Its features were so commonplace that often enough she found herself unable to recall them to her memory. Igor's features were molded out of common Russian clay, hurriedly molded, too, and yet every time she met him, she learned anew that there was something unrepeatable in their very ordinariness. It was a like a bowl of common white ware, cheap and thin, and it had a lighted candle put inside, and the cheap ordinariness of the white pottery became transformed with a glory. Igor's eyes were not beautiful, they were neither brown nor green nor even a definite hazel, they were not big, and usually they looked calm, sleepy almost. But sometimes he spoke of Russia or else mentioned something quite simple about an oak coppice or a river, and the ordinary eyes went on fire, and the light spread all over his face, and all that was commonplace in it was washed away by a glory for which Frossia could find no name.

Yet he often baffled her. She could more or less understand his lack of understanding beauty in detail—how he had marveled over her loving the porcelain bowls at a *stolovaya*—she could well gauge the roughness of his phrasing and the hardness of his judgments. He had often and often spoken to her of Tolstoy and Dostoevsky, urging her to find herself at home in the wealth they offered, but when he found her shaken by the concluding chapters of *Resurrection*, he said almost mockingly:

"Well, was it not a dream?"

"Don't you believe in absolute charity then?" she marveled.

"I do—in a sense. But remember your old Artemiy—a good furrow, a bad furrow, and that is life. That is also history. We are plodding through a very bad furrow just now—" And the now familiar light crept into his eyes so that she must listen, her earlier bewilderment quieted. "But the mind of man could never merely imagine comparisons. To me, and I am an unlettered man, the very idea of a comparison suggests something incomparable. Good, better, best, as we understand it, and I think the other best must be ultimate—you know it will cover all things and be compared with none because none can stand above it, Euphrosynia Pavlovna."

"Yes . . . yes—but when and how?"

"How could I tell you? It is all a puzzle. Look at us now—no bread, no fuel. . . . Typhus has come here. Day by day I sit there in my office, and I don't now just examine their permits, Euphrosynia Pavlovna. People who come to me are sick to the very depths, and they want to talk, and I must listen to them. So I hear stories. Those people have forgotten peace and abundance. They had never known comfort and ease. But they don't just hang on: they live. They do things. Even your timid apologetic Mark Alexandrovich, who is afraid of thirst and bullies and spiders, is doing something. And why? I cannot tell why. The Russian way must be maddening to any foreigner. A woman from Moscow told me that she had heard an American exclaim in very poor Russian: 'Most of you should have died. Why did you not die?' Well, millions have died, but many more millions are living, and I think, Euphrosynia Pavlovna, there is charity in living—"

Frossia might have said she was beginning to see it, but she said nothing.

It had been a difficult year, and her first three terms at the Rabfak suggested separate scenes from an elaborately staged nightmare. For months she had sat at her desk in the room with lily painted walls, and felt that they were all leagued against her—in spite of their lessened outward hostility, in spite of genuinely awakened interest and keenness to learn the language. Their oddly assorted committee had suggested excursions, Comrade Golubev had rather dryly endorsed the suggestion, and spoke no more of it. The initiative was left to Frossia. She remembered that her students, apart from the set lessons at the Rabfak, led lives of their own. Of leisure they could not have much. She learned that most of them were housed in a hostel, *obshchezhitie*, in an annex to the main building. Bedding, light, fuel, and rations were issued free. Yet they were responsible for housework, the stoking of stoves, cooking, and laundry. The fuel was kept in the back yard, but candles, soap, and rations were not always distributed on the premises: the students must often tramp for miles to the nearest food depôt. Their committee had grandiloquently suggested excursions. The students shrugged and retorted that they got quite enough exercise.

Frossia paid a call at the hostel. It was the stables converted to domestic use by means of rather flimsy wooden partitions. Cubicles ran right and left. Each had a hole of a window, a paillasse for a bed, and a crate which served for chair, table, and wardrobe. Between the cubicles ran a fairly wide passage furnished with a double row of trestles. The passage got its light from the cubicles, and their doors must of necessity stay open. At one end of the passage Frossia saw a huge iron stove and just to the left of it one cubicle was converted into a kitchen.

She went there one morning. The hostel was deserted, there were a few books strewn about the trestles, but the cubicles looked tidy, bleak, somehow unlived-in. She glanced at some of the books. Geology, trigonometry, practical engineering, a book on hydrostatics, a battered English grammar, several French textbooks . . . She picked up the English grammar when she heard someone cough, and a girl came forward. She was the ugliest person Frossia had ever seen. Her round face was nearly flat, she had almost no cheekbones, and her nose was a flattened button pressed into that round, deeply tanned pancake of a face. Her harsh frizzled black hair was brushed well away from the forehead. Her eyes slanted, her teeth were the only magnificent thing about her, white and exquisitely chiseled, but the thick, loose lips spoilt their beauty. She wore a bright blue overall, startling green beads, each the size of a pigeon's egg, and brown kid gloves were taut on her hands.

"Is this hostel A?" asked Frossia.

"Yes," said the girl in a hoarse voice. "I am the monitor. But we have not got a bed—so it is no good your trying to get one."

"I don't want to live here."

"No? Well, what do you want?"

"I have merely come to see the hostel—"

"You have seen it. I have been watching you, poking your nose in everywhere. There is nothing else to look at. We have no velvet armchairs to offer you."

"And why should you have them? And why," asked Frossia a little angrily, "should I want to sit in them?"

"You look that kind. . . . What are you doing here anyhow?"

"I teach French."

"That is funny." She looked uglier than ever when she tittered: her eyes disappeared altogether, there was nothing but brown skin, black hair, and a thick crimson line of her mouth. "How funny . . . Yes, I should say that is about the only thing you could do—chatter in French—"

"And what are you doing?"

"Why do you ask?"

"Can I not be interested in what you do?"

"Mathematics," said the girl, twisting the green beads. "Yes, mathematics, I said. Don't tell me it is funny, because everybody thinks it is, and I am too tired to hear it. I come from Ufa, I went to the village school and learnt that two and two made four, I learnt my multiplication table, and then came to grief. Do you want to know why?"

"Of course I do." Frossia put down the battered English grammar.

"The mistress set a problem. She was a bitter, unkind, stupid woman. She said: 'If you send one pound of mushrooms by rail from Tver to the Urals, paying two kopeks per verst for the transit, how much would you have to pay for the mushrooms on delivery?' Do you understand it?"

"Yes, but I have no idea of the distance between Tver and the Urals—"

"The distance did not matter. I knew it all right. She set me the problem, I must stand up and chalk it on the blackboard. Her back was turned. I wrote: 'Nothing at all.' She looked. Her face went purple. 'What do you mean, nothing?' she said. 'Have you not learnt your multiplication table?' I said: 'There is nothing to multiply because there could be no such delivery, the distance is so great that all the mushrooms would get rotten, and whoever heard of anyone paying anything for rotten mushrooms?' I said, and that was the end of my schooling. They expelled me, the teacher said I had the devil in me, and I minded geese for four years. But I knew I would learn mathematics some day. Nothing ever happens without some purpose to it. So I got here."

"And are you happy?"

"Well, it is the devil's own life sometimes, we all live together, and some chatter when I want to study, and we have had no soap for months, and the rations are thin, and I am nearly always hungry —a peasant mouth was born wide—I could eat the rottenest mushroom sometimes." Suddenly she asked: "Have you any gloves to spare?"

"Any what?"

"Gloves?" The girl from Ufa held up her hands encased in dark brown kid. "It is the first pair I have ever had. They are lovely, but they have split. I reckon they are too small for me. You cannot buy them anywhere. Listen, if you had a pair, my *batka* would send you a sackful of millet."

"But why do you like gloves?"

"I cannot say. It would not worry me to walk on my bare toes in this city, but something on your hands gives you such a nice feeling—" She measured Frossia with a shrewd glance. "I am wasting time talking to you like that. You are gentry. You know all about these things. They mean little to you. . . . Yes, I know, the way you hold your head, the way your hands are shaped, and then French—"

"I will see if I have any gloves—but I want no millet, please—"

"We shall see," said the girl from Ufa. "Well, is life not queer? There was I walking to Ufa, no trains round about that country, I walked one hundred versts, wore out two pairs of bast sandals, and came to Ufa, and had nothing except my silver cross and some coppers. I had not told my *batka* I wanted to go. . . . Well, I got to the station. The engine frightened me, I had never seen one. I sat down with my bundle and cried. They asked me for papers. I had none, and they put me into a cell. . . . Bugs and rats and what not . . . The rats ate my bundle. The next day they took me straight to a commissariat and asked for papers again. I said: 'Antichrists, can you not see I am a peasant girl; what can I know about any papers?' Well, they said they would send me back to my village. I got angry. They said permits were necessary for traveling. Then someone had enough wit to ask what I wanted. I said I meant to get to Moscow and go to a proper school. They asked: 'What do you want to learn?'—'Counting,' I said, 'long rows of figures and suchlike.' They laughed and let me go—"

"To Moscow?"

"Bless you, no. . . . I stayed on in Ufa. A man got drunk. He had some money on him. I took it, went to the station in the dark, and hid in a truck. We came to Moscow. They caught me. I spent a week in prison. Then a man came to see me, a clever man, a lawyer. I told him what I wanted to do. I told him about my taking the money from that man in Ufa and all. They sent me here. I am doing trigonometry now."

A bell clanged in the distance. The girl from Ufa seized an armful of books.

"Pasha Dobrina, my name is, comrade. Please don't forget about the gloves—"

"No, Pasha," said Frossia.

10

Frossia discovered that her students had most Saturdays free, and she asked if she might come and spend a day at the hostel. Her idea was taken doubtfully, they said they had all their weekly chores to do on Saturday afternoon, the wood to chop, the washing, the cleaning. . . .

"May I share in the work then?" said Frossia, and there was a thin chorus of assent.

"What are you doing it for?" marveled Elena Ivanovna, and Frossia replied: "Just to give them some French practice."

But the morning yielded few opportunities for any such practice. Frossia found all the men outside chopping wood for the coming week. The girls were busily, if sketchily, swabbing the trestles in the passage, and Frossia joined them. The trestles were soon finished, the stone floor looked dirty enough, but nobody suggested that it should be washed. A small boiler was brought in, water heated on the *plita* in the kitchen, and then soiled garments were simply rammed into the boiler, stirred with a shovel, pulled out, wrung once or twice, and then hung out to dry. To Frossia most of the clothes looked but little less dirty than they had been, but Glafira Antonovna, the woman with the squint, said, observing an obstinate inkstain on a man's tattered gray shirt: "Anyway, warm water has been over it, and that is something."

Frossia looked round, hoping to see Pasha Dobrina among them. She was not. Frossia asked after her, and they laughed.

"She never wastes time over washing and cleaning. She must be at a library somewhere. She knows she gets little peace here on Saturdays." And now they swarmed round the kitchen door. Swabbing and washing had been rather breathless affairs. Cooking promised more leisure, and they began hurling questions at Frossia:

"What is French for herring?"

"Is salt a man or a woman, I have forgotten—"

"Sorry, Euphrosynia Pavlovna, someone dropped a ladle. . . . I never heard you. Say it again."

She had brought her own rations, but they waved her little parcel aside, and she must share their own dinner of lamentably underdone millet and oversalted fish. Glafira Antonovna lent Frossia a none too clean wooden spoon. Six basins of millet, one for eight people, were put on the trestles. The fish was thrown into a kind of a tin trough which traveled up and down the passage. Each person had a small portion of coarse rye bread. Frossia politely refused her share, and the girl sitting next to her seized the bread and pushed it almost into Frossia's mouth. "It is a sin to refuse bread," she said in a coarse Novgorod accent.

The millet mess was eaten to a solemn rhythm, nobody diving into the basin out of their turn. They carried spoonfuls of yellow gluey stuff to their mouths slowly, carefully, never spilling a grain. The spoonful eaten, the spoon would be licked clean before the owner's next turn came round. Nobody talked. The fish trough came along with several roughly grilled pieces of gold-brown *vobla* on it, and the fish was eaten with fingers. Presently a great iron kettle appeared, full of weakly brewed black currant leaf tea. There was neither sugar nor saccharine. Tea was drunk out of most varied tumblers, handleless teacups, tin pannikins, jam jars, even flower vases. Frossia's neighbor drank hers out of a glass jar which still boasted a glazed label—"Brothers Eliseev. Choice cherry conserve."

The tea drunk, things were cleared away. No washing up could be discussed: they had used all their hot water for the day. The trestles were woefully dirty once again, and the smell of *vobla* bones rather strong. But they were preparing to enjoy half an hour of genuine leisure, and asked if Frossia could sing. Frossia gave them two brief French songs, and the second was finished to the muted accompaniment of distant snoring. She, too, felt sleepy; it was hot in the passage, it smelt heavily of fish, wet tin, and rather sketchily washed human flesh. She stopped singing. The snoring swelled into an emphatic chorus. She chose the cleanest trestle and curled herself on its bare boards.

An hour later they flung themselves to work again. The iron *plita* must be cleaned, and the men went on chopping the wood. The cleaning of the range left the girls with deeply sooted faces and hands. They ran out into the yard to wash under the tap, and Frossia was left alone when Pasha Dobrina burst into the converted stable.

"My gloves? You have not forgotten my gloves—"

Frossia had not forgotten.

"But I have had very little time since I met you—"

"H'm, and I had no time to think about my dinner. Do you think those beasts left me a crumb?"

Frossia was uncertain, but her own rations—cold boiled potatoes and some smoked *vobla*—were still untouched, and she offered the package to Pasha who looked at it suspiciously. She did not think she could take it, she mumbled. It was strange to see anyone offer food to people.

"No poison in it, is there?"

"Why?"

"You need not look so angry. I heard of a boy dying in Moscow—of poison he died. Nobody gave it to him, but all the same it was poison. He got into a barn somewhere, and there was some bread left about in small pieces with pink powder on it for rats. The boy had not seen any bread for months. He fell on it, and he died in ten minutes, they said."

"Will you eat my potatoes?"

Pasha bit into one.

"It must have been noisy here," she asserted, her mouth full of flaky silvery flesh. "I stayed away on purpose. But it is quiet enough in the evenings. We put two candles on each trestle, and for two hours nobody is allowed to talk. Then they get on with their nonsense—"

"What nonsense?"

"Well, languages. Languages are nonsense because they are so easy. You think you are clever because you can say 'soup' and 'potato' in so many different languages, but it is all words. You need nothing but memory for languages, and not too much brain. And if you are a Russian you must know some languages. They say ours is so difficult that no foreigner can ever learn it. But science is not like that. It does not belong to one people. It is the world's. You get hold of something in Russian—you don't know mathematics —so it is no use my explaining it to you," she flung into brackets. "Well, as I was saying, you learn it or you discover it in Russian, and a Chinaman or a Spaniard or a Swede will know the same fact, it does not matter what language it is put in. And there is another thing: you can learn a language well—or not so well—or even badly. You can speak broken Russian, or broken French. But you cannot juggle with science. You cannot present a broken truth or prove a bit of a proposition. . . . There you are," and Pasha finished both potatoes and *vobla,* wiped her mouth, and scampered away. The

291

men came in, tired and taciturn, and the girls returned, their faces clean and their hands red from the cold water. Frossia realized her day among them was over. She put on her coat. Pasha was in her cubicle at the end of the passage. Some students began tossing books along the trestles, and candles were being brought out. Frossia, coated and shawled, said good-by. Some answered, *"Dosvidania,"* *"au revoir,"* others muttered, *"proshchayte,"* "good-by." Frossia remembered having broken of their scant bread, and thanked them. But Glafira Antonovna shouted:

"Well, come again. You might help the fellows to chop wood some time."

"I might," said Frossia, and lifted the clumsy wooden latch. A bourdon of voices rose behind her, but their concern was not with her, she knew it, as she stepped into the bitterly cold open air.

Spring was coming once again, but that evening it was still winter, and thick snow coated the road. Frossia, aching for her bed and the blankets round her tired body, must accept the stillness all round her for temporary assuagement of her fatigue of flesh and mind. The snow was slippery, there had been a slight thaw some days before, and she dared not fall. In the fitful light of a late afternoon she plodded on, happily certain of her bearings and strangely satisfied with her day. She had not reached the slender Exchange Bridge at the farthest end of Petrograd Side when all weariness slipped off her. She would have run back to the Rabfak to spend another day in backbreaking tasks. She crossed the bridge. To the left of her the giant silhouette of the old and now useless lighthouse reared itself to the dark clear sky. She could not see the rich crimson of the tower, but the remembered color stole into her mind with an increasing depth. At the foot of the lighthouse the darker splash of small Exchange Gardens made her remember their once formal beds of wallflowers. They did look so formal, they were all chained off the paths, and I used to swing on those chains. . . .

There could be no flowers at that time of the year, and, as Frossia knew, some of the chains had gone rusty, others were missing, but her heart warmed to the childishly slight memory, and briskly she turned to the right towards Maly Prospect and her balconied home. She had not got there before wet, untidily flaked snow, "the kind which can never make up its mind to become honest rain," began falling all round her. The tip of her nose wet and glowing, her chin thrust into an inadequate collar, Frossia wondered why even that tiresomely wet snow could not disturb the serenity she had met on her long tramp home.

With the coming of warmer weather Elena Ivanovna suggested that the Zabalkansky were to meet less often at the flat. "Let us all go out," she said, "and leave the rooms to the spiders. None of us can travel much, but good air is there in the parks, and young grass and flowers, and it is possible to talk anywhere," she said. But most of the Zabalkansky people worked somewhere or other; they could give little more time than an occasional Saturday afternoon. Pavel Pavlovich grumbled. The only bearable places in Petrograd, he declared, were the Hermitage, the Academy of Arts, and the Alexander III Gallery, but Elena Ivanovna retorted:

"It is something to marvel at, Pavel Pavlovich, if an artist like you is going to be bored with an hour spent in the Summer Gardens. Aren't old trees in April as worthwhile as old pictures?"

He still grumbled, but Paulina Pavlovna was conciliatory. It was a beautiful idea, she murmured, and it would give them all much pleasure. Paulina Pavlovna meant to continue her small trite speech, and to lift the very ordinary scheme of Elena Ivanovna's to the higher plane of sorrily untutored metaphysics, but her brother broke in by bowing to them all and saying he had not really meant what he had said, and they were all content.

Frossia could not join them every Saturday afternoon. Her own lessons now took more and more time to prepare, and kindlier weather brought unkindly revelations of her thin wardrobe: things which had merely looked drab in the uncertain winter light, now proved to be soiled and tattered. So she worked away at her needle and her books as much as she could. But on her free afternoons she loved to join in the wanders of the Zabalkansky. She had not much to learn of the city, she had known it all her days, and now she felt that it lived from Vasilyev Island to Viborg Side, where the poor and unblessed had once lived in their darkness, from Kazan Quarter to Kolomna, from Moscow Gate to Narva Gate, with all its rivers, bridges, squat blue and gold domes, and slender copper spires. The great dark red archway at the end of Morskaya Street, the wide spaces round St. Isaac's, the brave silhouette of Annunciation Church sharp white against the dull red of Marine Barracks, great houses and great churches, and then waste patches, ranges of humbly timbered hovels, tapering off to squalor, but sooner or later, even the most squalid and unsavory lane came within the neighborhood of running water, and you knew that all squalor was somehow cleansed and redeemed. Then came Nevsky Prospect, three miles of it, a regal avenue, broken by bridges of a beauty to match its space and splendor, and the last bridge crossed, you came to the wide Znamensky Square, and Nicholas Station was soon left behind, also the overwhelming grandeur of important buildings, and you were in the Nevsky of humbler roofs and wooden palings, a much more narrow road which had something homely and Norwegian in it, and so you were led to the white gates of Alexander Nevsky Monastery with its clusters of several domes and its particularly quiet corner where a plain stone slab told you that the great Suvorov lay there.

One sultry afternoon, after a long tramp along the quays, Frossia crossed Nicholas Bridge. At the shuttered door of Konradi's chocolate shop she saw a sheet of paper faintly fluttering in the small breeze which came from the river. Frossia picked it up and thrust it into her pocket.

She found the flat in a turmoil because Parfen Nikitich, the undertaker, was giving one of his parties, and Frossia soon saw that she must eat a cold supper in her own room: both passage and kitchen seethed with Parfen Nikitich's guests, and Frossia had no desire for either company or trivial chatter. She sat by the open window, a book in her lap, trying to shutter her mind against discordant singing and loud laughter which rang from the kitchen. Then she remembered the paper she had picked up. She smoothed out the sheet. It was part of a letter, written in a very tidy small hand on both sides of the sheet. There was neither date nor signature. She read through various family details which said nothing to her, and then came to a separate paragraph, read it once, pondered over it, and read it again aloud in a soft voice fraught with wonder.

". . . because we must hold on to the Truth within and without us so that those who come after may say 'our fathers had a hard time of it, but they did succeed in keeping tryst with the highest good because they knew that never can good be overpowered by evil.' This is hard to learn, my dear, but . . ." Here the sheet came to an end, and Frossia slipped it back into her pocket, and sat still, and when Parfen Nikitich banged on her door and invited her to join them, Frossia forgot all about her earlier reluctance, and went.

One of the guests was a small swarthy man with a sickle-shaped scar on his right cheek. The undertaker offered Frossia a glass of tea and a potato cake. The swarthy man said:

"This is a grand party—"

"Yes."

"You live alone here?"

"Yes—"

The swarthy man sighed.

"I have nine children, and a wife, and the wife's mother, and an old aunt who is blind." He paused. "Thirteen of us—in three rooms. My eldest son is twenty-four. He is a lunatic. He has fallen in love—just fancy. . . ."

"Is that so impossible?" Frossia tried hard not to smile, his distress seemed so genuine.

"But you don't know. She is not one of us. Her father was a real *dvorianin*. Her mother escaped abroad. The girl is a student at the university. She has short hair, and wears men's boots, and says she is a true proletarian—but she is not."

"Perhaps she wants to be—"

"But you don't know. Perhaps she does. Kostia says so. He brought her along a week ago. We live in a very poor way. Well, my wife could not keep the place tidy if she worked the whole day at it. Imagine—thirteen people in three rooms. Zhenia—that is the girl's name—behaved well enough, but she is not one of us," he repeated stubbornly. "If she were, she would not spend all her time in telling us that she was. I call that acting." And he mimicked almost savagely: 'Andrey Ivanovich, I am all for the proletariat.' The kind that says so, is not—"

He had not finished, and Frossia waited politely. Andrey Ivanovich bit into his second potato cake, washed it down with hot tea, and went on:

"Now there is a different man I know, a grand man. He is a painter. He is always working at some great picture or other. He lives in Moyka, his name is Pavel Pavlovich Ratov. He never talks nonsense, but I know he is my brother for all he used to be a gentleman. Do you know why?"

"I think I do," Frossia murmured, but he would not listen to her. He set down his empty glass, wiped his mustaches, and said:

"Because Pavel Pavlovich never talks nonsense. He never mentions differences. They are not there for him to look at. He came to my place, it was a hot day, of course the rooms were stuffy—and what else can you expect with thirteen people living in three rooms? Well, Pavel Pavlovich sat down on the edge of the bed, and he never pretended it was a chair, nor did he say, 'You know, it is good to be sitting on a bed. . . . I would rather sit on the edge of a bed than in a chair.' That is what Zhenia says. No, Pavel Pavlovich takes everything as it comes. He will paint you a grand picture, clear snow off a street, and do real cobbling, and grumble and curse and use words you cannot always understand—but it is all of a piece with him. Do you see what I mean, *grajdanka?*" He got up. "You come and see us," he added genially. "You are good at listening.

295

We could entertain you. My eldest girl can sing, and Kostia can recite some Pushkin."

The guests left. The moon rose. Maly Prospect shed its squalor, and the ugliest timbered house borrowed beauty from the sky's silver treasure house. By moonlight Frossia read the letter once again. Then she slipped the sheet behind Taglioni's picture and went to sleep. The house was never really quiet. She heard the textile worker's cough. Mark Alexandrovich was groaning, and the undertaker's snores rose and fell all down the passage. A board creaked, then another. The wind rose. Clouds sailed across the silver-lit sky. The pure silver was soon shrouded in shadows, and Frossia slept.

CHAPTER TEN

"THE NEVA IS RISING"

Twice a term Frossia must make a journey to the *Gosizdat* along Catherine Canal where she had once sat, sorting out an endless avalanche of French and German pamphlets. "And you never really read them," marveled Igor. "Goodness me, Euphrosynia Pavlovna, you are made of strange stuff." And she defended herself by retorting: "It was all so dry and technical. . . ." There had been a time when she would urge Michael to look for work in some such place where his talents, however thin, might have answered some need of the hour. Now she went there in search of books for her ever-growing groups at the Rabfak.

She passed a small shop where, in incredibly remote days, her grandmother would take her to buy hats—Madame Rosalie's. Madame Rosalie had gone, the black and gold sign was hanging askew as if someone had wanted to wrench it off and left the job half done. Through the dirty windows Frossia could see little else than mounds of thick gray-brown dust on the shelves and the bare floor boards where once a rich blue velvet carpet had lain. She could easily imagine the place crowded with fussy, important mothers, patient, black gowned attendants, Madame Rosalia herself, all suspiciously golden hair and false diamonds flashing on the high bosom sheathed in pearl-gray satin. You were neither body nor mind at Madame Rosalie's, you were just a head for her to adorn. Frossia remembered a wickedly expensive dove-gray bonnet with a touch of darker ribbon and a slim wreath of marguerite buds, and another, a warm golden straw hat with a cluster of deep crimson roses, and a picture hat in white marquisette, its brim all wired, tiny clipped blue feathers encircling the shallow crown. "Not feathers, *Madame la Princesse*," pronounced Rosalie. "Surely not feathers for *mademoiselle*, but a motif of pale rose ribbon placed this way— *justement comme ça.*" Her podgy white hands busily sketched the motif in the air, but Frossia's eyes pleaded, and the hat was bought, its blue feathers inviolate, and they left smiling at Madame Rosalie's patent efforts to conceal her disapproval. Outside, by the curb, a small boy tugged at her grandmother's sleeve, and was given a small silver coin.

"Grandmamma, how much was that hat?"

"I did not ask, *ma chère*. No, wait a moment. I believe it was eighteen roubles, but you liked it—for a wonder. Cheap hats are always impossible—"

Frossia pulled at the shabby green shawl on her head and hurried on to the *Gosizdat*. It had been almost a pleasure to remember the multicolored traffic which had once flowed through Madame Rosalie's black and gray doorway, but sterner and no less interesting tasks now awaited Frossia. At the *Gosizdat* she filled a form with her name, status, and business, all in decreed block letters, was told she would have to wait, and wandered off to the nearest table to examine some of the books when a voice made her start.

"Why? Are you working here?"

It was Cherny, thinner, deeply bronzed, and very shabby, no longer in uniform, but the scar was there, and interest, if not friendliness, in deeply sunken black eyes. Meeting him here in a common, rather crowded waiting room was something strangely at one with those memories of Rosalie's, and the finding and losing of Michael, shadows on stone and snow, the first night in a deserted summerhouse in Moshkov Lane, her own absurd unsubstantial dreams about a legend, Anna von Packen. . . . But all those were curiously remote—not so much in mere time as in experience. Seasons had gone, weaving their own web, and they had not shared the seasons, had not observed the texture together.

"No," Frossia answered Cherny, "I teach French at a Rabfak. I am here to get a few textbooks. And you?"

"I am in Orel—working at the local Proletcult. I am not a policeman any more. I got a bullet in my thigh in a street brawl in Odessa. I am off to Orel tomorrow. But they want books, that is why I came here. They want Bedny and Ehrenburg and Alexey Tolstoy and some Pushkin and something of Engels, too, and Lenin's speeches. Where are you living?"

She told him. He asked after a few people they used to meet in common, but their names came to him with an effort, and her replies were brief.

"I am staying in Ligovka. Will you come and have supper? They say Palkin's is open. They might fry *vobla* nicely there—"

"Thank you—I could not. I am at the Zabalkansky tonight. Will you come?"

298

"No," answered Cherny. "And you have not asked me if I am married—"

"Are you?"

"Married? No. I live with a woman, a student, Nina Yakovlevna Baranova. She made me take up that work at the Proletcult. We get on all right. I met her in the train going to Odessa. There was very little accommodation in Odessa, things happen that way, you know. I am not sorry—though she does love arguing a bit too much. She has read a lot. A student, what will you? She can argue, and I cannot. I see one thing at a time. Nina Yakovlevna sidetracks all along. She will say: 'Cherny, I want three girls to learn Hungarian and Chinese. Women are good at propaganda, but they must be good linguists. Cherny, do you hear, I want Aniuta, Varia, and Masha to be put down for Moscow. Varia will do well in Hungary. She is that type.' And I say: 'Baranova, you have forgotten that it is very dangerous for our people to be in Hungary at all. That admiral is there, and he hates us.' She will reply: 'Cherny, that is where you are stupid. You must risk adventures and dangers to succeed in anything. A cabbage leaf is never in peril, and it remains a cabbage leaf.' Now Nina Yakovlevna is learning Hungarian herself," added Cherny. "Some day she will go there, and I shall be all by myself."

"She sounds nice," Frossia said politely.

"Well, she is a bit like a sergeant major of the old army. We have one small room. There is not much accommodation in Orel. There is little comfort. Sometimes we receive a little sugar, sometimes a little saccharine. Nina Yakovlevna locks everything up. She doles things out—mostly on alternate days. 'You must not think of your stomach too much,' she says. 'It is bad for the brain—'"

"I suppose it is," agreed Frossia, and held out her hand. "Good-by and give my respects to Nina Yakovlevna."

"Well, I might," he hesitated. "I have never mentioned your name to her. She would have thought it all so strange. I am glad to have seen you again, but you must not be hurt, Euphrosynia Pavlovna—you mean nothing at all to me now. . . ."

"So I was right that time," said Frossia, and Cherny turned on his heel and limped away.

2

It had been a heart-breaking summer, Nikolashka thought, looking at the empty shelves in his depôt, staring at the huge breadknife now used so seldom. The depôt had once been a chemist's shop; dusty jars and boxes still littered some of the shelves. Nikolashka always thought that an odor of camphor, glycerine, iodine, cinnamon, and methylated spirit still lived in the place. From the topmost shelf multicolored glass bowls looked down on the dust below. Often of a morning Nikolashka counted them. There were five, crimson, cobalt, bottle-green, orange, and violet. They were dusty enough, but they still broke into splendor whenever the sun smote them.

A heart-breaking summer, Nikolashka thought dully.

His two assistants had long since gone. One—a lad of twenty odd—had joined the agricultural drive in the country round Chernigov. The other, a pleasant, deep-bosomed woman, had decided that Crèche work was far more important.

"Of course, Comrade Nikolashka, bread is also important when we get it."

And they got none. Not oftener than twice a week could it be distributed now, sometimes even once, and then no more than two miserable ounces per head, two ounces of bread which crumbled almost as soon as the knife bit into it. Some people's two ounces were mere handfuls of oddly hued crumbs, brown and yellow and olive green, and they had no paper to carry them away in. Yet they went on queueing up for the bread which had more straw than rye in it. They took it, and sometimes made no comment. Probably, they felt too tired, but Nikolashka wondered sometimes if he would have welcomed a real riot in his shop. Noise and articulate wrath might have put a temporary halt to the deadness of the place. Once only an old man, wrapped in a threadbare gray coat, with a matted iron-gray beard and a wart on his left temple, sniffed as his two ounces of straw and rye and, probably, bark, were given to him.

"It makes a pain in your belly," he whimpered, "just as though you have eaten wood and iron."

"We may come to that, grandfather," a woman answered in a thick hoarse voice, and Nikolashka brandished his knife.

"Now then, who is the next? None of that, citizens—"

The old man stopped whimpering.

"And who do you think you are—the chief of commissars? Take it. . . . Let it choke you." He flung the handful of crumbs away from him, scattering them all over the wide counter, and shuffled out of the shop. Nikolashka waited, tense and almost relieved, but the rest of them kept still, almost meekly waiting for their thin dole.

Heart-breaking, that is what it is, he thought. All of them standing and waiting—as if ice, not blood, were in their bodies, and it is going to be a heart-breaking winter. Stands to reason you cannot bake bread out of straw—though some of them have tried hard enough. Wood and iron in the belly!

Yet, hunger notwithstanding, life flowed on in the city. Niko-lashka, worn out and often dispirited, kept to his two rooms in the Fifteenth Line of Vasilyev Island, stopped coming to the Zabalkan-sky Club for a time, but his customers often broke into conversation. From them he heard about the American Relief Administration in Morskaya Street. The Relief people, it was said, were soon to travel all over the country. They brought quinine and blankets, tinned milk and woolen socks, white flour and bandages, bacon, and sugar. Nikolashka listened incredulously. It all sounded like a fairy tale told by a simple-minded old nurse by a drowsy child's crib. White flour and sugar . . . He sucked his maimed thumb and shook his head. Such things were about as possible as a saffron loaf made of moonlight, but Frossia came, and she told him a few details, and he knew he could believe what she said. The Americans and the English were in the city. It was now possible for people to receive food parcels from abroad.

"Euphrosynia Pavlovna," Nikolashka said pleadingly. "You have had more than your share of short commons. Why do you not try and get work with the Americans?"

"Why? There is my own work."

"Yes, teaching French at the Rabfak and going hungry most of the time—"

"We are not always hungry. Why, Nikolashka, we had fifteen pounds of potatoes issued yesterday, good potatoes, too, not that nasty frozen kind which turns black as soon as you try to boil it—"

"What is fifteen pounds of potatoes?" he demanded. "It is just like you, Euphrosynia Pavlovna, to be so stubborn that you would turn rain into sunshine if you had a chance."

"That would be nice." She smiled. "No, I could not do relief work, Nikolashka, and I mean to be candid with you: I am greedy, I would do it for food alone. I have heard that they feed their em-ployees so well that some of them sob over their first meal there. . . . Well, I would not waste time on sobbing. I would just eat and eat. . . . But I could not do it. . . . I don't really know what I am talking about . . ." She broke off. "What about you, Niko-lashka? They are certain to want people who know all about corn and flour." Frossia could not even begin to imagine Nikolashka's lot thrown among efficient, busy, and definite people, but she felt that all the time he was searching for some door to be opened to him.

"No," he said almost sullenly. "Why mention it, Euphrosynia Pav-lovna? I used to be a flour merchant. Now I sell bread when I get a chance. But I could not go to the Americans. I am grateful to them, but I could not be among them. I would be worse than a needle lost in a haystack. I reckon we may pull through, what with all these folk sending food and medicines across their ocean. But there are worse days ahead, and that is why I feel I had better keep out of it. . . . A whole fleet could not feed all our millions here at home, and I would feel ugly inside, not properly grateful, you know what I mean, and that is shoddy and sinful. . . . But we are a queer people," and his face brightened again. "They say a cat has nine lives. We Russians must have about eighty-nine. Yet we are muddlers. We expect seven men to waste their strength pulling at a straw, and we put an elephant's burden on an ant's back, and the ant's back does not break. Why? You could not tell me. I could not answer you. What I think and what you think does not matter. It just happens, like the sun rising or the rain falling." He flicked a half-dead fly off the counter. "But you are right, Euphrosynia Pavlovna. I have gone as stale as yesterday's crumbs on the floor. I shall not go to the Americans, but I mean to make other plans, and I shall give a party, and you must all come." Now his face was smiling, and Frossia smiled back, remembering how he loved to dispense hospitality. But parties could not be given regularly because of his bare larder, even though Nikolashka contrived them sometimes, collecting provender for weeks and months with an ant's patience.

So Nikolashka chose a date, and invitations went round by word of mouth. All were bidden—Pavel Pavlovich and his sister, Elena Ivanovna, and several people from the Zabalkansky, Mark Alexandrovich and the undertaker, and Igor, and Olga Semenovna, the midwife. Pasha Dobrina was invited from the Rabfak, and Kostia, the freckled boy, and Glafira Antonovna, with her squint, and some others. Paulina Pavlovna accepted the invitation and said wistfully she wished Nikolashka's dear Irina Nikolaevna could be among them that evening, and Nikolashka replied cryptically: "Well—she might. Miracles happen everywhere." Later Frossia said to Igor:

"Now they are all busy talking about Irina Nikolaevna. They all say they would like to meet her at last. But I have no need to meet her, Igor Vladimirovich. I know her. I have known her for nearly four years. I see her plump and rosy-cheeked and very comfortable, nodding her head and saying a deep pleasing 'Yes' to any question and any statement made in her presence. She has thick brown hair, worn in one plait round her head, her eyes are dark gray, and she looks her best in a white kerchief and a loose blue woolen dress. She tucks up her skirts when she walks about in the farmyard. She is very kind to cows, hens, and pigs, perhaps, and is impatient with cats and dogs. She laughs in a nice fat way, and her greatest treat is a game of cards, 'little fools,' very likely, oh, yes, she must love *durachki,* and a cup of acorn coffee at eleven in the morning."

"Well," said Igor, "I have certainly met her now, Euphrosynia Pavlovna—"

One afternoon they all went to the Fifteenth Line of Vasilyev Island, and met at the gate into the yard, and all were shy to go in first. They just stood or shuffled about, looking at one another, their eyes asking, "What about you and what about you?" There was Pasha, wearing Frossia's gift—white suède gloves up to the elbow, worn with a loud yellow check cotton dress, and Glafira Antonovna neat in faded red print worn under a man's shabby gray jacket. Kostia was obviously proud of a freshly ironed white blouse. Pavel Pavlovich had shaved tidily, his red shirt had not a single button missing, and there was good old lace on Paulina Pavlovna's carefully mended lilac poplin. They were all there, as Frossia saw, hurrying down the street, all with glossy expectation in their eyes, all aware of their tidiness, their humble finery, and good manners. Even the undertaker looked respectable in a brown coat with enormous brass buttons. There were some whom Frossia did not know—men and women from the meaner streets of the Island, quiet, gray people, withdrawing, polite, and painfully grateful for the least notice taken of them.

Nikolashka, himself festive in a snow-white shirt tucked into black breeches, met them at the top of the stairs. The two rooms had not enough chairs for the company. Some of the men made for the window sills. Paulina Pavlovna and Elena Ivanovna were shepherded to the solitary sofa. Others were guided to the few chairs and trunks thoughtfully ranged alongside the walls. The communicating door was left open, and a very long table joined the two rooms. It was spread with odds and ends of clean enough napery. Two bunches of late mauve asters were stuck into jam jars. Salt in huge white china bowls, and a miscellany of plates, saucers, and mugs littered the table from end to end. The place was friendly and warm, an agreeable smell of hot food came from the tiny kitchen beyond, and Frossia's heart was so light that she found herself exchanging jokes with the undertaker.

All the guests were to be settled in their appointed places since there was no room for anyone to move about at their will. The company sat and kept quiet. Frossia guessed at the disappointment in some faces. They had expected to meet Irina Nikolaevna, but the thin trickle of talk ran on strictly formal lines: this was a party, an occasion, a solemnity of a kind, and its beginning, at least, was not to be spoiled by lack of courtesy. Personal questions must not be asked at such a party.

From the doorway Nikolashka beckoned to Frossia. She rose and threaded her way between chairs, trunks, and the long table. Nikolashka's face was beaded with glossy sweat and his whisper rang importantly:

"Euphrosynia Pavlovna, I beg of you—come and have a look at the things in the kitchen. You know what it is like—me being a widower and all that. . . . I wonder if there would be enough. I have used all I had." He went on mumbling and pushing Frossia into the steamy kitchen. The old fashioned *plita* was all crowded with dishes and saucepans. Nikolashka raised a lid. Frossia looked and almost closed her eyes. This was a moment she welcomed and feared and resented. But she could not help herself. She looked again.

"Nikolashka, genuine *pelmeny!* Where did you get the flour and the meat?"

Nikolashka was busily dishing them into a huge pale green soup tureen—a whole mound of *pelmeny,* little lumps of specially made pastry stuffed with meat and onions and boiled in water. There they were, and also two big jars of pickled cucumbers, two whole loaves of bread, a mountain of tiny mushroom patties, and raspberry jam for dessert.

"Nikolashka," gasped Frossia. "Have you been to the Americans? Or robbed the Food Commissariat? Or used a magic wand?"

"I have never had any traffic with speculators," babbled Nikolashka, opening a jar of pickled cucumbers. "Well, if you must know, Euphrosynia Pavlovna, I have had the mushrooms for months—they came from Irina Nikolaevna. Jam came from a pal in the Health Commission. I don't know how he got it, but he gave it to me without any bribery. And the rest . . . Ah, well"—he shrugged—"I mean to share it with you all—"

The great tureen was carried in. Alas, the steaming succulent *pelmeny* were not eaten hot. The astonished company fell to a slightly nostalgic discussion of vanished culinary glories. Nikolashka wrung his hands and looked almost desperate, Frossia felt for him, but it was not for the host to check his guests' talk. They remembered *bliny,* those famous Carnival pancakes, thin and golden, eaten sometimes with sour cream, and oftener with caviare, and *kulebiaka,* a pastry roll stuffed with sturgeon, and small partridges cooked with wine, artichokes and cranberry jelly. Nikolashka's humbler acquaintances remembered *tvorog* and *vatrushky* and quite ordinary *sitny, baranky,* those cracknels baked in the shape of huge curtain rings, deep yellow and crisp, lavishly sprinkled with carraway or poppy seeds. The undertaker alone sat silent, and at last he could endure it no longer.

"*Pelmeny . . . Pelmeny . . .* They are getting cold, good people," he groaned. This was an act of appalling discourtesy, and a few frowned at him, but in a moment they all fell to.

A generous helping of raspberry jam on a saucer before her, Frossia pinched her own elbow. It was all glorious, unreal, and somehow disturbing. She looked from one pleased shining face to another. Even the ethereal Paulina Pavlovna was much more concerned with her fifth mushroom patty than with any exalted matters. And the rest were unashamedly happy, greedy, eating lustily, using their fingers—since of forks there were none, and, there is absolutely nothing humiliating in this, thought Frossia almost angrily. We have had a wonderful meal, and we have been greedy, and how could we help it? And she ate her jam with real pleasure, undisturbed by any further reflections.

The last crumb was eaten. Nikolashka wiped his high forehead, tugged at the collar of his shirt, coughed, and said in a sonorous voice:

"Citizens and friends, Irina Nikolaevna—"

All started, hands to their mouths. Some looked at the door. Others stared at the windows. Paulina Pavlovna glanced at the ceiling.

"Irina Nikolaevna," repeated Nikolashka just as solemnly, "here she is—written with her own hand." He put a couple of sheets on the table. "Euphrosynia Pavlovna, I beg of you—will you read us Irina Nikolaevna's letter—"

Frossia read:

"My dear and greatly respected Papashenka, Mavra and I bow to you, and hope that you are in good health, and they all say here that good health will be hard to keep living in a town, and I agree with them, and they also say it is time I wrote you a letter, and I agree with them. And the nut harvest will be grand, and all rye and barley have gone, and nobody can say why, and there have been bad fires round here, and drought, and flies, and other plagues, and I am going away, and I mean to settle down with Uncle Kuzma at Riabchino. And Uncle Kuzma writes that his cattle are doing well, and they have salted all the pork, and put another field under wheat, and Uncle Kuzma writes that he has not seen you, greatly respected Papashenka, for a long time. I wrote and said you knew all about grain and flour, and Uncle Kuzma wrote and said you always like salted pork and cucumbers, and you take a train to

305

Viazma, and Uncle Kuzma will send a horse to bring you to Riabchino, and I cannot come to town again, I am afraid of big cities and houses, and Mavra says your store will soon be closed on account of there being no bread, and I agree with her, and bring your boots and some blankets, and the copper samovar, and nothing else, and I wrote to Uncle Kuzma and I said he must keep his sheepdogs on a leash for a time, and I know you will agree, and I kiss you and remain your loving daughter Irina."

"So I am going to Riabchino, good people," said Nikolashka.

There was a little more tea left, and they replenished their mugs and tumblers, and drank it silently until Elena Ivanovna said in a slow deep voice that she hoped God would go with him, and the company echoed it in a muted chorus. They discussed Nikolashka's brother-in-law, and Riabchino, and Irina Nikolaevna's excellent letter, and the prospect of crops, and none of them, not even Frossia, said, "We shall miss you badly, Nikolashka," because it lay so deeply in their hearts that they could not bring it to their lips.

Presently it was all over. In the shadows of the yard Frossia heard Igor's voice behind her:

"Now we have all met Irina Nikolaevna, and she *is* afraid of dogs."

3

"But, Comrade Golubev, you will not see my point. University students have gone to work with the Famine Relief, permissions have been given them to break off their studies, but I am the chairman of the students' committee in this Rabfak, and university students do not interest me. I am a proletarian, Comrade Golubev, and I feel convinced that famine need not be fought by sacks of flour and flitches of bacon alone. Famine, you will agree, is largely due to misdirected national consciousness. Here, in this Rabfak, we are all learning hard. Therefore why should any of the students be wrenched from their studies to go and be at the beck and call of American capitalists?"

Gleb Semenovich rather wanted to spit into Zolotov's face, but he said quietly:

"Comrade Zolotov, those American capitalists have come to save millions of our own people, and—"

"This is not the point. The difference between us is, I think, that—"

Gleb Semenovich said softly:

"Comrade Zolotov, this need not develop into a platform discussion. You object to the students going to work in famine areas.

You have stated your grounds. Well, you are their chairman. It should be easy for you to make them see your point of view—"

"But some of the students have already volunteered," grumbled Zolotov. "They are not properly educated yet. Why, this morning I talked to one of the volunteers, one Bielov. He is a second year student, a biologist. I understand he has been doing very good work. In about fourteen months he was to go and study at a German university. He is the son of a doctor, no proletarian, but honest and keen, and has no twisted class bias. Now he is going as a male nurse with a relief unit to Perm. He said there was typhus, probably plague. I said: 'this is rather foolhardy. Your physique is none too good. What will happen if you catch typhus?'—'Well,' he said, 'sometimes life is more important than science . . .' I said: 'But you are a brilliant biologist. . . . You are a scientist,' and he said: 'Precisely because of it.' This is muddled thinking. The Faculty let him go," he added gloomily.

Golubev said nothing. He was weary. He was busy. When someone knocked at the door, he shouted "Come in," and frowned at Pasha Dobrina.

"I see students in the morning only," he reminded her severely, but she grinned and waved one hand gloved in none too impeccable white suède.

"I am not here as a student, Comrade Golubev. I have heard that Bielov and some others are leaving for Perm with a Relief unit. I want to join them."

"You cannot," broke in Zolotov hotly, "I know you. You are a third year student, you will be taking your finals next spring. No, certainly, you cannot go."

"But I want to go," Pasha said to Gleb Semenovich. "That is simple enough. Peasants are dying, and I am a peasant. My place is among them. Mathematics can wait for a time."

"Suppose you did not return?" said Gleb Semenovich, and Pasha shrugged.

"Suppose a bear grew wings . . . Dear Gleb Semenovich, it is all a question of time, is it not? And time is an idea! There will certainly come a morning when it shall stop for you and for me. . . . Well, why worry?" She shrugged again.

"I had no idea you had changed mathematics for philosophy," Zolotov said acidly, annoyed by her shrug.

"What do I do, Gleb Semenovich?" Pasha would not look at Zolotov. "I know no English. I could not go to Morskaya Street and say to those Americans that I want to join them. I want to do everything in order."

Zolotov turned his back on them both. Gleb Semenovich explained the procedure to Pasha. She had better fill in the application to the Faculty, he would see that it went to them.

"It might take a day or two," he warned her.

Zolotov turned round stormily.

"Why must you waste yourself, Comrade Dobrina? Does it mean nothing to you that you have studied and—"

"It means much," Pasha said calmly, smoothing one soiled white suède glove, "though it has not all been paradise. The hostel roof has begun to leak. . . . Food has been scarce and often vile. . . . We have had smoked *vobla* with maggots in it. And hardly any soap all through the summer. But it has been fine all the same. I have loved it all. Don't worry, Comrade Zolotov, I shall be back and pass my finals with honors, too."

"But not next spring?"

"Well, no, the year after—maybe."

"So you are determined to waste one whole year."

Pasha grew angry.

"Stop talking nonsense! This is no committee meeting and you are not in the chair. I have told you why I want to go. Why do you think I made my way here from Ufa, and crouched in filthy cattle trucks, and spent nights in cells with bugs and rats for company? Why?"

"How could I tell?"

"No more could I . . . I cannot explain it. It is about as simple as the multiplication table and as difficult. . . . I have done with words. . . . Thank you, Gleb Semenovich." She bowed to Golubev and went out, banging the door behind her.

"She is out of date," hissed Zolotov, "I know that kind of jelly talk. She means Russia and patriotism and love for the people. . . . Yet we have had her nearly three years, and we have tried to educate her—"

"What do you want her to think about?" Gleb Semenovich pointedly picked up his pen and a sheet of paper. "She is not a Chinese girl. Why should she not think of Russia first?"

"There is also," said Zolotov in his best platform voice, "the Third International." Gleb Semenovich dipped his pen and said rudely:

"Well, that might be out of date before very long—"

"And what will remain, comrade?"

"Russia," said Gleb Semenovich unhurriedly, even though he was impatient to get rid of his visitor. "Yes, just Russia. Take away the Tsars, the police, the church, all hereditary ranks and distinctions of caste, all the rest of those pretty things. Layer on layer of pretty

things—take them all off. A museum might find room for those relics.
. . . But Russia is no museum piece," and Gleb Semenovich began
his long delayed letter, and so deeply absorbed he looked that even
Zolotov could not misinterpret his attitude and moved towards the
door. In the passage near the entrance hall he met Pasha Dobrina.
She bared her teeth at him in an almost friendly grin, but Zolotov
scowled and hurried away.

4

The studio in Moyka, for all its bleakness, could be made to look
almost comfortable once the mournful, moist October evening was
shut out and the iron stove stoked with as many logs as Paulina
Pavlovna's economical mind allowed. They were alone, having their
supper of gruel fritters sparingly fried in vegetable oil. Paulina
Pavlovna kept an eye on a simmering saucepan. They had no extra
kindling for using their big copper samovar.

Pavel Pavlovich said, pushing away his emptied plate:

"I went to Sennaya Market this morning"—he fumbled for his
pipe, remembered that he had no tobacco, sighed, and crossed his
huge arms—"just to watch the scene, you know. . . . There is not
much of a market left."

"The Sennaya," murmured Paulina Pavlovna. "Oh, dear, it is
such a distance from here, Paul, and you promised to be careful
with your boots. This winter," she said severely, "I shall have to
ration you. You will go out on Tuesdays and Fridays only, and you
must never tramp too far afield. The cobbler said he could not
put another patch on your left boot. If only you were a woman,"
she sighed, "then you might wear some of my satin slippers. I have
seven pairs left, and I stuff bits of felt into them, though, of course,
their soles are much too thin for wearing in winter—"

"Satin slippers!" sniffed Pavel Pavlovich. "Am I a lunatic then
to be condemned to satin slippers? What was I saying? You always interrupt, Paulina. Well, then, in the Sennaya I ran into a
woman—with a squint in her eye, one of Euphrosynia Pavlovna's
pupils. She came to Nikolashka's party."

"I remember." Paulina Pavlovna removed the saucepan and
measured out a spoonful of dried black currant leaves into it,
"Glafira something or other. She ate so many mushroom patties that
her face went nearly green. Frossia had to fetch her a glass of
water."

"I was not talking about mushroom patties," Pavel Pavlovich said
crossly.

309

"Well, you ate nearly a dozen—but then you are a man."

"Leave off discussing food, Paulina! That Glafira told me odd things about Euphrosynia Pavlovna. Do you know—they almost hissed her out of the room the first time she went to teach them, and she never told us anything about it. Now they almost love her. She spent a whole day at their hostel, helping them with their chores, and one week she gave up a whole Saturday to join them in a *subbotnik*. It was a hard job, too, unloading a timber train off Ligovka."

"Yes," said Paulina Pavlovna, "Frossia is like that. I don't like many things about her life. I don't like her living in that house, the undertaker man is just a nasty little reptile. . . . I did not like the boy she had in Moshkov Lane all those years ago, but he is dead now, and that makes all the difference. Also there was that dreadful Lettish woman, so fat and always painted. And all the weird jobs Frossia has had. . . . But now I am rather disturbed, Paul. Frossia is quieter, she is almost settling down, and that is dreadful in anyone so young. . . ."

"Nonsense," said Pavel Pavlovich, "she will never settle down—not in the sense you are afraid of."

Suddenly they heard steps on the stairs. He grumbled:

"I feel lazy and unsociable tonight. It must be someone from the Zabalkansky. . . . The light shows from under the door, and there is nobody to say we are not at home—"

"But we are at home, Paul."

Both listened. The steps were mounting the stairs. They were slow and halting steps as though someone were either weary or painfully uncertain of their welcome. They stopped just outside the door. The brother and sister expected a knock. None came. The door merely opened, and for a few seconds neither could recognize the visitor. Her head wrapped in a loose drab shawl, her body in a soldier's shabby and dirty overcoat, her feet in broken black boots, she stood, swaying a little and peering round her. Then Paulina gasped:

"Why, Lilian?"

"May I come in?" Lilian said huskily. "Just sit down for a few moments? I must not come near anyone. . . . I don't know what is the matter with me, my head is swimming, I am so cold and I am burning—yes, just burning from head to foot. . . . I called at the Marine Hospital, but they are overcrowded. . . . Could you telephone somewhere? Oh, I forgot there is no telephone left in life—" She groped towards a bench by the door, and almost collapsed, her head held in both hands.

"Quinine," said Paulina Pavlovna. "I have some quinine, Paul. And hot water. . . . Nonsense, Lilian, you must come to the stove. Why, we thought you had left Petrograd. . . . Where is Serge?"

Lilian pushed the thick brown shawl off her forehead. Her face looked red, her lips white, her green eyes were made of clouded glass. She spoke jerkily:

"Serge? Killed in a railway accident." She took some hot water from Pavel Pavlovich but refused to leave the bench by the door. "No, you must not come near me. . . . Yes, Serge got killed in the south. . . . Somehow I made my way to Moscow and then came here. . . . It is terrible, you know, people are dying like flies. . . . Sometimes it is famine or plague or typhus, but they always die—"

Her voice trailed off in an inaudible whisper. Her disheveled head lolled on one side, her clasped hands stayed still. The eyes of clouded green glass closed, and Pavel Pavlovich looked at his sister.

"You will have to look after her," he whispered. "Frossia and Elena Ivanovna will be at the Zabalkansky. I shall fetch them."

In about twenty minutes he brought Frossia. Paulina Pavlovna had lifted Lilian off the hard bench, spread a blanket under her, and tucked a pillow under the unkempt head. Lilian was unconscious. Frossia glanced at her and ran out of the room.

"Paul," began Paulina Pavlovna, but he stayed her.

"It is all right. Frossia always knows what to do."

They had not long to wait. Frossia returned with a neat clean-shaven man in khaki under a spotless white coat. The man could not speak Russian, and none of them could understand his French. But little needed to be said. The man brought in a pile of yellow blankets, picked up Lilian as though she were a pencil, wrapped her from head to foot, and carried her out. Frossia followed him. Some time after midnight she came to Moyka for the third time, and explained:

"He was an American doctor. I fetched him from Morskaya. They were all so kind. My English is halting, but they understood me. He came in a car. They have taken her to Petropavlovsky Hospital. It is typhus. She must have caught it in the train somewhere. The doctor gave me a bottle of disinfectant for you." She brandished a small package in her hand. "It smells like formaline." She uncorked it. "Poor, poor Lilian . . . She was chattering all the way to the hospital. She was a small child once again, in her mother's arms, and seeing her first military review. . . ."

"Never mind your disinfectant," said Paulina Pavlovna almost sharply. "I have made some nice hot tea for you."

That autumn came like a lover, slowly, beautifully, each new day flinging fresh colors on the city's canvas. There were bleak days, mournful days, even "clumsy" days as Frossia called them, but the wind kept away; in the Summer Gardens the ancient limes were allowed to go bare in a dignified quiet manner, their copper-crimson leaves patterning the ground so slowly and gently that it was almost like the weaving of a carpet. In Peter's Park the old oaks burned deep bronze and orange through calm mornings and still evenings, and far away, the scarred and blinded faces of be-spoiled palaces along Palace Quay and English Quay continued living their own hidden life somewhere in a strange place where past, present, and future were at one. In Galernaya Street a ven-turesome old woman watched her late dahlias petal out in the courtyard, and kept the gate open for the benefit of the passers-by, and those who came to see Elena Ivanovna in the afternoon, saw the luxuriously colored globes so still in the day's quiet, and they were heartened. Even in the bleakest, most forlorn slums at the back of Vasilyev Island some tree or other was determined to snatch some glory from the fading hour of the year, and clothed itself in brilliantly colored raiment until not a street, lane, or back yard were there but had their share in the polychromatic scheme.

Frossia loved her daily pilgrimage to Kamennostrovsky. It took her by way of the narrow wooden Exchange Bridge, its green, weathered timbers reddish in the morning and dark copper in the afternoon. Across the frail bridge, the few garden patches of Petro-grad Side looked kingly in their rainbowed stillness. Down the wide Bolshoy Prospect, the main street of the Side, trees there were none, but lanes and alleys, branching off the avenue, gave enchant-ing glimpses of beauty all the more precious because of its seclu-sion. The Prospect ended, and Kamennostrovsky was before her, and not a house but had something to offer. There were charred walls, broken windows, sunk roofs, and gaping windows, but the glory of autumn shone above all such untidiness and desolation, grass turned deep yellow in among wounded stones, and gardens stood in sculptured triumph.

The soft weather gave comfort to many. Queues still threaded the streets, but the long vigils were easier to bear in pleasant autumnal sunshine. Stillness made away with the rattling of insecure doors and windows, and those who had no work could go and sit on benches and not shiver. There was dust in abundance, but no wind to carry it about. Small dark blue steamers still plied their unhur-

ried way between Vasilyev Island and Ochta. Pavel Pavlovich, un-
heeding his sister's plaintive admonitions about shoe leather, wandered far and wide to observe the festally colored scene.

Elena Ivanovna and Frossia begged the buxom old lady in Galernaya Street for some dahlias. The woman was neither friend nor
close neighbor, they did not even know her name, but they asked
for some dahlias, and she gave them a generous bunch, and together they tramped to Petropavlovsky Hospital. They were left
waiting in a porter's lodge, a long narrow room which smelt of
carbolic and soapsuds. A small slate hung between two windows.
One brief word was chalked on the top, it was chalked in clear
block letters so that nobody could have misread it—"Died,"
"*Umerli.*" Below, in smaller, less distinct lettering, followed a string
of names, all of them obviously traced at different times by different hands. Frossia went up and read: "Liliana Parnikova." They
did not call her "Garonne" or "Grammère," she was simply Parnikova, the name which was in her labor book because she had never
had the right to any other.

"So it will be the mortuary, dear heart," said Elena Ivanovna.
"But we must wait for the porter to come back. They might not
like us to go there."

"Yes," said Frossia, "we must wait."

Elena Ivanovna remarked the four corners of the comfortless
room. There was neither ikon nor cross to be seen. Unabashed,
she went up to the little slate, crossed herself unhurriedly, and said,
her deep voice unlowered:

"Give rest to the soul of thy servant, Liliana." Here she stopped,
remembered Lilian's real Christian name, and said again, "Give
rest to the soul of thy servant, Ludmila." And Frossia started. She
had almost forgotten that Lilian was christened Ludmila, but Lilian
did not like such a simple baptismal label and had herself changed
it to Lilian—which was "chic," as she said. Then Frossia heard
Elena Ivanovna say: "To thy servant Ludmila, oh, Lord, and forgive all her sins, committed consciously and unconsciously. Give
rest to the soul of thy servant Ludmila in the place of light where
is neither sickness, nor grief, nor sighing, but life without end."
She crossed herself and murmured: "Yes, *golubushka*, we must
wait."

The porter was back. He had no information to give them. They
pointed to the slate.

"I see." He turned back to his desk. "Wait a moment . . . Parnikova? You never inquired about any Parnikova. You used a foreign
name. Why, I wrote it down to show to the sister." He scratched

313

his tousled head, tried to look important and menacing, and failed completely.

Elena Ivanovna explained briefly. He nodded.

"Yes . . . She did not know which wife she was. . . . We get a good few of them here. Little wonder. . . . The whole country has gone upside down. . . . Plenty of rotters roaming around. Never mind, *grajdanki*, we will go on grinding the corn and get our flour in the end." He grinned, and Frossia remembered Artemiy Sorokin, and smiled back.

The porter waited for them to go. But Elena Ivanovna lingered, touching the luxuriant lacquered leaves of the dahlias. "The living will enjoy them. The dead need prayers—not wreaths." She put the cluster on the little desk and asked, "Could we go into the mortuary?" and then explained their request. "You see, she was the daughter of rather special friends, and her parents are dead."

"Of course, of course." The little porter bustled about, ringing bells. "Wait, I will get a nurse down. . . ."

The nurse came. They were taken down a stone-flagged corridor. A small door was unlocked at the end. It felt cold, it looked dim. Frossia made out several trestles, just mere shapes neatly covered with pieces of rough gray linen. Little labels hung by the head of each trestle, and the nurse threw back one of the coverlets, saying: "Here she is—"

"Are you sure?" Frossia almost whispered, and checked herself in time. The pale yellow shriveled features were certainly Lilian's. The rest belonged to a Ludmila she, Frossia, had never known. Death had left her naked—both in flesh and memory, and tired and peaceful. Mockery, pretense, greed, and uncleanness of mind and of body, all these were wiped away. The thin, incredibly changed face had nothing but traces of ended suffering and a serenity you could not associate with mere flesh. Lilian's dead face looked as though in her very last tortured moment something had entered her body and stamped itself on the worn frail envelope. Peace was in her face and also a faint astonishment at a discovery her silenced lips could never communicate.

"Are you being responsible for the funeral?" asked the nurse, and Elena Ivanovna whispered: "Yes, I am," and she took no further heed of either Frossia or the nurse. She pulled the coverlet further back, and Frossia looked at Lilian's bony hands lying by her sides. Elena Ivanovna raised them and crossed them on the sunken chest. Lilian's flesh looked pale and dry as though it had gone through a great furnace and come out outwardly unscathed, inwardly burned to embers. Elena Ivanovna made the sign of the cross over

314

the blue-veined eyelids, replaced the coverlet, and knelt by the trestle. Frossia knelt, too. The nurse walked away to a corner and waited for them. Elena Ivanovna pressed her forehead to the stone slabs of the floor and prayed in silence. Then they both rose, and the nurse came towards them.

"It was typhus," she said conversationally, "also she had t.b., and something else. She had not a chance. . . . Her labor book says she was twenty-seven. She looked almost fifty," she went on, suggesting that Elena Ivanovna should see the almoner and arrange about the funeral, and Frossia murmured:

"Please, would you mind if I went now—"

"Goodness, no, *golubushka!* Come and see me this evening. I shall arrange with Father Faddey for a requiem. Maria Nikolaevna would have liked it."

Frossia went straight to Warsaw Station, and found Igor, who looked busy and slightly preoccupied with a sheaf of documents on his desk. But she disregarded the papers.

"Igor Vladimirovich, poor Lilian died last night."

"It is best for her—surely?"

Frossia leaned against a bookshelf.

"Is it? Somehow her face and this strange still weather are the same. It is all so disturbing, Igor Vladimirovich—"

"You should never have gone into the mortuary, Euphrosynia Pavlovna. Why must you always distress yourself?" He glanced at her and marveled. "Why, you had no great love for her, and your face looks stricken—"

"I am foolish. But Lilian always made the worst of everything. That is something you cannot even pity—so terrible it is. No, I had little love for her. But she must once have had something clean in her. Yet she went miles out of her way to wallow in mud." Frossia paused. "Her mother used to say it was all the fault of the revolution, but if there had not been any revolution, Lilian would have been the same. Igor Vladimirovich, why do these things happen? Why do people like her get born at all? They never enjoy life. They hurt anyone who comes near them. Why?"

He put his papers away into the drawer as though her question were important and urgent enough to sweep away all his other occupations, and she liked it.

"Do you think I could tell you, Euphrosynia Pavlovna? Or anyone? We read books, we worry over so many puzzles, we ask ourselves questions, and we never rest, we cannot, perhaps it is more wholesome that we should not rest, and we always come back to the same thing. But do you remember the letter you found once

315

in Nicholas Square? Well, the other day I read an article on Browning, the English poet, in an old number of *Niva*. It was not a good article, it did not give you enough, but it quoted some lines of his in Russian, and they made me quiet. I cannot remember them, and I cannot read English, but I will get you a copy from some library, and perhaps you will be kind and translate them for me fully and neatly. It was something about evil being nothing of itself. . . . Well, I cannot puzzle it out, but I think it is something of an anchor for our restlessness to rest on. Euphrosynia Pavlovna, you said that people like Lilian hurt anyone who comes near them. Yes, I allow that, but unhurt people are not much use in the world. There again you will be asking why it should be so, and I cannot tell you. But you know and I know that it is true. Unhurt people," said Igor, "are like blank pages in an exercise book. . . . No, that does not fit—they are like plants that nobody knows what to do with. They can hardly ever understand other people's grief, and they offer pity where none should be given. Would you have had your own life all lemon jelly and apple jam? Of course you would not—but don't ask me why."

They came out of the dim stuffy office and stood at the door leading on to one of the station platforms. People with bundles, sacks, and other clumsy luggage were eddying backwards and forwards all around them. All were moving, talking, gesturing. Most looked weary enough, but their bodily fatigue did not stain them. Over them and around them lay the fragrantly woven cloak of a gorgeous autumn afternoon. A woman in black went past, carrying a wispy little bunch of mauve and pale pink asters. A man spat angrily as he dropped an awkward bulging bundle for a second time. A small tattered boy, dirty thumb in his mouth, stared at a uniformed guard talking to his equally tattered mother. Papers fluttered in everybody's hands, fawn-breasted pigeons sat on the carved lintel of the waiting-room door, and a woman in a bright orange shawl sat down on her big bast hamper and started plaiting her little daughter's hair.

Why, they look at home everywhere, thought Frossia, and answered Igor: "Lemon jelly? Oh, no! You see I have never liked it, nor apple jam either—"

6

That strangely still weather broke off with an equally strange abruptness. One night—very early in October—thin snow fell, then more and more of it. It coated roofs and pavements for the space of one morning till the sun sailed high in the sky and melted the frail white carpet. That same evening the sun sank in a deep crimson, angrily violet sea, and a slight wind came from the west, a wind which had winter, not autumn, in its bitter, biting breath. The balconied house in Maly Prospect had little sleep that night. Every timber in it moaned and groaned to the ever increasing fury of the wind. The rooms and kitchen were unheated. Frossia shivered. The young textile worker coughed until everybody wondered whether his poor tired lungs were breaking to pieces. Olga Semenovna, the midwife, wrapped herself up in all the shawls she possessed, and prophesied in a dark mutter:

"All will be snow white in the morning. It is winter, mark my words, and no warning given, and the Domkom says there will be no fuel for a fortnight, and we shall lie frozen in our beds."

Parfen Nikitich, shivering in spite of his evil-smelling sheepskins, retorted:

"Snow? It is far too cold for snow at this time of the year. Black frost—that is what it is. . . ."

Yet no snow fell. The narrow quay gleamed wet after the thaw. Runlets gurgled in the gutter.

Next morning it was difficult to get up. Frossia awoke to find her body stiff and numb. Her breath stole up to the ceiling in vapory spirals. The window was coated with thin ice traceries. She rummaged in the chest for her valenki, ruefully remembering the gaping hole in the right sole. Water in her jug was almost all ice. Olga Semenovna had spoken truly: winter was indeed upon them. Frossia ran to the kitchen. Parfen Nikitich had already lit the *plita* with what little kindling there was. She boiled some water for her breakfast. The undertaker said grimly:

"Take those valenki off. It is skates you need this morning—"

Frossia almost upset her precious pannikin.

"Why, of course, yesterday's thaw—"

"Yes . . . I had one look out. . . . Sheer glass all over the street, and the cold so sharp no sun is likely to melt it today."

An hour later, coated and shawled, her feet still thrust into clumsy and shabby valenki, Frossia opened the front door. The outer staircase was coated with thick ice, but she clutched at the railings, and found her way down into the road, and turned right, towards the Exchange Bridge. Within three yards she slipped, steadied herself, slipped once more, and fell. The wide street, with its torn pavements, was ice-coated from end to end. The long since choked gutters had not absorbed the thaw. The sun came out, a pale remote wintry sun, it shone on the ice, and the ice sparkled and stayed firm. The scene was beautiful, unreal, and cruel.

317

Frossia had no watch, and she could not have gauged the time it took her to crawl along Maly Prospect, a distance which usually meant six or seven minutes' brisk walk. She fell again and again, and wondered if it would be better to grope along the pavement where an occasional hoarding would offer support, but she could not get near the pavement.

Her third fall left her slightly bruised, and she felt giddy. The road was a sea, and she could not swim. She seemed the only living soul in that motionless cold world. There were no people, no animals, no traffic. Her own movements provided the only break in the stillness, and her uneven fumbling steps crunched on along the jagged ice, and the echo ran up and down the street, mocking and frightening her. Her face was beaded with sweat long before she reached the end of the Prospect. Here, by the dull red bulk of the Stock Exchange, she saw some life. A few people were struggling along, some towards the University Quay, just round the bend, others on to the slender Exchange Bridge which she, too, must cross. Some crawled and crouched, a few were lucky possessors of skates, one man went by on all fours. But all alike were preoccupied with their own immediate concerns and perils. Frossia tried to smile at the man crouching on all fours, but he scowled, and she felt rebuffed and unwanted.

With Maly Prospect behind her, courage failed her almost utterly. The cold, slippery world under her feet seemed a far more perilous menace than hunger and darkness. The ground Frossia was trying to tread was an enemy, ready to pounce on her, defeat her, maim her in body and spirit. I shall never get back home if I do get to the Rabfak this morning. . . . And I left my locker open, and things will not be safe, she thought, trying to find excuses to match her failing spirits. Then she saw a tall girl emerging from the bend by University Quay. Frossia had sometimes met her at the Zabalkansky. The girl lived somewhere near Moyka and taught English at the Third University not far from the Rabfak.

The girl saw Frossia and stood still as if she were chained to the ice underneath. She is terrified, her face is so white, and I, too, am frightened, and how stupid both of us are—to be beaten by a sudden frost, but this strange weather makes you all small and helpless inside, thought Frossia, and started moving towards the other.

"What luck! We are both going to Kamennostrovsky."

"But the bridge has a hump, you crawl up and then you have to go down, I could never do it—Nicholas Bridge was enough of a nightmare."

"Well, you need not crawl down. You can just slide."

"You see," explained the girl, "I had my arm broken three years ago. I go nearly sick every time I fall—I always think I might smash something else. It is not pleasant—"

"It is not. Few things are," Frossia agreed. "But I am probably far worse than you are. Now I will catch hold of your left arm, see, just like that, and every time you feel you are slipping down, don't resist it, just let yourself go, and it will not hurt so much. Come on." And crawling and slipping and falling, they reached the bridge, and neither spoke until they had crossed it. It was a nightmare crossing: the crown of the bridge proved impassable, they found a smoother lane nearer the pavement, but the lane sloped rather perilously towards the railings, most of which were long since broken. Two or three times Frossia felt her companion's arm stiffen, then go suddenly limp, and Frossia must forget her own terror of the black water below, and steady and guide and reassure by touch alone. Neither spoke. Neither cared to look at the other.

But Exchange Bridge lay behind them, and they found easier going ahead. It could not have snowed hard in Petrograd Side, there were occasional dry patches here and there, though no trams were running, and they had to tramp all the long way to Kamennostrovsky Prospect.

"In the old days," said the girl from the Third University, "they would have come out with sand and ashes and spades, and roadmen would have broken up the ice—"

"Yes," replied Frossia, maneuvering round a dangerous patch, "but you and I would not have known much about it. Do you like your work at the Third?"

"Yes, but I am leaving soon. I have volunteered to go as an interpreter with the ARA."

"How very funny," said Frossia. "Forgive me, please, but it is funny—here I meet you terrified of a patch of ice under your feet, and yet you go off to work in famine areas."

"But that is not frightening. If you want to know the truth, I am doing it for food. I get so tired of going hungry so many days in the week—that is the main reason," she said almost defiantly, but Frossia would not accept it.

"Yes, you will get food, but you may also get typhus—or plague."

"Well, there is typhus here, and plague is not very far away."

"I"—Frossia spoke with an armored determination—"I would not go to the famine areas for all the bacon and sugar in the world— even though I don't know much about conditions out there. Of course, every queue is full of stories—"

"It is not only stories. I have seen photographs and reports.

319

Things are ghastly. There have been cases of cannibalism even. In most villages people are so starved that you must not give them any solid food for days and days. Even plain bread and milk might kill them."

"And yet you are going—"

"Yes," said the girl impatiently, "and I have told you why."

"That is nonsense," Frossia muttered under her breath, but the girl from the Third changed the subject.

Frossia reached her Rabfak almost two hours late. In the hall she met Gleb Semenovich.

"You are late, but you will not find any of your pupils here. They have gone to Comrade Uritzky's memorial meeting at the Smolny. Zolotov should have told you. It was arranged last week."

"So I need not have come," Frossia said in a dull, defeated voice, but he shook his head.

"On the contrary, Euphrosynia Pavlovna. I must see you about an urgent matter. Follow me—"

She went into the bleak cold office. She thought: If they mean to dismiss me now, I shall never trek it home. I might stumble off Exchange Bridge. . . .

Gleb Semenovich could not offer her a chair. There was but one in the room. Frossia scrambled on the wide window sill. Her tired feet dangled in their shapeless, heavy valenki. She was hungry and now that the exhausting pilgrimage was over she felt bitterly cold.

Golubev sat at his desk and spoke in businesslike accents. He used few words. He said that the Faculty approved of her work. Her groups had made more progress than any others.

"But there is just one thing, Euphrosynia Pavlovna. We should like to see you a permanent member of the Faculty—but for one obstacle. This is a Rabfak. . . . Yet you hold yourself aloof from so many activities."

She understood. She slipped off the window sill and walked up to the desk.

"You must not mind what I say. Régimes mean nothing to me. I could not fake any interest in those activities. Your zeal is wholly spent on certain political doctrines. I could not share them. . . . I have nothing except my country, Gleb Semenovich. Yes, just Russia, *tolko Rossia*." On her lips the words rang a finely graven musical phrase. "And if you were to ask me what I mean by it, I could not tell you. It is not a song, or a river, or clothes, or language, or field, or mountains. . . . It is all of them, it is above them—it is a dance under falling snow and a dance under June sunlight," she broke off. "I have answered you. I must not go on talking nonsense—"

"I shall tell the Faculty," said Gleb Semenovich. "Mine is the casting vote, you know. We want you for a member."

"Why?"

"I could not tell you," he said, and dismissed her.

Frossia went away, her heart lightened. The journey back to Vasilyev Island repeated the nightmare of the morning, but her high spirits waged a successful battle against all purely physical fear. She had won a niche at the Rabfak, they needed her, they used her, they respected her, they were prepared to tolerate her admittedly odd opinions. Frossia's feet slipped and stumbled on the treacherous, inimical ice. She fell more than once. Her shoulder was bruised and her knees ached, but her sense of triumph lent wings to her feet. When she came to Maly Prospect the undertaker stared at her.

"Why are you smiling? And we thought you would break your neck—"

"I have gold spurs to my feet," cried Frossia, and went into her room, the cryptic remark unexplained.

7

One afternoon the wind grew stronger. People went home from their factories and shops and commissariats, and the wind roared and sang in their ears, and some of them said it was a good wind, it had a curious mildness in it in spite of its strength, and it was good to feel the wind come from the sea again, they said, after all those weeks of unnatural quiet. The younger folk smiled and raised their faces to the wind.

Frossia went to Nicholas Station to see Pasha Dobrina off. Pasha wore a bright green coat and black kid gloves given her by Paulina Pavlovna. The left hand thumb was split, but this did not grieve Pasha. For her luggage she had one small wicker basket, a blanket, and a string bag with food and a bottle of milk. She was first going on to Moscow and then farther, on to Perm. Frossia told her about the girl at the Third University who had already left for Kazan.

"An interpreter," said Pasha wistfully. "That must be a fine job. I am no good at languages."

The second bell clanged up and down the crowded platform, Pasha climbed into the carriage, leaned over, and kissed Frossia rather loudly.

"You never laughed at me," she said solemnly, "and it was good of you. I know I am so ugly that people always laugh when they see me. Why is ugliness funny?"

321

"It never is," Frossia said sincerely. "It often is attractive."

She went back down Nevsky Prospect. The wind made her fly. She was glad she wore a shawl on her head: no hat would have stayed on. The wind soughed, moaned, groaned, soared round her, behind her, above her head. She must run in the middle of the road: the pavements were already littered with roof tiles and torn-off hoardings. A chimney collapsed somewhere behind her, and the noise was almost deafened by the fury of the wind. The roar was terrific all down the Sixth Line of Vasilyev Island. Some of the elms lay across the road, and Frossia picked her way carefully among tangled boughs. Round the Maly Prospect corner she was nearly swept off her feet, and a half-wrenched door off a derelict house fell down with a crash just behind her. Along the Maly the old timbered buildings were groaning. Once within the balconied house Frossia found all the tenants huddled in the small kitchen. Twilight had come, but they would light no candles, and the *plita* was cold.

"I did try to set it going, but the smoke ate into my eyes," complained Parfen Nikitich.

"I have an oil stove," offered Olga Semenovna, scratching her hair, "just enough oil to boil something in one saucepan. But what good would that be?"

"None at all," grumbled the undertaker, and Frossia lost her temper.

"This is not a churchyard, Parfen Nikitich. If you don't want hot food you need not join us." She smiled at the midwife. "Well, of course, it will be a communal stew, and we must pool whatever we have got."

"No dishing out," decreed the midwife. "We must eat out of the saucepan."

"Yes," agreed Frossia, and saw a shadow steal across Mark Alexandrovich's face.

A candle was lit. The midwife brought the stove and the oil. The textile worker offered a tiny bag of millet and a small raw fish. The undertaker had onions and four dried mushrooms. Olga Semenovna limited her bounty to two potatoes. "I have given the oil, have I not?" she said challengingly, and nobody disputed it. Mark Alexandrovich brought a handful of dry vegetables and some rye flour in a saucer.

"This is not enough," said the undertaker severely. "Two spoonfuls of flour! Would you have had as little for your own supper?"

"I have nothing more than a few rye rusks," lisped the unhappy Mark Alexandrovich, "but, please, Parfen Nikitich, I may be hungry but I am never greedy. Two or three spoonfuls will be quite enough for me, I assure you."

"Two or three, you say? A dozen or two, you mean. . . . Well, I shall watch you." But Frossia silenced the undertaker once again by exhibiting her own richly varied offering: some millet, three big onions, a cupful of rye flour, a tiny piece of lard, and about six large potatoes.

"Now there will be enough for two, Mark Alexandrovich. You must eat as much as you like."

They curtained the kitchen window with a couple of ragged blankets, nursed the oil stove, and prepared their stew. In about an hour all was ready. They were cold, their fingers looked blue in candlelight, their stomachs were empty, but even the mournful textile worker brightened up at the sight of the steaming saucepan. They produced their wooden spoons and ate unhurriedly, five people round an upturned crate for their table in a cold candle-lit kitchen, with all the timbers cracking and groaning around them.

The saucepan was emptied. The spoons were licked clean. The stumpy candle burnt low.

"What about bed?" suggested Frossia. "We must not waste candles."

Olga Semenovna swore under her breath.

"Bed? You will be lucky if you sleep tonight. Can you not hear the wind? My sister-in-law lives in Gavan. She is certain this wind means no good—"

"We always get storms in the autumn," insisted Frossia, but the elder woman scowled at her.

"Storms? That is all you know about it. You look too young to remember 1902. That was a flood. . . . Why, the whole of Gavan was under the sea, and Ochta, and Viborg Side. I remember postmen and milkmen rowing along the Fourteenth Line, and children laughing at them. That was funny, you see, but what happened at Gavan was no fun. The sea just walked in, and what help was there? Whole streets of tiny wooden houses were like so many nuts cracked by the water. In some of the streets water rose to fifteen feet, they said, and there were corpses floating about for days. Fun! When it was all over, fine ladies drove about in carriages, all furs and silks, and set up a fund, but they built some more wooden houses everywhere in Gavan. Was that sense, I ask you? They never learnt any better. Wooden hovels were good enough for the poor," and she spat on the floor.

Soon they were silent, and after a lengthy pause they discovered they must shout at one another to be heard at all. The wind rose to a frenzy as if all the noise in all the innumerable worlds were gathered together into something compact and terrific.

"It is a bad storm," Frossia murmured just to comfort herself.

The kitchen grew unbearably cold. They exchanged brief good nights and crept to their warrens. The feeling of exultation, produced by the savory stew, had long since died. There was nothing but the wind left in a dark and cold and howling world. Frossia wished they might all have stayed together. Their company, she knew, would be hardly congenial, but such as it was, it promised more than the solitude of her own little room. She wished she might find herself across the river, in Galernaya Street, with Elena Ivanovna or even Paulina Pavlovna, but the evening had long since closed in, it would have been insane even to try and brave the wind across the bridge, and, rather disconsolate, Frossia crept into her dark and cold room. She could not hear Mark Alexandrovich's habitual moans, nor the textile worker's cough. All other sound was vanquished by the wind. Frossia felt she was alone and, huddled under her ragged blankets, she remembered a prayer once mentioned by Igor, not a prose prayer but one in verse. They had a beautiful Latin name for it, he said, "the Golden Sequence," and it answered. Igor's Latin was very rough and halting, he had merely picked up a few words here and there, mostly guessing at the sense of more obscure sentences. Frossia knew no Latin at all, and he had translated a few stray lines for her. Now she found odd comfort in remembering them. "Come, Thou Father of the poor." Well, she belonged to such now. She was a pauper, she could not see in the dark, but her belongings were battered and few. Frossia closed her eyes, determined to shut herself away from the freezing darkness.

At dawn they all learned that the Neva had risen during the night.

8

"The Neva is rising." Two words in Russian—"*Neva podymaetsia*," and enough in those two words to weld the whole city together in panic and in charity also. But always, always would the same fatal mistake be made at the beginning of each inundation, and thin air clasped for solid hope. The wind might veer to another quarter, or else fall, or else the Neva itself calm down and the fury, woken from the sullen deeps of the Gulf, be broken against other, more remote shores. There was Peterhof, Oranienbaum, the flat sandy reaches beyond, the treeless plains of old Ingermanlandia. The sea might choose them for its prey, or, perhaps, turn sharply northward, and spend its wrath on the rocky shores of Finland. People were busily remembering:

"Why, in September 1898 the wind was so dreadful that roofs got torn off and two spires toppled down, and the Neva certainly rose a bit, but after two days calm came, and the Neva never broke its banks that time."

Others were more skeptical.

"The Neva never does burst the banks. It simply flows over them. It did in 1902. It was just the same three days of storm, and the Neva rose slightly, and then the wind dropped, and the Neva went back for a time, and nothing was ready when the disaster burst upon the city."

"Not at all," said a fussy woman, "the flood then came without the least warning. How could anyone be ready? I remember it so well—my husband took me to the Opera. It was so still that you could hear a leaf fall to the ground."

"That is imagination. The flood happened late in March. The trees were not even in bud."

"Excuse me. My husband always said I had an exceptional memory. It was in late May. Just before Ascension Day. We went to mass in a boat."

"No, it was late in September. You must have gone in a boat on the day of Our Lady of Pokrov—the first of October."

"No—in May."

That day it was still possible to come out into the street if you walked in the middle of the road, though hoardings kept tumbling down and roof slates went hurtling through the air. The communal store, once governed by Nikolashka, opened out of hours. Generous rations were issued. They had bread, five whole pounds of it, herrings, salt, a little saccharine, a little millet, potatoes, and vegetable oil, as well as a small bag of dried carrots and beetroot. "Iron rations," the manager warned them. "Please be careful with them, grajdane—"

"Why is so much given all at once?" marveled Frossia, gratefully receiving her share, and he replied briefly: "The Neva is rising."

A decree was nailed to the wall of a corner house. It admonished the citizens to remain calm, not to wander away from their homes, and it told them that a dam was being built at the westerly point of Gavan. It ended by a terse reminder that summary capital punishment awaited those caught looting in any flooded areas.

"A dam?" someone mocked. "And what is a dam to the Neva?"

In the balconied house the midwife and Mark Alexandrovich were together in the kitchen, discussing the unexpectedly lavish rations.

325

The textile worker had gone to his factory in Viborg Side. The undertaker sat astride a crate in his own room, patching a sadly frayed shirt. Frossia heard Olga Semenovna mutter in the kitchen:

"Iron rations! Don't eat them all at once, he said. And what is the good of food rations to a swollen corpse, I ask you, Mark Alexandrovich? You need not look so startled. It has begun. It can finish in one way only. Maly Prospect has not a chance. Once Gavan is under water—thank heaven my sister-in-law has gone to Ligovka, she would be safer there—well, I ask you, once Gavan has gone, we are doomed. And it is no use trying to run away anywhere, Mark Alexandrovich. The bridges are up, they say. That young man will never return from Viborg Side. Well, I don't know about you, Mark Alexandrovich, but I mean to die with my stomach comfortably filled. What about peeling some potatoes now? I could produce some more oil for the stove if you like to give me your saccharine instead. I heard a doctor say saccharine was none too good for elderly folk."

Frossia could endure no more. She must go out. The wind almost threshed the air out of her lungs, but she struggled against its fury, and reached the commissariat in the Sixteenth Line. The sentry glanced at her suspiciously and barred the way, but she explained about her work at the Rabfak, and was taken into a small room with a man in khaki and a telephone. They let her use it. Golubev said there was no need for her to worry, all the students were being mobilized in case of an emergency, and lectures were suspended. Besides, said Gleb Semenovich, how could she get to them? Exchange Bridge . . . Here the line groaned, wailed, and died as if someone had bitten it in two. Frossia looked at the man across the desk.

"He said something about Exchange Bridge. . . ."

"We have no information—"

"Is the Neva still rising?"

"Yes."

He spoke politely but briefly. The commissariat was like a beehive. The ground floor of the building was being rapidly converted into a rough rest center with heterogeneous bedding piled all over the place in high mounds. Outside, along the Sixteenth Line small clusters of people kept to the middle of the street, and threw fragments of stories at one another. Exchange Bridge had all its wooden spans broken in the night. Nicholas Bridge was up, Palace Bridge floating down the river, its timbers were also rotten, and the island was cut off, whispered those hurrying, frightened men and women. A thin dark-eyed man in a worn sheepskin muttered grim prophecies about the punishment to fall on a city of infidels, but nobody stopped to listen to him. Only a pale-cheeked woman in a green felt hat with bedraggled ostrich feathers said derisively:

"Infidel yourself! We have had many a flood in those old holy days!" And someone tittered.

But the stories grew as if they meant to keep pace with the ever rising fury of the gale. Gavan was wholly under water, and so was Ochta, half of Viborg Side had already disappeared, and Alexander Bridge lay under the Neva.

A platoon of soldiers marched past. They looked bored and weary, and they went by as though the welfare of the island were of no concern to them. Then an ancient trailer came along with two boats, their keels upwards, and women murmured:

"The Neva has risen! The boats are for Gavan—but what is the use of two boats among thousands?"

Presently the wind came to a brief lull. A young army sergeant, his left arm in a sling, blood on his face, passed down the street. They rushed to him.

"What has happened? Is there fighting?"

"Fighting? What fighting? A slate hit me! Please, *grajdane*, don't crowd in the streets. The hospitals will be full as it is. Why must you add to the casualties?"

"Is the water high?"

"About ten feet."

"Where?"

But he would not answer and hurried away. Frossia returned to the balconied house. She had no faith in stories, she disregarded richly embroidered details about the collapse of several bridges, but she longed for a place of her own, for familiar voices and faces, for someone to say: "Now, Frossia, this job must be done at once," and she had nothing to do at the moment.

She went into her room, avoiding the kitchen occupied by the midwife, the undertaker, and Mark Alexandrovich. She could smell some cooking, and guessed that the two men and Olga Semenovna were busily using up their iron rations. Frossia slipped into her room almost on tiptoe. Their end of Maly Prospect lay at some distance from Gavan where, apparently, the river had already broken through; there seemed no immediate danger to their walls, and now she had been out and watched the scene in the street, she realized that she could not stay safe and inactive anywhere. Galernaya was all fringed by rivers and lesser streams. Boats had been rowed down Galernaya in many an earlier flood. Frossia thought she would somehow try and get across, and find herself among her intimates.

Here she paused in the middle of the room, her hands idly twisting a handkerchief. Unless Igor happened to be at the Zabalkansky she could not reach him: she did not know his address.

"But Elena Ivanovna would know it, and the Ratovs are certain to," she said aloud by way of reassuring herself.

She stayed indoors for about an hour. The kitchen door was ajar. They had eaten well. Now the midwife was fingering a pack of greasy cards, and Mark Alexandrovich, obviously afraid of solitude, sat and listened to her chatter.

"Here is the knave of diamonds again. For a young man it means promotion in business. For an elderly person a legacy."

"Legacies are abolished by law," he reminded her nervously, and she chided him:

"Cards never lie. Here is the queen of hearts. What did I tell you? The knave of diamonds and the queen of hearts . . . A most rare and fortunate combination, Mark Alexandrovich. You must have been born with a silver spoon in your mouth. It means a fortune, heart's contentment, and union with your beloved. Now for the third throw," and she frowned. "Oh, queen of heaven, it is all spoilt now. The king of spades. What an unpleasant card. . . . It stands for perversity in fortune and tribulation in the heart, but the king is always better than the queen. The queen of spades is a poisonous card, Mark Alexandrovich—"

Frossia stopped in the doorway.

"I am going out."

Both stared at her.

"In the devil's own weather, Euphrosynia Pavlovna? Have you mislaid your wits?"

"I must. I have friends on the other side—in Galernaya and Moyka."

"Galernaya is under water," asserted Olga Semenovna.

"So they say. I must really find out." And Frossia turned and went back to her room. Tidying up seemed an odd occupation for such a turmoiled day, but she thought: I might not come back. I should hate anyone to find things in disorder. Her wardrobe could not occupy her long. What had she? One shabby dress and another, her rose gown, one change of underwear, one pair of shoes, and she was wearing them, two much-darned shawls, and a coat. She examined her locker now almost full with the iron rations she had not yet touched. Her pannikin, mug, knife, and spoon were all clean. The narrow shelf above her bed held the two leather-bound books, *History of French Dancing* and *Euphrosynia's Legend*, Taglioni's portrait, and four family photographs in tarnished silver frames. These Frossia must dust once again, her fingers slow over them and her eyes slightly clouded. She pulled out a small green leather portmanteau from under the bed. It housed her few treasures: some faded intimate snapshots, two or three unimportant trinket, her mother's tiny gilt scissors, an extravagantly embellished thimble. She looked over them hurriedly and pushed the porman-teau out of sight.

There was nothing else for her to do, but a black-bound volume of Browning lay on the bed, and she remembered there were some lines in a poem that Igor had wanted her to find, and she had never found them. She could not read English with much ease, and poetry was all the more difficult. Now coated and shawled, she picked up the book, almost furiously determined to find the place, and she came upon it.

"There shall never be one lost good. . . ."

She read the lines three times over, not certain of her accent, but the meaning stole into her mind, and the words, she knew, would be lodged in her memory. Then she stuffed her pockets with chunks of bread and came out. From the kitchen Olga Semenovna shouted to her:

"Mark Alexandrovich had the ace of hearts three times running, and no spades at all. Just imagine . . . Now we are going to have a nice game of *durachki*."

Frossia smiled, ran to the front door, and wrenched it open. It slammed to behind her, and she had to clutch hard at the timbered railings.

9

It was late afternoon. The sky hung curtained in thick sullen gray. The sun had never come out that day, and sometimes the wind dropped for a few instants, but such lulls were heavy with the menace of more bitter wrath to fall upon the city. Frossia rounded a corner and ran along the Fourth Line. She came to Sredny Prospect, and found herself checked by a sad procession coming from Gavan. There were carts and sledges which thundered over the cobbled pavements, women in men's coats and caps, men in women's shawls, all pushing, jostling, tramping, hurrying, all in-tent on escaping from the bitterest foe they had ever met. Here Frossia heard no fantastic stories. What they had seen could not be exaggerated by the most fertile imagination. Nor did they talk much.

Carts and sleighs had mostly rubbish piled on them, photograph albums, a small bead screen worked in the Japanese fashion. A tin saucepan gave shelter to a small soiled yellow silk fan. A mirror in an ornamental brass frame reposed on top of a cart in among a piebald assortment of rags, brooms, and chipped enameled basins. The refugees did not talk much, but there ran subdued wailing up and down their tattered ranks, accompanied by a muted refrain about lost identity papers. At the corner of Sredny a red guard picket awaited them. Those fleeing from the inundated streets were to go to a certain house in the First Line, well away from the treacherous neighborhood of the quays, where mattresses and hot food would be given them, but they must hurry, urged the guards roughly though not unkindly. If they did not hurry those behind them would never get through.

"*Kormilets,*" sobbed a middle-aged woman, a boy's gray coat inadequately covering her bent shoulders. "All the labor books were in the locker. I could not get to it, and now four of us have no papers, we are nameless, we are nobodies. . . ."

"Go on, mother," said the guard. "What is a paper when life is in danger? They will sort you all out."

Frossia, her heart hammering, stood and watched. Pushing a small cart, laden with comparatively neat bundles, came an elderly woman, whose breeding could not be disguised under the humblest of rags. She was asked for her labor book, and produced it calmly. Over the man's shoulder Frossia caught the name, and marveled. It had been a great and ancient name, it was still a proud name. The man obviously knew it, too. He held the labor book for a second or so, looked at its owner, standing there, at the head of her cart, herself clad in tatters, standing there with as much self-possession as if she were coming out of her drawing room, and the man handed back the book.

"The First Line, *grajdanka.* You will get a mattress and something hot to eat."

She inclined her head. Frossia could not have called it a nod. The cart went on its way. The guard turned to a comrade.

"Anyway, no wailing from such as she," he commented.

As soon as the procession had gone Frossia hurried on. But at the next corner she was stopped by a picket. Nobody was to go any further. "We have had enough panic as it is. Things are not much better on the other side," they said. "You could never cross. Go back, *grajdanka—*" And crestfallen, Frossia turned away when suddenly a hunchback came out of a house; she recognized Nikita Fyodorov, and shouted at him:

"Comrade Nikita—"

He did not hear at first. Frossia thought: No, I am not going back to listen to Olga Semenovna's card chatter. . . . I must find something to do, and she shouted all the louder, and he heard.

He did not at first recognize her. Then he smiled broadly as if they had parted the day before.

"Euphrosynia Pavlovna! Meeting you here is a pleasure—" He grinned so pleasantly that she knew she could believe him. "Of course, there is plenty to do. Come with me to the Mines Institute. We have started a refuge center there, and a soup kitchen." He explained things to the picket, and they let her pass.

The situation was indeed grave, Nikita told her, as they were fighting their way against the ever strengthening wind. Gavan was nearly all under water, even Little Neva had burst its banks, Exchange Bridge had fallen down. He had heard about boats down along Palace Quay and Galernaya Street, but the houses there were of stone, and things were easier. But Gavan, Ochta, Viborg Side! He waved his long arms.

"Have you any gum boots? No? Well, I might lend you a pair. The water is not very far from the Mines Institute, and you must stay put and do your job and not wander anywhere. Korabelnaya Street is a ghastly sight. The first to be flooded it was, and that in the night. Few had a chance to get away. We sent lifeboats down, but what good wasting a lifeboat for a cargo of corpses?" he added grimly. "The day will be over in about an hour, and think of that hell in the dark! There is neither gas nor electricity in the city."

They found the Mines Institute a beleaguered fortress. Water was already licking the outer walls. The huge gates were reinforced halfway up with cobbles and hastily improvised sandbags. "The boys worked the whole night at them," explained Nikita. The enormous courtyard was dotted with bonfires, and the wind sent wild tongues and pillars of flame in all directions. Banisters, window frames, doors, and paneling, anything at all served for fuel, and everywhere were huddled groups of refugees, rag-wrapped and shivering. Three of the big lecture halls, Nikita said, were turned into kitchens.

"Keep the fires going," rang the order.

Fires indeed had to be kept going. There was no oil for lamps. There were not enough candles to go round. There was no other means of lighting at all. But the outdoor fires were hard to start and harder still to keep going because of the wind. They were dangerous, too, since tongues of flame would shoot upwards, then veer in another direction, zigzag, spiral, and sparks flew here and there.

"Not enough candles to go round," said Nikita. There was not enough of anything to go round. Frossia knew it as soon as her eyes had taken in the wild, turmoiled scene. A single ragged blanket must be adequate to cover four cold and possibly soaked human bodies. Of course it was not enough, and all were shivering. Children were crying, men flung ugly oaths at whatever came in their way. Most of the women kept quiet. And, plunging deeper into the yard, Frossia heard one or two of them attempt to croon a lullaby.

In a hall an enormous cauldron stood bubbling and steaming on an improvised iron stove. Two thin white-kerchiefed women, in men's coats and high boots, stood, each armed with a huge ladle, and stirred. One of them muttered: "It looks a bit thin to me. . . ." The other dipped her ladle, breathed hard, and sipped.

"Little sister, we have lost our wits! It is just boiling water with some grease in it. We never put any millet in. Where is it?"

"Behind you—in a sack. Hurry up with it. We may all be drowned before we are fed," shouted an old man from a bench by the wall.

They pounced on the sack. It held sand. The two women wrung their hands.

"But it was given us for millet."

Frossia heard and tore down the narrow dark staircase. In the yard she came on Nikita by pure luck, tugged at his sleeve, explained about the empty cauldron and the sand in the sack. He swore foully.

"They call themselves cooks, those two, and they waste all that fuel on water! There must be millet somewhere, we had stores brought in yesterday. But I am busy, Euphrosynia Pavlovna. Just you go round, shouting for Comrade Zherebzov. And when you get the stuff, mind you cook it. Those daughters of Satan might pour it all down the drain."

Frossia threaded her way around the huge courtyard, shouting, "Comrade Zherebzov! Comrade Zherebzov!" Sometimes she got no reply at all. Sometimes a voice would shout back at her that nobody had seen the man for hours. An old woman mumbled:

"He is not here. He has gone to Gavan—with a lifeboat. He is drowned most likely. What do you want him for?" And Frossia would have given up the search, had it not been for her remembering the cold hungry folk huddled along the walls of that lecture hall, all of them hoping for good hot millet. After something like an hour she found Comrade Zherebzov up one of the numberless dim staircases, on an evil-smelling landing. Zherebzov, a small brown man, in a dirty khaki shirt, sat on the floor, surrounded by a bevy of women with babies, women alone, women with grown children. He had an open box by his side, a candle, and a basin of darkly colored water, lint, swabs, a bottle of iodine, and huge bloodstained scissors. He was bandaging a baby's thin leg, and spoke to Frossia without looking up: "What do you want?" in so sharp a voice that Frossia explained as briefly as possible. The candle stood on the floor. In the dimness she could not see the women's faces, but some took to muttering, and she felt their resentment at her intrusion. Comrade Zherebzov was dressing their children's wounds, there were so many of them, he worked single-handed, and now came this interruption. But Zherebzov had no intention to cease from his work. He finished bandaging the leg, handed the baby over to its mother, rapped out "next," held out his hairy arms for a tiny girl, her face all caked with blood, and snapped at Frossia:

"Get down on the floor. Hold her," he added. "Millet can wait. This job is urgent—"

Frossia held the child, and hoped her arms were not shaking too much. The man's rough calloused hands seized a sponge, washed off the blood, and he stared at a deep oblong wound across the tiny forehead. He stared for a mere second, then snatched at some cotton wool, dipped it in a bottle, smeared the gash, swathed the head with gauze, and rapped out again: "Next—"

Frossia shivered. The smell on the landing gave her nausea. Her arms were numb but, fascinated, she watched the man. He was brusque, almost unfeeling, he handled the children as though they were so many parcels ready for the post, yet she knew that for him those parcels were the most important things in the world, and she almost forgot her message and the hungry people in the dim hall.

After about an hour the last wound was dressed. Zherebzov got up and led the way to an equally dirty room. He held the candle high. Frossia could see mounds of sacks strewing the floor. He pulled at one of them. "There is the millet. Enough for two hundred or more. Do you think you could carry it?"

"Yes," said Frossia, but she never knew how she succeeded in hauling it down one staircase and up another and into the hall. There she was met by wild abuse. Nikita's brusque injunction that she was to cook the millet could not be followed. The sack was pulled off her shoulders. The two cooks, ladles upraised in their hands, rushed towards her, and for a second Frossia thought they meant to strike her.

"You have been nearly two hours," they screamed at her, "nearly two hours—"

She ran away. She found a comparatively quiet corner of the yard, and slept, her coat folded round her. Towards dawn the wind slackened, and soft rain patterned the gloomy scene. In murky gray light she saw Nikita coming towards her.

"Well, I am glad to see you. Take these gum boots. We have a boat in the Twenty-sixth Line. Do you know anything about first aid?"

"A little—"

"It is Korabelnaya Street. They say not much could be done there, but I am going." He shrugged his sunken shoulders. "Some say the Neva has stopped rising. Are you tired?"

"Well—"

"I don't know if I am or not. I have not taken my clothes off or anything for three nights. That is nothing. Hungry?"

She was, and he pressed a hard-boiled egg and a rusk into her hand. The egg was an incredible luxury, and she ate it carefully.

Outside the gates a strange world awaited them. It was murky. It was also strangely warm. The wind still blew from the west, but its fury had grown much thinner. The air seemed watery-green as though they were all enclosed in an aquarium with no visible boundaries to it. Even outside the gates black slimy water lapped round their ankles. By the time they came to the Twenty-sixth Line, it reached up to their knees. In the uncertain light Frossia saw darkly patterned shapes floating round.

"We could not pick up everybody," said Nikita. "But the river must be falling back. You could not see much of a roof here yesterday."

The light grew, and Frossia saw the derelict roofs, standing along a derelict street. It all seemed too unreal to frighten her, though she kept avoiding to look at the shapeless swollen objects floating down the street.

"There is the boat," said Nikita and shouted, "Egor, ah, Egor . . . I have brought a nurse along. . . . Water is going back."

The small wizened man in a boat stopped rowing towards them. Between them and the boat lay a distance of some ten or twelve yards, but here the water lay deeper. Frossia's short skirt was soaked, the water squelched in her gum boots and rippled round her thighs with a strange sucking noise, and she stopped. She could not tell Nikita of her fear. She thought that if she were to take another step she would be certain to miss her footing and fall, and the waters would close over her face and make her one of those dreadful shapes she dared not look at.

"Come on, Euphrosynia Pavlovna," urged Nikita, and she smiled and plunged forward, and the boat was reached. But Egor was not sure about going down Korabelnaya Street. "It is a lane of floating timber and corpses," he said. "Stands to reason all those hovels cracked like nuts. Some were down long before the flood came. Think of that gale—a fortress might have been battered by it. There was a small house in Korabelnaya, just four windows and a doorway. . . . Well, the gale came, the house cracked—you could hear it from one end of the street to the other, and the next gust brought it down, roof, chimneys, and all. Just as if a child had puffed at a house of cards. . . . Except that the noise was enough to deafen you. . . . Yes, they say the water is falling back, but you could not walk down Korabelnaya. The wind is freshening, and I have to row against the wind," he grumbled.

"Comrade Petiuchov said I was to go," insisted Nikita. "He is sending three more boats along."

Egor shrugged, turned the boat, and rowed hard. Presently roofs, however derelict, were left behind. Now there was nothing around them but planks, poles, uprights, piled up masses of wreckage, and Egor said briefly: "Korabelnaya, *grajdane*. There might be one or two houses left at the end, but I don't think so," and they rowed past a wrecked house, its roof torn off, its windows, all glass gone, gaping stupidly. Through the dark mouth of the doorway they could see furniture standing two feet deep in dark slimy water. By a half submerged chest along a wall was huddled a woman's body.

"Nobody left there," said Nikita grimly. "Well, I can now report to Comrade Petiuchov. We have done our job. It is no good going by rumors, Egorka. People will say anything. A woman told me that she knew the spire of Peter and Paul was under water. I ask you, Euphrosynia Pavlovna! The old body must have been thinking of Noah's flood . . ." But Frossia broke in:

"Comrade Nikita, do you see the chest in the room? There is something on it. It moved a moment ago. I saw it move, I tell you." She spoke faster and faster, and both men stared hard.

"The light is dim, but I think you are right, Euphrosynia Pavlovna. It must be a child. If only its mother had had enough sense to scramble on the chest."

"The doorway is too narrow," said Egor. "I could not bring the boat into the house, and neither of you could manage her on your own. The wind is getting worse again."

Frossia looked at Nikita.

"The water will be up to your waist," he said gravely, "perhaps higher. But you are tall." He smiled a little ruefully. "A pygmy like myself would get drowned like a dog. Can you swim?"

"No—but I am going—"

"There will be steps to the house," Egor warned her. "Three or

335

more—else the water in the room would have been as deep as here. Feel for the steps and don't stumble—and I will turn the boat round."

"It is not right somehow," began Nikita in a doubtful voice, but Frossia had already leapt overboard.

The boat was in the middle of the street. The water rose to meet her, slimy, swirling, gurgling, hostile water, sucking at her skirt, and then venturing higher, lapping her waist, her breast. She breathed deeply and plunged on. It was only a matter of some few yards. She felt for the steps, counted them carefully. There were four of them. Once she was in the room, her thighs were clear of the water. She could move more easily.

The room was dreadful. Another huddled body lay to the left of the doorway, the outstretched hands clenched like claws, the face downwards. But on the half-submerged chest in a tin tub, all swathed in dirty coverlets, she found the child, raised her shaking arms, touched it, heard a thin plaint, and knew deep joy. Carefully she lifted the tiny bundle and cradled it in her arms. She tried to think of some words, a shred of a lullaby to croon in its ears. She opened her lips and knew her voice had gone. Now she must return, and slowly she made her way towards the door. One, two, three, four steps . . . How easy they were though a burden now lay in her arms! Frossia raised her eyes and saw Egor plowing towards her.

"Alive?" he shouted. "Well, a good morning's work done, *grajdanka*. I left Nikita with the boat. She is quite steady."

But the boat seemed miles away. The steps were behind her, all dark danger slipped away, and Frossia knew her strength was failing her. She held the tiny bundle out to Egor. "Please—carefully—very carefully," and Egor, grinning sheepishly, took the child and turned his back on her. She followed. It was not very far. The water ran up to her waist again and then higher and higher still. The water was a slimy green dragon, lying in wait to pounce and to destroy utterly. It had already destroyed much, but not enough to slake its hunger. "Must I go, too?" Frossia thought stupidly, and knew herself slipping. "I must not ask Egor for help. He is carrying the child, and Nikita is with the boat. . . . With the boat," she repeated to herself, stumbled again, and knew the waters were closing over her face.

CHAPTER ELEVEN

". . . AND USE IT FOR A WELL"

The long room was in half-darkness except for a screened-off corner where a young nurse sat, yawning over some temperature charts. It was nearly midnight, the night doctor would soon come along. But the ward was tidy and everything done, and the nurse could afford some leisure for her own thoughts. I am lucky. Was it not awful in the last war trying to learn nursing? Where was I? At St. Mary Magdalene's. "Who are you? A Negress, surely?" "No, a creole, my father came from Martinique, my mother was a Circassian," but that did not help. They nicknamed me "Negress," *negritianka.* . . . How it hurt. . . . They would not let me learn anything. Four years did I spend there, and I was not allowed to do anything except scrub floors and mop up messes. *Negritianka* can do it—the dirtiest job going, yes, call *negritianka.* Now I am lucky. To be in an important German Hospital, run on German money. Where do they get their money from? They were beaten in the war. . . . Yet here we have creosote and expensive preparations in the pharmacy, and we are given white bread and good fish. . . . And nobody calls me *negritianka* any more. I am the French sister. She yawned again, and made some notes on the margin of a sheet. Even here, in this expensively run place, they must be careful with paper. There was hardly any paper in the country, Dr. Smirnov had said. Irma made her notes in a small legible hand. She had been to a proper school, and she never forgot it.

Yes, she was fortunate with the people in her first ward. Twelve bodies she had in her charge, all of them with pulmonary trouble. Eight were pleasant but ordinary, and there was nothing exciting either about themselves or their treatment. But she also had Varvara Filipovna, a dear middle-aged soul, once a nurse at St. Nicholas's Home, who knew much about mental treatment. Varvara Filipovna could say such unexpected and pretty things. Once she said: "Sister Irma, you remind me of a magnolia—you are all dark and yet there is cream about you, and your skin is pure cream-ivory velvet." A magnolia . . . Poor Varvara Filipovna would never again see any flowers in bloom. They were now in October, but Varvara Filipovna's lungs were like twin sieves, and she knew it herself, you could not hide much from a nurse, but she merely talked about her days at St. Nicholas' and a garden remembered from a brief spring visit to the Crimea. "Oh, those almond trees, Sister Irma . . ."

Irma also had Klara Karlovna, a frail spinster from Riga, once governess to a cotton king's family along the banks of the Neva, by Schlüsselburg. Klara Karlovna was very religious. She forgave everybody. She had forgiven the Germans for the cruel pillage of Riga. She had forgiven the Soviet for the shooting of her employer. But she had something odd in her forgiving ways. She had a small pink china vase, and Irma broke it and was very much upset. "I forgive you, Sister Irma," said Klara Karlovna in her slightly acid and tremulous voice, and Irma knew that the breaking of the vase meant the breaking of a small separate world for Klara Karlovna.

Then there was little Tania who talked least of them and said most. Little Tania was twenty, but she was shrunken to the size of a ten-year-old girl. They had discussed her going to the south late in the summer, but she could not have traveled any distance. She had no longer strength to do, she merely retained her strength to be. She lay, looking at you with her huge sherry-colored eyes, two burning dark golden-brown stars in the thin ivory frame of a wasted face, and you sensed that the ugliest chipped enamel trough, crammed with gray cotton wool and soiled dressings, had some beauty in it because little Tania had looked at it. When Varvara Filipovna smiled tearfully over her almond trees in the Crimea which, as she knew, she would never see again, little Tania's smile almost brought almond blossom into the ward. When Klara Karlovna enlarged on her experiences of freely exercised forgiveness, little Tania's burning eyes strayed to the window and searched the skies as if she were bent on discovering in among the pure clouds something of a hidden quality which alone could cleanse and redeem the indubitable oddness of Klara Karlovna's pardoning. Little Tania once said to Irma: "There is much in life to live for," and when she knew that her own scant sands were running out—even though nobody told her—but she knew it all the same, she murmured so softly that Irma alone caught the small whisper: "Need anyone become a mere corpse just because they are dead?"

Next to little Tania, the last bed against the wall, housed a newcomer. They had brought her in the day before. She had narrowly escaped drowning in one of the flooded streets in Gavan. She was first carried into the reception ward, and Irma thought she had

escaped altogether—the face was blue with fine purple streaks running along the temples and round the closed mouth; her clothes
were torn and sodden, there was blood behind her left ear and another small clot of it on the pointed chin, and the burnished casque
of her hair lay all dull, matted, soaked like hemp which had been
out in the rain too long. They took off her clothes, wiped her with
methylated spirit, put on a clean flannel nightgown, combed out
the hair, and washed the blood off her face. The reception sister
whispered to Irma: "Have you ever seen anyone quite so lovely?"
Irma had not. For a fleeting instant she was bitterly conscious of
her own thick lips, her heavily cream skin, and largely imagined
ungainliness of both bone and flesh, and then she was ashamed
of it.

Case No. 12 was wheeled into the ward. There stole a tiny breath
of faint color into her cheeks, and the purple streaks lost their
dreadful lividness, but she lay unconscious. Sister Irma and a doctor ministered to her, and the other patients whispered about her.
Klara Karlovna maintained that the newcomer must be a Baltic
German.

"Look at the chiseling and the complexion. It shows rare breeding. In the Baltic provinces we have some of the best, the oldest
German blood. . . . Why, she may be an Ostensaken or—"

Varvara Filipovna protested.

"Why should she be a Baltic German? This is a pure Russian
shape. Look at the forehead, the chin. Have you never seen a really
beautiful Russian girl?" And little Tania whispered to reconcile the
two of them: "Maybe she is Russian. Maybe she is a Baltic German. She is very lovely and that is enough."

Presently Irma learned details. She was a Russian, Euphrosynia
Bozert, she taught French at a college in Kamennostrovsky Prospect. She lived in a house in Maly Prospect. The house was utterly
demolished the afternoon of the day when Little Neva had burst
through by Exchange Bridge. . . .

"Bozert—" said Klara Karlovna. "I seem to have heard the name
somewhere, but it does not sound very Russian to me."

"Her father was a court jeweler," eagerly remembered Varvara
Filipovna. "But they came to Russia generations ago, and her
mother was a pure Russian."

Early in the afternoon Case No. 12 woke up, looked round, saw
nothing, and closed her eyes again. They gave her a little hot milk,
they brought another hot water bottle. "Dry . . . Is it dry?" she
murmured, and was again unconscious, and little Tania murmured
back, "Yes, sleep, please."

They all kept quiet. They realized No. 12 was a grave case. In normal days such a case would have had a room to herself, or a cubicle, at least, a screen round the bed. But the hospital was over-crowded, and the only screen on the premises had to be used for another, grimmer purpose. So they kept quiet. They tried to cough quietly. Even the nurses glided about in carpet slippers and did not bang against beds and lockers in their usual fashion. Everyone spoke in muted voices. Irma felt flattered at such a display of self-discipline. The doctor called twice that day. Little Tania asked him shyly about the baby.

"What baby?"

"The one she saved in Gavan." They had already heard an out-line of the story from a garrulous and excited nurse.

"I am afraid I cannot tell you."

"But we must know," insisted little Tania. "We must know what to tell her when she wakes up. Please, Doctor Freydt, could you not find out?" He nodded and passed on, and later Sister Irma brought the news that the infant was safe and taken to an orphan-age, apparently none the worse for its experience.

"So she saved at least one life," said Varvara Filipovna. "That is a grand thing for anyone so young."

"Cannot middle-aged people do as much?" demanded Klara Kar-lovna. "Why—"

But they would not carry on an argument in whispers, and it died a swift death.

Now it was nearly midnight, the ward lay still, and the night doctor appeared in the doorway. Doctor Freydt, a busy dry Ger-man, made his rounds fussily and hastily, and kept himself aloof from all lesser concerns which kept the ward alive. But this was a Russian doctor, Nikolai Nikolaevich Smirnov, fat, rosy, kindly, with a secret passion for dolls and an open attachment to rather loud tie-pins. The one he wore now, and the white coat was unbuttoned the better to show it, was a cluster of bright green stones. He beamed at Sister Irma.

"I heard you were here all through the day," he said accusingly.

"The night sister is ill. We could not get anyone else, and we have a serious new case in the ward."

"You are a born nurse," he beamed, and Irma burned with pride, but he added, "You are also the world's prize fool," and her heart sank, but Nikolai Nikolaevich smiled so genially that she knew he approved of her readiness to bear a twenty-four-hour burden, and the world was a bright room once again. They tiptoed to No. 12. Little Tania was awake and watched them intently. Then she

340

closed her eyes. It was better to stay in the dark. Little Tania never said prayers. She was shy about prayers. She merely talked to her God very much as she would talk to her mother. She had talked to her God all her life, and such talk meant no effort to her. It was far easier talking to God than trying to converse with some people. Little Tania said: "You are seeing her at this very moment. You have made her so beautiful to look at, and she must be beautiful within also because she has saved a human life, and that is yourself, and all beauty lives in you. So, please, don't let any of it be wasted," she said, kept her eyes closed, and presently fell asleep.

2

It was winter. The snow lay so thick that it banked the window ledges with thick shining swathes, and this dimmed the rooms, but lights must not be switched on until it was quite dark, said Sister Irma, and Frossia lay quietly. She was getting on well, they said, but it was warmer in bed: even a German hospital could not get enough fuel for central heating.

The winter was still very young, but sometimes Frossia thought that it was a winter five hundred years ago since that autumn morning, all wet and pallid green, when she handed a small whimpering thing to Egor, followed him across the treacherous slimy water, and the water pounced on her, and all ceased until she knew herself warm and dry, and wondered how such things could be, and also knew that she was so tired that it was impossible to think at all. So she slept and slept.

It was winter. Not far from the cream-yellow walls of the hospital in the Fourteenth Line, snow hid the ugly ravages of the flood, thin ice began covering up the destruction meted out by mad swollen waters, and the dead in Gavan and elsewhere slept secure from flood and from frost. In the German hospital new people were admitted. They came, coughed, struggled for breath, and coughed again. Sometimes they conquered, sometimes they were defeated. The single ambulatory screen traveled from ward to ward. So many screens had been used for fuel the winter before, explained Sister Irma. In Frossia's own ward two young girls died in the same night. Their beds were at the other end of the long room, and she, lying low on her pillows, could not see them die. The bed stood empty for nearly a week. It seemed that admission into the German Hospital was surrounded by many difficulties. Sister Irma said vaguely that it was no easy matter to feed the patients, but this could not be the true reason because food was good and almost abundant. Milk and cocoa they had every day, and soft-boiled eggs sometimes, and small white rolls with every meal. At first Sister Irma had to be severe with Frossia.

"No. 12, you must not stare like that. Just eat your roll, will you?"

Frossia said feebly: "But I must know if it is genuine, sister—"

"Eat it," whispered little Tania.

She ate, wondered, and slept. She woke, ate again, wondered, and slept again. It was all a puzzle, but she felt as peaceful as though she had been bedded in down.

She got better. She could sit up, observe things, get near to the other people. She met little Tania, and Varvara Filipovna, and Klara Karlovna, who said with something of a rebuke in her soured voice:

"You will be out fairly soon."

"Why, you may soon be out also," Frossia said politely.

"No"—Klara Karlovna did not wince—"and it is better so. It is much nicer to die warm and comfortable."

Varvara Filipovna avoided such topics, but she showed great interest in other things.

"Bozert's was in Morskaya Street, was it not? I had never been inside. But the windows were a fairy tale. I remember one day off I had just before Easter, and I went all the way from St. Nicholas's just to look at Bozert's windows. They had an Easter window all done with countless eggs of gold and silver and precious stones. And some were the size of a pigeon's egg. Those were made of jasper and malachite. In the evening they had dear little pink lamps all behind the window, and soon there was a crowd staring at it all. There was a small necklet, I remember, all made of tiny jeweled eggs—something like mosaic," she ended wistfully, but Klara Karlovna had different reminiscences to offer.

"M. Kotunin's wife bought all her pretty things there," she said loftily. "I sometimes went with her. 'Klara Karlovna,' she said to me once, 'if you were not a mere governess, I would buy this opal pendant for you. I can see you like it, and I can well afford it, but what use would such a pendant be to you? Where would you wear it?' Those were her very own words, she could not help saying such things sometimes, wealthy people have few feelings for their dependents, and, of course, I forgave her."

They were all uncomfortable, aware that the pendant episode had soured many a day in Klara Karlovna's past, and Frossia said she was very sorry but she had never cared much for jewels, and Varvara Filipovna chimed in brightly:

"Just like a young lady in Bligken's chocolate shop. I asked her once how many sweets she ate every day. 'None,' she said. 'We are allowed to eat as many as we like, and I simply gorged at first, but now I cannot touch them: they make me nearly sick,' she said."

Klara Karlovna was interesting even if querulous, and Varvara Filipovna amusing in a faintly wistful way, but Frossia soon learned to love the least sound of little Tania's voice. It came seldom enough. Talking tired little Tania more and more.

Visitors were allowed three times a week. There were other grave cases in the ward, and callers had no more than twenty minutes allotted to them, and they must sit close to the patient's bed and not talk too loudly. Little Tania's mother, a small bent woman with a kindly brown face, came regularly. There was little talk between them. They looked at each other, Tania's thin white fingers clasping the other's reddened, roughened hand. A daughter came occasionally to see Varvara Filipovna, a big loud woman, even her clothes were worn in a loud manner, they always rustled, and when she tried to speak softly, she hissed. Nobody ever came to see Klara Karlovna. "I am a lone pebble," she confessed to Frossia. "Oh, yes, I have relations, two nieces and their families, but do they care? Friends? Friends are faithful enough when you are well and can smile at them. Oh, yes, my dear, I have had a lot to go through in my long life." She smiled her acid tight-lipped smile, and Frossia wished she might love her a little if only out of pity.

Nobody came to see her. She grew anxious. So many threads seemed snapped, and her earlier background receded into vague and misty spaces. Maly Prospect, the Rabfak, the studio in Moyka, the Zabalkansky, places where she had lived and worked and belonged, too, in a certain sense, were not there any more. Something ended when the waters washed over her face, and she must face a new beginning, and she fretted, and asked Sister Irma: "Has nobody at all been to see me? To ask for me?" And she always asked in a whisper, unwilling lest others, however friendly, should decipher the secret lettering of her anxiety and offer her sympathy which might only deepen her hidden wounds. Sister Irma soothed her by saying that she must not fret.

"Things have been rather chaotic—you know. There are so many people missing, and others ran away from the city as soon as the flood began. All traveling restrictions were done away with during the flood. Perhaps, some of your friends have gone away. You know it was a shocking disaster, the city has not got over it yet. Here the water did not come further than the basement, but in other places—" and she checked herself. "What about writing to some of them? You are fit enough to write now. I shall fetch you some paper and a pencil—the matron will not have ink in the wards."

Frossia felt shaken and rather stripped that day. She had not even got a pencil of her own to write a note with. Indeed she had no possessions at all. Other people's lockers were strewn with their unimportant but none the less intimate belongings. Hers alone was tellingly and cruelly bare. Even the gray celluloid comb she used had been provided by the hospital. She ended her note to Elena Ivanovna with a plaintive postscript—"If you can, will you please go to Maly Prospect? I have been here three weeks, I think. I have nothing of my own," and she added a brief list of such things as her tired mind could remember.

One early afternoon, two days later, a red-cheeked nurse clattered down the ward and said something to Sister Irma who immediately vanished. Nearly everyone in the ward was either asleep or lying quietly. Varvara Filipovna was putting out her favorite patience which hardly ever came out, but Varvara Filipovna went on perseveringly, and now she muttered under her breath: "Just like that ace of diamonds to turn up and spoil it all. . . . And it was nearly out."

Klara Karlovna, steel spectacles on her hooked nose, looked on disapprovingly. She was trying to read her German psalter. Frossia knew that book. It was old, printed in Stuttgart in 1714, in thick black Gothic lettering, and bound in black leather, now worn to a shining green.

Sister Irma was back.

"What am I to do?" She bent over Frossia's bed. "You have visitors. They are downstairs. I thought you said you had no people of your own. What am I do? That is what I said to myself. There are ten of them. They are all over the hall. The porter said they could not come up, this is not a visiting day, but you know what I did? I went to the matron, and she said 'Yes,' but you can see two only and not for more than twenty minutes."

"Who are they?"

"Well, this is difficult—how could I remember ten strange people? But there is an elderly woman who looks rather motherly, and a youngish man who appears ordinary and is not—this is very muddled, but perhaps you will know what I mean, and I noticed he had some books under his arm. Then—"

"I want those two, please. Thank you, Sister Irma, I just want those two—"

She knew she would have to wait for some time. Varvara Filipovna had told her that all visitors must sign a book, get a special

344

pass, and have their parcels examined before they were allowed to come up, and their ward was in an annex, there lay innumerable stairs, landings, and passages between them and the entrance hall which faced the Fourteenth Line, and Frossia was grateful for the delay. It gave her leisure to pick up now one broken thread, now another, and still another, and weave them together, and look at the web for a moment. "Ten," she marveled, and tried to count: Elena Ivanovna, Pavel Pavlovich, Paulina Pavlovna, Igor Vladimirovich, Pasha Dobrina—possibly—but no, Pasha was still away, then Gleb Semenovich, perhaps, Nikita, Mark Alexandrovich, Olga Semenovna . . . Surely not the undertaker . . . In the end she gave up counting. She simply waited.

You cannot do without people, she thought. Your own family may be taken from you, and you must needs find other people to be intimate with. Was I not foolish in always being afraid of people, in trying to keep my funny little differences all to myself? I did not know then that no two people can ever be the same. What is this happening to me? she thought, watching Varvara Filipovna shuffle her greasy pack of cards. I cannot tell. She waited, tense with excitement, and her eyes were starry when Elena Ivanovna and Igor came into the ward.

3

Her ten visitors were: Pavel Pavlovich and his sister, Elena Ivanovna and Igor, Nikita and Egor, Glafira Antonovna and Kostia, and two acquaintances from the Zabalkansky.

"But if you only knew the inquiries we were making," said Elena Ivanovna. "Someone said you had gone to your Rabfak that day, and we searched every hospital on the other side. We never thought of this place, they say this is very difficult to get into. And we know all about you, and we are proud, *golubushka*." She bent down and kissed Frossia, and Igor put the books down on the locker.

"Euphrosynia Pavlovna, this is Pushkin and also Gogol's *Dead Souls*."

They had much news to give her. The balconied house in Maly Prospect was gone. They could tell her nothing about the tenants.

"But you are getting better, and when you are discharged, you come to me," said Elena Ivanovna. "I have had a few bits of furniture spoiled by water, but nothing much. The water was just about three to four feet deep in Galernaya. It will be farther for you for the Rabfak, but there is a tram from Annunciation Square straight on to Mikhaylovskaya Street, and you change there—"

"Yes, I change there."

"I have a good room at the back—with a nice bed in it, and you and I will run the Zabalkansky together." She sighed. "Some of them will need cheering up, *golubushka*."

They brought her gifts: two Anton apples, huge red-cheeked things, a small bottle of lemon essence, and beads for stringing in a funny box with a glass lid. "From the Gostiny Dvor," said Elena Ivanovna. "I must have bought them years ago. Here is needle and thread for them, and here is something to amuse you, *golubushka*," and she produced a tiny white china polar bear and a blank exercise book with a pencil.

Frossia thanked them rather brokenly, but the twenty minutes had flown on wings, Sister Irma appeared in the doorway, and they went. Frossia lay back, exhausted, but contented and at peace until Klara Karlovna said:

"Is your old home gone?"

"Yes—"

"And all your things?"

"I believe so—"

"Then why," demanded Klara Karlovna, "don't you cry about it? Losing possessions is so sad. It happened to me—oh, many times, and on each occasion I felt the world had been broken. Of course, your things might not have meant so much to you—"

"Well, I think I loved them all, but why should I cry?"

Klara Karlovna shrugged, but little Tania looked at Frossia, and Frossia knew there was a secret lying between them, a warm and lovely secret. Little Tania said nothing, but Frossia could read her mind clearly. Yes, I understand. Things get given to you, and they are cherished, and then they are taken away, perhaps destroyed. . . . Things should not matter so much in this turmoiled, extraordinarily patterned world. But people do matter. Your small polar bear might be smashed any day by some careless nurse in the ward, but a friend gave it to you, and her thought for you cannot be spoiled by anyone's clumsy touch. You know this now. Frossia read all this in little Tania's face, and blushed, and she held up her ridiculous box of beads with its glass lid.

"Look, I have thread, too; good strong thread, and two needles. I am going to make you a necklace, Tania. Which will you have— rubies, beryls, emeralds, amethysts, or sapphires? I have them all in this box."

Little Tania chose rubies, and Klara Karlovna vented her secret annoyance by mocking at the beads.

"Such common glass beads they are. I know this kind of a box.

346

You used to buy them in those poky little shops—back of Gostiny Dvor, in Perinnaya Line. They were common and very cheap. Nursemaids always bought them."

"You could not buy them now for a million," said Frossia, "and they are lovely. They do sparkle."

"Please," said Varvara Filipovna, "I used to love them, too. I have not seen them for years. I should also like a necklace—made of those big green ones."

"Oh, emeralds," said Frossia, and set to work.

4

Even Klara Karlovna was sorry when they discharged Frossia. It was still winter, she murmured, snuggling closer under her dark blue blankets, and in the hospital you got a bed and food and warmth of a kind, and what was she going to do outside, asked Klara Karlovna?

"Work," said Frossia. "You see I am a teacher. I teach French at a Rabfak in Kamennostrovsky. I have nearly one hundred pupils." And she sketched a few details about college life and business, but Varvara Filipovna sighed.

"None of it will last. I ought to know. I have spent twenty-eight years in a mental hospital. This country has become one huge asylum. Our minds have gone, I mean ours—middle-aged folk. It is hard enough for the old, it is worse for the young, and the children. My daughter says she had heard of someone receiving letters from abroad, real letters properly stamped. There is no hunger abroad, but what do the Russians do? They wash dishes, or mend foreigners' underwear, or sell hats and flowers. And they are hungry often enough, and it is bad to feel hunger amidst plenty. But here we have nothing, and we shall have nothing. We shall merely grow hungrier and hungrier, and then die—all of us. And you talk of work!" She fingered her brave green beads. "I know what work means. You must have quiet to work well. The country has no quiet anywhere. Nobody could really work."

"There may be no work for you and for me," murmured little Tania. "But Euphrosynia Pavlovna is different, she is well again and she is strong, and she is so well educated, too—"

"They have no use for real education," retorted Varvara Filipovna. "This is a madhouse," and she wept over her dinner of fish soup and potato cutlets. They forgave her the outburst: they remembered that her loud-spoken daughter was leaving for Kiev in a few days, nobody would come to see Varvara Filipovna again till the spring, so the daughter had said, and Varvara Filipovna knew she could not be certain of any spring coming near her door again. So she looked miserable and sniffed and wept, and even a game of patience could not console her.

Frossia's last day was rather awkwardly stilled. The others, the comparatively inarticulate patients, lay and listened to Varvara Filipovna, and Frossia knew they all tacitly agreed with the peevish and mournful monologue. Frossia ceased to listen and occupied herself with other things. She gave the china bear to Sister Irma, and distributed the gaily colored beads between the two nurses. Elena Ivanovna had sent her a parcel of clothes, all of them old but neat. She was all ready to leave, dressed in the shabby blue blouse and skirt and a thick brown overcoat, but it was too early, and she found she had a whole hour on her hands. She opened *The Dead Souls* when she heard little Tania's voice.

"Are you very sad?"

Most of the others were asleep by now, and little Tania spoke in a whisper.

"No. . . . Why should I be?"

"Because of those words . . . Poor Varvara Filipovna! They were not harsh words. They were pitiful. Illness is worse in middle age. When you are young it is sometimes unbearable, and it becomes a glory to bear it at all. And when you are old, it is like the opposite bank of a river, its lights growing clearer and nearer with every new pain. But in middle age it is nothing but a burden. . . ." She paused for breath, she had never talked so much. "You don't think we live in a madhouse?"

"No," said Frossia without hesitation. "Not unless we imagine it to be one—"

"I understand German a little," went on little Tania. "Poor Klara Karlovna! She reads her old psalter as though it were a time-table. Once, months ago, she read that psalm with a verse in it about going through the vale of misery and using it for a well, and she read it through as woodenly as if it were something about a mug of water on her locker. . . . But I have thought of it ever since." Little Tania had talked too much, her ivory-white cheeks went a faint threatening flush, and Frossia begged her to stop.

It was not Elena Ivanovna whom she found waiting in the hall below, but Igor. He had to go to the Zabalkansky, he said, and they might just as well walk together. They came out, and Frossia closed her eyes for a second: the snow was almost blinding, and she hoped Igor would offer her his arm, but he never noticed her halt, and walked straight on, hands in the pockets of his very shabby overcoat. She caught up with him and told him odd fragments about the people in her ward. She also mentioned Varvara Filipovna and her despair.

"I can understand her, Euphrosynia Pavlovna. Surely, you can also. There is hope in some, there is despair in others. This is inevitable, and it is a mystery. Like good and evil, darkness and light. I can understand her, but I cannot pity her—"

"Not pity her?"

"No. . . . Nor any others like her. Their despair is their joy. They feed on it. It sustains them. Sometimes I think despair has its own uses. There are many more people who must hope if they want to go on living, and when they hear such mournful talk, they want to rush to the defense of their hope. They get frightened that their own hopefulness might get dimmed by their neighbor's despair, and somehow their own hope grows all the stronger because of it. I know nothing of medicine, but I have heard that when one poison has entered the body, it is good sometimes to introduce a second which kills all the danger from the first."

They were nearing Nicholas Bridge when Frossia said:

"I hear you have salvaged some books of mine, a photograph, and a volume bound in red leather. Igor Vladimirovich, I have no other possessions in the world. It ought to frighten me, and nothing in me seems to mind," and she glanced at the river she had not seen for some months.

Igor said slowly:

"Do you remember that day at Peterhof when I broke off a branch of lilac for you and when you and I ate a meal in the park—"

"Yes, and then we came back, and found poor old Touras with her broom in this square, and you thought me such a fool."

"You were a fool," said Igor. "But I was not thinking of that. Now the park and the lilac and all of it . . . All now belonging to the nation, and all of it yours and mine just as the river and the city and every stone in the city are no less yours or mine because they belong to all. Is a master's great picture any less yours because it hangs in a museum and millions are free to feast their eyes on it?"

"This is rather deep philosophy, Igor Vladimirovich—"

"This is an answer to your question. You have no possessions, you said this should have given you cause for fear, and you don't in the least resent being stripped. You would have minded five, even four years ago."

"But where is the answer?" Frossia challenged him, but they had now crossed the bridge, and must negotiate the slippery corner of the English Quay, and Igor said no more until they came to the house in Galernaya, and Elena Ivanovna welcomed them in the richly traditional manner—a chunk of bread on a wooden platter and a rough earthenware saltcellar over the bread. There was a rich crop of news about everybody for Frossia to listen to. Klava had written from Pskov briefly but full of pride over Frossia's feat. Nikolashka was safe and busy at Riabchino, happy to be under his brother Kuzma's roof and happier still to be together with his incomparable Irina Nikolaevna. Dasha's mother had sent a barely legible scrawl from the south of Russia, full of half-ended allusions to hens, hunger, a soap factory, and a brief remark that Dasha's strength was coming back to her. The house in Maly Prospect was ruined indeed, but there were no casualties, even Mark Alexandrovich, for all his slender wit, had succeeded in escaping. Elena Ivanovna thought that the undertaker and Olga Semenovna had left Petrograd. Pavel Pavlovich and other habitués of the Zabalkansky were coming in later. "Nikita Fyodorov has sent in a large parcel of smoked fish, and it is going to be a feast."

Later that evening they were all settled in two dim rooms. Elena Ivanovna had no further supply of any fruit syrup, and they had to drink plain hot water. Glafira Antonovna had tramped all the way from the Rabfak. Her budget of news was delivered at a breathless speed. Things were rotten, food bad and scarce, fuel most inadequate. The hostels were now abandoned. Hostel B had had its roof torn off in the gale, and there was no fuel for any outside buildings at all, so the students ate, slept, and worked in lecture halls. But even there water and ink froze by night. Manual work on Saturdays was now compulsory. Kostia, the fair, freckled pupil of Frossia's, had joined an agricultural commission, and gone to Kharkov.

"Is Pasha back?"

Glafira Antonovna had not heard. She sipped her hot water out of a cannister and mumbled:

"You might not like coming back, Euphrosynia Pavlovna. None of us have done much work for months. There has been so much else to do, and a winter day has a short life."

"Of course, I am coming back," said Frossia. Glafira Antonovna shrugged and ate her smoked fish in silence.

Frossia wandered from one room to the other, and she talked to them all. She observed their clothes, gestures, faces, voices. She had not met any of them for more than three months. They all looked changed, hungrier, more passive. They talked less. The exultant theme of Frossia's return gradually wore thin among them, and conversation drifted into the grooves of ordinary queue topics, American lavishness, barter, hunger, disease. In earlier days Elena

Ivanovna would have discouraged it. She would have banged a soup ladle on the table and shouted: "Now then—what about a song, good people?" But even Elena Ivanovna's mind was obviously not set on any singing. Talk rang muted, brittle, and Frossia could not mistake its note of general weariness.

Is it the flood then? They must all have suffered? Or is it this winter? She marveled, and moved nearer one of the guests.

"Have some more hot water, Nina Andreevna."

"What did you get to drink at your hospital?"

"Mostly condensed milk, sometimes cocoa—"

"Varenka," the woman shouted at her daughter across the room. "Just imagine—condensed milk and cocoa at that hospital."

The club stirred at these words. In candlelight Frossia could read incredulity and something like envy on their upturned faces. In the darker kitchen at the back she came on Igor fussing over the small *plita*.

"Elena Ivanovna wants some more hot water, but the fire is nearly out."

"Igor Vladimirovich, what is the matter with them all? They are so quiet—they all look tired."

"Well, we are all tired, Euphrosynia Pavlovna. Look at yourself—"

"But I mean to go on."

"They do, too. In their own way. But the lips cannot sing a song when the heart wants to sob."

"Nina Andreevna almost hated me when I said we had had milk and cocoa at the hospital."

"Nina Andreevna," he said slowly, trying to rouse the all but moribund fire to a brief lease of new life, "Nina Andreevna is more exhausted than all of us. She had had eight months in Shpalernaya Prison, and has never complained about it. She is over sixty, and has not slept in a proper bed for more than six years. Her two sons were killed in the first Kronstadt rising, and killed in a horrible manner. Her daughter, Varenka, is nearly blind. But Nina Andreevna would give her last crust to a hungry man from the Tcheka. . . . You are growing impatient, Euphrosynia Pavlovna, and impatience is more tiring than hurry—"

As day succeeded day, Frossia learned of more and more changes which had come over her environment. The prevailing mood was discontent, nostalgia for the irrevocably vanished past and, above all, weariness of flesh and mind. Cradled in comparative comfort at the hospital, Frossia had battled with a severe illness, and was now back in her world and once again at work. But the changes

351

she saw everywhere gave her no rest. Again and again she would try and get Igor to see her own bewilderment, but he argued that she was wrong.

"This weariness has nothing novel in it. It has been growing for years. What is there to perplex you? You are just tired out, Euphrosynia Pavlovna, and that is all."

"But where will it end?" she cried, and he would not answer.

For some years the country had lived its own strictly enclosed life among wreckage, shut off from all communication with the outer world, but now there were letters from abroad, foreign parcels, foreign relief units, business men from America and Sweden and Germany in their midst. Nostalgia frequently mingled with more or less inarticulate gratitude. Roofs which did not leak, drains which worked, clothes which did not fall to pieces, all and any amenities of outwardly civilized life, seemed heaped up along the fringe of an inaccessible horizon. They teased, they tormented imagination, and then they vanished. But all alike yearned for such things. And Igor merely repeated:

"Leave them to their weariness. They have earned a right to feel tired." And once he quoted Artemiy Sorokin: "Let the corn be ground, and you shall have your flour in the end," and Frossia, stung into anger, left him alone.

5

Her bewilderment grew apace with Pasha Dobrina's return. Pasha came back some two months after Christmas, a strangely altered Pasha, no longer either defiant or garrulous, no longer interested in kid gloves and odd bits of loud finery. Pasha returned to the Rabfak and began her work for the finals in May, and she avoided everyone so that all the students grumbled and said that the foreigners had spoiled her altogether. But she did not avoid Frossia. They met in a passage. Frossia reproached her for keeping away, and asked:

"Well, what was it like?"

Pasha did not answer. She merely said in a heavy mournful voice:

"I am having my finals in May. They are letting me go to Germany in July. To study at a University there. I am going, and I might not come back."

Frossia heard it without astonishment. She led Pasha away. There was a shed in the back yard where students kept their choppers and saws. It was empty, and she drew Pasha inside.

"What has happened to you?"

"Nothing." Pasha sniffed angrily. "I am just sick of it all."

352

"Not of your studies, surely?"

"No. . . . But what good are they? The stomach always comes first, and when there is nothing to put into the stomach—"

"Pasha, a great many people were hungry here."

"Don't you talk to me! I might have listened eight months ago . . . I cannot now. You are in clover here. I have gone from town to town, from village to village. Famine does not make you weak all at once. Once you begin feeling really weak you are as good as dead, and then you do die. But before you are weak you are strong to do dreadful, vile things. . . . Don't talk to me of horrors. . . . I have lived them. In some villages there were no real people left—they were just animals, and a hungry beast will sometimes pounce on its own kind. . . . There were other villages, and they were worse. . . . I saw a woman point at a beech and scream: 'We must kill this damned cow . . . She has given no milk for weeks,' and they went for the beech with axes, and they felled the trunk and smashed up some of the boughs, and they ate them. I tell you—they ate them. You need not look at me like that. I am not telling stories . . . I saw it. . . . And children . . . Children . . ." Pasha was sobbing now loudly, unashamedly. "They gave us the revolution, 'for yourselves, they said, let all the important people die, they don't matter, for yourselves,' they said, 'for the peasants, the workers . . .' And who are dying now? The peasants in thousands, in hundreds of thousands . . . They never asked for sugar or jam or tea. They wanted bread only. And they have no bread. They are dying. 'It is the bad crops,' they say, 'we have had four years of lean harvests.' That is a lie. Harvest has not been bad all over the country, Russia is too big for that, I know my statistics, corn did grow in places and grow well, and was harvested—and then it rotted away. They say the rolling stock is in bad repair. They could not have enough transport, they say. That is true enough. It is a muddle from end to end, and peasants are dying, and I am a peasant, and do you think it means nothing to me?"

"You helped, Pasha—"

"What did I do? I could not help. I learnt some nursing in a hurry, and went about distributing medicines and food. Was that enough? I tried to go hungry myself, I refused my own rations, what good did it do? And typhus"—she went on sobbing—"and not a single damned louse had sense enough to bite me. . . . Here I am, safely back at my studies"—she clenched her rough, unshapely fists—"and Gleb Semenovich cooed to me: 'You will be going to Germany in the summer to do a year's work as a state student. You will have a proper foreign passport issued to you,' and I said: 'Thank you, comrade,' and I thought: None of you are my comrades any more—my comrades are the dying, the dead, the peasants who have no bread. . . . You are antichrists, fiends in the flesh," and she went on sobbing, and Frossia thought:

Igor Vladimirovich might help her. I cannot. I might have done so a few months ago, a year ago. I cannot now. I might put my arm round her shoulders and kiss her, but this would not comfort her. She needs no comfort. She needs something else. She is right and she is also wrong about it all, and I should be able to find something between the two and make her see it, and what can I say? And she said aloud: "Pasha, I am trying to understand—"

"You could not," sobbed Pasha. "Have you ever seen people dying when there was no need for them to die and you could not stop it . . . ? Have you?"

It was dim and cold and quiet in the shed. It was some seconds before Frossia replied, her eyes on the dully gleaming saw under her feet:

"I have. My own people . . . There was no need for them to go. . . . But they chose to . . . I could not stop them. . . . But I loved them."

Pasha, still sobbing, looked up. For a full instant her swollen eyes stared at Frossia's face, she said nothing at all, she got up and strode out of the shed. From that day on she avoided Frossia for nearly a month. Then one brilliant March morning she stole past her in a passage and muttered:

"I reckon I had a lot of wild talk in me when I came back."

"It was not wild, Pasha, it was natural."

"Well, things are quieter," Pasha mumbled, her ugly face crimson, "not that I feel any happier. Who could be? But I think a year in Germany will be enough. I feel I belong here, don't I?"

"Yes, you do."

Pasha gave her hand a hurried squeeze and vanished down the stairs.

That afternoon Elena Ivanovna wished to go to the General Post Office. She had to buy some stamps, and she held that stamps had no virtue in them unless they were bought at the General Post Office, and Frossia offered to go with her.

They bought their stamps and were moving away when Frossia caught her own name traced on the board marked, "Letters to be called for."

"A letter—for me!"

The black-bloused girl behind the wire was brusque. She demanded to see the labor book, the ration cards. She scrutinized every entry in those documents, pushed a form towards Frossia to sign, and after several minutes' delay handed her the letter. It was a thick gray envelope, its stamp belonged to Paraguay. It had left Paraguay a year before. Its Petrograd postmark was nearly four months old. Frossia could not recognize the handwriting, and Elena Ivanovna said:

"Let us get home. The light is failing and the wind is freshening again. There might be several sheets inside. It is never safe to open a letter in the street." They hurried home, Elena Ivanovna produced a candle, and Frossia's fingers shook as she struggled with the envelope.

"It is from Yulia," she stammered. "I did not even know she was alive—"

"And who is Yulia?"

"My Aunt Alina's daughter. My aunt has been dead for years and years. Yulia went abroad to Italy, I believe. I could not even remember what she looked like—"

"You read your letter and I will get the supper," suggested Elena Ivanovna, but Frossia protested: she must share her very first letter from abroad, and Elena Ivanovna must listen. She carried the sheets nearer the candle and read aloud:

"My dear Frossia; it is more than seven years since I heard from the family, and I am writing to you rather than to Father, Grandmamma, or Uncle Paul. Where are you and how are you? I came here from Italy four years ago together with a friend, and we have started a girls' school." [There followed a boringly detailed description of the school and its routine.] "My friend died some months ago, and I am wondering whether Father and you, possibly, could come out to me. It might be arranged and, later on, perhaps, Grandmamma and Uncle Paul could join us. I hear that various Relief Missions will soon be going to Russia, and something might be done through their help. Anyway write and give me your news as soon as you get my letter, and I will try and write again later on. This is a lovely country, and my pupils are exceptionally nice wellbehaved children, but naturally things are not always easy."

"Well," said Elena Ivanovna, "she writes warmly enough. But why ever has she not written all these years?" and Frossia wrinkled her forehead to remember half-forgotten details.

"There had been a quarrel—I think. Yulia is much older than I am, and she takes after her mother. Aunt Alina went to London, my uncle was at the Embassy, and Aunt Alina was always doing odd things—helping 'political' refugees and buying books banned in Russia. My uncle had to leave the diplomatic service, and they came back, and my aunt died soon afterwards. But I never really knew Yulia—she was always something of a socialist, cropped her hair, and talked about bombs. Fancy her being in South America—"

"You had better go and discuss it all with Igor Vladimirovich," suggested Elena Ivanovna, and Frossia was not astonished at the suggestion.

"But I don't know where he lives," was all she said as they sat down to a supper of pea soup and tea.

6

Elena Ivanovna promptly supplied the address.

"It is one of those Christmas Streets. Yes, I have it all written down—49 Fifth Rozhdestvenskaya Street. I have always thought it funny that one city should have ten or twelve Christmas Streets."

"Yes, it is funny," agreed Frossia.

They washed up, and each settled to her own work. Elena Ivanovna was knitting a sock. Frossia began mending her gown which had got torn at the hem. The letter from Paraguay still lay on the table. They would all say: "Euphrosynia Pavlovna is fortunate, she has a cousin, she has been asked to go to South America," and Paulina Pavlovna would once more remember that she had once been to Chile. A letter from Paraguay . . . A door into another world. There would be revolutions, excitements, in South America nobody could live without excitement, but there would be no stark bitter winter, no snow, no shivering by a half-dead fire, no standing in wearisome queues. She could indeed write to Yulia: "Yes, I have been teaching for three years. They say I can teach. I like it. My French is as good as ever, and I could learn Spanish to teach other subjects." She would write to Yulia: "It is quite natural that I should come out to you. You are my first cousin, and I have nobody else left in the world. You understand, Yulia, you and I have no one else in the world. I have no news to give you of anyone. I must tell you all about it when I am with you. I am all alone," and she would say no more than that. She would also say: "If I come I will bring a family document. Do you remember the legend of that young Euphrosynia who fell in love with an Englishman and he was killed, and she died in the snow? I can bring that, Yulia, she was your ancestress and mine also." She would not say that once she had hoped to translate that legend into a ballet. . . . Then she tried to imagine Yulia, and could not. Frossia's Uncle Nicholas was tall and somber, a good diplomat, but a mere shadow to her. Yulia called herself a socialist, but she had a school for obviously well-to-do children. Could Yulia share in a saga which embraced Elena Ivanovna and Pasha Dobrina, little Tania and Nikita Fyodorov, Cherny and Igor Vladimirovich, Madame Touras,

Michael, and the people in the balconied house in Maly Prospect? Frossia found it difficult to imagine that she could. Also Yulia never once mentioned Russia. This was odd. She could not, of course, speak of controversial political matters, but she might so easily have written: "Bow for me to Russia, to dear beloved Russia." But Yulia had not done so, and the Russian of her letter, even if good, was not altogether flawless. Probably, Yulia still thought in French— like so many of her kind.

No. 49 Fifth Christmas Street was a small, two-storied, ocher-painted house. Its eight windows had cheap lace curtains. It looked humble enough but clean and somehow reserved as though people who lived inside had secret lives of their own. An old bearded man opened in answer to Frossia's bell. Yes, Igor Vladimirovich Titov lived there, he rented a room in the ground floor flat from Anna Petrovna Savvina. Did she then wish to see Anna Petrovna? he asked.

"No," said Frossia, "I have come to see Igor Vladimirovich—"

"Come and wait then," muttered the old man, shuffled down a passage, led her through a small entrance hall, and gestured to a door on the left. "Go in and wait then. Igor Vladimirovich will not be long."

It was a small square room furnished with a few pieces of drably varnished cheap deal. It had one window with the bleak scene of the back yard for view, a camp bed, two chairs, a domed trunk, and a big table pushed against the wall. Above the table a crowded bookshelf ran the whole length of the wall. Frossia went up to look at the titles: *Latin grammar, Russian,* Bielinsky's *Essays,* Karamzine's *History,* Shakespeare in Russian, an Old Slavonic *New Testament,* John of Kronstadt's *My Life in Christ,* Homer, Pushkin. These she had expected, but there were other volumes mostly on history and philosophy, names all unknown to her. She opened one of them, saw the thickly penciled notes on the margin, and put it back.

The cheap lace curtains struck the only note of comfort in the room. There was neither cushion nor carpet. The hard bed had a single flat pillow. The green papered walls were bare of pictures. There were no ornaments on the big table except a white china saucer with an oblong green bead in it, and Frossia looked at it hard. "I should like a necklace of those green beads," had said Varvara Filipovna, and those were oblong beads, too. . . . The table was littered with papers, a map, a large inkstand, odds and ends of blotting paper, and a ridiculous bright pink penwiper in the shape of a rabbit.

The door opened, and Igor came in, beating the wet mushy snow off his badly patched boots. He showed no surprise when he saw her.

"Good morning to you, Euphrosynia Pavlovna. . . . It is cold for late March, is it not?"

"I have had a letter from Paraguay," she said, handed it over, and waited till he had finished, and then she added quietly: "I am not going to Paraguay—"

Igor put the letter side by side with the pink rabbit. They both look ludicrous, thought Frossia.

"Your reason for not going is a wrong one."

Frossia looked at him, but she had come of her own free will, and he would not spare her.

"You are not going because of me, and this is not enough. If you knew yourself belonging here truly, you would stay even if you had nowhere to go, no warm corner of your own, no friend to call you by your name. Things are hard now, they will be harder still, but you would stay because of your hope and your faith, and faith and hope should never be straitly housed, Euphrosynia Pavlovna—"

"Straitly housed," she echoed, but he had not done.

"I have no right to ask you anything, but you must remember that I am not of your world; I found the alphabet difficult to learn at an age when you spoke several languages. . . . And I am clumsy, I shall always be clumsy, and I have no right to ask questions, but I am going to ask one. You lived here in the old days, you have been here in the new days. . . . You have had your share of every-body's misery and your own also, probably deeper than most other people's. Did you ever before think of going away—years before this letter came? I know you will tell the truth—"

"Not till now," she said, her eyes full on his face.

"And now that you have had it—"

"I have thought about it—as if it did not concern myself. . . . You spoke once about Time. You said it was all really one, past, present, and future, it was only our dim understanding of it that made for divisions. . . . Well, the old days are in us now, and the future, too, yours and mine and everybody's." Still she was looking at him, and he stammered:

"But I dare not . . . Euphrosynia Pavlovna, it was unworthy of me to say such things. . . . I am a hard man. . . . Mine has been a hard life. . . . I dare not—"

"I have dared," Frossia reminded him. "I have dared to come home at last."

July, 1940—May, 1942

358